• Myths, Gods & Immortals •
Aphrodite
New & Ancient Greek Tales

Publisher & Creative Director: Nick Wells
Editorial Director: Catherine Taylor
Editorial Board: Gillian Whitaker, Catherine Taylor, Jocelyn Pontes, Jemma North, Simran Aulakh and Beatrix Ambery
Special thanks to Karen Fitzpatrick

FLAME TREE PUBLISHING
6 Melbray Mews, Fulham,
London SW6 3NS, United Kingdom
www.flametreepublishing.com

First published 2025

Copyright in each story is held by the individual authors.
Introduction and Volume copyright © 2025 Flame Tree Publishing Ltd

Unless otherwise stated, all translations are by the author. The Extracts from the Electronic Text Corpus of Sumerian Literature (ETCSL; http://etcsl.orinst.ox.ac.uk; eds. Black, J.A., Cunningham, G., Ebeling, J., Flückiger-Hawker, E., Robson, E., Taylor, J., and Zólyomi, G.; Oxford 1998–2006) are copyright © J.A. Black, G. Cunningham, E. Robson, and G. Zólyomi 1998, 1999, 2000; J.A. Black, G. Cunningham, E. Flückiger-Hawker, E. Robson, J. Taylor, and G. Zólyomi 2001; J.A. Black, G. Cunningham, J. Ebeling, E. Robson, J. Taylor, and G. Zólyomi 2002, 2003, 2004, 2005; G. Cunningham, J. Ebeling, E. Robson, and G. Zólyomi 2006. The authors have asserted their moral rights. The online article 'Phoenix Goddess Temple's "Sacred Sexuality" is More Like New Age Prostitution' can be found at https://www.phoenixnewtimes.com/news/phoenix-goddess-temples-sacred-sexuality-is-more-like-new-age-prostitution-6447544

25 27 29 30 28 26
1 3 5 7 9 10 8 6 4 2

ISBN: 978-1-83562-268-1

All rights reserved. No part of this publication may be reproduced, stored in a retrieval system, or transmitted in any form or by any means, electronic, mechanical, photocopying, recording or otherwise, without the prior written permission of the publisher.

Publisher's Note: The stories within this book are works of fiction. Names, characters, places, and incidents are a product of the authors' imaginations. Locales and public names are sometimes used for atmospheric purposes. Any resemblance to actual people, living or dead, or to businesses, companies, events, institutions, or locales is completely coincidental.

Content Note: The stories in this book may contain descriptions of, or references to, difficult subjects such as violence, death and rape, but always contextualized within the setting of mythic narrative, archetype and metaphor. Similarly, language can sometimes be strong but is at the artistic discretion of the authors.

Cover art by Flame Tree Studio based on elements from
Shutterstock.com/Ironika.

A copy of the CIP data for this book is available from the British Library.

Printed and bound in China

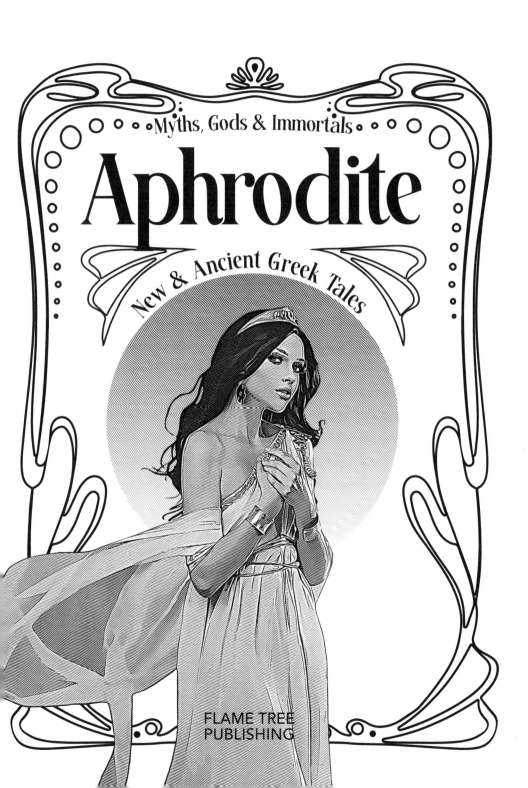

Myths, Gods & Immortals

Aphrodite

New & Ancient Greek Tales

FLAME TREE
PUBLISHING

Contents

FOREWORD
Dr. Anja Ulbrich 6

ANCIENT & MODERN: INTRODUCING APHRODITE
by Stephanie Budin 10
1. The Persona of Aphrodite 11
2. The Origins of Aphrodite 52
3. Aphrodite's Sisters (and Their Lovers) 78
4. Aphrodite's Aftermath (Dealing with the S-word) 99

MODERN SHORT STORIES OF APHRODITE
Those That Hunger For Warmth
Benjamin Cyril Arthur 127
Obaasima Aphrodite
Bernice Arthur 144
Aphrodite Will Take Your Order
Andrea Modenos Ash 159
The Heart of a Warrior
Angelina Chamberlain 175
Best Served Cold
C.B. Channell 192

CONTENTS

A Mortal Breaks Aphrodite's Heart
Ev Datsyk 199

Pandemos – Skotia – Areia
Voss Foster 209

Hymn to the Pain
Luna C. Galindo 223

Feasts of the Fair and Fowl
Ali Habashi 234

All's Fair
Xoe Juliani 246

Venus Descending
Vanessa Ziff Lasdon 261

The Constraints of Love
Russell Hugh McConnell 279

Aphrodite's Promise
Melody E. McIntyre 289

Someone will remember us
Fiona Mossman 301

Sorry, But We Really Don't Need a Love Goddess Right Now
Noah Ross 314

The Love Goddess's War
Zach Shephard 330

Froth
Lauren Talveryn 348

BIOGRAPHIES **361**
MYTHS, GODS & IMMORTALS **367**
FLAME TREE FICTION **368**

Foreword
Dr. Anja Ulbrich

From antiquity to the present day, Aphrodite, and her Roman successor and counterpart Venus, has intrigued and inspired authors (and artists), to which this title is the latest testimony.

No other Greek goddess features in so many ancient myths and stories in a leading role, has exercised the minds of everyone from ancient authors to modern researchers to such an extent and inspired literature and iconic pieces of art, leaving such an enduring legacy in European culture.

In ancient Greek literature and poetry, Aphrodite is a relative newcomer to the familiar pantheon of the twelve Olympic Greek gods and goddesses. In contrast to Hera and Athena, both already mentioned in Mycenaean Linear B tablets of the thirteenth century BCE, Aphrodite makes her first appearance in the eighth and seventh centuries BCE.

According to Hesiod's *Theogony*, however, Aphrodite belongs to an older, second generation of gods, and is a direct descendant from the Sky god Ouranos and the earth goddess Gaia, the original primary divine couple, whose nightly sexual encounters had produced many children. One of those encounters, albeit with a violent twist, resulted in the 'birth' of Aphrodite, rising as a fully formed nude maiden from the foam of the sea. After sailing the seas, she made landfall in Cyprus, allotted to her as her home by the Greek gods, where, she was greeted by the Seasons. A

FOREWORD

Homeric hymn picks up the story, telling us that the goddess was then accompanied to her main sanctuary in Cyprus in ancient Paphos (modern Kouklia), considered by Greeks and Romans as the 'navel' (centre) of the world alongside the Apollo sanctuary in Delphi, for a fully immersive spa and makeover experience involving incense burning, fragranced oil, beautiful clothes and rich jewellery.

Aphrodite's Greek birth myth encapsulates and reflects an array of information on her origins, multifaceted nature and universal powers. She was much more than simply a 'goddess of love and beauty' as she is predominantly known today. Greek and Roman authors clearly allude to her Oriental origins and shared traits with her Middle Eastern predecessor and sister goddesses, such as Ishtar and Astarte, and stress her prominence and universal powers on her home island of Cyprus. The latter is also expressed in her frequently used alternative names, such as Kypris (the Cypriot goddess), Queen (wanassa) or Lady (medeousa), 'the goddess' (thea), Paphia (goddess of Paphos), Golgia (the goddess of Golgoi) or Kypria, which were also used by the ancient Cypriots themselves in the preserved dedicatory inscription to her from Cyprus. The predominance of Kypris is also reflected by her over 150 archaeologically attested sanctuaries, both by the votive sculpture referring to her different powers, and the prominent location of those sites in cities and settlements, e.g. on an acropolis, in palaces, at city gates, near harbours, roads and tombs, as well as in the natural landscape, e.g. on the coast, promontories, riverbanks and hill and mountain tops.

Aphrodite's myths, her additional names (epithteta), the identity of her worshippers and the location of her sanctuaries indicate that she exerted powers over all realms of the natural world and many areas of human activity within it. As goddess of the skies, she was worshipped as Ourania, especially by mariners, due to her ability to calm the sea and winds (Eleemon). Nature blossoming as response to her first landfall in Cyprus makes her a goddess of vegetal fertility and thus agriculture.

Yes, at the heart of her various powers lies love in its broadest sense, revolving around erotic love, sex, marriage and procreation of humans, animals and even plants. The bulk of ancient stories refer to her supreme physical beauty, flirty personality and her many love affairs with almost all of the male gods, most prominently Ares (the god of war), with whom she had several children. She also fell in love with a few mortal men as punishments imposed on her by her boss or father Zeus for stirring up romantic strife and rivalries among the Olympians and cuckolding her husband, also chosen for her by Zeus to reign her in, the hardworking but ugly god of metallurgy, Hephaistos – the two were completely incompatible personalities.

Aphrodite was the winner of the first ever beauty contest with her fellow goddesses Hera and Athena as judged by the Trojan prince Paris. He was, of course, bribed by Aphrodite who granted him the love of the most beautiful woman on earth, Helena, who was already married to King Menelaos of Sparta, but through Aphrodite's machinations eloped with Paris to Troy. That set off the Trojan War as narrated in Homer's *Iliad*, during which Aphrodite actually fought in battle on the side of the Trojans.

FOREWORD

After being wounded in action, Zeus sent her off with the order to confine herself to the female, i.e. domestic sphere, particularly beautification, erotic love/sex, harmonious marriage, and children.

This famous story marks the moment when the Cypriot goddess, originally multitasking not only in love matters, but also in politics and actual warfare, animal and vegetal fertility and agriculture, fertility of the earth's natural resources, as well as seafaring and trade, was cut down to size to fit into the somewhat crowded Greek pantheon, where other goddesses already presided over some of those areas. Athena over the state, politics and warfare, Hera over marriage, Demeter over agriculture, and Artemis over nature and wild animals. In the Greek and Roman worlds, Aphrodite retained those roles which were not yet covered by other goddesses, particularly erotic love and sex and domestic harmony, but also as patron goddess of mariners either involved in maritime trade or navy operations. Her joint worship and frequent depiction with Ares, and her taking up arms herself, as reflected in her additional name Areia (with arms), are probably surviving remnants of her original role as state and war goddess, though frequently reinterpreted as agonies and battles in love relationships, already in antiquity.

And that is the main focus of most modern Aphrodite-inspired literature and stories, though Aphrodite's other powers do shine through.

Enjoy the read about mighty Aphrodite!

Dr. Anja Ulbrich
A.G. Leventis Curator of the Cypriot Collection

Ancient & Modern: Introducing Aphrodite

by Stephanie Budin

1.
The Persona of Aphrodite

This honour she has been appointed from the beginning
Her portion amongst humans and immortal deities
Girlish chit-chat and smiles and deceits
And sweet joy and friendship and gentleness.
– Hesiod, Theogony, ll. 203–206

t is the year 400 BCE and you live just outside of Athens in central Greece. Lately your sex life has not been all that great. Your husband has been busy in the fields with harvesting season and you are still recovering from the birth of your second child. You really do miss sex, but your body just is not responding in the way you want it to. So you pray to Aphrodite, the Golden One, to restoke your libido and restore the intimacy between you and your husband. Aphrodite gleefully fulfils your wish. To thank her you make the short trek out to her sanctuary at Daphne, at the fringe of Athens on the way to Eleusis. There you dedicate a small terracotta vulva to thank the goddess and to display to all other visitors the power of Aphrodite.

Aphrodite – the Golden One, Kypris, Kythereia, Violet-Crowned, Heavenly, Pandemos, Hetaira, Leader, Genital-Loving, Paphian – is the ancient Greek goddess of sex, love and beauty, pretty much in that order. But Aphrodite is more than just a deity of snuggling in bed. It might be better to think of her as a goddess who brings people (and other creatures) together. One way this happens is, clearly, through sex and love. Often this is a good thing, both in the sexual intimacy of lovers and also in the political harmony Aphrodite inspires among fellow citizens (yes, she does that). Sexual passion is still passion, however, and it can lead to other passions which, when not controlled, can lead to violence. Nor is 'control' a concept well applied to this goddess, as we shall see. So Aphrodite, like all deities, has her dark side.

She also has qualities that do not seem to pertain to sex at all. For example, she protects people travelling by sea. You might think this would be exclusively Poseidon's domain, as god of the sea, but there it is. She is also a patroness of male adulthood, a sign of the maturity that marks the proper role of all Greek men as responsible husbands and fathers. Finally, outside of Greece but absolutely in Cyprus and the Near East, Aphrodite is understood to be a queen, occasionally paired with Zeus instead of Hera. We shall see more of that aspect in Chapters Two and Three. But to begin at the proper beginning…

SEX AND LOVE AND BEAUTY

Above all else, Aphrodite was the divine embodiment of sexual pleasure. The ancient Greek word for 'sexuality' is literally *aphrodisia*, and sexual intercourse is *ta erga Aphroditês*: 'the works of Aphrodite'. The Greeks loved her for it. As the seventh-century BCE poet Mimnermos claims of the goddess in 'Fragment 1', ll. 1–3:

> *What life, what joy without golden Aphrodite?*
> *I should die were these things not a care to me:*
> *Secret love and sweet gifts and the bed.*

As noted in the opening of this chapter, Hesiod, one the earliest known Greek poet-authors (the earliest form of Greek literature was poetry), claimed that her role in reality included smiles, joy and sweet love. Even the fifth-century Athenian playwright Aeschylus – generally viewed as a bit of a misogynistic curmudgeon – had to admit in his play *Eumenides*, ll. 215–218:

> *In your argument Kypris is tossed aside dishonoured*
> *From whom the most beloved things come to mortals.*
> *For the destined bed is for man and wife*
> *Greater than any oath when kept properly.*

This aspect of Aphrodite's persona is very well expressed in one of her epithets, the descriptive 'nicknames' that often accompany ancient Greek names: 'Philomeides'. The word is actually a pun, as it means both 'Smile-loving' and 'Genital-loving'. Aphrodite is absolutely both. She loves and promotes the emotions that bring joy to all living things, making them smile. She also loves and promotes genital friction. And if that friction happens to bring a smile to the face as well…

Aphrodite was also known to be the embodiment of feminine physical beauty and the sexual desire it aroused. As an Archaic poet hymned the goddess in a Homeric *Hymn to Aphrodite 6*, ll. 5–18:

> ... *The gold-crowned Horai [seasons] received her*
> *Joyfully; about her they tossed divine clothing;*
> *Upon her immortal head they placed a lovely*
> *Well-wrought crown of gold, in her pierced ears*
> *Flowers of copper and precious gold.*
> *About her soft neck and silvery breasts –*
> *They decorated those with golden chains, just like*
> *Those with which the gold-crowned Horai are adorned*
> *Whenever they go to*
> *The lovely chorus of the deities or to their father's house.*
> *But when they had placed all this adornment upon*
> *her flesh*
> *They led her to the immortals. And they on seeing her*
> *welcomed her*
> *And received her with open arms. And each god*
> *Prayed that she would be his wife and that he would lead*
> *her home,*
> *Such did they marvel at the sight of violet-*
> *crowned Kythereia.*

One might ask: What's not to like?

The problem is that when it came to sex – which Plato himself claimed to be a form of madness – the ancient Greeks were not always all that sure how they felt about Aphrodite, even as we are not sure in modern times. The problem, as the Greeks understood it, was that Aphrodite was *too* powerful. She literally had all mammals by the short hairs, and every other life form by whatever parts were non-euphemistically their genitalia.

Not even the gods could resist mighty Aphrodite. Her longest-preserved Homeric Hymn (not really composed by the eighth-century Homer credited with the *Iliad* and *Odyssey*, but writing in his style) begins:

> *Muses, relate to me the works of golden-*
> *throned Aphrodite,*
> *Of Cyprus, who in deities stirs up sweet desire and*
> *Who subdues the race of mortal men*
> *And air-borne birds and all wild creatures,*
> *And as many creatures the mainland rears, and also the sea.*
> *To all these are the works of well-crowned Kythereia*
> *a concern.*
> – Hymn to Aphrodite 5, ll. 1–6

After mentioning that a grand total of three goddesses on Olympos – the virgins Artemis, Athena and Hestia – are immune to the goddess of love, the poet continues in ll. 34–40:

> *Of the others there is nothing which can escape Aphrodite,*
> *Neither of blessed deities nor of mortal humans.*
> *And even the mind of Zeus delighting-in-thunder she*
> *leads astray,*
> *He who is greatest with the greatest share of honour;*
> *But whenever she wishes, tricking his wise mind*
> *Easily, she has him mingle with mortal women,*
> *Forgetting Hera, his sister and wife.*

Nor is it just the gods: Aphrodite works her will on humans, too. In her only completely preserved poem the sixth-century poet Sappho (the one from Lesbos) prays to the goddess to induce the non-reciprocating object of Sappho's affections to respond in kind. Aphrodite assures her in *Hymn to Aphrodite*, ll. 13–28:

> *And you, O blessed one,*
> *Smiling on your immortal face,*
> *Asked on what account I am suffering again, and*
> *On what account was I summoning again,*
> *And what did I want most in my raving heart*
> *to happen.*
> *'Whom do I persuade on this account*
> *To lead you back to her dearest love?*
> *Who, O Sappho, wrongs you?*
> *For if she flees, soon will she follow;*
> *And if she does not receive gifts, then she will give.*
> *And if she does not love, soon she will love even if she does*
> *not wish it.'*
> *Come to me now, release me from this grievous care!*
> *What my heart desires to come to pass, make happen.*
> *And you yourself be my ally.*

And, yes, Aphrodite even wields power over animals, as shown in the Homeric *Hymn to Aphrodite* 5, ll. 68–74. When the goddess goes to seduce the Trojan prince Ankhises on the slopes of Mount Ida in Anatolia:

THE PERSONA OF APHRODITE

> *She came to well-springed Ida, mother of beasts,*
> *And walked straight through the mountain dwelling.*
> *The grey wolves and bright-eyed lions fawned over her,*
> *Bears and nimble leopards insatiate for game*
> *Approached her. And she seeing these was delighted in her mind*
> *And into their breasts cast desire; through her all of them*
> *Lay together in pairs in the shadowy haunts.*

In other words, as Aphrodite walked along the paths of the mountain, all the wild animals started having sex in her wake.

Not only does Aphrodite cause irresistible sexual desire for others, she is herself, as the epitome of beauty, the ultimate source of compulsive erotic desire. This especially comes across in Book 8 of Homer's *Odyssey* in the so-called 'Song of Demodokos'. It all started when Helios, the sun who sees everything, told Hephaistos, the smith god, that his wife Aphrodite was cheating on him with Ares, god of war. Every day when Hephaistos left for work in the forge, Ares would come over for a not-so-quicky in Hephaistos's own bed. So Hephaistos forged some chains that were very strong, very thin – invisible really – and set them about that bed one day before 'heading off to work'. In comes Ares, and he and Aphrodite begin their daily dalliance when they are caught in the chains in total *flagrante delicto* (you can picture the scene). The cuckolded husband calls all the other Olympians to come laugh at the pair and to complain. The gods show up; the goddesses do not; nor is there any mention of Zeus, father to both of the deities caught in the act (and, for that matter, the cuckolded husband). Poseidon, feeling bad for his nephew, arranges compensation for Ares if Hephaistos will let them go. As for the other gods ('Song of Demodokos', *Odyssey*, ll. 334–342):

> King Apollo, son of Zeus, spoke to Hermes:
> "Hermes, son of Zeus, Messenger and Giver of
> Good Things,
> Truly then, even bound in strong chains would you wish
> To lie in bed next to Golden Aphrodite?"
> And Messenger Argeiphontes [Hermes] replied:
> "How I wish! O Far-Shooting King Apollo,
> Even if three times the chains were about us,
> And all you gods and goddesses saw,
> Even so I'd still bed Golden Aphrodite!"

Eventually Aphrodite and Ares are set free. Ares runs off to Thrace, while Aphrodite goes for a soothing bath and spa day at her sanctuary in Paphos. However, the point is that even the gods are subjected to the will and appeal of Aphrodite; trying to curb this tendency (calling out the adulterous couple) only promotes it more (inadvertently causing the seduction of Apollo and Hermes – both also sons of Zeus, for the record). Especially if bondage and voyeurism are involved…

Even *statues* of Aphrodite can arouse irresistible lust. The first sculpture ever made of Aphrodite in the nude (or of any goddess in the nude, for that matter) was the so-called Knidian Aphrodite, created by the sculptor Praxiteles around the year 350 BCE. According to tradition, he was commissioned by the residents of the island of Kos to make them a statue of the goddess for her sanctuary on the island. Praxiteles made two: one properly dressed, the other naked. He asked the people of Kos which one they preferred, and they chose the clothed one. At this point the people of nearby Knidos insisted on buying the naked statue, which they set up in an open-air sanctuary overlooking the sea. Then, according to Pliny's chapter about stones and stone-working in his book *Natural History* (translation by John Bostock, 36.4.21, 1855):

Superior to all statues, not only of Praxiteles, but of any other artist that ever existed, is his Knidian Venus; for the inspection of which many persons before now have purposely undertaken a voyage to Knidos. The little temple in which it is placed is open on all sides, so that the beauties of the statue admit of being seen from every point of view; an arrangement which was favoured by the goddess herself, it is generally believed. Indeed, from whatever point it is viewed, its execution is equally worthy of admiration. A certain individual, it is said, became enamoured of this statue and, concealing himself in the temple during the night, gratified his lustful passion upon it, traces of which are to be seen in a stain left upon the marble.

In other words, some man become so enamoured of the statue that he sexually assaulted it one night and ejaculated on its thigh. Aphrodite kept the stain there, either as a sign of her disapproval or a sign of her power.

To be perfectly clear: Aphrodite wields power over *everyone*, for good and bad. Sweet love and gentleness are all fine and well, but uncontrollable sexual urges can (and do) start wars. Sex is a double-edged sword and the Greeks appreciated this fact. To quote 'Fragment 941' from the fifth-century BCE playwright Sophokles (most famous for his works on Oedipus of Freudian fame, speaking of problems caused by uncontrollable sexuality):

> *Children, Kypris is not only Kypris,*
> *But she is called by many names:*
> *She is Hades, she is indestructible life,*
> *She is raving madness, she is desire*
> *Unconquerable. She is lamentation. In her is everything*
> *Earnest, peaceful, leading to violence.*
> *For she sinks deep into the heart of those with*
> *Soul within. Who is not gluttonous for this goddess?*
> *She enters into the floating race of fish,*
> *Is within the four-limbed offspring of dry land,*
> *Controls the wing amongst the birds…*
> *Throughout beasts, mortals, gods above,*
> *Whom does she not wrestle and throw three times?*
> *If it is just – and it is! – for me to speak the truth:*
> *She dominates the heart of Zeus sans spear,*
> *Sans iron – all the plans of mortals*
> *And gods Kypris cuts to the quick.*

In no context is this more apparent than in Aphrodite's part in the start of the Trojan War, perhaps her most famous role in Greek mythology. According to an epic called the *Kypria* (named for Aphrodite of Cyprus and now mostly lost), the whole conflict started at the wedding of the goddess Thetis to the mortal king Peleus (both of whom became the parents of Akhilleus of the Achilles heel). In a lamentable social faux pas, Eris, the goddess of strife, was not invited to the wedding. In revenge (and true to her nature) Eris tossed a golden apple into the reception inscribed 'For the Fairest'. Three goddesses immediately went for the apple: Hera, queen of the deities and goddess of marriage; Athena, goddess of warfare and wisdom; and Aphrodite. No one wanted to get involved with *that* dispute, so they sent the messenger god Hermes to abduct Paris, a prince of Troy, to judge the divine beauty contest. Since bribery was allowed, Hera offered the young man Asia, Athena offered him wisdom and Aphrodite offered to get him into the sack with the most beautiful mortal woman there was: Helen, queen of Sparta.

Obviously neither Hera nor Athena had had much experience with young men (really, Athena thought he would value *wisdom*? You don't value wisdom unless you already have it). In the end Paris chose Aphrodite – who then had to give him Helen in exchange. Problem One was that Helen was already married to a king named Menelaos. But if Aphrodite is already going to annoy Hera by challenging her at a beauty contest, she certainly won't mind bothering her again by unravelling a very politically significant marriage. One way or another, Aphrodite helped (or forced) Helen to elope with Paris and leave Sparta for Troy. Problem Two was that Helen was actually the queen of Sparta; Menelaos was only king because he married her. To stay king (Helen had brothers) he had to win her back.

And so began the 20-year saga of diplomacy, negotiations, failed diplomacy, raising an army, and ten years of conflict only the last few weeks of which actually feature in Homer's *Iliad*. Just to bring everything full circle: the Judgement of Paris occurred right after the marriage of Thetis and Peleus, and their son Akhilleus was the primary hero of the Trojan War to recover Helen. For the sake of an apple and bragging rights Aphrodite started a kerfuffle that lasted over 20 years which drained Greece of its manpower, caused the downfall of Troy and pretty much brought about the end of the Bronze Age. Like I said, the Greeks had ambivalent feelings about her.

SEX WORK AND CIVIC HARMONY: APHRODITE PANDEMOS

This ambivalence infused more than just matters of adultery and *casus belli*. Rather like in modern times, some ancient Greeks saw a divide between affectionate love (*philia*, 'friendship' for the Greeks) and bodily lust (*eros*). In Plato's philosophic dialogue *The Symposium* ('Drinking Party'), the philosopher of the fifth and fourth centuries BCE claimed that there were in fact two separate Aphrodites – 'Heavenly' (*Ourania*) and 'All People's' or 'Common' (*Pandemos*). With them came two separate types of love as shown in lines 180 d–e and 181 a–c:

Surely there are two goddess Aphrodites. The one then is the older and is the motherless daughter of Ouranos [Heaven]. This

one we named Ourania [Heavenly]. The younger one is the daughter of Zeus and Dionê. We call her Pandemos [Common].
...

Now the love of this Aphrodite Pandemos is truly common and does its work at random. And this is the kind of love the worthless members of humanity feel. For, first off, this type loves women as much as boys, and they love their bodies more than their souls. And when they can they love the most witless people, based purely on sight – not caring if they are good or not. From this it happens that they do things randomly, equally good, equally not good. For this love comes from the goddess who is younger by far than the other...

The love associated with Heavenly Aphrodite is mainly intellectual and totally lacks the corporal element, which is where we get the expression 'Platonic love'. The love associated with Aphrodite Pandemos is, according to Plato and his kind, base and carnal. Thus the notion emerged that this Aphrodite Pandemos presided over all those aspects of crass, non-amorous sexuality, especially prostitution. This divide between asexual Heavenly Aphrodite (good) and carnal Pandemos (bad), as espoused by Plato in *The Symposium*, then entered the Christian tradition. It has been haunting sexuality studies ever since (see Chapter Four).

Sex Workers and Companions

That Aphrodite Pandemos presides over lust rather than love has led to the idea that this version of Aphrodite was the patroness of sex workers, the very embodiment of purely carnal sex. Yet the only real evidence we have for this correspondence is a story about a sixth-century BCE Athenian politician named Solon when he was organizing Athenian society. Preserved in a work called the *Deipnosophistai* ('Witty Diners'), compiled by a man named Athenaios around the year 200 CE, we read how (§13.569 d–f):

Philemon, in his work The Brothers, *records that it was Solon who first purchased girls and set them up in houses [brothels] because of the urgency of young men, just as Nikandros of Kolophon says in book three of his* Kolophoniaka. *He says that Solon was the first to construct a sanctuary of Aphrodite Pandemos using the proceeds of these houses.*

Athenaios goes on to mention that it was understood at the time that Philemon was joking – *The Brothers* was in fact a comedy – but that later authors such as Nikandros lost sight of this and thought that it was true. A number of modern scholars do too…

Not unreasonably, Aphrodite came to be associated with sex work in general, even to the point that one anecdote, also preserved in Athenaios (to be perfectly clear, *most* of our data about ancient Greek prostitution come from Athenaios), explains how Aphrodite got her epithet *Pornê* or 'whore' in §13. 572 e–f:

There is a sanctuary of Aphrodite Pornê in Abydos, as Pamphilos says. For when the city was oppressed in slavery, the garrison in it was once offering sacrifice – as Neanthes narrated in his Mythics *– and getting drunk the soldiers raped several hetairai, of whom one, seeing that the guards had fallen asleep, seized the* *keys and climbed the wall to alert the Abydians. Immediately they arrived in arms to kill the garrison and seize control of the walls. And having regained their freedom they showed their gratitude to the whore by building a temple of Aphrodite Pornê.*

In reality, Aphrodite's association with sex work – Pandemos or otherwise – is exaggerated. It mainly comes about because of a later misunderstanding of another profession in ancient Greece, that of the Companion (*Hetaira*, another epithet of the goddess). A *hetaira* is a woman who literally sells her companionship to men. In a society where men tended to marry much younger women (a 30-year-old man would often marry a girl aged between 13 and 15, for example) and keep their wives as uneducated as possible, many men found they needed a woman with whom they could talk, enjoy a night's dinner, discuss politics and philosophy. It didn't hurt if that woman also happened to be extremely beautiful. A loving, even sexual relationship might evolve. But to be absolutely clear, what the man was paying for was the woman's companionship, not sex. This is why the women were called *Companions.* In later centuries, such as the time of Athenaios, the distinction between a prostitute (*pornê*) and a companion (*hetaira*) faded, mainly because the profession of the *hetaira* disappeared in the Roman age.

Rather than prostitution, Aphrodite was associated with *hetairai* – the beautiful, witty, desirable women with whom men tended to fall in love. She was *especially* associated with a very famous companion: the fourth-century *hetaira* Phrynê. According to ancient authors this Phrynê served as the model for Praxiteles' Knidian Aphrodite (the statue mentioned above with a stain on her thigh from an over-enthusiastic fan), as well as the Aphrodite *Anadyomenê* (rising from the sea) painted by the artist Apelles. In Phrynê's hometown of Thespiai the sanctuary of Eros contained three statues by Praxiteles – one of Eros himself, one of Aphrodite and one of Phrynê. When once Phrynê was prosecuted in Athens for impiety (like Sokrates, who was found guilty and had to drink hemlock), our friend Athenaios records in *Deipnosophistai*, 13.590 e:

When Hypereides [her lawyer] was advocating for Phrynê, as he was achieving nothing by speaking and saw that the jury were likely to vote against her, leading her into their view he tore off her under garment and bared her breasts, making such a lamentation in his closing remarks in full sight of her that he made the jury afraid of this prophetess and priestess of Aphrodite.

Phrynê was neither a prophetess nor a priestess of Aphrodite (a position reserved for citizen women in Athens). However, the literary anecdote does give a sense of how closely the *hetaira* was linked with the goddess.

Beyond Phrynê, the connection between Aphrodite and *hetairai* is revealed by the fact that enslaved companions were liberated into the goddess's care. In ancient Greece a common mode of manumission was to have a deity 'buy' the slave, who henceforth remained under that deity's protection. Slave owners could also free their slaves under the auspices of a deity. In both cases the freed slave was known as a *hierodule*, or 'sacred slave', and his/

her freedom was sacrosanct. Apollo and Artemis often served this function, but Aphrodite did too for certain women. In Corinth, a city where Aphrodite was an important goddess with a temple on the acropolis, Strabo informs us in his work *Geography* (8.6.20) that:

The temple of Aphrodite at Corinth was so rich that it possessed more than a thousand hierodules, hetairai, whom both men and women used to dedicate to the goddess. The city was frequented and enriched by the multitudes who resorted there on account of these women. Masters of ships freely squandered all their money, and thus the proverb,
'It is not in every man's power to go to Corinth.'

When enslaved companions were liberated, they were placed under the protection and patronage of Aphrodite.

Rather than sex work, Aphrodite *Hetaira* brought people together in companionship. As the Athenian Apollodoros was recorded saying in his work *About the Deities* (Atheniaos 13.571 b), 'They say that Aphrodite *Hetaira* brings together male and female companions, that is, *friends*.'

A Civic Goddess

Apollodoros of Athens went on to note, in the same work *About the Deities*, that in Athens Aphrodite, whose shrine was next to the ancient *agora* (town centre), bore the epithet *Pandemos* because it was there, originally, where all the people (*panta ton demon = pan demos*) gathered for political assemblies. In later years the travel writer Pausanias visited Athens and remarked in his book *Description of Greece* (1.22.3): 'Concerning Aphrodite Pandemos, when Theseus united the Athenian *demes* into one city he instituted her cult as well as that of Peitho (Persuasion). The ancient statues are no longer visible in my day, but the ones that are there now are by eminent artists.'

The word *demos* refers to what we would call 'the people'. It was a technical term referring to an important political subdivision in classical Athens. A man's official name consisted of his own name, his father's name and his *deme*. To belong to a *deme* meant to be an Athenian citizen. Aphrodite Pandemos, rather than a 'common prostitute', was understood to be the goddess who united all those citizens in a political context. In fact, Aphrodite could even be the *leader* of the people/*demos*. A dedicatory inscription (*IG* II2 2798) found in the Athenian agora dated to 230 BCE was dedicated by the city council (the *boulê*) to Ἀφροδίτει ἡγεμόνει τοῦ δήμου καὶ Χάρισιν ('Aphrodite Leader of the *demos* and the Charities'). It is generally understood that this dedication, erected after the re-establishment of the city's independence, was meant to invoke the unity of the citizens in a new era of prosperity.

Nor was it only Athens. In the city of Didyma on the western coast of Asia Minor the prophet of Apollo dubbed Aphrodite *Katallakteria* – 'She who reconciles'. About a century later, in the year 17 BCE, the archivists in the northern African city of Cyrenê dedicated a statue to Aphrodite *Nomophylakis* – 'Guardian of the Laws'. On Paros, a Cycladic island, military generals in the third century BCE erected an inscription to Aphrodite, Zeus *Aphrodisios*, Hermes and Artemis *Eukleia* (*IG* XII 5, 220). This citation of Aphrodite as first recipient, plus the reference to Zeus in Aphrodisian mode, seem to indicate that these military men were invoking a spirit of concord and harmony in the land. Aphrodite was a goddess who promoted civic goodwill, reconciliation, law and peace. Or, to quote Apollodoros of Athens, Aphrodite makes friends.

SEX MAKES BABIES – FERTILITY

All ancient goddesses, every last one of them, are defined at some point or another as a 'fertility goddess'. Aphrodite is no exception. In this case it actually makes sense, insofar as sex makes babies and Aphrodite is a goddess of sex.

However, a few points must be kept in mind. First of all, ancient peoples – in Greece and elsewhere – believed that *males* were the source of new life and fertility, not females. We have known about semen for a lot longer than we have known about the ovum, and most people figured out that women seldom get pregnant without male intervention. So when it came to fertility the ancients were more likely to think in terms of gods than goddesses.

Second, and following up on that issue of 'male intervention', the ancient Greeks understood that pregnancy resulted from sexual intercourse, which was absolutely Aphrodite's domain. Aphrodite's role in fertility was thus not so much as a creatrix of new life, but as the one who encouraged beings to have sex (with its standard results). The clearest association between Aphrodite and fertility/reproduction in the epic tradition appears at the end of Hesiod's *Theogony*. Here children born of goddesses through unions with mortal men are described as occurring 'through Golden Aphrodite' (*dia khrysên Aphroditên*), clearly referring to reproduction through sexual intercourse rather than the parthenogenic reproduction prevalent in earlier verses of this work. Likewise, in the *Homeric Hymn to Aphrodite* (5, ll. 50–51), the goddess causes mortal sons to be born to the 'deathless gods' through their sexual unions with mortal women.

The notion that Aphrodite induces sexual intercourse that leads to fertility extends beyond just deities and humans. As noted above, her visit to Mount Ida caused all the mountain creatures to start mating in her wake, leading, no doubt, to a surplus of cute baby animals not long after. Aphrodite was even credited with earthly fertility, insofar as she caused Ouranos (the heavens) to mate with Ge (the Earth). (Granted, there is an alternative version where Aphrodite rather specifically *stops* Ouranos from mating with Earth by emerging as the resurrection of Ouranos's castrated penis; see Chapter Two). Some of the fifth-century Athenian playwrights explained it quite poetically. Aeschylus, in his lost play *Danaids* (preserved in Athenaios's *Deipnosophistai* 13.600 b), has Aphrodite declare:

> *Pure Heaven loves to accost the land,*
> *And Love seizes Earth to have in wedlock.*
> *Storm falling from Heaven resting in ambush*
> *Impregnates Earth: she bears to mortals*
> *Flock fodder and Demetrian livelihood.*
> *The season of trees from moist union*
> *Is perfected. Of all this I am the cause.*

A similar fragment comes from Euripides, likewise quoted by Athenaios, 13.600 a:

> *Earth loves storm, whenever the dry land –*
> *Fruitless in drought – needs moisture.*
> *August Heaven, filled with rain, loves*
> *To fall upon Earth – because of Aphrodite!*
> *Whenever these two are mixed into one*
> *They together for us grow and rear all things*
> *By which the mortal race lives and flourishes.*

And as Euripides noted in his play *Hippolytos,* ll. 447–450:

> *She moves upon the aether, she is in the billowing*
> *Sea, Kypris is. All things grow through her.*
> *She is the sower and giver of love*
> *From which we all on earth are sprung.*

So, yes, Aphrodite absolutely has a role to play in fertility, namely the fun part: sex. However, she is *not* a mother goddess. She did have some children of her own, notably the deities Eros (Love), Himeros (Desire) and Harmonia (Harmony) – generally understood to be the children of Ares rather than her husband Hephaistos (except for Eros, who was either her son or, according to Hesiod, one of the four primordial deities who existed before Aphrodite). Yet we get a taste of how Aphrodite actually felt about maternity in the story of her seduction of Anchises (*Homeric Hymn* 5).

Basically, Zeus was tired of Aphrodite constantly causing him – and the other gods – to fall in love with mortal women and have affairs with them, thus getting him into trouble with his wife Hera. This was *all* Aphrodite's fault, right? In order to give her a taste of her own medicine, Zeus caused Aphrodite to fall in love with the young Trojan prince Anchises. In love she duly fell. Off she rushed to her temple in Paphos for a bath, some perfume, a quick fashion makeover, co-ordinating jewellery, the whole nine yards. And so attired off she went to Mount Ida to find Anchises, who was herding his cattle because back in the day princes still worked for a living. She set herself right in front of the prince, looking for all the world like a decked-out Manhattan debutante in the middle of a field of soy beans in Nebraska. Needless to say, Aphrodite had to explain herself. She came up with this tall tale that she was a demure virgin from nearby Phrygia. She had been out playing and dancing with her female friends when all of a sudden Hermes showed up and carried her away to Troy to be the wife – by the will of the gods! – of Prince Anchises, whoever that might be.

So there's Anchises, all alone with some cattle on a mountain, and before him appears the most beautiful creature in the universe (inscribed golden apple available upon request). She is brimming over with desirability, and if the prince had *any* qualms at all, this irresistible creature just told him that the *gods have already decreed that she will be his wife*. They go back to his shack and have a *lot* of sex. Then Anchises falls asleep. When he wakes up, Aphrodite has removed her mortal disguise and appears before him as a goddess. He immediately begs her not to hurt him. She calms him down, but complains that she is pregnant, and she is *not* thrilled about this fact (ll. 247–257):

> *But for me this will be a great disgrace among the*
> *Immortal gods for all days everlasting because of you.*
> *Before they continually feared my words and wiles, by which*
> *Ever I made all the gods mingle with mortal women;*
> *For all minds were tamed by me.*
> *But now indeed no longer will my mouth be able to boast*
> *Of this amongst the immortals, since I greatly erred,*
> *Wretch, most unblameworthy, having gone out of my mind,*
> *And I put a child under my belt having lain with a mortal.*
> *As for him, as soon as he sees the light of the sun,*
> *Deep-bosomed mountain nymphs will rear him.*

Aphrodite's response to maternity is to hand the child – Aeneas – over to babysitters as soon as possible. In later years, during the Trojan War, Aphrodite proves to be amazingly ineffective at helping Aeneas on the fields of battle (see below), far less so than when helping her darling Prince Paris, whom she manages to whisk off the field, bring back to the castle, clean up, put into bed, then fetch Helen to come and have sex with him. To be clear, Aphrodite is a much better mother figure to Paris than she ever is to her actual son Aeneas. No, Aphrodite is *not* a mother goddess.

VIOLENCE

A debate that has emerged among scholars in recent decades is the extent to which Aphrodite might be a war goddess, or at least seriously involved with violence. This is understandable.

She spends a lot more time with Ares than Hephaistos, and even has the epithet *Areia* in Sparta (where, to be fair, everything is more martial than normal). Furthermore, as we saw with the Trojan War, the goddess is pretty good at starting conflicts. As discussed in Chapters Two and Three, she is closely associated with, even evolving out of, some Near Eastern goddesses who are themselves martial deities (Ištar, Aštart). Perhaps most importantly, though, ancient authors recorded numerous depictions of Aphrodite bearing armour and weapons, with epithets such as *Hoplismenê* (Armed), *Enopl(i)on* (Armed) and *Strateia* (Pertaining to Warfare).

To be perfectly clear, *no* ancient testimonials exist that claim that Aphrodite could fight or was effective on the battlefield. Quite the opposite: In Book 5 of Homer's *Iliad* (ll. 330–333, 426–430), we read what happened when she did try to help her son Aeneas in the midst of battle:

> *And he [Diomedes] swung the pitiless bronze at Kypris,*
> *Knowing her to be a deity without warcraft, not of those who,*
> *Goddesses, range in order of the ranks of men in the fighting,*
> *Not Athena nor Enyo, sacker of cities.*
> ...
> *...And the father of men and gods [Zeus] smiled and spoke*
> *To golden Aphrodite, calling her to him,*
> *"No, my child, not for you are the works of war. Rather*
> *Concern yourself with the lovely works of marriage,*
> *While all these things here will be of concern to Athena and*
> *swift Ares."*

As far as Homer was concerned, Aphrodite was definitely not a war goddess.

In contrast to this, however, are numerous attestations in literature and art of the goddess armed for battle. In his *Description of Greece,* Pausanias, the Roman-era travel writer, finds that on the island of Kythera (3.23.1), 'The goddess herself is an armed *xoanon* [ancient wooden statue]'. Likewise in Corinth (2.5.1) the statue of Aphrodite on the acropolis is armed – *agalma de autê te hoplismenê*. And in Sparta? *Everyone* knew about the armed (*hoplismenê*) statue of Aphrodite in Sparta. Pausanias, of course, tells us about the 'ancient temple and *xoanon* of Aphrodite Armed' (3.15.10), while from Antipater of Sidon in *Greek Anthology* 16.176, in the first century BCE we hear:

> *Even Kypris is Spartan. She is not dressed as in other towns*
>   *In soft garments;*
> *But in full-force she has a helmet instead of a veil,*
>   *Instead of golden branches a spear-shaft.*
> *For it is not proper for her to be without arms, the consort*
>   *Of Thracian Enyalios [Ares] and a Lakedaimonian [Spartan].*

Quintillian, writing in the first century CE, posed in his *Institutio Oratoria* the fascinating question: '*Cur armata apud Lacedaemonios Venus?*' 'Why is Aphrodite/Venus armed amongst the Lakedaimonians?' (2.4.26). Plutarch apparently came up with the answer, for in his *Institutions of the Spartans* 239 a, he states that:

> *They [the Lakedaimonians] worship Aphrodite Armed (enoplion), and the statues of all the gods, both male and female, they make with spear in hand to show that all the gods have excellence in warfare.*

Nonnos, in his fifth-century CE 'Dionysiaka', was a tad more paranoid, warning the traveller not to 'approach Sparta, where the war-like citizens have a bronze statue of armed Aphrodite, lest she, that spear-wielding one, thwack you with your own iron!' (35, 175–177). Finally, writing in the sixth century CE, Julianus of Egypt tells us in his 'To the Armed Aphrodite in Sparta' in the *Greek Anthology*, 16.173:

> *Always Kythereia has learned to carry a quiver*
> *And bow, and the work of the crafty archer.*
> *Revering the laws of steadfast Lykourgos*
> *She brings charms to Sparta for those armed for close combat.*
> *But you in the chambers, Spartan girls, revere the arms*
> *of Kythereia:*
> *Give birth to courageous children.*

There were, of course, some naysayers. According to Leonidas of Tarentum, writing in the third century BCE and preserved in the *Greek Anthology*, 9.320:

> *Eurotas once said to Kypris, 'Either take up arms,*
> *Or quit Sparta, the polis mad for arms.'*
> *She, laughing, replied, 'I shall be ever unarmed,'*

> *She said, 'and I shall dwell in Lakedaimonia.'*
> *Our Kypris is unarmed. Shameful are those tale-tellers who say*
> *That our goddess bears arms!*

So what was going on?

It is a combination of chronology and fashion statement. In terms of chronology, not a single reference to Aphrodite Armed (*hoplismenê, enoplon*, etc.) exists before the Roman era. The closest we come is Leonidas of Tarentum (a Spartan colony in Italy), who is at best arguing *against* such a notion. The Greek city of Corinth was destroyed by the Romans and only rebuilt a century later, so anything that Pausanias saw there was, perforce, Roman in date and culture. When considering an armed Aphrodite, we have to accept the fact that what we are actually seeing is the Roman goddess Venus.

A martial Aphrodite/Venus had a significant role to play in the rise of the Roman Empire, starting with the propaganda of the dictator Lucius Cornelius Sulla Felix (aka Sulla, born 138 BCE). According to Appian's *The Civil Wars* (1.97), it was once prophesied to Sulla that:

> *Believe me, Roman, Kypris has given great power,*
> *Caring for the line of Aeneas. But you to all*
> *The immortals make annual offerings. Don't forget:*
> *Lead gifts to the Delphians. And there is someplace they go*
> *Under snowy Tauros, a wide city*
> *Of the Carians, who dwell there naming it for Aphrodite.*
> *In that place bring an axe, and you will receive power for yourself.*

Sulla made the dedication at the Anatolian city of Aphrodisias, with the inscription 'Autocrat Sulla dedicates this to you, Aphrodite, who saw you in a dream *arranging the army in battle array and fighting in the panoply of Ares'*. Sulla even went on to give himself the epithet *Epaphroditos*, 'the man by Aphrodite', to complement his Latin title *'Felix'* (Happy). When he returned home from the East he dedicated a temple to Venus Felix, inscribing, according to Plutarch (*Life of Sulla*, 19.9), her name beside those of Mars and Victory. Venus the war goddess had arrived.

As did Sulla, so too did Pompey. In August of 55 BCE Pompey dedicated a theatre/temple to Venus Victrix (Victor), he being the first to give this epithet to the goddess. Both Pompey and Julius Caesar invoked this goddess before battle (Appian 2.281; Plutarch *Life of Pompey*, 68.2; Pliny *Natural History*, 35.115). Beginning in 45–44 BCE, the coins of Julius Caesar show the goddess with weapons and emblems of victory. Julius Caesar considered himself to be a direct descendant of Aeneas, the child of Aphrodite and Anchises (see Chapter Three).

Later, however starting with Octavian Caesar (aka Augustus) around 30 BCE, we begin to see iconography of a different kind. On his coins the goddess is still portrayed with arms – a shield, helmet and spear – but she is naked except for a *himation* (shawl) around her lower legs, emphasizing the contours of her buttocks. She stands upright against a pedestal, holds the helmet and does not actually carry the shield (it is leaning against the pedestal too).

It is *this* portrayal of 'martial' Venus that gains the monopoly in Roman iconography, where slight variations on this theme and pose appear on coins, mirrors, gems and large-scale sculptures. The primary difference between the coin imagery and the statuary is that on the sculptures the goddesses is frequently completely naked, save for a very consistent baldric, and she often is shown holding (the remains of) a sword. On many occasions Venus is surrounded by little Cupids, flying about and playing with the weapons. There is nothing especially martial or threatening about this armed Venus, who seems rather to be amusing herself with her lover's tools (the 'panoply of Ares') than about to go into battle. One is a bit more concerned that one of those Cupids will cut himself.

This is the 'armed' Aphrodite that Pausanias saw in Greece: not a militaristic goddess per se, but a thoroughly Romanised Aphrodite/Venus, bare-ass nude and posing with the weapons of Ares. Only in Sparta does the potentially martial nature of this erotic goddess call for more than a passing comment. And let's be real here: We are talking about Sparta. Winnie the Pooh would be shown with arms and armour.

So Aphrodite is not a martial goddess. She is a goddess, however, and deities have the power to protect their worshippers (a major cause of worship throughout world religions). That was absolutely the case in Corinth during the time of the Persian invasions in the early fifth century BCE. At this time, according to an anecdote by the second-century CE philosopher-biographer Plutarch and a *scholion* (annotation) to a poem by the fifth-century BCE poet Pindar, the wives and women of Corinth prayed to Aphrodite, their protective goddess on the acropolis, to cast desire into their husbands to fight well. A good choice, as Aphrodite is very good at casting desire. Thus Plutarch recorded in On the Malice of Herodotos, 871 a–b:

And in truth of the Greeks only the Corinthian women offered that fair and divine prayer, that the goddess [Aphrodite] should cast desire at their men to fight the barbarians... For the matter was made famous, and Simonides composed the epigram when bronze images were set up in the temple of Aphrodite... The epigram is as follows:

*These ones, for the sake of the Greeks and straight-
    fighting citizens,
Stood having prayed to Kypris divine;
For holy Aphrodite did not intend to betray
A Greek acropolis to bow-toting Medes.*

The prayer worked, by the way: The Persians and Medes did not invade Corinth (they did raze Athens). This might suggest that Aphrodite was more effective in protecting her city than Athena was, although one might also consider the fact that it was the Athenians and *not* the Corinthians who provoked Persia. Aphrodite was the recipient of prayers to save a city at a time of military invasion, and she was successful. But this is not because she is a war goddess (in contrast to Athena who most assuredly is, a sacked Athens notwithstanding). She is simply a goddess, in this instance a goddess of Corinth – the goddess whom a group of women chose to approach to protect, specifically, their husbands by casting desire at them...to fight.

SHE SAVES SAILORS BY THE SEA SHORE

Perhaps it is because she was born in the sea and brought by wave to Paphos (see Chapter Two) that Aphrodite became associated with the sea, sea travel and the protection of those at sea. Several of the goddess's epithets pertain to this aspect of her cult: *Thalassaiê* (She of the Sea), *Pontia* (of the Deep Sea), *Pelagia* (Open Sea), *Galenaiê* (Calm Sea), *Euploia* (Smooth Sailing) and *Limenia* (of the Harbour). It was specifically the shrine of Aphrodite *Euploia* at Knidos where Praxiteles' famous nude statue of Aphrodite was displayed. It is just such a scenario – a statue of the goddess overlooking the sea – that is invoked in a lyric poem by the third-century BCE Arkadian poet Anytê of Tegea in 'Poem 22', *Greek Anthology*, 9.144:

> *This is Kypris's spot, since she loves to be here;*
> *From the mainland she always views the shining sea.*
> *Because she brings voyages to good fulfilment for sailors*
> *The sea reveres her, seeing her gleaming xoanon.*

As a generally gentle goddess overlooking the sea, Aphrodite was also invoked as a goddess who protects those travelling by sea – a bit of an anti-Poseidon, if you will. The best description of this function of the goddess is preserved, yet again, in Athenaios's *Deipnosophistai* 15. 675 f–676 c. He narrates how a man named Herostratos survived a sea storm when travelling from Aphrodite's city of Paphos to the Egyptian city of Naukratis:

During the 23rd Olympiad Herostratos, a citizen of ours, making use of trade and sailing about the various lands, arrived at Paphos of Cyprus, and purchasing a small idol of Aphrodite, a span in height and of old-fashioned craftsmanship, went bearing it to Naukratis. And while approaching Egypt a sudden storm fell upon him and he didn't know where on earth he was; all the sailors fled to the image of Aphrodite and besought her to save them. And the goddess (for she liked Naukratis) suddenly made the area before her full of fresh myrtle, and a sweet scent filled the ship, while previously those sailing despaired of safety, being really seasick and retching profusely. And when the sun appeared they saw their anchorage and arrived at Naukratis. Herostratos set out from the ship along with the idol, also bearing the miraculously appearing fresh myrtle; he dedicated them in the sanctuary of Aphrodite. He sacrificed to the goddess and dedicated the idol to Aphrodite, and summoning about the hearth of this sanctuary those who came with him and his closest neighbours, he gave them each a crown from this myrtle, which he then called 'Naukratitis'.

Centuries earlier than this we have references in Sappho to this function of the goddess. Sappho's brother Kharaxos was a sea-trader and thus came often into Poseidon's harm's way. So it is not surprising that Sappho wrote lyrics begging for her brother's maritime safety. In one short fragment ('Fragment 5') Sappho pleads:

> *Kypris and Nereids, unharmed to me*
> *Grant that my brother arrive here,*

*And that all that his heart wants
Be brought to fruition.*

(Granted, in another fragment she chews out her brother for spending so much money to liberate a *hetaira* from Naukratis, which brings several Aphrodisian themes full circle…)

Aphrodite's protection of those at sea even extended to sea battles. Over the course of the Peloponnesian War between Athens and Sparta (431–404 BCE) the Athenian admiral Konon won a victory over the Spartans in a sea battle off the coast of Knidos. In thanksgiving for this victory Konon founded a sanctuary to Aphrodite at the Piraeus, the primary port of Athens. As recorded by Pausanias in his *Description of Greece,* 1.1.3:

By the sea Konon built a sanctuary of Aphrodite, having totalled Lakedaimonian triremes by Knidos off the Carian Chersonese. For the Knidians revere Aphrodite above all, and they have various sanctuaries of the goddess. The oldest is of Aphrodite Doritis; next comes that of Aphrodite Akraia ('On High'). The most recent is to the Aphrodite most people call 'Knidia', but whom the Knidians themselves call Euploia.

The specific dedication to Aphrodite, possibly as *Euploia*, was no doubt owing to the importance of this goddess at the site of victory.

The correlations between Aphrodite and the sea show up all the time in art. Perhaps the most famous depiction of the goddess is Botticelli's painting *The Birth of Venus* (less formally known as

'Venus on the Half-Shell'), where the newly born goddess, fully nude but with strategically placed hair, rides a giant shell to the coast where one of the Seasons (*Horai*) greets her with clothing. This Renaissance painting reflects numerous similar depictions of Aphrodite from late Classical and Hellenistic times, where the goddess appears with swans, geese and dolphins and frolicking with Nereids – the divine, nymph-like daughters of the sea god Nereus who populate the oceans just as nymphs populate the forests. Another popular motif was the *Anadyomenê* of Aphrodite, where the newly born goddess is shown emerging from the sea. One especially famous depiction is on the Ludovisi Throne (*c.* 470 BCE. In this scene the (clothed) goddess is being helped out of the water by two females, possibly Horai or Charites/Graces. The scene calls to mind yet another anecdote from Athenaios (13.590 f–591 a) once again referring to Aphrodite's mortal avatar Phrynê:

And truly, Phrynê was more beautiful in her unseen parts. Because of this one could not easily see her naked. For she covered herself with a khiton close to the body and she did not use the public baths. During the Eleusinian festival and the Poseidonia – in full view of all of the Greeks! – she removed her himation [overgarment], and having loosened her hair she stepped into the sea. And from her Apelles painted his 'Aphrodite Anadyomenê'.

GROW UP!

Because she is a goddess of sex, in modern times we tend to associate Aphrodite with pleasure. There is a very good reason for this and I am *not* saying that it is wrong at all. As discussed above, however, sex leads to babies, which was a rather important function of at least heterosexual sex in ancient Greece (and everywhere else). Having children in the ancient world was not a personal choice. Ancient societies were based to one degree or another upon family units (the household, the clan, etc.), and it was critically important, from a political perspective, to keep those families extant. On a very personal level it was necessary to keep one's family alive. It was the family that owned property, provided labour, gave help and security and was the foundation for one's identity in society. It was thus *imperative* to have children to keep the family going.

This is one of the reasons why modern debates about ancient 'heteronormativity' are so absurd. Yes, of course, those living in ancient times were deeply focused on heterosexual unions: they needed babies. Furthermore, those babies needed to fit into society in ways that society could deal with, which usually – but not necessarily – involved institutions such as marriage or adoption. To put it simply, everyone needed to make babies in order to keep society going.

This had nothing to do with what we nowadays call 'sexuality'. The ancient Greeks seem to have understood that humans were, for the most part, pretty much bisexual, with people being attracted to their own sex or the opposite sex at different levels of eroticism over the course of the life span. A young man (who, keep in mind, might not marry until he is 30) might have an erotic – or even just an intensely emotional – relationship with another male, either his own age or older, before marrying a young girl and having those oh-so-necessary babies, before possibly ending life with a partner of either sex, depending on attractions and inclinations. So long as he had those babies in wedlock, nothing else really mattered. It was a bit more restricted for girls, of course, because they had to reserve their childbearing for a very specific man (that is, their husbands), but this was not an issue when it came to other females. So it is not surprising to find Aphrodite implicated in same-sex relationships in ancient Greece, especially manifest in the poetry of Sappho of Lesbos.

In her one surviving complete poem, the *Hymn to Aphrodite*, Sappho writes:

> Ornate-throned, immortal Aphrodite
> Child of Zeus, wile-weaving, I beseech you,
> Do not with ache and anguish overwhelm,
> Mistress, my heart.
> But come here, if ever before
> Hearing my prayers from afar,
> Listening, leaving your father's house
> Of gold, you came.
> On a yoked chariot, beautiful swift sparrows brought you
> On fluttering wings to the dark earth from heaven
> Through the middle air.
> Quickly you came. And you, O blessed one,
> Smiling on your immortal face,
> Asked on what account I am suffering again, and
> On what account was I summoning again,
> And what did I want most in my raving heart to happen.

> *'Whom do I persuade now,*
> *To lead you back to her dearest love?*
> *Who, O Sappho, wrongs you?*
> *For if she flees, soon will she follow;*
> *And if she does not receive gifts, then she will give.*
> *And if she does not love, soon she will love even if she does not wish it.'*
> *Come to me now, release me from this grievous care!*
> *What my heart desires to come to pass, make happen.*
> *And you yourself be my ally.*

For the record, Aphrodite could also send overwhelming heterosexual desire to young women. To quote Sappho again in 'Fragment 102':

> *Sweet Mother, I cannot beat the loom beam,*
> *Being overcome by tender Aphrodite with desire for a boy.*

(I have the strong impression that the speaker here was told to get her butt back into gear and finish her weaving in spite of her debilitating heartbreak!)

So Aphrodite could, and did, promote all sorts of love and erotic inclinations. In the end, however, at least some of that libido *must* be heterosexual, because of the need for babies. Aphrodite as the goddess who inspires reproductive heterosexuality was prominent in coming-of-age rituals in ancient Greece, often alongside Hermes, the god of crossing borders. As discussed in Chapter Two, these two deities were worshipped together at the longest continually used sanctuary in the Aegean (Kato Symi Viannou on Crete). Here it appears that young men were initiated into adulthood via camping. In Locris in southern Italy (a Greek territory in ancient times), terracotta plaques show children offering toys to Aphrodite and Hermes, a step on the road to adulthood.

Yet perhaps the best ritual pertaining to adulthood, heterosexuality and the power of Aphrodite is to be seen in the tale of Hippolytos, preserved in a play of that name by the Athenian playwright Euripides. The story is in the genre of the biblical Potiphar's Wife. The Athenian hero Theseus has returned from Crete after having slaughtered the Minotaur. He did this with the help of the Minoan (Cretan) princess Ariadnê, whom he then abandoned (and who ended up as wife to the god Dionysos, so she absolutely married up). Theseus went on to marry Ariadnê's sister Phaidra, whom he took home to Athens to be stepmother to his illegitimate son Hippolytos, conceived during his tryst with the amazon Hippolyta (aka Antiopê). However, according to Euripides, Aphrodite is extremely annoyed with Hippolytos for disdaining the goddess and being the single most frigid man in Greece. Hippolytos had *no* interest in sex at all. He spent his days hunting in the company of Artemis and – this is the really problematic bit – actively insulting Aphrodite. In revenge, Aphrodite caused his stepmother Phaidra to fall desperately in love with Hippolytos. Consumed by love sickness, she finally confesses her love to the young man. He violently rejects her. Phaidra writes a letter to Theseus in which she claims that Hippolytos tried to rape her, then kills herself.

Theseus, apparently not knowing his son very well, believes the lying letter and calls on Poseidon to have Hippolytos trampled to death. The end.

Euripides was, and is, generally understood to be rather cynical when it came to the deities, and this play is often mentioned in that regard. Not only was Aphrodite so petty as to kill a man just because he didn't like her, but Artemis did not lift a finger to protect her friend and hunting partner. She merely took revenge by killing Aphrodite's favourite mortal Adonis (see Chapter Three).

However, this interpretation misses the significance of Hippolytos's sexual denial. He was the boy who refused to grow up; like Peter Pan he lived in world of fantasy, surrounding himself with young men and a single female, herself virginal and wild. In so doing he actively shunned women, marriage and sex, and consequently reproduction, the maintenance of the household and the *polis* (city-state). He rejected the responsibilities of adulthood, including those of marriage and fatherhood. Put simply, Hippolytos is not merely frigid; he is an irresponsible citizen. This is not to be tolerated, even by the deities.

In the end, Hippolytos was made an object lesson. A cult was established for him in Troizen (the location of Euripides' play) where girls went to offer a lock of hair as they prepared themselves for marriage. Euripides' Artemis proclaimed in ll. 1424–1429:

> *For you, o suffering one, in recompense for these evils*
> *Great honours in the city of Troizen*
> *I shall give; for unwed girls before their weddings*

> *Will cut their hair for you, who for a long age*
> *Will cull the great sorrow of their tears.*
> *Always will you be recalled in the music-making*
> *of maidens…*

This practice was recorded as late as the second century CE in Pausanias's *Description of Greece*, 2.32.1:

There is a most notable temenos *[sanctuary] dedicated to Hippolytos, son of Theseus, with a temple in it and an ancient statue. They say that Diomedes made these and additionally that he was the first to sacrifice to Hippolytos. Among the Troizenians is a priest of Hippolytos who serves for his entire life, and they offer sacrifices annually. And this other thing they do: Every maiden cuts a tress for him before marriage, and bringing it to the temple dedicates it.*

Hippolytos was destroyed, and henceforth girls mourn him and learn from his negative example. They pass by his temple to leave a token symbol of childhood on their way to reproductive adulthood. Aphrodite's sexuality can certainly be fun, but it can also be a duty, and she will remind her devotees that they cannot avoid their necessary work. To have sex responsibly is to be an adult.

What in modern times we might view as a 'frivolous' goddess – she who presides over the prattle of love-struck girls and flirtation – was actually an extremely powerful deity for the ancient Greeks. It turned out that libido was far more difficult to deal with in civilized society than, say, blacksmithing, and that sex plays a more important role in society than we moderns give it credit.

Not only did Aphrodite have power over all living things (or at least anything that reproduces sexually), but that power extended into other aspects of mortal life. Along with deities such as Hermes and Artemis, Aphrodite helped children to mature into socially responsible adults; they would then go on to give rise to the next generation of socially responsible adults. Aphrodite had a prominent role in the initiation of certain historically rather important wars, but she could also protect people during military conflicts. The women of Corinth certainly depended on this aspect of their acropoline goddess. If one were lucky (and it was good luck), Aphrodite could simply prevent conflicts from happening in the first place, promoting social harmony in the state and among fellow citizens. While all creatures may have been enthralled to the goddess's erotic power, many erotic slaves were liberated into her care and she was protective of their newfound liberty. Aphrodite even guarded people travelling by sea, with no erotic connotations whatsoever – that one was simply a freebee. Not bad, all in all.

Nevertheless, as noted at the beginning of this chapter, the Greeks remained a bit wary of this extremely powerful goddess. More so than with any other deity, they were constantly aware of her *foreign* nature: her origins in Cyprus, or even beyond. Somehow Aphrodite was simply less Greek than the other deities. We'll consider why in the next chapter.

2.
The Origins of Aphrodite

First amongst the divine Kythereians
She floated; then she arrived at sea-girt Cyprus.
The fair hallowed goddess stepped forth, and about her
Tender feet grass grew forth.
– Hesiod, *Theogony*, ll. 192–195

t is the year 1200 BCE, and you live in Pylos on the western coast of southern Greece. You are walking through the palace known for your kinsman Nestor, heading to the archives where the palace records are kept on clay tablets, written in an early form of Greek in a writing system known as Linear B (those Minoans to the south, in Crete, wrote in Linear A, not that you can read it). You come across a list of deities to whom sacrifices are to be made. This list would look quite familiar to your much later descendants, who lived in Athens in the time of Plato: Zeus, Dionê, Hera, Hermes, Artemis, Poseidon, Eileithyia, Enyalios (also known as Ares), the Erinys (Furies), the Lady of Athens (Athena), Paiawon (aka Apollo), Dionysos, Hephaistos and the Earth (*Da*) Mother (*Mater*) Demeter.

But one of the Olympians is missing: Aphrodite, the goddess of sex and love. The Golden One has not yet arrived in Greece.

Considering the details of Aphrodite's birth, this might not be all that bad. According to Hesiod's *Theogony*, the eighth-century poem of the 'Birth of the Gods', Ge, Earth, mated with her son Ouranos, the sky. Unfortunately he would not stop, not even when Ge wanted to give birth. Needless to say, she got a bit cranky. Ge made a sickle and had her youngest son Kronos castrate Ouranos, solving the problem. Kronos then threw Ouranos's penis into the sea (ll. 188–191):

*And as soon as he had cut off the members with flint and cast them from the land into the surging sea, they were swept away over the sea for a long time. And a white foam (*aphros*) spread around them from the immortal flesh, and in it grew a maiden.*

And so Aphrodite was born – created by an act of sexual violence and castration. Perhaps not the most auspicious beginning.

The goddess on the sea floated past the southern edge of Greece and past the island of Kythera with its view of Sparta. She eventually made landfall on the island of Cyprus, not far from Paphos. It was at Paphos that the Greeks first encountered Aphrodite, and it was here that they placed her home (*Odyssey*, Book 8, ll. 364–366):

She, laughter-loving Aphrodite, went to Cyprus, to Paphos, where are her temenos and fragrant altar. There the Graces bathed her and anointed her with immortal oil, such as gleams upon the gods that are forever. And they clothed her in lovely raiment, a wonder to behold.

KYPRIS – THE GODDESS OF CYPRUS (I)

Leaving aside Greek tales of horny rain gods, Cyprus is the actual birthplace of Aphrodite. Her lineage here extends back into the Early Bronze Age (2250–1900 BCE) when, around 1900, the residents of Cyprus, the Copper Island, began to make use of humble terracotta figurines of women. These women in clay were a far cry from Golden Aphrodite. Schematic and rectangular, they had rudimentary eyes and nose, occasional breasts (or not), and no legs to speak of – just the bottom of a skirt. About one-third of them carried a baby in their arms. But every one of them was elaborately dressed. The figurines were covered with incised facial decorations, holes for earrings, elaborate necklaces and textile patterns upon the body that hint at richly woven clothing. They may have had minimal bodies, but they certainly knew how to dress! These figurines came to light throughout the island, in homes and burials, used by the living and placed with the dead.

Sometimes these figurines appeared in larger pottery compositions, in bowls or sculptures, often standing opposite a man. These larger compositions have always been found in burials. In fact, at one tomb at the site of Karmi-Palealona, possibly dating as early as 2000 BCE, what appears to be a large-scale, low relief of such a figure appears on the wall of the corridor leading to the tomb.

What did they mean, these abstract, terracotta women, elaborately dressed and occasionally holding infants? As noted, the bodies were minimal, just enough to show that they were female, but there is clear emphasis on the decoration, both clothing and jewellery. Some scholars have even suggested that the textile patterns on the dress are reminiscent of a tartan, perhaps a way to show membership of a family or clan. Perhaps, just possibly, these women in clay represented the family itself – schematic portrayals of a beloved great-grandmother who in the house, in the grave, even from beyond the grave continued to watch over her descendants.

Certainly this is a far cry from Aphrodite *Kallipygia* – She of the Lovely Derriere. However, over the centuries these terracotta figurines morphed and evolved. First they became a bit more three-dimensional (the first step towards getting a derriere). Then, in the Middle Bronze Age (1900–1600 BCE), they became naked (now we're getting somewhere!). Now these rounded figurines, still adorned with necklaces and holes for earrings, show fully modelled breasts and occasionally a hole that may represent a navel or even a vagina. They acquire modelled arms that lie upon the torso, drawing attention to these sexualized attributes. Our Cypriot great-grandmother is becoming increasingly erotic.

By the Late Bronze Age (1600–1050 BCE) our figurines have become utterly eroticized. Now completely nude, they have large, fully modelled breasts adorning the chest, highlighted by a criss-cross between them and the hands lying upon the upper abdomen above an incised navel. Broad hips accommodate a *giant* pubic triangle, highlighted further by incised cross-hatching and an incised vulva. The body is still adorned with earrings and necklaces, and even now many carry a baby in their arms. The figures also have very large noses and are commonly referred to as 'bird face figurines'.

By the end of the Late Bronze Age our terracotta female changes for one final time. Still in possession of breasts, pubic triangle, navel and jewellery, her hips and nose shrink to normal proportions (these are now called 'normal face figurines', to distinguish them from their more avian sisters). The babies disappear. What we now find in Cyprus, in Paphos even, is the image of an eroticized nude woman with prominent breasts and genitalia, adorned with jewellery, but not really a mother figure. Aphrodite has arrived.

So what happened? How did we go from great-grandma to *Philommeides* – 'Genital-Loving Aphrodite'? Basically, Cyprus got a lot of influence from the lands to the east, such as Syria and Mesopotamia. This influence included the introduction of some extremely erotic goddesses, notably the powerful Mesopotamian goddess Ištar.

OURANIA – THE HEAVENLY ONE: NEAR EASTERN INFLUENCE

Starting in the Middle Bronze Age, and in full flow by the Late Bronze Age, Cyprus developed increasing contacts with Near Eastern civilizations, especially those of Syria and Mesopotamia. From around 1400 BCE sanctuaries with Near Eastern precedents start to appear on the island, along with numerous goods, both elite and common, from their eastern neighbours. Two aspects of this contact implicated the evolution of Aphrodite: iconography and divine personae.

The iconography concerns the terracotta figurines discussed above. These changed from demure mum to more erotic ladies through contact with Syria, where such figurines became increasingly prominent from 2000 BCE. These terracotta females were rendered in the nude, with elaborate coiffures, earrings, necklaces, even bracelets and anklets. They might have arms out and a criss-cross over the chest, or their hands might be actively holding their modelled breasts. Some of the figurines had emphasized pubic triangles filled with stippling motifs and even a carefully rendered vulva. It is not difficult to see how they came to influence the Cypriot tradition, but there is one crucial distinction: the Near Eastern models *never* carried babies. Syria and Mesopotamia before it were making figurines of highly eroticized females who had nothing to do with maternity.

Nor was it just iconography that was making its way westward in the Late Bronze Age. Near Eastern deities also started to be worshipped on the Copper Isle. Around the year 1400 an official from the Syrian coastal city of Ugarit (modern Rash Shamra), who was residing on Cyprus, wrote a letter to his king. It begins:

> *To the king, [my] lo[rd],*
> *speak thus:*
> *From the officer of the one hundred, [your servant]*
> *At the feet of my lord, [from afar,]*
> *seven and seven times [I have fallen.]*
> *I myself have spoken to Ba'al...*
> *to eternal Šapaš, to Athtart,*
> *to Anat, to all the gods of Alašiya...*

– Translated by Neal Walls. *In Copper Production and Divine Protection: Archaeology, Ideology and Social Complexity on Bronze Age Cyprus*, edited by A. B. Knapp Göteborg: Paul Åströms Förlag, PRU V, 8, 4–8, 36, 1986

Alašiya was the name used for Cyprus in the Bronze Age. Ba'al (Lord), Šapaš (Sun), Athtart (Astarte) and Anat were all deities worshipped in Ugarit. By 1400 deities in Cyprus had become so close to those in Syria that they were simply called by the same names and officially recognized as 'the gods of Alašiya'. One of these deities was Athtart, a Western manifestation of the more Eastern Ištar.

Ištar

If one were looking for a goddess who could be described as 'highly eroticized with nothing whatsoever to do with maternity', Ištar would be a good choice. All that one would need to add would be a healthy (or perhaps not so healthy) dose of violence, as Ištar is the Mesopotamian goddess of sex and war. Her name and persona developed through a merging of two separate Near Eastern deities – the Sumerian goddess Inana and the Semitic god Aštar. Inana was a goddess of both love and warfare; Aštar was a god of war. Both were associated with the planet Venus, the morning and evening star. When the Sumerian-speaking residents of Mesopotamia came into increasingly closer contact with their Semitic, Akkadian-speaking neighbours, these two deities fused into the single goddess Ištar.

THE ORIGINS OF APHRODITE

Sumerian Inana's eroticism was most frequently expressed in the tales of her and her young bridegroom Dumuzi. In hymns and narratives, the young Inana would call out to her young man to love her and satisfy her sexually:

> *You are to place your right hand on my vulva while your left hand rests on my head, bringing your mouth close to my mouth, and taking my lips in your mouth: thus you shall take an oath for me. This is the oath of women, my brother of the beautiful eyes.*
> *My desirable one, my desirable one, your charms are lovely, my desirable apple garden, your charms are lovely. My fruitful garden of meš trees, your charms are lovely, my one who is in himself Dumuzi, your charms are lovely.*
> – 'Balbale' Hymn to Inana and Dumuzi B, ll. 21–30, from *The Electronic Text Corpus of Sumerian Literature*

In later years, after the death of Dumuzi (either by raiders or through the machinations of Inana herself, see Chapter Three), and once she had evolved into the less young and innocent Ištar, the goddess developed an even greater libido:

> *'The young men of your city gather to me!' Celebration is the foundation to the city!*
> *'To the shade of the city wall let us go!' Celebration is the foundation to the city!*
> *Seven (at) her bosom, seven (at) her hips. Celebration is the foundation to the city!*

Sixty and sixty climax in her vulva. Celebration is the foundation to the city!
The young men got tired, Ištar did NOT tire. Celebration is the foundation to the city!
– Above is the author's translation. 'Ein spät-altbabylonisches pārum-Preislied für Ištar', by Von Soden and Oelsner, *Orientalia*, Nova Series, 60, no. 4, 341.

In addition to her amorous inclinations, Inana/Ištar had numerous qualities that made her extremely popular throughout the Near East. As noted, she was a war goddess, granting victory in battle. Perhaps related, it was she who bestowed legitimate kingship. Her early links with the planet Venus made Inana/Ištar an astral deity, a heavenly goddess. In some places she was even understood to have healing and prophetic qualities. All in all, she was a useful goddess to have around.

The cult of Inana/Ištar spread throughout the Near East. In western Syria, she was often called by her more Semitic name of Athtart/Aštart, the feminine version of Aštar mentioned above. Aštart went on to have far more of Ištar's martial, rather than erotic, qualities, but her image was still that of a beautiful young naked woman. This image, plus Ištar's libidinous reputation, was enough to instigate the eroticisation of goddesses farther west (for example, in Cyprus). When Near Eastern iconography and Near Eastern goddesses arrived in Cyprus in the Late Bronze Age, they induced the formerly demure Cypriot ancestress to morph into the powerful – and powerfully erotic – goddess of Cyprus, Aphrodite.

KYPRIS – THE GODDESS OF CYPRUS (II)

She was not actually known by that name on the island. The earliest attestation of the name 'Aphrodite' is in the works of Homer and Hesiod, Greek sources dating from the eighth century BCE. But this was not the name the Cypriots used for their goddess. Furthermore, they did not worship her as a nude female after the Bronze Age. The naked female figurines so common throughout the Bronze Age ceased to be produced on Cyprus by the end of that period.

Influences from Aegean traders and, later, settlers changed the female iconography on the island completely. At first, of course, it was simply the shrinking of the hips and the disappearance of the baby; vibrant nudity remained. Over time, however, this nude female was replaced by the so-called 'Goddess With Upraised Arms', a Cypriot version of an idol common in Late Bronze Age Crete. This Cypriot image had a columnar base rather than legs and pubis. Her arms were held up on either side of her head in a gesture of blessing rather than touching the body itself. Modelled breasts were still present, but the overall impression is of a woman wearing a long robe.

Furthermore, it seems that the Cypriots came to worship their island goddess in physical form as a baetyl (literally 'house of god'): a stone that embodies the divine presence. This was especially so at Paphos, where a cone of green-grey microgabbro 1.22 metres in height was revered as the cult image of the goddess well into Roman times. As noted by the Roman historian Tacitus in the first century CE, 'The statue of the goddess does not have human form; it is a circular block, larger at the bottom and growing smaller to the top, as a cone. The reason for this is obscure' (*Histories*, 2.3). Archaeologists discovered this baetyl upside down in a rock-cut pit in the floor of Sanctuary II at Old Paphos; it probably belonged originally to the twelfth-century BCE temple. Similar baetyls have come to light in Kition and Enkomi. Both sites were the locations of significant Cypriot sanctuaries as well as copper foundries. So, no longer a nude female, but a rock. Only in later years, under Greek influence, will statues of Aphrodite as an elegantly dressed woman be revered on the island. Not until the fourth century, with the creation of Praxiteles' *Aphrodite of Knidos*, will she again appear in the nude.

And, as noted, she is not really 'Aphrodite' yet. When we start to be able to read inscriptions from Cyprus in the tenth century BCE (before that Cypriots wrote in a script called Cypro-Minoan, which they got from Crete; it remains unreadable today), we find numerous references to highly localized goddess titles throughout Cyprus, many that we shall come to associate with Aphrodite. First, and most importantly, we find a goddess in Paphos called *Thea*, the Greek word for 'goddess', and *Wanassa*, the Mycenaean Greek word for 'queen'. A final title she holds here is *Golgia*, literally meaning 'The One of the City of Golgoi'. If we go to Golgoi we find this goddess again, this time known as *Golgia*, *Thea Golgia* and *Paphia*, 'The One of the City of Paphos'. In Idalion she is still *Golgia*; in Khytroi she is *Golgia* and *Paphia*. By the fourth century BCE Khytroi is also producing inscriptions to *Aphrodite-Paphia*, while the southern Cypriot city of Amathus reveals, finally, the title *Aphrodite-Kypria*: Cypriot Aphrodite.

It seems that in the early Iron Age the Cypriots, now joined by the Greeks, worshiped a goddess whom they recognize as the 'Queen of Paphos' – or simply as either 'the Paphian' or just 'The Goddess'. She also has a significant cult site in Golgoi. Over time this deity comes to acquire her Greek name of Aphrodite. She is equated with the Queen of Paphos and eventually associated with the entire island – hence the name *Aphrodite-Kypria*. So, Aphrodite evolved on Cyprus, but she was not called by that name on the island until the fourth century, when the Cypriots began using the Greek name for her instead of a series of titles (*Wanassa, Thea,* etc.).

For the record, the name Aphrodite is not Greek. While the ancient Greeks believed that the name was related to *aphros*, the word for 'foam', this is just a folk etymology. We have no idea where the word Aphrodite comes from or what it means.

APHRODITE COMES TO GREECE

The earliest evidence for Aphrodite in Greece dates from the eighth century BCE. In literature she appears in the works of Hesiod (*c.* 750 BCE) and Homer (*c.* 700 BCE), as noted above. In terms of epigraphy (inscriptions), the first attestation of her name is on the so-called Nestor Cup from Pithekoussai (off the western coast of Italy). Dating from 730–720 BCE, the inscription reads:

> *Of Nestor, in this wine cup a pleasant drink;*
> *Who would drink this beverage, immediately*
> *Will desire for fair-crowned Aphrodite seize him.*

As soon as we hear about Aphrodite, we read that getting drunk will make you horny. This cup was discovered in a child's grave. You have to wonder about the parenting skills...

Kythera (and Asia...)

As far as the Greeks themselves were concerned, Aphrodite originally came from Cyprus – especially Paphos, as described above. When she made her way westwards, her cult (the physical manifestation of her worship) first appeared in southern Greece.

According to all the ancient literary accounts, the place where Aphrodite first graced Greek soil was the island of Kythera, ten kilometres off the southern coast of the Peloponnese. The three primary testimonials come from Hesiod, Herodotos (fifth century BCE) and Pausanias (second century CE). In Hesiod's *Theogony* ll. 192–195 we read how:

> *First amongst the divine Kythereians*
> *She floated; then she arrived at sea-girt Cyprus.*
> *The fair hallowed goddess stepped forth, and about her*
> *Tender feet grass grew forth.*

The goddess is thus thought to have floated past the island of Kythera on her way to Paphos. This technically gave Greece (rather than Cyprus) dibs on the goddess, even if she did ultimately make landfall on the island of copper.

Later authors already had some notion of the more eastern origins of their goddess of sex, looking past even Cyprus to the Levant and then Mesopotamia. Even so, they believed that when this eastern cult reached Greece, it first appeared on Kythera. We thus hear from Herodotos in his *Histories* Book 1, 105 that:

The sanctuary of Aphrodite Ourania in Ashkelon … is the sanctuary, as I discovered through inquiry, which is the oldest of all the sanctuaries of this goddess; for the sanctuary of Cyprus originated there, as the Cypriots themselves say, and as for the one amongst the Kythereians, the Phoenicians are its founders, who are from Syria too.

So, according to Herodotos, the oldest sanctuary of the goddess is actually at Ashkelon, a city on the southern coast of Palestine/Philistia. From there Aphrodite's cult spread both to Cyprus and, farther west, to Kythera, introduced and spread by Phoenicians. Going even farther east, we read in Pausanias's *Description of Greece* 1.14.7 that:

Nearby is a sanctuary of Aphrodite Ourania. It was established that the first people to revere Ourania were the Assyrians, and after the Assyrians the Paphians of Cyprus and those of the Phoenicians who dwell in Ashkelon in Palestine; Kythereians worship her having so learned from the Phoenicians.

Ironically, there is as yet no evidence of Phoenicians on Kythera during the early Iron Age, just the time when Aphrodite was introduced into Greece. It is highly likely that later Greek authors such as Herodotos understood the eastern origins of their goddess but had to reconcile that with the dictates of Hesiod, who associated their goddess with Kythera. Aphrodite thus bears the epithet *Kythereia*, but the role of any actual Phoenicians is still in debate.

Crete

By contrast, there is rather more evidence for early Aphrodite on the island of Crete, appearing in archaeological, epigraphic and even literary form. Concerning the last, we read from the poet Sappho in 'Fragment 2':

> *Hither to me from Crete to this holy temple,*
> *Where is your beautiful apple grove*
> *And altars smoking with incense.*
> *Cold water gurgles through apple tree branches,*
> *And the entire area is shaded by roses,*
> *And quivering leaves pour down*
> *deep slumber.*
> *There a horse-rearing meadow has blossomed with*
> *spring flowers,*
> *The gales blow gently...*
> *There indeed you, Kypris, take up...*
> *In golden kylikes gracefully pour nectar*
> *Mingled with (our) festivities.*

THE ORIGINS OF APHRODITE

The problem with the physical data is that the archaeology and the texts do not quite line up in terms of chronology. In other words, the sanctuaries associated with Aphrodite are actually much older than any references to the goddess's name in Greece.

Take the sanctuary at Kato Symi Viannou in south-central Crete, for example. A sanctuary existed here from around 2000 BCE, continuing in use until the rise of Christianity. From the sixth century BCE inscriptions from the sanctuary make it clear that it was dedicated to the joint worship of Aphrodite and Hermes – possibly a site where young men went through coming-of-age rituals. But was the site *always* dedicated to these two deities? There is no evidence for either deity in Crete as early as the second millennium (Hermes shows up in the Linear B corpus much later and farther north).

Furthermore, the sanctuary shows signs of a significant re-organization in the seventh century BCE. It would appear that the sanctuary at Kato Symi Viannou was originally dedicated to one or more Minoan deities – the Minoans being the non-Greek population who lived on Crete before the Greeks arrived. This is confirmed by the presence of Minoan religious artefacts at the site, such as Minoan-style worshipper figurines and the famous *labrydes* (double axes). Only later were the deities of Kato Symi Viannou 'reimagined' as the now more familiar deities Aphrodite and Hermes, these deities dis/replacing earlier Minoan gods whose names are lost to time.

Sparta (Already Occupied)

This actually happened a lot: Greek deities displacing and replacing earlier deities. It is exactly what occurred when Aphrodite arrived in Sparta. Before the arrival of Aphrodite, the Spartans had their own goddess of love and beauty: Helen of Sparta (aka Helen of Troy). An anecdote from Herodotos bears this out. In telling us about the most beautiful woman in fifth-century Sparta, he relates in *Histories* 6.61 that:

For her appearance being plain – and she being the ugly daughter of wealthy folks – her nurse, having seen that her parents thought her appearance was a disaster, considering everything decided on the following. Every day she carried the girl to Helen's sanctuary. This is in the area called Therapnê, above Apollo's sanctuary. So the nurse carried her, setting her before the statue and invoking the goddess to deliver the child from ugliness. And indeed once, when the nurse was leaving the sanctuary, a woman, it is said, appeared and asked to see what the nurse carried in her arms. The nurse said that it was a child. The woman asked her to show it to her, but the nurse said that she could not – for she was forbidden by the parents to show the child to anyone. But the woman demanded by all means to see the child and, seeing the woman making so much of seeing the girl, the nurse revealed her. The woman stroked the head of the child saying how she would be the most beautiful of all Spartan women.

This shrine at Therapnê was just to the east of Sparta. To judge from the votive remains the cult began in the early seventh century, when an inscription records that 'Deinis dedicated these objects to Helen, wife of Menelaos'. Later, in the early fifth century, a large limestone stele was set up at the shrine, which 'Euthikrenes dedicated to Menelaos'. The shrine is now generally understood to be a joint cult of the Homeric hero Menelaos and his wife, the heroine Helen. However, the evidence from Deinis indicates that it was originally dedicated to Helen, and the evidence from Herodotos makes it pretty clear that Helen was not originally worshipped as a heroine (or a wife), but as a goddess of beauty.

When Aphrodite showed up, though, Helen got demoted. Despite being still revered as a goddess in Sparta (according to Herodotos), in the rest of the Greek world she was ousted by Aphrodite, who became the more universal goddess of love, sex and beauty, not to mention the bane of Helen. As the goddess fulminated at the heroine in Homer's *Iliad*, Book 3, ll. 414–417:

> *Don't provoke me, bitch, lest I get angry at you*
> *And hate you as now I violently love you.*
> *I can make you a baneful scourge in the midst*
> *of both sides –*
> *Trojan and Danaan – and then you will end badly.*

Helen turned out all right in the end. She survived the Trojan War (of which she was the cause) and returned home to be queen of Sparta. In fact, her husband Menelaos was granted eternal life because he was her husband. According to Homer's *Odyssey*, Book 4, ll. 561–570:

> *For you it is not ordained, O Menelaos, fostered by Zeus,*
> *To die in horse-pasturing Argos and to follow death,*
> *But to the Elysian Field and the ends of the earth*
> *The immortals will lead you. There is*
> *gleaming Rhadamanthus,*
> *Where the easiest life exists for humans,*
> *Never is there snow, nor great winter storms, nor shadows ever,*
> *But always Ocean sends forth gentle breezes of the blowing*
> *West Wind to refresh humans.*
> *This because you have Helen and are son-in-law to Zeus.*

But as far as Greek religion in general was concerned, Helen was no match for Aphrodite.

Not all Greek deities got out of the way so easily. Hera, for one. Still in Sparta, we read in Pausanias that:

Here there is a sanctuary of Hera Hyperkheiria (Upper Hand) made, according to an oracle, when the Eurotas River greatly overflowed their land. The old xoanon they call Aphrodite Hera; it has been held customary that mothers sacrifice to this deity upon the marriage of a daughter.
– Description of Greece, 3, 13, 8–9

Just as Helen was the original Spartan goddess of beauty, Hera was (and remained) their goddess of marriage. When Aphrodite arrived it appears that there were some…negotiations regarding who would take over this aspect of Spartan culture. Should it be the original goddess of marriage or the newly arrived goddess of love?

The Queen of the Deities held firm and came to be worshipped as a goddess of marriage, with a helping of love and sex on the side.

On the one hand Aphrodite nudged and occasionally displaced some goddesses when she arrived in Greece. On the other, she also teamed up with some gods, most notably Hermes, Hephaistos and Ares.

HOOKING UP: APHRODITE'S FRIENDS WITH BENEFITS

The link with Hermes is the one least represented in mythology, although the result of that union was the intersex hero Hermaphroditos (more popular in Roman times than in Greek). More likely than not, Aphrodite got paired with Hermes because of their joint cult at Kato Symi Viannou, when they took the place of much earlier Minoan deities.

When Aphrodite and Hermes were worshipped together, it was often in the context of coming-of-age rituals. There has been much speculation about the Greek cult at Kato Symi Viannou, where copious bronze figurines and plaques depict a pair of males – one older, one younger – engaging in hunting and camping activities. This iconography is complemented by other artefacts that came to light in the sanctuary. The pottery finds are mainly gustatory in nature: chalices and goblets for drinking, libation vessels, conical cups and dishware. These fabricated items go nicely with the other remains found within the precinct: carbonized wood mixed with animal bones. It was originally thought that the bones were the remains of sacrificial victims.

However, as nothing at the site would appear to constitute an altar, and as the bones themselves were not burnt, the hypothesis of sacrifice has been tempered into one of a sacred meal celebrated at Kato Symi. Some kind of ritualized picnic seems to have taken place there, with the head of the sacrificed animal being perhaps reserved for the deity or deities.

These finds appear to illustrate an anecdote from Epheros, an author of the fourth-century BCE who wrote about the customs of Greeks living in the Peloponnese and Crete. According to him, it was customary in Crete for an older *erastes* (lover)/ *eispnelas* (inspirer) to take a fancy to a younger *eromenos* (beloved). The *erastes* would inform the *eromenos's* family of his intentions; if they approved, he would 'kidnap' the object of his affections. The *erastes* then took the boy out to the country for two months along with other male companions. There they camped and slept together, with the older man educating the younger. At the end of two months the lover returned the beloved with many fine gifts, including clothing and weapons. Such a coming-of-age ritual was deemed most prestigious for the boy.

If Kato Symi Viannou was indeed the site of such a ritual, then Hermes' role here was both as a god of nature and a god of (traversing) boundaries – in this case from childhood to adulthood. Aphrodite's role may have had to do with the introduction to adult sexuality that this transition entailed.

Aphrodite and Hermes were likewise revered together at the site of Locri Epizephyrii in Italy. The sanctuary itself was mainly dedicated to the goddess Persephonê (and possibly

Hades), but numerous *pinakes* (terracotta plaques) found in the sanctuary depict either Aphrodite alone or the goddess accompanied by Hermes. In these images, the deities (or, more likely, their cult statues) are approached by older children offering the deities their childhood toys. Such sacrifices were made by children when they celebrated their transition into adulthood.

Aphrodite's links with Hephaistos and Ares seem to stem from her origins in Cyprus. Bronze Age Cyprus brought forth bronze statues of a war god. In one especially famous depiction, this divine statue wore a warrior's helmet with horns (a sign of divinity in ancient Near Eastern art), carried a spear, and was set upon an oxhide ingot as a statue base. Oxhide ingots were the main shape taken by units of copper when transported within and beyond the island. Thus in one image we have a god (horns) associated with both war (the spear) and metal (the ingot). When the Paphian came to Greece, it seems the Greeks could not quite decide which god this was. Could he be Ares, god of war? Or Hephaistos, god of metallurgy? So Aphrodite simply paired up with them both.

In the Greek context, of course, the union with Hephaistos made no sense at all. He was unattractive, frequently sooty and, according to Homer (*Iliad*, Book 1), already married to one of the Charities. Greek gods might fool around a *lot*, but they were absolutely (if serially) monogamous. The Greeks themselves rationalized this pairing through a story in which Aphrodite was basically used as a bribe. Once upon a time, according to scraps of a poem by the seventh-century lyric poet Alkaios ('Fragment 349') and the Roman-period author Pausanias:

> *These things are said by the Greeks, how Hera cast out Hephaistos when he was born, and later when he was feeling vengeful he sent her as a gift a gold throne bearing invisible chains. When she sat in it she was caught. Then when none of the other deities could persuade Hephaistos to come back, Dionysos could – Hephaistos thought he was the most trustworthy. So Dionysos got him totally drunk and led him back to heaven.*
> – Description of Greece 1.20.3

Artistic representations of this tale, such as on the François Vase, not only portray Dionysos leading a very drunk Hephaistos into the company of the deities, they also show Aphrodite being offered to the inebriated smith. In gratitude for her release Hera, the goddess of marriage, gave Aphrodite to her difficult son. So the marriage of Aphrodite and Hephaistos makes sense in a context of Freudian-level mommy issues and an extraordinary amount of alcohol. No surprise it didn't work out well.

Of all her consort gods, Aphrodite was ultimately paired most closely with Ares. This makes sense in light of the Cypriot evidence, as well as the fact that opposites attract. In addition, Ares was seriously attractive. The goddess frequently cheated on her smith husband with this god of battle, as recounted in Book 8 of Homer's *Odyssey*, the so-called 'Song of Demodokos', ll. 266 ff, which begins:

> *But striking the lyre Demodokos took up the fair song*
> *About the great love of Ares and well-*
> *crowned Aphrodite;*
> *How they first mingled in the halls of Hephaistos –*
> *Sub rosa – he [Ares] having given many gifts dishonoured*
> *the couch and bed*
> *Of King Hephaistos…*

Using the same invisible fetters trick that he used on his mother Hera, Hephaistos bound the two together in bed and invited all the other Olympians to come and laugh at them. His brothers Apollo and Hermes immediately decided that they wanted to have sex with Aphrodite too. Hephaistos really hadn't thought this one through…

Apart from shacking up in epic, Aphrodite was paired with Ares in cult and even epithet. The two were worshipped together in Argos, Sparta and the Cretan site of Sta Lenika-Olous. In Sparta, Pausanias informs us in 3.17.5 that:

> *To the left of the Bronze House they set up a sanctuary of*
> *the Muses, because the Lakedaimonians go out to their*
> *battles not by trumpet-call but rather to the tune of flutes*
> *and the stroke of lyres and kitherai. Opposite the Bronze*
> *House is a temple of Aphrodite Areia; the xoana are as*
> *old as any in Greece.*

Furthermore, archaeologists excavating the Spartan acropolis brought to light a knife blade inscribed *Lukeios Arewiai*, 'Lukeios [dedicated this to] Arewia'. *Arewia* is a very old form of the epithet *Areia*, suggesting that this epithet of the goddess is very old indeed.

In Crete, at Olous, excavators found a temple dedicated to Aphrodite and Ares that dates back before 700 BCE. The sanctuary was identified by inscription as *to arkhaion Aphrodision* – 'The Old Sanctuary of Aphrodite' – but it eventually also housed a cult of Ares.

In the end, Aphrodite was not entirely a Greek goddess, and the Greeks seemed to have recognized this. Kythereia was originally the Paphian, possibly originally Assyrian, and she was brought to southern Greece by Phoenicians. The farther east the Greeks looked, the more cognates they could find for her: Kypris, Aštart, Ištar.

Yet this really did not matter. On the one hand, the Greeks believed that a number of their deities were in some way 'foreign'. Ares was from Thrace, of course, while Dionysos was from... somewhere else, possibly India. The Greeks actually had a tendency of 'removing themselves' from deities who made them feel uncomfortable – a goddess who literally had them by the short hairs certainly did that.

On the other hand, the Greeks understood that their deities were universal. Basically, for the most part, everyone worshipped the same deities; they just used different names and according to local fashions. So what if the Egyptians call Zeus Amun, or the Lydians call Rhea Cybelê? The fact that

THE ORIGINS OF APHRODITE

the Phoenicians call the Queen of Cyprus Aštart while we call her Aphrodite isn't really a big deal. In fact, Aphrodite 'overlapped' with many non-Greek goddesses in a process known as 'syncretism', the topic of the next chapter.

3.
Aphrodite's Sisters (and Their Lovers)

'Amongst the primeval Phrygians I am Pessinuntia, Mother of Gods.
Here the autochthonous Athenians call me Cecropian Minerva,
There the wave-swept Cypriots call me Paphian Venus.
The bow-toting Cretans call me Dictynian Diana;
For the tri-lingual Sicilians I am Stygian Proserpina.
For the Eleusinians ancient Ceres;
Juno for some, Bellona for others;
Hecatê here, Rhamnusia there.
And those of the land where the sun first rises –
The Ethiopians and the Egyptians strong in ancient doctrines –
They celebrate me with proper rites
And call me by my true name – Queen Isis.'
– Apuleius, *The Golden Ass*, Book 11.5

It is 300 BCE and you are a Greek merchant sailor taking a voyage. The ship leaves from the harbour at Piraeus in Athens, where you made an offering to Aphrodite *Euploia* for safe sea travels, just as your mother always taught you to do. Your travels take you to Crete, Egypt, Palestine, Anatolia and Cyprus. On your journey you find many versions of your patron goddess. In Egypt they call her Hathor (and worship her with beer!) and in Sidon she is the warrior Aštart. Merchants from Babylon and Armenia call her Ištar (who also likes beer), Nanaya and Golden Anaitis, while in Cyprus she is the Paphian, Golgia, or simply Anassa – Queen.

ORIGINS AND SYNCRETISM

Perhaps no deity from any ancient pantheon summons images of her foreign siblings as Aphrodite does. To be perfectly clear, all deities have cognates: deities who are like them or related to them in nearby and not-so-nearby regions and societies. This happens for two reasons. First, it is the consequence of a splintering effect, as a deity's worshippers spread out into the world and the deity changes to accommodate new life situations and challenges. Second, it is caused by syncretism, in which different peoples come to equate separate deities who were not (necessarily) originally related.

The splintering can happen at many levels, leading to a family of related deities who may not look very similar. Consider the Norse god Oðinn, for example, who becomes Wodan for the early Germans, eventually evolving into Wotan. The names are close enough and the worshippers similar enough, although it must be noted that the sly, crafty traveller worshipped by the Vikings is rather different from the beefy war god presented in *Das Nibelungenlied*. Less obvious is the sky god Dyaus Pitar, who reaches way back into Indo-European antiquity. Travelling west he became Zeus for the Greeks, Jupiter for the Romans and eventually the war god Tyr for the Vikings. All the names are etymologically related even if on the surface the resemblance is, well, negligible.

Syncretism goes the other way, from many to fewer. At its simplest, 'syncretism' is the process through which deities merge identities. This typically occurs when peoples with different pantheons come into contact with each other and, consciously or unconsciously, try to get their religious systems to mesh. The word has come to have a range of related meanings over the past two centuries, ranging from a general notion of 'relationship' to an equation of deities equivalent to a kind of monism, in which many deities of the same sex are all recognized as actually being one. Such is the case with the quotation from Apuleius at the head of this chapter: All goddesses are Isis! Let us consider three different types of syncretism.

First, there is *interpretatio* syncretism. Here people simply understand that two (or more) differently named deities in different pantheons are really just the same being. Thus Etruscan Fufluns is Greek Dionysos; Gaulish Epona is Athena. This is especially evident in the Greek and Roman pantheons. We tend to think that the Greeks and Romans worshiped the same deities, just by different names. Yet there are actually considerable differences between them. For example, in the Greek pantheon the lunar goddess is Selenê, a completely different goddess from Artemis. In the Roman pantheon Diana has absorbed attributes of both goddesses and become the lunar goddess of the hunt. Keep this in mind when we get to Aphrodite and Venus!

'Amalgam' syncretism occurs when a mixing of two or more deities, possibly from different pantheons, creates a new divinity. Thus in Hellenistic Egypt the Greeks combined the Egyptian deities Apis (a bull) and Osiris (God of the Dead) with some notions of their own deities Zeus and Dionysos, creating the new deity Serapis.

Finally, there is what I call 'eclipse' syncretism, in which a new deity enters a pantheon and takes the place of an earlier deity, effectively shoving that deity out of the pantheon entirely. We saw an example of this in the previous chapter with Aphrodite and Helen. Artemis did the same thing to Iphigeneia, and so did Apollo to the young Cretan god Hyakinthos.

One thing that is extremely important to understand is that the *basis* for the syncretism – why ancient peoples saw similarities – is not always obvious. Nor are the commonalities between the syncretized deities ever 100 per cent. Some syncretisms are simply baffling. For example, the Mesopotamians worshipped a goddess of sex named Nanaya – who, as you can probably imagine, was soon syncretized with the erotic Ištar. Later, Nanaya was also syncretized with the chaste Artemis. How did *this* happen? Well, already in the late second millennium BCE Nanaya had come to be seen as the partner of the scribal god Nabû; together the couple were the chief deities of the city of Borsippa. In later years the Greeks identified Nabû as Apollo, so they equated Nanaya with Artemis. We read in Strabo's *Geography* (16.1.7) that even in his day Artemis and Apollo were the primary deities of the city. By the first millennium Nanaya was depicted with a bow and quiver on her statues. She also appeared on coins with moon crescents – not because she originally was conceived of as a lunar goddess of the hunt, but because the Greeks had already started to merge her with Artemis, after which the Romans equated her with Diana. A goddess of sex thus develops into a virginal moon goddess via syncretism. However, this does *not* mean that the original Mesopotamian goddess had any of these features.

It is extremely common for deities to have close and not-so-close relations throughout the world's pantheons. Why, then, is Aphrodite so notable for her close rapport with foreign goddesses? It is because her ties, especially to Near Eastern goddesses, are so obvious, both in the visibility of her origins (see Chapter Two) and in her relations with other mythological beings. In *no* case is this more blatant than in Aphrodite's rapport with Adonis.

ADONIS AND APHRODITE AND DUMUZI AND INANA

According to legend the founder of Aphrodite's city of Paphos was King Kinyras, whose own family originally came from either Syria or Assyria, more or less depending on how far the Greek imagination could travel. According to the second-century CE author Apollodoros in his *Bibliothekê* ('Library', Book 3.4), King Kinyras had a daughter named Smyrna. She angered Aphrodite, who caused her to fall in love with her father. In a plot that involved a *lot* of darkness, Smyrna managed to seduce her own father and had sex with him over the course of 12 nights, at which point Kinyras thought to light a lamp. Realizing that he had, by this point, impregnated his own daughter, he tried to kill her. Smyrna managed to run away and was turned into a myrrh tree, the origins of incense.

Ten months later the myrrh tree gave birth to a lovely baby boy, Adonis, whom Aphrodite took and hid in a box. Not being especially maternal and having no desire for the other deities to know what she had done, she handed over box-plus-baby to Persephonê, goddess of the underworld, for safekeeping. Adonis grew up and became very handsome, with the result that both Aphrodite and Persephonê fought over him. Brought in to negotiate, Zeus declared that Adonis would spend one-third of the year with Persephonê in the underworld, one-third above ground with Aphrodite and one-third wherever he wanted (which turned out to be with Aphrodite). This weird balance ended only when Adonis was gored to death by a boar, at which point he spent the rest of eternity in the underworld like everyone else. A ritual emerged whereby in July Greek women would lament the death of Adonis. They planted seeds in shallow containers and placed them on the roofs of their houses to grow, wither and die. So much for Adonis.

This story, with many strange twists and turns, goes all the way back to Mesopotamia. In a tale that existed in both Sumerian ('Inana's Descent to the Underworld') and Akkadian ('Ištar's Descent') mythology, the goddess Inana/Ištar travelled to the underworld to visit (and potentially overthrow) her sister Ereškigal, Queen of the Dead. But as Inana descended she passed through seven gates. At each gate she was required to remove one item of apparel, so that she arrived before her sister completely naked. Ereškigal attacked and killed her sister, turning her into a mouldy slab of meat hanging on a hook.

However, Inana had made preparations in case of just such an eventuality. She had instructed her personal assistant to reach out to several other deities above ground to orchestrate her rescue. Inana's uncle Enki duly helped out, creating magical beings from dirt under his fingernails. These beings – known as *galatura*, *kurgarru* and *assinnu* – went to visit Ereškigal. They were so kind and friendly to the goddess that she offered them a wish, whereupon they asked for the slab of meat on the wall. They successfully revived it with the Waters of Life. Then they all beat it out of there and had the sense not to go back.

What happens next gets complicated. Early on in the love life of Inana and her boyfriend Dumuzi, either a shepherd or a farmer, the young man is killed. Inana mourns his death together with Dumuzi's mother and his sister Geštinanna. However, according to a different, probably later, version of the story, Dumuzi is still quite alive when his wife makes her underworld journey. Furthermore, Ereškigal made it clear that the only way Inana could leave is if she sent a substitute to take her place. When Inana comes back, escorted by Ereškigal's personal demonic henchmen, they find that the only being on Earth not mourning the dead Inana is, well, Dumuzi. Inana is not amused. She immediately hands Dumuzi over the Ereškigal's demons to drag to the underworld. However, according to yet another version of the tale, Dumuzi's sister Geštinanna agrees to trade places with her brother twice a year. Dumuzi thus spends six months in the underworld and Geštinanna the other six. According to this story, Dumuzi dies and is resurrected annually.

This tale travelled westward. In the Bible, in Ezekiel 8.14 the prophet complains that just outside the temple in Jerusalem the women sit mourning the god Tammuz, the Semitic equivalent of Sumerian Dumuzi. In the Phoenician cities of Sidon and Tyre the queen goddess Aštart – a Western version of Inana/Ištar – is paired with the 'dying-and-rising' gods Ešmun and Melqart (who was himself syncretized with the Greek Herakles). When the tale reaches Greek soil, Dumuzi/Tammuz becomes known by his Semitic title *'adôn'* ('Lord'). He is paired with Aphrodite, the Western cognate of Inana/Aštart. She shares Adonis with Persephonê in annual alternation (the Geštinanna version) and then loses him to death entirely.

So it is not just because Aphrodite so clearly evolved out of Ištar/Aštart that their connections are especially appreciated. Other aspects of their narratives and cults (for example, the mourning of Tammuz/Adonis) continued to exist. For example, Aštart became the queen goddess of various Phoenician city-states, including the Phoenician city of Kition on Cyprus. The Queen of Kition (Aštart) was clearly the Queen (*Wanassa/ Anassa*) of Paphos (Aphrodite) and so the two syncretized, both being the Queen of Cyprus. In some respects Ištar and Aphrodite even wore the same clothes! Many depictions of Inana/Ištar from the ancient Near East show her wearing a crisscross over her chest; it appears in the more detailed images to be a baldric for attaching weapons. When this element of couture arrived in Greece adorning the Golden One, it was understood to be Aphrodite's *kestos* – a kind of sash. According to Homer's *Iliad,* 14, ll. 214–217 it was:

> *... An embroidered sash,*
> *Ornate. Within it every charm is wrought.*
> *Within is friendship, is desire, is fond discourse,*
> *And consolation, which steals the sharp mind even of*
> *the wise.*

So Aphrodite and Ištar could even dress the same.

Well, sort of. One of the important things to keep in mind with the equation of deities is that the equation was never 100 per cent. As noted above, the Greek Artemis was still not entirely the Roman Diana. And there was a *lot* that differentiated Aphrodite from her Eastern sisters. For one thing, we recognize both Inana/Ištar and Aphrodite as sex goddesses, but in context this meant different things. Aphrodite was a goddess who not only embodied sexual desire herself, but who also inflicted desire onto others. This was a very important aspect of her persona, as shown in Chapter One. By contrast, while Inana/Ištar had a voracious sexual appetite herself, it was not necessarily in her persona to inflict libido onto others. One might say she and Aphrodite had different jobs. Furthermore, as we saw in Chapter One, Aphrodite had none of Inana/Ištar military capabilities. Inana's martial baldric had become Aphrodite's sash of desire.

The lack of total correspondence can create problems in later scholarship. For example, throughout the Middle Ages we knew a lot more about Latin Venus than Greek Aphrodite, and then far more about Aphrodite than Phoenician Aštart into modern times. We already knew, thanks to Greek authors and inscriptions, that Aštart was basically Aphrodite, so we assumed that she must be an erotic goddess. She actually is not. While Aphrodite inherited all of Ištar's eroticism, Aštart got the martial side. They were simply not the same all the way. You cannot reconstruct Aštart through Aphrodite (although many people have tried…).

APHRODITE EVERYWHERE

If Aphrodite came to be equated with Near Eastern goddesses such as Aštart and Ištar because of very real family ties, the same cannot quite be said for the many, many other goddesses whom the Greeks came to identify as 'Aphrodite'. Herodotos of Halikarnassos, the fifth-century BCE historian, wrote about the many peoples who shared the Earth with the Greeks, with a special focus on the customs and religions of his neighbours. He found specifically Heavenly (*Ourania*) Aphrodite all throughout the Orient. When discussing the Arabs of the Saudi Peninsula, he notes in his *Histories*, Book 3.8 that:

They believe in no other gods except Dionysos and Heavenly Aphrodite; and they say that they wear their hair as Dionysos does his, cutting it round the head and shaving the temples. They call Dionysos Orotalt and Aphrodite Alilat.

The reference to Alilat is probably a cognate to the Arabic goddess Al-Lhat. Her cult spread outwards, such that eventually the Persians 'learned later to sacrifice to Aphrodite *Ourania* from the Assyrians and Arabians. She is called by the Assyrians Mylitta, by the Arabians Alilat, by the Persians Mitra' (1.131). (For further discussion of Mylitta, see Chapter 4). Even the barbaric Skythians living in what is now the Ukraine had their own name for this goddess, as well as several other Greek deities (4.59):

In the Skythian language, Hestia is called Tabiti; Zeus (in my judgement most correctly) Papaeus; Earth is Apia; Apollo Goetosyrus; Heavenly Aphrodite Argimpasa; Poseidon Thagimasadas.

More likely than not most of these goddesses resembled Ištar more closely than the Paphian, but the equation held.

In some instances, however, the equations, the syncretisms, were more difficult to fathom. It was rather like Nanaya mentioned above, who could be simultaneously Aphrodite and Artemis. Nor was she the only one. Consider the Irano-Armenian goddess Anahita, for example. Anahita seems to have emerged as a Zororastrian adaptation of the Mesopotamian goddess Ištar. Yet she also absorbed the attributes of an independent water goddess and came ultimately to be known as *anahita*, the 'Immaculate One'. The Graeco-Roman deity to whom she was most often syncretized was Artemis/Diana in the function of a 'pure' fertility goddess. So much is attested in Plutarch's *Lucullus* (§24), the *Annals* of Tacitus (3.63), and the Anatolian epithet of Artemis as Artemis *Anaitis* (ancient Greek doesn't have an 'H' sound in the middle of words). Her role as a fertility goddess in Armenia specifically is attested in Agathangelos's *History of the Armenians*. He calls her 'the great Anahit, who gives life and fertility to our land of Armenia'.

Only one ancient source, the late fourth-century BCE historian Berossos, syncretized the goddess with Aphrodite. It appears that this was owing to Anahita's epithet 'Golden', in reference to her famous golden statues in the cities of Erez (Pliny, *Natural History*, 33.4.24) and Armenian Ashtishat (Agathangelos, 809). That Berossos came to associate Anahita with Aphrodite through similar statue iconography seems apparent in his 'Fragment 12'. There he discusses the origins of Persian cult statues, claiming that King Artaxerxes 'first set up the statue of Aphrodite Anaitis and showed respect to it at Babylon, Susa and Ekbatana, in Persia and Bactria, and at Damascus and Sardis'. The fact that Anaitis was a specifically Eastern name for the Greek goddess has also been preserved by Berossos. He notes that when Zororaster-Zarades, the founder of Zoroastrianism, changed the religion of the Persians and brought in some Greek deities, he did not:

preserve their names, but Zeus was Bel, Herakles was Sandes, Aphrodite was Anaitis, and others are called by other names as is told by all those who wrote of the ancient history of the Assyrians and the Medes.
– 'Fragment 13'

Things can become weirdly complicated as a result. The Mesopotamian goddess Ištar enters into the Irano-Armenian pantheons and is combined with an unnamed river goddess, thus becoming Anahita the Pure. This purity aspect gets her associated with Artemis and later Diana. However, the statues of this 'Pure One' are made of gold in two cities, so Anahita is also the 'Golden One', apparently linking her to Aphrodite. The path from Ištar to Aphrodite via Anahita is not even remotely the same as the path from Ištar to Aphrodite via Aštart.

Interestingly, what worked for the Levant and Mesopotamia failed in Egypt, where Aphrodite had minimal syncretisms before the Hellenistic period. Her cult was there, of course. The city of Naukratis on the Nile was founded by the Greeks in the 26th Dynasty (seventh to sixth centuries BCE), and one of the major temples in the city was dedicated to Aphrodite. As a matter of fact, the profession of *hetaira* – professional female companion – may have actually originated in this town. The first professional *hetaira* we know of is Rhodopis, a contemporary of Sappho and thus datable to the early sixth century BCE. According to Herodotos, Rhodopis ('Rose-face') plied her trade in Naukratis:

Rhodopis came to Egypt brought by Xantheus the Samian, but once she arrived she was released from her profession for a lot of money by Kharaxos of Mytilenê, son of Skamandronymos, brother of Sappho the poet. Thus Rhodopis was liberated, and she remained in Egypt and was so utterly charming that she acquired a huge fortune, such as it would be for Rhodopis ... the hetairai in Naukratis are quite lovely, for the very woman about whom this story is told became so famous that all the Greeks learned the name of Rhodopis ... Kharaxos, who freed Rhodopis, went back home to Mytilenê, where Sappho excoriated him in song.

– Histories, 2: 134–5

In spite of this, Aphrodite only came to be syncretized with Egyptian goddesses once the Greeks took over following the conquests of Alexander the Great in the fourth century BCE. The most likely reason for this is that by this time various Hellenistic queens had come to identify with/link themselves to various goddesses, the most popular of these being Aphrodite. This was especially the case with Queen Arsinoë II, one of the Ptolemaic rulers of Egypt in the late fourth century BCE. In an effort to forge cultural links with the Egyptians, she associated herself not only with Aphrodite, but also (through her) with the native Egyptian goddesses Hathor and Isis. Both of these goddesses were very closely connected to the god Horus, and thus to notions of kingship and sovereignty in the Land of the Nile.

Hathor was an obvious choice for syncretism with Aphrodite, being the ancient Egyptian goddess of sex (and music and Westerners and trees...). One of her titles was 'Mistress of the Vulva'. At the New Kingdom (1600–1200 BCE) sanctuary of Deir el-Bahri men left her votive offerings of wooden phalluses in prayers for... virility (I imagine it looked like a field of dildos).

In later years temple records mention that large phalloi were carried in one of the processions held in Hathor's honour, while another Hathoric festival was known as 'the opening of the bosoms of the women'. An ancient Egyptian tale ('Re and the Destruction of Mankind') relates how the solar deity Re once became angry with humankind and ordered Hathor, in her more ferocious guise as Sekhmet, to kill everyone. The goddess raged and started to slaughter people. At this point Re changed his mind, so the gods now had to decide how best to stop the frenzied goddess.

They got several hundred gallons of beer and dyed it red. Hathor/Sekhmet then drank it up, believing it was blood. She got drunk and passed out, resolving the problem. In commemoration of humanity's salvation the ancient Egyptians held very large drinking celebrations as part of their worship of Hathor. By the second century BCE a temple of Aphrodite-Hathor was established on the southern island of Philae by King Ptolemy VII and his consort Cleopatra, a permanent attestation of the union of these two goddesses.

Isis was a somewhat stranger choice for association with Aphrodite, especially as she was more commonly syncretized with Demeter (Plutarch's *Isis and Osiris*). In the Ptolemaic period, however, Isis acquired some new attributes, one of which was the protection of sea travellers (the Egyptians mostly stuck to the Nile before the first millennium BCE). As such, she became the Egyptian equivalent of Aphrodite *Euploia*. Artistic depictions of 'Isis, Lady of the Sea' showed her resting on a rudder and holding a cornucopia, sometimes standing opposite the Pharos of Alexandria, one of the Seven Wonders of the Ancient World. Eventually Isis herself acquired the epithet *Euploia*.

VENUS

Just as Diana is not really Artemis, Aphrodite is not really Venus. These are two separate goddesses who were syncretized probably no earlier than the late third century BCE. Before this the Roman goddess Venus (Turan in Etruscan, the closest neighbour of the Romans) appears to have been a goddess of gardens, flowers and springtime. The earliest known Roman temple to her was constructed in the city of Rome at the base of the Aventine Hill at the beginning of the third century BCE by Q. Fabius Maximus Gurges. Dedicated to Venus *Obsequens* (Accommodating), it was clearly in exchange for the goddess's help in some matter.

The true merging of Aphrodite with Venus occurred at the end of the third century BCE, when the cult of Venus *Erycina* was introduced into Rome from the sanctuary of Aphrodite at Mount Eryx in Sicily in 217 BCE. According to Livy's *History of Rome* (22.9–10) this introduction was decreed by oracle during the Punic Wars to help the Romans in their fight against Hannibal. Sicilian Eryx was already a site of considerable cultural mixing and divine syncretism. From the first millennium BCE the island had been inhabited by three groups of people: the indigenous Elymians, the Greeks (mainly in the east) and the Phoenicians (mainly in the west). The sanctuary in western Eryx was thus originally dedicated to the Phoenician goddess Aštart. Needless to say, when the Greeks spread out over the island they identified this Phoenician Aštart with their own goddess Aphrodite (just as later the Romans turned her into Venus). According to the first-century Greek geographer Strabo in his *Geography*, 6.2.6:

Also inhabited is Eryx, a lofty hill. It has an especially revered sanctuary of Aphrodite; in past times it was filled with female hierodules whom many people from Sicily and elsewhere dedicated according to a vow. But now, just like the settlement itself, the sanctuary is depopulated and the plethora of sacred bodies has left.

The sanctuary was well known for the practice of manumitting slaves here under the auspices of the reigning goddess, be she Aphrodite or Venus – a *hierodule* is a manumitted slave under divine protection. Writing at roughly the same time as Strabo, the Roman philosopher and politician Cicero made mention of the so-called *libertae Veneri Erycinae* – Freedwomen of Erycine Venus; *libertae* here is the Latin equivalent of *hierodouloi*. In his *Divinatio contra Q. Caecilius*, 17.55–56, Cicero sheds considerable light on the status and functions of these Venerii, the freed slaves of Erycine Venus:

There is a certain woman, Agonis of Lilybaeum, a liberta *of Venus Erycina, who was quite well-to-do and wealthy before this man was quaestor. An admiral of Antonius abducted some musician-slaves from her in a violent, insulting manner, whom he said he wanted to use in the navy. Then, as is the custom of those of Venus (*Venerorum*) and those who have liberated themselves from Venus, she invoked religion upon the commander in the name of Venus; she said that both she and hers belonged to Venus. When this was reported to quaestor Caecilius – that best and most just of men! [total sarcasm here] – he commanded that Agonis be called to him. Immediately he appointed a commission to see 'If it appeared that she had said that she and hers belonged to Venus'. The justices judged that it was surely so, nor was there indeed any doubt that she had said this. Then the cad [i.e. Caecilius] took possession of the woman's goods, sentenced her into servitude to Venus, then sold her goods and pocketed the money. And so because Agonis* *wanted to retain a little property by the name of Venus and religiosity, she lost all her fortunes and liberty by the outrage of this cad! Verres later came to Lilybaeum, heard the matter, annulled the judgement, and bade the quaestor to count up and pay back all the money he got for selling Agonis's goods.*

Significant aspects of Aphrodite's sanctuary in Eryx continued into the Roman period, as Venus and Aphrodite merged traits and personae.

But it was not just Venus who transformed under the influence of Aphrodite: Aphrodite also acquired new traits through the new interest the Romans took in her. Most importantly, Aphrodite the rather ineffective maternal figure (see Chapter One) suddenly became the national mother.

It was because of that tryst with Anchises mentioned in Chapter One. The offspring of that union was the Trojan prince Aeneas, who managed to escape the fall of Troy at the end of the Trojan War. Vergil's *Aeneid* tells how, accompanied by his son Ascanias, Aeneas actually carried his father Anchises out of the burning wreckage. The *Aeneid* then tells how these three men, along with a small band of Trojan survivors, fled the Troad and eventually founded a 'New Troy' in Italy. Or, to put this another way, Aeneas, son of Aphrodite, is the ur-founder of the Roman Empire. As far as the Romans were concerned, Aphrodite/Venus had an important role to play in this; she guided her offspring to Carthage and finally to the Italian Peninsula, all the while providing safe sea travel. As Vergil recorded in Book 1, Venus addressed her son:

'Whoever you are, you are not, I think, hateful to
heavenly favour:
Still breathing you have come to Tyre city.
Continue this way, and carry on to the door of the queen here.
For I tell you that your comrades are returned to you,
And the fleet lies in safety through good winds on the
northern shore.'
...
So she spoke, and turning away a rosiness shone from the
nape of her neck,
And her ambrosial hair breathed an eddy of divine fragrance.
Her dress flowed down to her feet,
And truly the goddess was revealed by her gait.
When he recognized his mother, so did Aeneas's voice trail
after her:
'What's with the constant head games with your son?
Why don't you give me your hand, join me hand in hand?
And listen, and tell me the truth?'
So he accused her and then set his step to the city walls.
But Venus enclosed them [Aeneas and Aschates] in a shadow
as they climbed,
And the goddess cast clouds about them,
So that no one might see them, or seize them,
Or cause delay, or ask them why they came.
She herself departed to sublime Paphos to rest and see
Her happy place, where her temple is, and
One hundred altars burning Sabaean frankincense.
– ll. 388–392, 402–417

Also, just so you know, Ascanias, son of Aeneas, grandson of Aphrodite/Venus, was also known by the nickname Iulus.

If the name Iulus looks familiar, it is probably because it is the name of one of the most famous and politically powerful families in Roman history. Iulius (Julius) Caesar stands out among them. With the founding of the Roman Empire by the Iulian clan (Augustus Caesar was also a member), the goddess Venus became a national mother, acquiring the title Venus *Genetrix* or 'Mother Venus'. Julius Caesar dedicated a new temple to this goddess, his ancestress, in the Forum Julium during his triumph (victory parade) in 46 BCE (Cassius Dio, *Roman History*, 43.22.2).

As went Venus, so too did Aphrodite, who became far more maternal under Roman influence. As early as the first century CE, Aphrodite acquired the epithet *Geneteira*, the Greek equivalent of Latin *Genetrix*. As a matter of fact, in the Greek city of Eresos on the island of Lesbos, there was a bilingual dedicatory inscription in honour of Augustus's daughter Julia, here named Julia *Aphrodite Geneteiria* in the Greek or Julia *Venus Genetrix* in the Latin (*Incriptiones Graecae* 122 537). In addition, by the first century CE Aphrodite had become *Promêtor* or 'First Mother' – a title she held especially in her own city of Aphrodisias on the western coast of Turkey, not far from the original location of Troy.

Aphrodite did not merely become more maternal because of her syncretism with Venus. As noted in Chapter One, she also became more martial, when Pompey and later Julius Caesar both came to revere Venus with the epithet *Victrix*, 'Venus Victorious'!

This manifestation of the goddess evolved out of a new construction of Aphrodite formulated by Sulla. When in southwestern Anatolia he had a dream in which he saw the goddess decked out in the panoply of Ares and leading his forces to victory. It should come as no surprise that this conception of the goddess emerged in Eastern territories – places where Sulla, no doubt, was influenced by Eastern martial goddesses such as Phoenician Aštart *inter alia*. However, the cult of Venus *Victrix* most assuredly did not remain purely Eastern. Dedicatory inscriptions were being made to this goddess from the first century BCE onwards in Spain, Italy, Sicily, northern Africa, Akhaia in Greece, Dacia-Romania, Pannonia-Hungary and Dalmatia-Croatia. In several instances, especially in Dalmatia, these dedications were commemorative monuments for women.

In a few cases there is evidence that the Venus *Victrix* in question was still being syncretized with more Eastern goddesses. The Venus *Victrix* recorded in Pannonia is commemorated with Heliopolitan Jove, suggesting that what we have here is a Latin syncretism with Syrian Atargatis, a later version of Aštart. Spain brought forth inscriptions to 'Veneri Victrici Africae Caelesti', the 'Heavenly Venus *Victrix* of Africa' (bringing to mind those countless references to Aphrodite *Ourania* and her eternal Eastern syncretisms) who could easily be an adopted Roman version of Carthaginian Tanit – Queen of the Punic pantheon.

All in all, Aphrodite is never far from her Eastern cognates, even when we switch orientation and look west.

4.
Aphrodite's Aftermath
(Dealing with the S-word)

> *Flawless as Aphrodite,*
> *Thoroughly beautiful,*
> *Brainless,*
> *The faint odor of your patchouli,*
> *Faint, almost, as the lines of cruelty about your chin,*
> *Assails me, and concerns me almost as little.*
> – Ezra Pound, 'Ladies'

he modern world has an ambivalent relationship with Aphrodite. In this it is not entirely different from the ancient world, but the reasoning is different. In ancient Greece, as we saw in Chapter One, the concern was that Aphrodite was too powerful, able to overturn the mind even of Zeus himself, King of the Universe. In more recent times, by contrast, the awkward rapport with the goddess has everything to do with our negative feelings about sexuality. Such negativity first emerged from the writings of Plato and other pagan Greek philosophers. During the first and second centuries CE it became entrenched in Western ideology by the likes of Paul of Tarsus and the early Church Fathers. Nowadays we can be completely negative about sex *in toto* and thus condemn the influence of Aphrodite, the goddess of sex.

Or we might take the more common approach and accept that it is okay for men to be sexual, but not women. Boys will be boys and men have needs, after all. Females are divided into the Eva/Ave dichotomy, either being virtuous virgins ('Ave', the first word in Latin of the prayer *Ave Maria*, 'Hail, Mary', is thus a reference to the eternally virginal holy mother) or total sluts ('Eva' referring to the biblical Eve who convinced Adam to expand his mind by eating the fruit of the Tree of the Knowledge of Good and Evil, an action that we have somehow come to believe must have something to do with sex). As the quintessentially sexual female, Aphrodite becomes the cosmic whore – Aphrodite *Pornê* – and we disdain her as such.

Or we might decide that Aphrodite is good because she promotes fertility, being a fertility goddess like all the other goddesses, even the virgins. So long as all that sex is to make babies, preferably for a legally married husband, then sex is fine. Even the staunchest Christian celibates could cope with that one. Granted, a certain amount of denial as to the actual persona of Aphrodite is necessary here...

Then again, we might decide that sex is a good thing, for males *and* females, and that the worship of Aphrodite raises human sexuality to a divine level. As a matter of fact, in some branches of neopaganism worship of Aphrodite may involve ritual sex. Or perhaps the spectre of sacred prostitution may be summoned – claiming, with varying amounts of good faith, that selling sex this way is a sacred act and should be protected as freedom of religious expression. Things often go downhill from here, for various reasons.

In short, we have an abundance of ways not to cope with Aphrodite in modern times. How did we get here?

APHRODITE, SEXUALITY AND EARLY CHRISTIANITY

Greek Philosophy and Sex

As noted in Chapter One, the Greeks were somewhat ambivalent about Aphrodite, believing that she simply had way too much power over humans. In his play *Hippolytus,* ll. 1–5, the Athenian playwright Euripides made the goddess declare:

> 'Great one, I am not without name,
> Goddess Kypris I am called by mortals and in heaven.
> Of all those who dwell within the boundaries of sea
> and ocean
> Seeing the light of the sun:
> Those who revere my power I honour
> And I overthrow those thinking haughty thoughts
> against me.'

On the flip side, the Greeks were conscious that Aphrodite provided some of the most wonderful things on Earth: love, sex, friendship. Thus the poet Nossis, who wrote in the third century BCE, celebrated her influence as recorded in the *Greek Anthology,* 5.170:

> *Nothing is sweeter than love, and all blessed things are second to it,*

> *Even the honey I spit out of my mouth!*
> *So says Nossis: She whom Kypris hasn't loved,*
> *She doesn't know what kind of flower is the rose.*

The general idea was that humans just had to submit to the dominion of Aphrodite and accept love, lust and heartache as part of life. We've all been there.

The problem was in the matter of social practicalities. You can't have your wife falling madly in love with some other guy (less of a problem if she loves another woman, but we don't have the data). Having men fight over a lover can lead to chaos and conflict (think of Helen and the Trojan War). Ancient Greek philosophers thus tried to come up with ways of minimizing tension between social harmony and the dictates of the Paphian. At one extreme were the Pythagoreans, who claimed that your best bet was to deny Aphrodite and Eros entirely and to refrain from sex except, exclusively, for reproduction. At the other extreme were the early Stoics, such as Zeno of Kition and Khrysippos. They argued that society would be better off having group marriages, something like the 'free love' of the 1960s mixed with a kind of early socialism. As Diogenes Laertius in his *Life of Zeno*, 7.13 recorded it:

> *It is resolved that among the wise the wives should be held in common, so that one might make use of another pretty much at random, just as Zeno said in his* Politeia *and Khrysippos in his* On Government *(and also Diogenes the Cynic and Plato). They would love all the children equally as a father and it would do away with the jealousy arising from adultery.*

For the Stoics, however, eroticism was not an end in itself; it was rather the means by which one builds up 'friendship' (*philia*) in society (*Life of Zeno*, 7.130):

The aim of eros is to make friendship through the perception of beauty – not sexual intercourse, but friendship.

Basically, people, both men and women, would be attracted to each other and to the younger men and women in their society. They would have sexual relations, build friendships, educate the young people and provide for social harmony, while also getting rid of classism and the hording of wealth associated with traditional marriages. One might say that the Stoics accepted Aphrodite in *all* of her manifestations: libido, friendship and political concord.

In between were philosophers such as Plato. In his *Symposion*, as we saw in Chapter One, he argued that physical love (libido, eroticism) was inherently base and associated with Aphrodite *Pandemos*. In contrast, intellectual love, associated with Aphrodite *Ourania* (Heavenly), was noble and good. In short, love and friendship are both very, very good; physical sex is problematic at best. Or, if you prefer, love with the mind is good, love with the body is bad.

As you might imagine, both of the extremes went down about as well as hippie free love and socialism did in the twentieth century. In fact, rather less well. The Greeks continued to practice monogamous marriage, with males permitted some nookie on the side. But both the Platonic ideology and the more radical ideas endured…

Early Christianity: Hellenic Judaism Meets Aphrodite

Like Plato, modern society values spiritual, intellectual and emotive love and friendship highly, but has all sorts of problems with the physical act of sex. Granted, part of this is because of the reproductive aspect of heterosexual intercourse: Societies prefer not to have a bunch of babies with no clear family or support network. However, this does not account for the negativity towards homosexuality throughout the past two millennia, or why we still debate whether birth control is a good thing. Even divorced from reproduction, people still have a problem with sex.

Much of this, at least in the Western tradition, might be traced to ideologies that emerged at the dawn of Christianity. The early Christians had very negative attitudes towards sex. These were folded into the religion that then came to dominate Europe (and beyond) for some 2,000 years.

Importantly, after the conquests of Alexander the Great in the fourth century BCE, the Near East – including the Levant – became very Greek in language and culture. All scholarship was conducted in Greek (even by the Romans). Even the Hebrew Bible was translated into Greek in the 3rd century BCE, a work called the Septuagint (LXX), because according to tradition the work was carried out by some 70 sages who were locked in their rooms and now allowed out until they finished. When Roman-era Jews and Christians studied the Bible, they studied it in Greek, *not* Hebrew. Early Christianity is what you get when you mix the Hebrew Bible with Hellenistic culture.

Enter Paul of Tarsus (aka Saul of Tarsus, aka Saint Paul). He was your standard Hellenised Jew, very active in his faith, who converted to the new branch of Judaism that became known as Christianity. Paul then took it upon himself to convert as many people as he could throughout the entire Roman Empire to Christianity, even including people who were not already Jews, namely Gentiles and pagans.

Sexual intercourse was already a bit problematic in this milieu. As far as the Greeks and Greek language were concerned, the word for 'sexuality' was *aphrodisia*, and sexual intercourse was *ta erga Aphroditês*, 'the works of Aphrodite'. So how does one have sex *without* worshipping the goddess? Remember: All those pagans and Gentiles still actually believed in the Greek gods. They just knew that, per the dictates of Judeo-Christian monotheism, they weren't supposed to worship them. So linking sex to the Greek goddess was already a stumper.

Paul made it worse by creating a miasma around physical sexuality, rather as Plato and the Pythagoreans had done. This happened in two parts, both neatly presented in his *First Letter to the Corinthians*.

Part #1: Paul became panic-stricken over the Greek word *porneia*. You have probably noticed that 'porn-' element of the word and figured out that it has something to do with sex. If you paid attention in Chapter One, you might even know it pertains to prostitution. And you are correct! The Greek word *porneia* does mean 'prostitution'. But for those 70 sages who translated the Hebrew Bible from Hebrew into Greek, it came to have a somewhat different meaning. In the Septuagint, *pornê* ('prostitute') is the Greek word used to translate the Hebrew *zônah*, meaning a woman who engages in illicit sexual activity — a prostitute or an adulteress (yes, the same word was used for both). In the works of the Old Testament prophets such as Hosea and Ezekiel, the land of Israel itself was conceived of as the Bride of Yahweh. Whenever the Israelites worshipped any god other than Yahweh, the collective people became a metaphorical adulterous wife, a *zônah*, a whore. 'Whoring' therefore became a *metaphor* for apostasy. When the Bible was translated into Greek, the concept was expressed with the word *porneia*. Paul didn't entirely get the metaphor, however, teaching instead that it was actually the illicit sexuality that *caused* apostasy, a turning away from God. So, illicit sex, fornication, *porneia* was deemed a grave sin that must be avoided at all costs.

Granted, this immediately brought up the issue of what constituted *illicit* sex. There were numerous dictates in the Pentateuch, such as no bestiality and no incest. But for Paul – and here is Part #2 – illicit sex was defined as sexual intercourse you had with someone who wasn't your very specifically Christian spouse. As noted above, Paul took it upon himself to convert as many people as possible to Christianity, including many who were not already Jews. As a result, Paul was less than insistent about having non-Jews follow Jewish laws. It can be *extremely* difficult to convince adult men to adopt a new religion – *any* religion – if you require them to be circumcised. If you tell people that they have to give up bacon and multigrain bread, they are going to look elsewhere. So Paul let most of the Jewish laws slide except for three. Monotheism was an absolute. You had to pay heed to the words of God's messengers (which in this case, conveniently, meant Paul). And you must not have sex with non-Christians. You see, if you convert one person in a marriage to Christianity, he or she will then nag the heck out of the spouse to convert as well. If somebody is in love with a Christian, then she/he has to convert to pursue the relationship. And while Paul was more than happy to allow Christians to divorce pagans, such was not the case for Christian couples. Once you converted there was (theoretically) no turning back. Basically, Paul used the lure of sex as a recruitment tool.

So, fornication is bad. Having sex with a non-Christian is bad. But eating meat that was sacrificed and consecrated to a pagan deity? Well, that's not so bad really. Even if it's bacon? No worries. The only *real* sins are fornication (sex) and apostasy (whoring). Sex is thus clearly the great evil. Needless to say, Aphrodite did not thrive in this environment.

By the second century CE the Church Fathers were well onboard with this. They condemned Aphrodite and her ability to bring individuals together in sexual, friendly, civic communion, mainly because *'ta erga Aphroditês'* involved the goddess. As Clement of Alexandria neatly described it in his work *Stromata*:

There are some who even call Common Venus a mystical communion. This is an insult to the name ... But they have impiously called by the name of communion any common sexual intercourse ... These thrice wretched men treat carnal and sexual intercourse as a sacred religious mystery, and think that it will bring them to the kingdom of God. It is to the brothels that this 'communion' leads. They can have pigs and goats as their associates. Those who have most to hope from them are the public harlots who shamelessly receive all who want to come to them. But you have not so learned Christ, if you have heard him and have been taught by him as the truth is in Christ Jesus; put off with the ways of your former life, which is corrupted by the deceitful lusts. ... But fornication and all impurity and covetousness and shamefulness and foolish talk, let them not be mentioned among you as is fitting for saints.

– Translation by John Ernest Leonard Oulton,
Alexandrian Christianity, The Westminster Press, 3,
27–28, Philadelphia, 1954, slightly adapted

It was the Pythagorean mentality that ultimately triumphed in Christianity. Sex was deemed evil but necessary in order to create the next generation of Christians (once it was determined that the end of the world was not particularly nigh). Sexuality was ideally reduced to sexual intercourse reserved exclusively for one's spouse, engaged in exclusively for reproduction. Homosexuality was out. Masturbation was out. Every sperm was indeed sacred.

And Aphrodite? She was already bad enough just because she was a pagan goddess. But she was also the patroness of the irresistible forces of desire just when we decided that sex was evil, which made her even worse. By the fourth century CE the early Christians even did away with her divinity. They redefined Aphrodite as nothing more than the paragon of prostitutes who turned other women to whoring. Such was the assessment of the fourth-century Christian author Lactantius in his work *The Divine Institutes* (1.17):

She [Venus] first, as it is contained in the Sacred History, *instituted the art of prostitution and was the instigator amongst women in Cyprus to prostitute themselves publicly. She ordered this so as not to appear alone amongst other women as immodest and desirous of men.*

Later in the same work Lactantius asks, 'How will [pagan worshippers] maintain their modesty when they worship a "goddess" who is naked and adulterous, the whore of Olympus?' (5.10.15).

Yahweh certainly did not have sex, especially once we did away with his wife Asherah. Apollo was at least symbolic of enlightenment and the iconographic stand-in for Christ before Christianity was legal. Dionysos went through a similar death and resurrection, thus getting the pagans familiar with the concept; he also provided sacramental wine. But nothing good could come from the Celestial Whore.

TRANSITION

Once the European Christians got used to the fact that they were Christians, they managed to calm down a lot about the pagan deities. In the literatures of the later Middle Ages and Renaissance, Latin Venus and eventually Greek Aphrodite re-emerged in ways far more typical of what we saw in Chapter One – a goddess of love (less so sex) with all the joy and heartbreak that entailed. In fact, as early as the 12th century Marie de France, in the court of Eleanor of Aquitaine, could summon the image of Venus as the patroness of courtly love in her lay 'Guigemar':

Venus, la deuesse d'amur   *Venus, the goddess of love,*
Fu tresbien mise en la peinture   *Was well wrought in the painting;*
Les traiz mustrot e la nature   *Revealing love's character and nature,*
Cument hom deit amur tenir   *How man should maintain love*
E leialment e bien server.   *And serve it loyally and well*
ll. 234–238

The use of Venus in painting to set the mood also appeared in Chaucer's *The Knight's Tale*, a story of hopeless courtly love set in ancient Greece. Chaucer describes the painting, and thus also the goddess, as follows:

> *For soothly al the mount of Citheroun,*
> *Ther Venus hath hir principal dwellynge,*
> *Was shewed on the wal in portreyynge,*
> *With al the gardyn and the lustynesse.*
> ...
> *Ne may with Venus holde champartie,*
> *For as hir list the world than may she gye.*
> *Lo, alle thise folk so caught were in hir las,*
> *Til they for wo ful ofte seyde "allas!"*
> *Suffiseth heere ensamples oon or two,*
> *And though I koude rekene a thousand mo.*

> *The statue of Venus, glorious for to se,*
> *Was naked, fletynge in the large see…*
> – ll. 1936–9, 1949–56

By the time we get to Shakespeare, Venus has become not merely an art theme but a character in her own right again. This is most evident in the long poem she shares with her lover Adonis (see Chapter Three). Here, yet again, we see the ambivalence of the goddess, the bringer of sensual delight but also suffering:

> *So soon was she along, as he was down,*
> *Each leaning on their elbows and their hips:*
> *Now doth she stroke his cheek, now doth he frown,*
> *And 'gins to chide, but soon she stops his lips;*
> *And kissing speaks, with lustful language broken,*
> *'If thou wilt chide, thy lips shall never open.'*
>
> *He burns with bashful shame; she with her tears*
> *Doth quench the maiden burning of his cheeks;*
> *Then with her windy sighs and golden hairs*
> *To fan and blow them dry again she seeks:*
> *He saith she is immodest, blames her miss;*
> *What follows more she murders with a kiss.*
> – §§8–9

The Latin West only slowly acquired Greek again after the Middle Ages, and it took still longer for that trend to trickle down from the universities to ordinary people. Aphrodite (not Venus) re-emerged in more popular culture mainly with the Romantic poets such as Shelley, Keats and Byron, who were themselves obsessed with ancient Greek culture. When they began to translate ancient Greek literature, Aphrodite resumed her place in modern society. Shelley's *Homeric Hymn to Aphrodite*, ll. 1–8:

> Muse, sing the deeds of golden Aphrodite,
> Who wakens with her smile the lulled delight
> Of sweet desire, taming the eternal kings
> Of Heaven, and men, and all the living things
> That fleet along the air, or whom the sea,
> Or earth, with her maternal ministry,
> Nourish innumerable, thy delight
> All seek ... O crowned Aphrodite!

APHRODITE IN MODERN PAGANISM (AND PERCEPTION)

Certain deities get more attention than others in modern neopagan religions. Oðinn and Freyja are popular in Asatru; Gerd less so. The Morrigu and the Dagda have their roles among the modern Druids, but Goibniu not so much. Aphrodite is absolutely a popular goddess in modern paganism, especially (but not exclusively) among those with a Hellenic frame of mind.

The main problem with the recreation of ancient religions – often unrecognized – is that the primary mode of worship was animal sacrifice. We're not just talking about pagan religions either (see the Hebrew Bible, for example). Ancient peoples ate a *lot* less meat than people do today; its consumption was often involved in religious rituals that sanctified the killing of the animal. A Greek public sacrifice known as a hecatomb involved the ritual sacrifice of 100 bulls, usually to Zeus (although, to be fair, *one* bull and 99 figurines would also do, if we're being practical). In Homer's *Odyssey* (Book 14) even the enslaved swineherd Eumaios remembers to offer a portion of the meat to Hermes and nymphs before he and the household servants eat their pork. In any given Greek sanctuary the altar was of far greater importance than the actual temple. Most religious rituals culminated with the slaughter of an animal at the altar, followed by a community barbeque.

This doesn't work out so well in modern times. People are now far more squeamish about killing animals, especially mammals, and it is frequently illegal in urban environments. As such, the new pagan religions have often avoided this (critical) aspect of the ancient pagan religions. For the best, to my mind. It does mean, though, that most people today do not seem to realize that killing an animal was central to ancient religions, and that the modern recreations are literally missing the *kreas* (Greek for 'meat'). The Carnival no longer has its *carne*.

And so the various branches of neopaganism needed to come up with new rituals. Conveniently, when it comes to Aphrodite, there is at least some ancient precedent: According to Tacitus (*Histories*, 2.3) it was 'forbidden to spread blood on the table of sacrifice' at Aphrodite's temple in Paphos. So bloodless sacrifice was the rule. Incense and cakes were often on the menu, just as in common modern practice.

Other rituals now associated with Aphrodite focus on the Beauty aspect of her persona. A candle-lit bath with scented soaps and oils is recommended in various online and printed pagan manuals. Sensual music, dressing in silks, luxury bed sheets, frankincense, flowers, seashells and spicy scented candles are *de rigeur*. One author mentions her Greek Goddess Barbie on the altar (no comment). Chocolate is anachronistic yet absolutely appropriate. For those more interested in the erotic aspects of the goddess, various types of ritual sex can be performed. One author mentions pole dancing… The clear focus here is on *sensuality*.

While all authors who write about sexual congress as an aspect of Aphrodite-worship emphasize the importance of consent and being age appropriate, one ancient and modern myth continues to lurk in the quest for erotic Aphrodite: the idea of 'sacred prostitution'.

THE SPECTRE OF SACRED PROSTITUTION

In 2018 the *Phoenix New Times* did a story on the Phoenix Goddess Temple, where the high priestess (termed a 'goddess') – Aphrodite by name – gave a healing session to one of the temple's acolytes. The article described what occurred:

C. gets butt-naked and belly-down on a massage table. Aphrodite runs her hands over his back, then takes off her sarong and drapes it over him. She's wearing only a black G-string .... She tells him she's going to run the sarong across his body a few times, and each time he should imagine some pain he's had going away. She rubs coconut oil on him while saying things like, 'We're all deserving of pleasure'. About 40 minutes into the session, C. turns over on his back. He doesn't have an erection. Aphrodite proposes a prostate massage. She puts on a 'finger condom' and inserts a finger into his anus, while simultaneously gripping and stroking his penis. Five minutes of this and C's whole body starts shaking. He lets out several loud moans, and Aphrodite cleans him up with a wet towel.

– Phoenix Goddess Temple's "Sacred Sexuality" is More Like New Age Prostitution', *Phoenix New Times*, Nicki D'Andrea, 2018.

According to the report, at the temple 'every room includes a massage table (which they call an "altar of light"), as well as a bed (called the "grand altar")'. Basically, it was a brothel that claimed to provide sacred healing, administered by unlicensed 'goddess' sex therapists. The various goddesses suggested donations of up to $650 an hour.

This is just *one* manifestation of the concept of 'sacred prostitution' in modern times.

For the record, there actually was no sacred prostitution in the ancient world – no tradition in which patrons offered money to a deity (usually understood as Aphrodite or Ištar) in exchange for sex with a 'sacred' slave or meretricious priestess. This misunderstanding of ancient religion is still rather popular in current constructions of antiquity. But it is inaccurate.

It all began when Herodotos, the so-called 'Father of History', wrote in the fifth century BCE of the city of Babylon that:

The most shameful custom among the Babylonians is this: It is necessary for every local woman to sit in the sanctuary of Aphrodite once in life to 'mingle' with a foreign man. But many do not deign to mingle with the others, thinking highly of themselves because of their wealth, and they set themselves before the sanctuary having arrived in covered chariots, with many a maidservant in tow. But the majority act thus: In the temenos of Aphrodite many women sit wearing a garland of string about their heads. Some come forward, others remain in the background. They have straight passages in all directions through the women, by which the foreigners passing through might make their selection. Once a woman sits there she may not return home before one of the foreigners, tossing silver into her lap, should mingle with her outside the sanctuary. And in tossing he must say: 'I summon you by the goddess Mylitta'. The Assyrians call Aphrodite Mylitta. The silver is of any amount, for it may not be rejected: this is not their sacred custom, for the money becomes sacred. The woman follows the first man who tossed her silver, nor may she reject anyone. When she should have mingled, having discharged her obligation to the goddess, she leaves for home, and after this time you might not take her, offering gifts no matter how great. Those who are attractive and tall go home quickly, while those homely in these respects wait

about a long time, being unable to fulfil the law; some among them wait about for three or four years. And in some areas of Cyprus the custom is similar to this.
— Histories 1.199

It certainly seems pretty straightforward. The problem is that we now know a lot about ancient Babylon. Thousands upon thousands of cuneiform tablets have come from the soil, dealing with everything from the Great Flood to interest rates on mortgage payments, and there is *nothing* like this attested anywhere. Hundreds of women sitting around a temple in the middle of one of the greatest cities in the world? Someone would have to feed them; someone would have to arrange for the port-o-potties, etc. But we got nothing. This combined with Herodotos's less-than-accurate description of Babylonian medical practice (you bring sick people to the marketplace where passers-by give them advice) eventually led to the realization that this 'most shameful custom' was hooey.

Before that realization, though, when we could read the Greek but not (yet) the cuneiform, scholars accepted Herodotos's account. So when early Assyriologists found the names of female cult functionaries in the new texts, they translated them as 'sacred prostitutes', even the ones sworn to virginity. So now, in addition to 'every woman in Babylon', there were *also* categories of professional 'sacred prostitutes'. Pretty soon you couldn't spit in the ancient world without hitting a sacred prostitute, they were found in such abundance (Babylon, Byblos, Corinth, Eryx, *ad nausium*).

In modern times, among neopagans and others, this was seen as a good thing. Harkening back to that problem that the body is evil, sex is evil and women most assuredly are evil, the notion of sacred prostitution seemed to offer a corrective to all of that. In that context, (presumably) joyful sex took place not as a sin, but as some kind of sacrament. Embodied sexuality, usually understood as provided by a female, became holy and wholly positive.

We thus wound up with some pretty interesting descriptions of sacred prostitution. In her book *The Sacred Prostitute: Eternal Aspect of the Feminine,* the Jungian analyst Nancy Qualls-Corbett provided a description that reads like some mash-up of Herodotos and Harlequin and Phoenix Aphrodite:

Imagine the sacred prostitute greeting the stranger, a world-weary man who has come to the temple to worship the goddess of love.... She tells him amusing stories of her training – how the temple priests and other ritual priestesses taught her the art of love-making... She came to the temple, she tells him, in order to fulfil the law of the land, which every maiden must do. With reverence she speaks of her devotion to the goddess as she approaches the small marble image of Venus.... The sacred prostitute leads the stranger to the couch prepared with white linens and aromatic myrtle leaves. She has rubbed sweet-smelling wild thyme on her thighs.... He is keenly aware of the passion within this votary to the goddess of love and fertility, and is fulfilled.

The woman and stranger know that the consummation of the love act is consecrated by the deity through which they are renewed.
– *The Sacred Prostitute,* 22–24: Inner City Books, 1988

Taking perhaps a more feminist approach, Cosi Fabian's chapter 'The Holy Whore', published in Jill Nagle's book *Whores and Other Feminists*, (48: Routledge, 1997) claimed that:

Sacred prostitute stories reveal an understanding of women as gateways to transformation. In them, women use combinations of sexual ecstasy, formal ritual, and informational teaching, and are seen to embody incarnations of their goddess.

What does recur in the majority of descriptions of (entirely modern) 'sacred prostitution' is the notion of *healing*. While Pagan sacred sex itself might be understood as a means of communion with a deity or a means of raising energy (or both, or more), once the word 'prostitution' appears in a text the focus switches immediately to healing rituals. Every sex practitioner or worker interviewed by Jennifer Hunter in her book *Rites of Pleasure: Sexuality in Wicca and NeoPaganism* immediately noted the healing function of sacred prostitution, with one interviewee claiming 'What has been called "temple prostitution" was, I believe, the practice of healing sexuality' (182: Citadel Press, 2004).

To be perfectly clear, there is not a single reference to healing in any of the ancient texts associated with the construct of sacred prostitution. The ancients did have both healing deities (e.g. Asklepios) and healing rituals, often involving incubation and revealing dreams. But the only ancient documents that had sex as part of a healing ritual were the ŠÀ.ZI.GA texts from Mesopotamia, used to treat erectile dysfunction. The sexual part of the therapy was provided by the guy's wife. You get my point.

Rather, the idea of healing as associated with modern sacred prostitution brings us back to the Phoenix narrative above: there needs to be an excuse to charge for it. A sexual-sacred union is an equal joining of two individuals with mutual benefit; there is no cause for an exchange of money. By contrast, a healing ritual, however conceived, can be seen as a *service*, for which a fee or request for a donation is perfectly acceptable. The healing aspect of sacred sexuality, which rarely bears comment in all other ritual aspects, suddenly becomes a major focus when money is involved. This actually does a major disservice to those who promote positive sexuality and those who fight for the rights of sex workers. Once sex, no matter how sacred, is paid for, we feel we must euphemise it into something else (for example, a 'healing ritual').

Beyond the way the myth of sacred prostitution complicates the interplay of divinity and sex (and sex work) in modern times, the current understanding of the myth as expressed by Qualls-Corbett (probably accepted as the norm by many people today) is a misrepresentation. It does not accurately portray what was actually understood to happen to so-called sacred prostitutes in antiquity. To provide just two narratives…

According to Lucian, the second-century CE author of *On the Syrian Goddess* §6:

The people of Byblos shave their heads [when mourning for Adonis], just like the Egyptians when Apis dies. Of the women, those who do not wish to shave perform this penalty. For a single day they stand for the sale of their beauty. The market is open to foreigners only and the payment becomes a penalty to Aphrodite.

Likewise in the *Epitome of Pompeius Trogus,* Justinus writes in 21.3:

When the Locrians were being pressed by the war with Leophron, tyrant of the Rhegians, they had vowed – if they were victorious – that on the feast-day of Venus they would prostitute their virgins. As the vow was intermisso *(paused, interrupted, neglected, omitted, ignored, left unfulfilled), when they were waging a losing war with the Lucanians, Dionysios summoned them into an assembly; he urged that they send their wives and daughters into the temple of Venus as ornately decked-out as possible, from whom 100 chosen by lot would enact the public vow and would – for the sake of religion – stand for one month in a brothel (before this all the men would swear that no one would touch any of them). So that the matter would not harm the virgins who were releasing the state by the vow, they made a decree that no virgin would marry until those girls were given to husbands.*

In the first passage, women who choose not to shave their heads are, for one day, sold as prostitutes and their earnings are given to Aphrodite. Lucian mentions no similar penalty (or any penalty, for that matter) for the city's men. In the latter narrative the people of Locris in southern Italy vowed to prostitute their virgin daughters in the hopes of preventing their war-time rapes. They returned to this technique years later under similar conditions. In the first passage the Byblian women's attempt to maintain their own bodily integrity is deliberately thwarted – give us your hair or we take your vagina. In the latter, virgin girls are offered the choice between rape and mandatory sex work. These are not tales of female power and liberation, nor are they sex-positive narratives; they are tales of the sexual oppression of females. Even the original passage from Herodotos stresses the lack of volition experienced by the Babylonian women: The wealthy who hide in carts, the less attractive who are stranded for years, the complete inability to negotiate.

It is critical to note that Aphrodite was not associated with sexual oppression. While irresistible desire (problematic as it is) might be one of her hallmarks, she is not linked to rape narratives. Although the patroness of *hetairai* (who could be enslaved, yet could also be liberated into her care), Aphrodite is less associated with actual prostitutes, who were usually impoverished slaves in ancient Greece (and Rome). Aphrodite *Pornê* only appears once in the literature, in Roman times, after the *hetaira* had passed out of the culture. Aphrodite embodied and promoted the joys of sex; when she went 'dark' the result was warfare and bloody death, *not* sexual violence or oppression.

SAFE SEX: DEALING REASONABLY AND RESPONSIBLY WITH APHRODITE

'I didn't think the Greeks had religion,' my mother-in-law once said. 'I thought they just had mythology.'

This is not an atypical view in modern society. There is a notion that only the current batch of world religions – Judaism, Christianity, Islam, Hinduism, Buddhism – are actual religions. Those ancient pagan religions were just collections of stories, not too distant from, say, *Cinderella*. Somehow, when Noah sticks two to 14 of every animal onto an ark before the flood rains come, it's religion; when Ut-Napištim does the same thing in the *Epic of Gilgameš*, it's mythology.

Furthermore, mainly thanks to somewhat impious Romans (especially Ovid) and those Church Fathers mentioned above, the pagan deities who show up in the myths, the stories, are always bad. Zeus sticks it into anything with an orifice, Hera is a jealous bitch, Ares is a war-crazed psychopath, Aphrodite is a whore. By contrast, the God of Abraham is always presented as good, kind and merciful, even when he's demanding the slaughter of babies and threatening to have his adulteress wife Israel gang raped (see Ezekiel for more on that one). We do not think very clearly about religion.

All religions are human-made. Someone wrote the Torah (actually, a lot of people), Siddhartha sat under that Bodhi tree, someone in the deep mists of time composed the Vedas, Paul of Tarsus was a major contributor to Christianity, Gerald Gardner helped to give rise to modern Wicca. And while we can all agree that humans are irrational and weird, they are rarely completely masochistic: they do not make up religions that work against them. All religions work, at least originally, within the *Weltanschauung* in which they emerged, and they tend to adapt – sometimes quickly, sometimes *very* slowly – to new conditions. Or not. The point is that people create religions that make sense to them and serve a purpose. To create maladaptive deities risks driving the entire society to neurosis.

Aphrodite is a perfectly reasonable goddess. In her is embodied the very real experience of the human sex drive, that hormonal response that defies logic and causes one to think with one's dick/clitoris. We've all seen it. The beauty of Aphrodite is that she creates a divine place for that in the world and in human psychology. *Of course* you're thinking with your dick! *No one* can resist Golden Aphrodite – not even Zeus! Your libido is perfectly normal, even inevitable, so learn to work with it. It is not bad and you are not bad for experiencing it. Aphrodite enables people to deal with their endocrine systems in a way that accords with nature. Furthermore, she allows positive emotions to prevail in social gatherings, leaving social harmony and friendship in her wake.

By contrast, those religions that claim that the body, and sex in particular, are evil create extraordinary stress. Even if sexual intercourse is carefully confined to marriage, guilt and shame still remain simply for *feeling* erotic urges. There is no

Aphrodite to 'take the blame'; there isn't even a god subjected to Aphrodite for people to relate to. Religions like these offer only a single outlet, reserved for procreation, with no scope to work masturbation or homosexuality or simple human desire into the divine master plan. This is going to drive people crazy. As John Heath observed so well in his book *The Bible, Homer, and the Search for Meaning in Ancient Myths* (317: Routledge, 2019):

Sex is a natural force and efforts to suppress it almost always backfire. Eros is the whack-a-mole of human psychology – you can try to smack it down, but it will materialize someplace else, usually arising as a bigger and more destructive beast.

Like all deities before they were subjected to hostile negative propaganda, Aphrodite *worked* for her ancient Greek worshippers. She not only gave an explanation for a constant and inevitable aspect of life but also revealed the joy that could be had by embracing this aspect of the mind and body. Contrary to the early Christian and current understanding of her persona, Aphrodite was more than just a goddess of libido. She made human society possible by allowing humans to stand living with one another. She was the basis of friendship and social harmony. She was the origin of all reproduction. She kept the world alive.

Modern Short Stories of Aphrodite

Those That Hunger For Warmth
Benjamin Cyril Arthur

Aphrodite visits you…

…Between the dust-laden streets of Accra's Jamestown, where fishing nets dry like abandoned spider webs and the air tastes of salt and diesel fumes, your world has shrunk to the size of your mother's compound house, its once-vibrant yellow walls now peeling like old scabs. Your siblings are scattered like seeds in the harmattan wind: Ama runs a hair salon in London, Kofi chases fortunes in Nigeria's tech boom, and Kwabena, the oldest, tends bar in Cape Coast's tourist traps. The love they send arrives like raindrops in a drought – too little, too scattered to nurture anything substantial. They know you're gay, they want nothing to do with you. Past promises of being there for you echo in your empty mobile notifications, each ping a hollow reminder of distance. The iPhone that once connected you to their world lies on your bed, silent as ever. Your attempts to reach out to them are met with biblical walls higher than Mount Everest. "You're a sin," they said, as if the years you lived together in one house meant nothing anymore, after you came out to them.

Gone are the days when you could knock on your neighbour's door. Their faces have hardened like concrete now, their doors closing faster at the sight of your approaching shadow. Even the shop owners, who used to smile at you, now turn away when you pass.

* * *

So Aphrodite comes to you…

She is stirring palm nut soup in your mother's kitchen when you walk in, her skin gleaming like polished golden mahogany in the afternoon light. She wears a fabric you've never seen before – neither kente nor Dutch wax print, but something that shifts like oil on water, the colours of sunrise trapped in cloth. Her hair is crowned with cowries that whisper ancient spirituals with every movement.

"Kwame," she says, and your name in her mouth tastes like the ripe mangoes of your childhood.

She ladles soup into your mother's cherished glass bowl, the one brought from the Cape coast years ago. Her fingers, when they brush yours, feel warm, like the moment before rain breaks the heat of a sunny Accra afternoon. You don't scream or panic; your mother was a fetish priest, you've seen worse.

In the bowl, you see reflections of market women selling at dawn. You see the Ghana that exists in the spaces between streetlights and smartphones, hidden love in the shadows of high-rises where old gods still dance and worshippers still offer libation and sacrifices. You see your mother and father before the car crash, when they were alive to love you.

"There are other hungers," Aphrodite tells you, "deeper than the belly's emptiness. You've been starving for so long, my child."

"Starving of what?"

"Of love."

"I followed my heart and now this is what I got, a life of loneliness."

"What you got or what you chose? Punishing yourself, are we?"
"Who are you?"
"I am everything?"
You roll your eyes. "Who are you? A ghost? A spirit?" you ask. There's a pause and then she begins to levitate. You sigh, "Very dramatic."
"I am love, I am beauty. I am the goddess, Aphrodite."
"And why are you here? Shouldn't you be in Greece, drinking red wine from someone's vineyard?"
"Your mother sent me."
The words hit you like a punch to the gut. You feel the air rush out of your lungs as your eyes go wide, mouth agape. A heaviness settles in your chest, an aching sorrow welling up from somewhere deep inside "My mother?" you ask, and she nods.
"Yes. Your mother."

* * *

It's 7:30 p.m. and you're in a small apartment waiting for the games to begin. You want to go home but Aphrodite has sworn to unleash hell on you if you come back before 10 p.m. You take off your shirt as you settle into the couch watching others play Uno. Not far from you, standing in a corner is the goddess herself, silently watching, waiting for something. The door suddenly opens and a stranger walks into the apartment screaming the words, *"Harry Potter is a classless, tasteless punkass bitch!"* to your friend Tina, who is carrying bottles of red wine and a tray full of fries and chicken.

As soon as your eyes fall on him, you see yourselves together in a house on casual days, like a Tuesday morning, when he is about to leave for work. You're making his coffee as he wears the blue shirt you bought him a week ago at the mall. You see days like Friday evening, when he is coming home from work tired. He sees you across the street, and he smiles, and you have this feeling like you've never felt so loved before you met him. It's like he's opening new chapters of your life with him popping up in every inch of it, for better or for worse, for richer, for poorer, to love and to cherish. You look away when his warm brown eyes, sweeping the room, finally land on you. A smile tugs at the corners of his full lips. He drops the cards and walks up to you.

"I'm Xolali," he greets.

"I'm Papa," you reply.

"I haven't seen you here before."

"I don't really do outings; I'm a couch potato. My whole life is basically a sixty-year-old stripper who threw her back out coming down from a pole."

He laughs and says, "You're funny."

You smile. As the night progresses, you can't keep your eyes off him. You watch as his fingers dance over the Uno cards; he laughs richly and melodiously when he calls out, "Uno out!" The game blurs into a haze of colour, but you focus entirely on the way his brows furrow in concentration, the flash of his teeth when he grins. Later, during a heated round of trivia, his knowledge of Harry Potter will leave you in awe. You will groan in mock defeat, secretly thrilled by the playful glint in his eye.

The clock strikes 2 a.m. and friends begin to depart. You find yourself gravitating towards him. Your heart pounds as you approach him, and the words tumble out before you can stop them. "I…I…Can I sleep in your room?"

His eyes widen slightly, then soften. Then, he nods and replies, "Yes. Why not?"

Later that morning, you will write a sentence in an empty journal, the first line of your novel.

Lips softer than life, sweeter than swimming in a sea of daydreams and obscure happiness.

* * *

He doesn't call. He doesn't text either…

You spend all week staring at your phone, and nothing.

You're in the kitchen with Aphrodite. You both had just come back from a protest, sweaty and hungry, smelling of teargas. You stir the soup with one hand, the other holding your phone while Aphrodite sits at the counter, her feet finally free of the torturous boots she's worn all day. You watch the steam rise from the pot.

"He's handsome, you say?"

"Very handsome," you reply.

"You know, beauty isn't everything."

"You're one to talk, goddess of beauty."

Aphrodite laughs. "This body is nothing but a vessel, it will wither with time. Fall in love with someone who looks like you on the inside. Someone who understands your heart, your kindness." She drops the ladle and picks up her glass of wine.

"You know what I was thinking about during the protest today?" she begins, tracing a finger through the condensation on her glass. "What if humans stayed as ideas in their mother's soliloquy?"

You look up from the soup, caught off guard by the poetry in her voice. "What do you mean?"

"Like, before humans were born, before they knew who they'd become, what if they never happened?" She pulls her legs up onto the stool, hugging her knees.

"Then we wouldn't exist."

"And wouldn't that be good. Fewer evil people, less corruption, no climate issues, no need to protest for clean water, no homophobia."

"Homophobia is a disease that has no cure. Born from hatred. If hatred can't be cured, I doubt homophobia can. Besides, if we don't exist, who will worship you?"

"True."

"I still can't believe you followed me to the protest."

"It's a protest for love rights, and as the goddess of love, I have to be there."

"I thought gods were homophobic."

"I have a gender non-binary child. Your mother clearly didn't tell you everything about me."

"Tell me truthfully. Can I find love despite everything, a genuine love that will stay with me till it's time for me to leave this earth?"

Aphrodite reaches across the counter and squeezes your hand. "Of course you can."

"It's not too late for you too, you know."

Aphrodite laughs, but it's a hollow sound. "Decades of living for others has made a depressed lesbian out of me, sucked me dry of love."

You look out through the window. The moon hangs full and bright, watching in its own quiet way.

"Come on," you say finally, wiping your eyes. "Let's eat before it gets cold."

She smiles, reaching for the bowl. "And then you can tell me about that man you met at game night, who couldn't take his eyes off of you."

"He's not into me."

"Why do you say that?"

"No calls, no texts, nothing."

"Doesn't mean he's not thinking about you."

"You can be so delusional sometimes."

"I am the goddess of love and beauty. Delusion is my anthem."

"I'm okay being alone."

"You're not. I can see inside you. The longing and yearning for love is louder than ever. Every living thing wants to be loved. Papa, no one was born to be alone."

You sit on the sofa and begin to eat. Five minutes into your dinner, your phone's screen lights up and, "hey. it's me, Xolali" appears. Aphrodite smiles.

"Don't smile!"

"Told ya."

You both giggle and then she puts down her bowl suddenly. "Okay, first things first. We're going upstairs to pick you out an outfit. Do you need lessons on seduction?"

"I don't need seduction lessons from a thousand-year-old goddess who doesn't know how to use an iPhone."

"That's fair."

* * *

You watch Xolali's profile against the night sky, the way his jaw curves like carved ebony, strong and precise. The evening air wraps around you both like a shawl, heavy with the scent of distant cooking fires from roadside chop bars.

"My phone was stolen that night," he says. "I had to wait for a week to get a new one."

"And there I was, thinking you're not interested in me."

"What would make you think that? I am very interested in you."

You walk past shuttered shops, their metal gates pulled down like sleeping eyelids. The streetlights grow fewer here, creating pools of darkness between their circles of yellow light. In one such shadow, Xolali's hand finds yours. His palm is soft except for the calluses at the tips of his fingers – markers of hours spent typing reports at his job. You marvel at how perfectly your fingers fit between his.

"What do you want?" he asks, and you stop walking.

"Huh?"

"I don't do situationships, or short flings, I…"

"I know, I also don't do short…I want to date you. I want love, I want it because I can return it."

Voices drift towards you from around the corner. Before you can process it, your hands have already separated, muscle memory born from years of careful navigation. You both step slightly apart as a group of young men pass, laughing about a football match. Your hand feels cold where Xolali's warmth had been.

The beach appears, the tide stretching its hands towards the unknown. The waves provide a constant soundtrack of surge and retreat. Palm fronds whisper overhead, their shadows dancing on the sand like ancient spirits.

"It's different at night," Xolali says.

You understand what he means. The darkness feels like a friend here, not an enemy to be feared. The moon hangs low and full, turning the ocean into a sheet of hammered silver. You can smell the salt, feel it on your skin. Xolali stops walking and turns to face you. In the moonlight, his dark eyes hold galaxies. You've never seen anything more beautiful than the way he looks at you now, like you're a poem he's trying to memorize.

"I've been wanting to do this all evening," he whispers, and then his hand is on your cheek, thumb tracing your jawline. When he kisses you, he tastes like the sobolo he was drinking earlier, spiced and sweet. Your hands find his waist, pulling him closer as the waves crash behind you. The kiss deepens, and you forget everything. When you finally part, Xolali rests his forehead against yours.

"We should go," he says, but makes no move to step away.

"Five more minutes," you whisper, drawing him back to you. Above, the stars wheel in their ancient patterns, watching over your secret moment of freedom.

* * *

You wake to the soft morning light filtering through unfamiliar curtains, and your heart nearly stops. There he is, right next to you, his face mere inches from yours. His dark lashes rest gently against his cheeks, and his usually groomed hair is delightfully mussed from sleep. You can't help yourself – you reach out, letting your fingers drift through the soft strands. He looks so peaceful, so different from his usual confident self. A small smile plays at the corners of his mouth as he sleeps, and you wonder what he's dreaming about. Your hand continues its gentle exploration of his hair, memorising this moment. This perfect, impossible moment. Then his eyes flutter open, those deep brown eyes. He smiles, shifting closer.

"Morning," he whispers, voice husky with sleep. That's when reality comes crashing back. The sound of rain hammering against the windows makes your blood run cold. Your jeans are on the clothesline. He'd hung them out to dry last night, confident in the weather forecast that promised no rain.

"Everything okay?" he asks, propping himself up on one elbow. He's looking at you with a warm and inviting expression. He reaches out and touches your cheek, obviously sensing your internal panic. "Stay," he says simply. "I'll make breakfast. The rain is supposed to clear up in a few hours anyway. I'll just give you my jeans. Bring it back tomorrow."

"The trouser is an excuse to get me to come back, isn't it?"

"I don't know what you're talking about," he replies, laughing.

* * *

The trotro lurches forward, then stops again. Your knees press against the seat in front of you, and the woman beside you shifts, adjusting her sleeping child.

The conductor's voice rings out: "Circle, circle, Kaneshie!"

You check your phone: 10:42 p.m. The late-night traffic crawls like a wounded animal through Accra's streets.

Through the clouded window, you watch the city's neon signs blur into streaks of colour. Every red light feels like a personal affront. The radio crackles with hiplife music, barely audible above the vehicle's protesting engine. A hawker approaches with sachets of water, and three passengers raise their hands. More waiting.

When you finally reach your stop, Xolali is leaning against a street pole, scrolling through his phone. The sight of him makes your heart stumble. He's changed his shirt – a crisp white one now – and the streetlight catches the silver chain at his neck.

"Almost 11," he says, grinning.

"Don't remind me," you groan, but you're smiling too. "What are you doing here? It's late."

He steps closer, just enough to be noticed. Just enough to be dangerous. "I've been thinking," he says, voice low. "Move in with me."

The words hit you like cold water. "What?"

"My place is closer to your office. The rent is reasonable. And…" he pauses, "I hate watching you leave every time."

Your mind races to all the ways this could go wrong. "Xolali, people will talk. The neighbours—"

"Will believe we're brothers," he interrupts, eyes gleaming. "You're from the Volta Region, just like me. Same tribe, same accent if you try. Nobody questions family living together."

You think about your current apartment, the nosy landlord who keeps asking when you'll bring a nice girl home. The long commute. The nights spent staring at your phone, wanting to call Xolali but worrying about what your roommate might overhear.

"Brothers," you repeat, testing the word.

"Mm-hmm. You can be the responsible older one who makes sure I eat proper meals," he says.

Then, he adds with a wink, "At least, that's what we'll tell the neighbours."

A taxi passes, its headlights sweeping over you both. You step apart instinctively, but Xolali's eyes hold yours. In them, you see shared mornings over coffee, quiet evenings on the balcony, a space where you don't have to count the inches between your bodies.

"The landlady is very religious," he continues, serious now. "She'll love having two God-fearing brothers as tenants. We'll go to church sometimes, just to keep up appearances. My best friend does the same with her girlfriend in Tema."

Your heart is racing. It's terrifying how much you want this. "You've thought about everything, haven't you?"

"Everything except your answer," he says softly.

Another trotro rumbles past, spewing exhaust into the night air. In its wake, the street feels quieter, like the city is holding its breath while waiting for your response.

You look at him – really look at him – standing there under the streetlight, offering you not just a home, but a way to make one together. It's dangerous and beautiful and everything you've always wanted.

"Yes," you hear yourself say. "Yes."

His smile breaks across his face like a sunrise, but he keeps his distance. Not here, not now. Later, behind closed doors, you'll celebrate properly. For now, he simply nods, pulls out his phone as if checking a message.

"Good," he says, loud enough for anyone passing to hear. "It'll be nice to have my brother around."

And in that moment, under the ancient stars that have watched lovers deceive the world since time began, you start planning your careful dance of truth and secrets, of love hidden in plain sight.

* * *

You stare at the walls of Xolali's bedroom, already imagining where things could go. Your books on the shelf by the window, a splash of colour on the walls – something warm, maybe a light amber or moss green. The space is neat, almost clinically so, with everything in its exact place: bed perfectly centre, dresser at a precise distance from the door, the rug positioned just so. This has been his sanctuary, his retreat, and it shows.

"So, I was thinking," you begin, testing the waters. "Maybe we could shift the bed slightly? Just so it's closer to the window."

Xolali's expression shifts, and you see his brows knit ever so slightly, a tiny crack in his calm.

"The bed stays there," he says, in that steady, careful tone he uses when he's about to put his foot down. "It's centred for a reason. Besides, if it's near the window, the light will wake us up too early. It's fine where it is."

You cross your arms, refusing to let him shut the conversation down. "But we can just pull the blinds. It'll be cozy, Xolali. You know, natural light…"

He shakes his head, exhaling, with a hint of tension in his stance. "It's not just about light," he replies, the edge of his voice sharp but careful. "It's my – our room, sure. But it has to stay… how it works. So I can…feel okay."

And you know what he means. You know his OCD routines, how he finds comfort in them, how certain things need to be just so for him to feel settled. But you can't ignore the feeling building in your chest, the quiet frustration of having to squeeze yourself into a mould that's already been shaped.

"Xolali, I'm not asking to turn your world upside down," you say, more softly now. "I'm just asking for a little piece of it. Just something that feels like…me."

His jaw tightens and he looks away, staring at the shelf, his fingers tracing the edge of his dresser with a deliberate slowness. Finally, he turns back to you, his eyes softer, with a flicker of vulnerability beneath them.

"What if we start with just the nightstand?" he murmurs, as if the suggestion costs him something. "You can add a book or… maybe a plant. One. But the bed stays."

You stare at him, feeling a sudden tenderness that catches you off guard. Because you know how much he's fighting right now – not you, but himself, his own fears, his need for control. You take a step towards him, closing the space between you. "One book and one plant," you agree, smiling. "I can live with that…for now."

There's a beat, a moment of stillness and then his shoulders relax. He chuckles softly, his eyes meeting yours with a warmth that makes the room feel like it's glowing. "You're relentless, you know that?"

"Only because I like you," you say, and then you're both laughing, tension melting away as easily as it had come. And before you know it, his hands are on your waist, pulling you closer. His lips meet yours in a kiss that's slow, soft and entirely consuming. The argument, the furniture, the room itself – all of it fades, and it's just the two of you, caught in each other, your hands tangling in his hair as he leans into you. The world beyond the four walls vanishes, leaving only the heat of his touch, the taste of his kiss.

"Fine," he whispers against your lips, breathless, giving in. "Maybe…maybe a small lamp, too."

You smile against his mouth, your heart pounding, and in that moment, you know you've found your place.

* * *

You love knowing that love hides in questions, like when his best friend asks you what your favourite food is. You told her it was waakye and she makes it for you the next day for lunch.

It's Christmas and you're staying at Tema, celebrating the launch of your first novel.

The aroma of spices fills the house as you help Tina, Xolali's best friend, clean up after lunch.

The Christmas tree lights twinkle in the corner of their apartment. Xolali's friends have somehow become your friends. They're telling stories about their university days, and you catch Xolali watching you from across the room, his smile soft and secret.

The conversation flows like honey, sweet and slow, but something pulls at you – a familiar tingle at the base of your spine. You excuse yourself and climb the stairs to the guest room, your feet knowing where to go before your mind does.

She's there, perched on the windowsill like she owns it, her golden skin catching the last rays of the setting sun. Aphrodite. Her presence still takes your breath away, even after all these years of her random appearances.

"My beautiful boy," she says, rising to cup your face in her hands. Her lips brush your forehead, and you catch the scent of grapes and roses. "You're not starving anymore."

The tears come before I can stop them. "You're leaving?"

"You don't need me now." Her smile is radiant with pride. "Look at you – surrounded by love, giving love, growing love. That's all I ever wanted for you."

You hold each other, and you try to memorise everything about this moment. When she finally steps back, her own eyes are glistening.

"Go back to him," she whispers, and then she's gone, leaving only the faintest shimmer in the air where she stood.

You take a moment to compose yourself before heading back downstairs. The scene that greets you makes your heart swell: Xolali is crouched by the front door, cradling a small, scraggly cat in his arms. The cat's fur is a patchwork of grey and white, and it's purring loud enough for you to hear from the bottom of the stairs.

"Can we keep him?" Xolali asks. Before you can answer, his face lights up with inspiration.

"Oh! We should call him Edem!"

You laugh, the sound carrying all the joy and love that Aphrodite knew you would find. "Where did you find him?" you ask.

"Outside, all alone. Starving."

You smile. "Lil Edem it is…" You touch the kitten and it purrs. "Welcome home, Edem."

Obaasima Aphrodite
Bernice Arthur

Many call me the goddess of love, beauty and pleasure, as if those titles alone were not enough. But can I blame them? Since that's all they see when they look at me – sex, a symbol of irresistible desire, a force of passion. It doesn't stop there; they inscribe my image in myths as a seductress, a temptress who had children with multiple men and whose power lies only in her face and form.

But they forget – love is not always gentle, beauty can be fleeting or hidden, and desire, ah, desire, is rarely simple. I am far more than the stories dare to admit. So no, no, no! I am not the Aphrodite they think they know…well, at least not anymore.

* * *

Aphrodite sat in the forge of her husband, Hephaestus, surrounded by the heat of the fires and the rhythmic clang of his hammer against metal. Sparks flew into the air as he worked, shaping steel into blades – cutlasses and knives destined for war. Her husband's hands were calloused and rough, embodying a different kind of power, one born of labor and creation. She watched him silently, the thoughts swirling in her mind heavier than the iron he forged. This was not her world of silk and roses, of whispered desires and secret glances. Strength was raw and visible in this space, yet she felt more at home than in any temple built in her name.

As Aphrodite sat there, her reflection in the polished surfaces of the weapons Hephaestus was crafting, she couldn't help but think about the whispers, the rumors that followed her like shadows. They said she was nothing more than a seductress, a goddess who bore 16 children by different lovers despite being married to the god of the forge. They talked of her affairs, her dalliances with Ares, the god of war, as if her legacy could be reduced to stolen moments of passion and infidelity. But what they never spoke of were her moments of strength, her moments of decision, the choices she had made to protect, empower and resist the very chains they sought to place on her.

Sitting in Hephaestus's workshop, she thought about what she had been reduced to: the goddess of reproduction and a trophy of seduction. But wasn't she also the goddess of survival? Of endurance? She thought of the women in the mortal world who prayed to her – for love or beauty, but not for strength or the power to be seen as more than their bodies or the children they bore. She had more to offer them than allure. She had more to offer the world.

Aphrodite rose from her seat, feeling the fire of the forge echo in her heart. She would not let the myths define her. The world would know her for what she truly was – a goddess of complexity, a force of nature beyond mere beauty. She would embrace the power she had always held but had never fully claimed. She would be more than the goddess of love; she would be the goddess of revolution, defiance and liberation from the narrow definitions imposed upon her.

She would rewrite her story.

As Hephaestus continued his work, oblivious to her inner struggle, Aphrodite knew it was time to break free from the traditional roles the world had cast her in. She turned away from the forge, and as she took her first steps towards the door, Hephaestus's voice broke the silence.

"Where are you going, Aphrodite?" he asked, confusion evident in his tone.

She paused, glancing over her shoulder. "To redefine myself," she said calmly, her voice steady with purpose.

Hephaestus frowned, clearly perplexed. "What do you mean by that?"

Aphrodite turned fully to face him, her gaze unwavering. "You'll know soon enough," she replied, a hint of finality in her words. Then, without another word, she turned and walked away, not once looking back.

As she disappeared into the vast, open sky, Hephaestus stood by the flames, his hammer idle in his hand. Confusion gripped him. What had she meant by "redefining" herself? And what is that even supposed to mean? With a frown etched deep into his face, he resolved to visit Zeus, the king of the gods, to share what had transpired.

But little did Hephaestus know that Aphrodite had already left the realm of Olympus with a greater purpose in mind. She was not simply retreating into her thoughts; she had a plan this time. She had vanished into the wilderness, to the untamed lands where the goddess Artemis reigned.

Artemis – the fierce and unyielding goddess of the hunt, independent and wild – had long stood as a symbol of everything

Aphrodite now sought. She represented strength, autonomy and resistance against the expectations placed upon women, mortal and divine. Aphrodite knew that if she wanted to dismantle the limiting roles the gods had imposed upon her, she needed allies who understood the power of reinvention. Artemis was the key to that change.

The wind howled through the dense forest as Aphrodite descended from the skies. The trees seemed to whisper secrets of their own as she landed lightly on the forest floor. The scent of pine and earth surrounded her, and in the distance, she could hear the soft footfalls of Artemis's hunting party. Wolves howled, and a symphony of nature followed, but there was no need for Aphrodite to search for her sister goddess. Artemis knew she had arrived.

From the shadows, Artemis appeared – tall and strong, her silver bow slung over her shoulder, her eyes were as sharp as the arrows she wielded. The huntress was clad in the skins of animals, her presence commanding yet still as wild and untamed as the wilderness she roamed. There was a certain stillness in her movements, like a predator waiting to strike. She stepped forward, her wolves circling Aphrodite with curiosity, their golden eyes gleaming.

"Aphrodite," Artemis said, her voice low and measured. "What brings the goddess of love to my woods? These lands are not for hearts and roses."

Aphrodite stood firm, meeting Artemis's gaze without flinching. "I did not come for hearts and roses, Artemis. I came for truth, for strength. I came to break free from the chains of the myths they've written about me."

Artemis tilted her head, intrigued. "The myths serve their purpose. The people need their stories. So why are you here?"

"I'm tired of being seen as a symbol for one thing and one thing only," Aphrodite replied, her voice filled with conviction. "They paint me as a temptress, a goddess who exists only to be adored, loved and desired. But there's more to me. I want to be seen for who I am, not for what they've turned me into. I want to challenge the way they see me – and the way they see all of us. Of all goddesses, you know what it means to defy expectations."

Artemis's eyes narrowed. "You seek to challenge Olympus itself?"

"I seek to challenge the limitations they've placed on me. I'm not just the goddess of love. I'm the goddess of power, of will, of choice. And if I am to rise beyond what they think they know, I will need allies. I need those who understand that the old ways no longer serve us."

Artemis circled her slowly, her wolves following her every step. "You've always been tied to the desires of others, Aphrodite. To love, to passion. Why do you want to break away from what has given you your power?"

Aphrodite smiled softly, a spark of determination lighting up her eyes. "Because I'm more than that. Love is not a weakness. Beauty is not my only gift. There is power in creation, but there is also power in destruction, in rebirth. I want to reclaim my story, Artemis. Just as you have."

Artemis stopped, her eyes gleaming with approval. "You speak boldly. You seek independence, like the wild. You want to roam free of the confines of their myths, like the hunt. You want to stand as something more than a goddess to be admired."

Aphrodite nodded. "Exactly. The myths have trapped and shaped us into roles that serve their needs. It's time we take control of our own fates."

Artemis studied her momentarily, her sharp eyes piercing Aphrodite's soul. Then she smiled, a fierce, knowing smile. "Very well. You've intrigued me, Aphrodite. You'll need more than words to redefine yourself and reclaim what's yours. You'll need the strength to fight those who stand in your way. Are you ready to embrace the hunt, to fight not with seduction but with strength?"

Aphrodite met her gaze with unwavering resolve. "I'm ready."

Artemis gestured toward the forest, where her warriors – women of strength and resilience – emerged from the shadows. They had been watching, waiting. "Then come, sister," Artemis said. "We will teach you not just to survive, but to hunt. To take what is yours."

For the first time in her immortal life, Aphrodite felt the exhilaration of what lay ahead. She wasn't leaving behind her powers of love and beauty, but integrating them with something more significant. She was becoming more than a goddess of passion.

* * *

Meanwhile, Hephaestus had taken it upon himself to involve the king of the gods, Zeus. The blacksmith of Olympus, usually patient and slow to act outside his forge, had been troubled by her words and the strange shift he felt in her demeanor. Her declaration of "redefining herself" weighed heavily on his mind. Hephaestus was not one to question the whims of the gods often, but something in her voice had unsettled him in a way that the flames of his forge never could.

Rising before dawn, Hephaestus left his workshop, the tools of his trade left behind for once, and made his way to Zeus's grand palace atop Mount Olympus. The sun had barely started illuminating the skies when Hephaestus arrived, his steps heavy with uncertainty. As the god of fire and craft, Hephaestus was not a frequent visitor to the halls of Zeus; he preferred the solitude of his forge, away from the politics and power struggles of Olympus. But today was different.

Zeus, the king of gods, was amid his concerns when he was informed of Hephaestus's arrival. He was seated upon his grand throne, overlooking the world below, deliberating on when to send rain to the mortals who were praying for its arrival. He heard their cries, their offerings and the sound of the distant storms rumbling in the heavens, waiting for his command.

"Lord Zeus," came the voice of Hermes, the messenger of the gods, entering swiftly into the room, "Hephaestus has come seeking an audience."

Zeus raised an eyebrow, intrigued. Hephaestus rarely sought counsel outside his domain unless something serious had arisen. "Let him in," Zeus commanded, his deep voice echoing through the marble halls of his palace.

Moments later, Hephaestus entered, his steps deliberate and slow as he approached the throne. His muscular frame, covered in soot and sweat from his endless work at the forge, seemed out of place in the gleaming splendor of Zeus's chambers. Yet, it was his troubled expression that caught Zeus's attention.

"Hephaestus," Zeus greeted him, his thunderous voice booming with authority. "To what do I owe this rare visit?"

The blacksmith god hesitated for a moment, choosing his words carefully. "My lord, it is about Aphrodite."

Zeus leaned back slightly on his throne, his gaze narrowing. "Aphrodite? What has she done now? Has she caused another stir with Ares?"

Hephaestus shook his head. "No, not Ares this time. She has... changed. She spoke of "redefining" herself, of becoming something other than what the myths have always said about her. I don't understand what she means, but I fear something is different."

Zeus studied him for a moment, considering his words. "Redefine herself?" Zeus muttered more to himself than to Hephaestus. "Aphrodite has always been the goddess of love, beauty and desire. What more could she wish to become?"

"That is exactly my concern, my lord," Hephaestus replied. "I've never seen her like this before. There was something in her eyes, a kind of determination that felt...unsettling. She is not content with her role anymore."

Zeus rose from his throne, walking towards the vast balcony overlooking the world below. The clouds swirled at his command, and he could feel the weight of the heavens shifting beneath his control. "The gods are not meant to change, Hephaestus," he said slowly, his tone heavy with contemplation. "We are eternal, bound by the roles the universe has set for us. To question that order is dangerous."

Hephaestus nodded, stepping closer. "That is why I came to you. If anyone could understand what this means, it's you. I do not know what Aphrodite intends, but something is shifting."

Zeus remained silent momentarily, his eyes scanning the skies, deep in thought. Aphrodite was, after all, one of the most powerful of the Olympians – her influence over love, desire and beauty stretched far beyond mortal comprehension. But this talk of redefining herself, of stepping outside the roles set for her, was something that even Zeus had not anticipated.

"Aphrodite has always been a force of nature," Zeus mused aloud, more to himself than to Hephaestus. "She has never been one to be contained by rules, but this…this could be something far greater than we realize."

He turned back to Hephaestus, his eyes sharp with authority. "We must keep a close watch on her. Whatever she is planning, it cannot go unchecked. The balance of Olympus – and the world – depends on the gods fulfilling their roles. If Aphrodite seeks to redefine herself, she could disrupt the order of things in ways we cannot predict."

Hephaestus, though still troubled, nodded in agreement. "I will do as you command, my lord. But there is one more thing…"

Zeus raised an eyebrow. "Yes?"

"She has gone to see Artemis," Hephaestus said. "I know not why, but Artemis seems an unusual choice if she seeks to form alliances."

At this, Zeus's expression darkened. Artemis, the goddess of the hunt and independence, was known for her strong will and defiance of traditional roles. If Aphrodite had aligned herself with Artemis, this was no mere personal transformation – it could be the beginning of something far more disruptive.

"Artemis," Zeus murmured, his voice now laced with concern. "The wild one. The free one. If they join forces…" His words trailed off, and Hephaestus knew Zeus's thoughts mirrored his own. Whatever was happening was bigger than either of them had first imagined.

Zeus turned sharply, his eyes flashing with the storms he commanded. "Keep an eye on her, Hephaestus. Whatever she plans with Artemis, it must not be allowed to threaten the order of Olympus. The gods do not change – our roles and powers are fixed for eternity. If Aphrodite seeks to defy that, she may become a danger. Not only to herself, but to all of us."

Hephaestus bowed, his resolve strengthened by Zeus's words. He would do what was necessary, even if it meant opposing the very woman he had once loved so deeply. As he left the great hall of Zeus, he couldn't help but wonder what Aphrodite's true intentions were – and whether anyone, even the king of the gods, could stop her now.

* * *

The next day was going to be a big day for Aphrodite. She had planned to meet with Athena and Artemis, hoping to convince them to build an alliance with her, not as mere figures tied to their old myths but as goddesses capable of reshaping their destinies. Together, they could challenge the status quo of Olympus, a realm steeped in tradition that had long been defined by the power of men.

As the morning sun rose over the horizon, casting golden light across the mountains of Olympus, Aphrodite set off with Artemis by her side. The air was thick with anticipation as they approached the temple of Athena, the goddess of wisdom and warfare. The weight of the mission hung heavy in the atmosphere. This meeting would begin a new era for the goddesses if everything went as planned.

But there was something in Artemis's silence that gnawed at Aphrodite. The once-confident goddess of the hunt had grown quieter since they last spoke. Perhaps it was the gravity of what they were about to do. Nevertheless, Aphrodite pushed the unease aside. She needed Artemis by her side for this, and together with Athena, they would be unstoppable.

The goddess's imposing figure awaited them at the steps when they arrived at Athena's temple. Dressed in armor, her eyes were sharp, gleaming with intelligence and calculation. Beside her stood Hephaestus, which sent an immediate wave of confusion through Aphrodite. Her heart thudded in her chest as she approached cautiously.

"Hephaestus?" Aphrodite asked, surprised to see him there. "Why are you here?"

Hephaestus, usually calm and composed, looked serious as he stepped forward. "I came to speak to you, Aphrodite. I need to understand this 'redefinition' of yours."

Aphrodite's eyes narrowed. Something wasn't right. She glanced at Artemis, who had not moved from her place, her expression unreadable.

"Is there something I should know?" Aphrodite asked slowly, sensing a shift in the air.

Artemis stepped forward, her bow in hand, but there was no warmth in her voice when she spoke. "Yes, Aphrodite. There is."

Before Aphrodite could react, Artemis leveled her bow directly at her, the gleaming tip of an arrow trained on her chest. The betrayal hit like a physical blow.

"I can't let you challenge the order of Olympus," Artemis said coldly. "You think you can just tear apart centuries of tradition? Change the roles of gods and goddesses at your whim? No, Aphrodite. You're a threat to the balance, and that balance is what keeps us all-powerful."

Aphrodite's heart clenched. She had trusted Artemis and believed in their shared mission of freedom. "Why? You, of all goddesses, should understand the need for change! You fight for independence, for strength. Why stand in my way?"

But Artemis's gaze was stern. "My independence is within the framework of Olympus. You want to dismantle everything that makes us gods, Aphrodite. I won't let you do that.

"And you, Hephaestus, can't you keep your wife in check?" Artemis spat, her eyes narrowing as she turned towards him. "What use will we be if every god and goddess starts tearing apart traditions that have stood for centuries? Take your wife from here and ensure she knows her place – love, beauty and nothing more. If she wants to play at being Miss Independent, what does that leave me?"

Her words cut through the air like a sharp blade, filled with scorn. Hephaestus stood silent, the fire in him simmering but uncertain. Beside him, Aphrodite's heart clenched, caught between the truth of Artemis's words and the fire of her own desire for change. For a moment, the confidence she had built flickered like a candle in the wind.

Hephaestus finally sighed and stepped forward, placing a hand on her shoulder. "Perhaps she's right," he said, his voice low. "Perhaps we should leave this behind and continue as we were – husband and wife. There's no point in challenging the world we've always known. You can still inspire love and beauty, and I will return to my forge. It's simpler that way."

Aphrodite looked at him, the weight of centuries pressing down on her. The rebellion, the hopes and the dreams she had nurtured over the last few days felt fragile now, crumbling under the force of tradition. The life they had lived, the roles they had played, felt inescapable at that moment. She glanced back at Artemis, who watched her with cold, calculating eyes.

There was no denying that Artemis had spoken a harsh truth. It wasn't just about them. The very fabric of Olympus depended on the gods playing their parts, on the careful balance of power and tradition that had stood for eons. To defy that was to risk everything – chaos, war and unraveling the world as they knew it. Maybe Hephaestus was right. Perhaps it was easier to turn back, to return to the roles assigned to them by fate.

With a deep breath, Aphrodite nodded, her voice subdued. "You're right," she said softly. "It's not worth tearing everything apart. I'll go back to what I know."

Artemis raised an eyebrow, slightly surprised by the sudden retreat, but satisfied. "Good. Go back to where you belong. We all have our place in this world. Don't forget it."

Hephaestus gently took her hand, and together they turned away, leaving behind the wilderness and the confrontation with Artemis. As they walked back through the woods, the fire that had once driven Aphrodite began to cool. The further they walked, the more distant the dream of rebellion felt. Yet, something inside her stirred, refusing to be extinguished entirely.

*   *   *

By the time they reached their home, the world of gods had resumed its usual rhythm. Hephaestus returned to his forge, and Aphrodite to her temple, where women prayed to her for beauty and love. It was a life they knew well, a life that made sense within the confines of Olympus. But something had shifted.

Despite her return to the role of the goddess of beauty, Aphrodite couldn't shake the feeling that she had abandoned a part of herself in those woods. That fleeting moment of rebellion, of wanting to be something more, still lingered deep within her. Though she had retreated from the challenge, she wasn't the same Aphrodite. The fire she had felt hadn't been entirely snuffed out; it smoldered beneath the surface, waiting for the right time to reignite.

She spent her days as she always had – answering the prayers of those who sought beauty, grace and love. But as she watched women across the mortal world, she began to see things differently. They, like her, had been confined to roles that did not reflect the fullness of their strength. Women prayed to be beautiful and adored, but Aphrodite saw the truth behind their prayers. They didn't just want beauty – they wanted power, freedom and the strength to define their lives.

And so Aphrodite made a silent vow. If she could not live out the rebellion she had dreamed of in Olympus, she would help others – mortal women – it was also strength she had once sought for herself. She would answer their prayers, but not in the way they expected.

No longer would she simply bless them with beauty. She would teach them that true beauty was more than appearance – strength, resilience and the courage to defy expectations. She would instill in them the power to be independent and more than the world had told them they could be.

As the days passed, a subtle change spread across the world. The women who prayed to Aphrodite began to see themselves differently. They discovered beauty in their strength, minds and ability to stand tall against a world that sought to limit them. They learned to love others and themselves, and in doing so, they became forces to be reckoned with.

Aphrodite watched this transformation from afar, her heart swelling with pride. Though she had retreated from the rebellion on Olympus, she had started a quiet revolution in the mortal world. She had become a symbol of empowerment for women who, like her, sought more than what tradition allowed. In a way, she had fulfilled her vow to never let anyone – gods or mortals – define her or the women who looked up to her.

Aphrodite Will Take Your Order
Andrea Modenos Ash

"Aphrodite will take your order," my mother says to the handsome middle-aged man in the black raincoat holding a rolled-up *NY Post*. She shuffles away and heads to the counter, where my father is short-order cooking on the other side.

"I need an Adam and Eve on a raft!" she yells. Lately my father is hard of hearing, but honestly, I think she's always talked that loud.

"What?" my father says from behind the grill; his weathered face is scrunched up trying to hear.

"I said, AN ADAM AND EVE ON A RAFT!" my mother screeches again. My father nods, and his stark white curls fall onto his cloudy blue eyes as he wipes the sweat from his brow, and then tugs at his matching white beard.

"One Adam and Eve on a raft," he repeats with a sigh, his accent as thick as olive oil. *"Ah gamoto!"* he cries as the flames shoot up from the pan drippings; he's burned his sensitive skin again. You would think after two thousand years of working a grill he'd be used to it by now. I hand the handsome man a menu.

"Thank you, Afro-di-tee," he says and winks at me. Well, well, maybe I'm the special of the day.

My mother shuffles back to the register. Once Hera could've stopped a raging bull in its tracks. Now her hair net falls on her sagging face as she helps me wait tables at our family-run Mount Olympus Diner in Astoria, Queens.

Once I could've stopped a bull too. No, I would've ridden that bull. And a hundred bulls afterwards. But now? My feet ache in my orthopedic black shoes and my old dingy bra has a wire loose cutting into the side of my boob. I catch a glimpse of my face in the reflection of the window. I bought a new brow liner and tried to match the young fertile woman's face on the package cover. I tried. I was not successful. I look like a crazy aging waitress who smokes too much, has a messed up thyroid and bad feet, not like the goddess of love and erotic pleasure who could feast on countless men a day.

"What can I get for ya?" I say. My accent and vernacular have become accustomed to this place, ever since my father moved us to NYC over seventy years ago. It was time to leave Greece, he said, and we set sail for America. It was the 1950s, cars and poodle skirts and Greek diners were all the rage. We were popular again, if only for a little while.

The man smiles at me. I smile back, and he reads the menu. The door opens and in pour a gaggle of high school girls, young and wrinkle free, full of juice and estrogen. The man peeks up, his eyes wide, staring at them. I am no longer on the menu. Was I ever?

"I'll take a chicken rice soup and a turkey club," he says, still staring at the girls.

"You got it!" I say, snatching the menu, and as I whip around, my dyed brittle black hair smacks him in the face like a horse tail swatting flies. As I head over to the counter, my orthopedic shoes squeak.

"Baba!" I cry over the hissing of the oil from his pans. "Soup and club, turkey." He nods. I have a few minutes before the order is ready, so I grab my purse to head out. I want to smoke a cigarette and dissolve the depression in my chest with nicotine. I grab a donut from the counter to eat after my smoke, but my mother stops me with a heavy grasp of her aging hands. Like a hawk she still is.

"You're getting fat!" she hisses. Dionysus, my brother, eternally thin, chuckles. I sigh and put the donut back. I try to leave but she stops me again.

"And go downstairs and get the unopened vat of mayo!"

"Mama! Let Dion do it! I'm on a break!"

"I'm busy!" my brother says never lifting his face from his phone, glued to his spot at the counter. He never moves. He just sits there, hunched over, a skinny, middle-aged man-child. He tells our parents he's "conducting business" but I know that he's on Grindr looking for a quick hook-up. I could do the same, but why bother? Once men would beg for me, go to war for me, throw themselves off cliffs for me, but now, huh! I will never beg a mortal, as much as my aching body sometimes wants to. I sigh mightily, and head down into the cellar.

As I walk past the paper goods, stacks of ketchup packets and the standard blue and white coffee cups with the Greek Key and "It's Our Pleasure to Serve You" written on them (whoever came up with that obviously never worked in a diner) and head toward the mayo, I smell a familiar stench.

Sulfur.

I stop dead in my tracks. It can't be. I whip around.

"Hello Aphrodite." The deep sultry voice echoes in the dampness, the face hidden in the shadows.

"Uncle Hades."

"It's been a while," he says, stepping forward into the dim light. His pallid thin face hovers close to mine, and he kisses both sides of my cheeks. He is deathly cold. As per always.

"What are you doing here?" I say. "If my father sees you…"

"I know, I know, your mother will cut my balls off," he says, half-smiling. "Diti, how are you?"

"Fine. You? How's the mansion in Brookville?" I ask with disdain.

"Good, the pool leaked but I got it fixed. I guess I can't complain," he says.

"No, I guess you can't!" I say with a little more hiss than expected.

"You all still live upstairs in that tiny apartment?" he asks. I glare at him.

"Of course. What do you think?"

"It's not my fault, Diti! You know that!" he says as he grabs my hand. I pull away from his icy clutch.

"I guess the fates had one last banger left in them before they crushed us, eh?" I say.

"None of us thought that new religion would take. What god forgives?" he says with such disgust, as if he ate a rotten fig.

"The new guy does, two millennia now. We've all accepted it and moved on," I say. My legs ache. I sit on a case of paper towels.

"What do you want?" I ask. He pulls over a crate, sits and leans toward me. A little too close; the sulfur stings my nose and eyes. I lean back.

"I have a proposition for you," he says.

"Two thousand years we don't see you, and now you want to do business?" I cry.

"Please, let me explain!" he whines.

"Do you know how long we wandered around Greece and the rest of the world until we came here?" I say, the unwanted tears burning in my eyes and spilling down. "Did you ever check in with us, even once? Do you know how Zeus, your brother, my father, is doing? Do you know that he has a heart condition and bad circulation and has to take pills for his blood sugar?"

"Diti, I tried!" he whines. "But your mother…"

"You got a second chance!" I interrupt his cries of victimhood. "The world thinks you're the devil. You still have power and live like a king while the rest of us work like dogs."

"Please, Diti!"

"Proposition this!" I say and give him the Greek hand gesture pushing shit into his face. I stand to leave, but my legs are shaky.

"Wait! I can get us back home," he blurts.

"Why, you're an Uber driver now?" I snort.

"You were always the funny one. I can get us back home, all of us. Trust me."

"Trust you? Why should I?!" I cry.

"Because. Look at you. You're miserable. Once you would've had us all howling in lust. Now you are full of…yeast. You're dried up, Diti. Don't you want to go home? Don't you want to go back to the mountain top?" Hades waves his arm over me and suddenly I am transported back to Mount Olympus. A warm breeze flows across me, carrying the smell of the sea and jasmine and thyme and chamomile and olives. The azure sky hovers above and the wine-dark sea lulls below. The hairs on my arms prickle. I remember how I would split my time between my grotto in Cyprus, and with family on Mount Olympus with scores of adoring lovers and supplicants, celebrations and sacrifices, gifts and songs.

And then flashes before me of the destruction of my temple, when the new god was crowned. Our power was gone in a second; we were discarded like old gyro meat covered in flies. My parents, once divine royalty, were now homeless, penniless, terrified. My father looked so frail, so weak, so…human. The vision fades into a mist.

Hades smiles. That was his trickery. He still has powers to persuade, to coerce.

"I don't want to go back," I whisper.

"Yes, you do," he says.

I look down at my swollen feet.

"Why do you even care what I want?"

"Because I want to be free of this prison and go back to the way it was," he says, jumping up. "With your father in charge, and with me back in my own Underworld with Persephone and the shades. I don't like this new gig. It's too hot. And the people here are annoying."

"Not more annoying than the diner."

"Diti, I can't do this anymore, I can't be on the earth plane for too long – look at me!"

His face is blotching. He wheezes.

"I think I got asthma!"

I roll my eyes.

"And I have some sort of food allergy!" He rolls up his black sleeve, revealing hives. He scratches and his skin peels and oozes. I hand him a paper towel. He dabs at his dripping sores.

"So," I say, trying to break the awkward silence, "where is Persephone these days?"

"She's in Portland, on an organic oregano farm or something," he says, folding over the paper towel. "Uh, she sends her love." He tries to hand it back to me, but it's goopy. I shake my head no. He shoves it in his pocket.

"Why come to me? Why not Dion or my father?"

"You're the only one with half a spark left in our family. You're the only one who can do this."

"Do what?"

He smiles again, his face turning dark, his teeth sharp. He leans in. The sulfur is overwhelming.

"Tonight, at midnight, meet me at College Point Boulevard off of Main Street."

"By the slaughterhouses? Why?"

He leans in further and his eyes glow red.

"The sacred white bull has been found!" he hisses, and with that, he disappears in a dramatic burst of grey smoke. It chokes me, and I rush back up the stairs without the mayonnaise and get yelled at by my mother.

* * *

That night after we close and head upstairs, I cook dinner. Lamb, potatoes with lemon and oregano, zucchini and carrots. Greek salad with feta, olive oil and red vinegar. I serve the food to my parents and brother. I pour their glasses full with water and red wine. My father and Dionysus inhale their food in two minutes, sopping up the leftovers with bread and then get up, leaving their dishes and mess on the table, and head into the living room to watch the Mets. My mother helps me put everything in the sink and then shuffles off behind them. I spend the next hour washing all the dishes and pots and pans, wiping down the counters, the sink, the table, sweep and mop the floor and as my father and brother groan at the baseball game, my mother serves them walnuts and assorted fruit.

Exhausted, I head in to join them, but then a howl comes from down the hall. Hephaestus, my brother and ex-husband, cries out from his room.

"Aphrodite! I crapped my pants!" he cries. My mother shoots me a look.

"Go clean him up!" she huffs, cracking walnuts and handing them to Dion. He is like a child with his hand out, scarfing down the shelled nuts while swiping on his phone. Typical Greek son, babied for eternity.

I sigh and head down the hall. Hephaestus sits in his wheelchair, his body twisted, his CPAP machine hanging off his face. The smell is unbearable.

"I crapped my pants!" he cries again, and I help him from the chair to the bed, roll him on his side and clean him up. I roll him on his back and prop him up; I adjust his feeding tube and his oxygen, turn the TV onto the Mets game and head out to throw the shitty diaper away without even a thank you.

Outside in the alley, I light a cigarette and exhale mightily as I toss the garbage bag into the metal can and slam the top on it, hard. Hephaestus. I remember when they forced me to marry him. *That will keep her under control*, my father and brothers and uncles said, laughing. It was all a joke to them. Hades laughed particularly hard. I was the goddess of unfettered passion, yet I had to be controlled and humiliated.

How long have I been what they wanted? And not what I've wanted to be?

My grandfather Cronus was a tyrant. Under his rule, my siblings and I had to go into hiding or else the paranoid old man would've had us killed. When my father finally murdered him and gained the throne, it was a new day for our family, a golden age.

We were excited with the possibilities, no more chthonic gods who would rule by animalistic brains. No, my father would usher in logic, philosophy, art, democracy, beauty and freedom. Or so we thought. Behind closed doors, the new boss was the same as the old boss. Tyrannical, angry and power crazed, we had to do his bidding, all of us, especially his daughters. Of course, his sons got away with more than we did, as in a typical Greek family. My sisters and I were held on short tethers.

"Aphrodite, you are the one they will look to, to release all their uncontrollable urges," my father had said. "You must always be that so humans can grow, evolve."

"But what if I don't want to?" I cried. Then thunder clapped and the skies turned dark, and stones fell from the sky, hitting me, cutting my face.

"Yes, Baba," I conceded, my head bowed. I was trapped. I couldn't be a maiden or a crone or a loving mother. I had to be primordial lust only; Zeus wouldn't let us be more than one thing. Even Athena, his favorite. She's a professor at Oxford now, but still the eternal virgin, living alone with nine cats and a closet full of Birkenstocks. That's what people don't understand. They think I wanted to be full of lust and sex all the time when mostly I just wanted to eat figs, listen to a good epic, maybe climb a tree, nurse a baby, sit at the loom, swim in the sea with the dolphins and have a lover caress me gently at night.

But now? What is it that I want, besides eating a donut? I flick the cigarette into the street.

Midnight at College Point Boulevard? A sacred bull? Hades has lost his mind.

* * *

Back up in the apartment I'm ready to pass out on the couch, but just as I am about to sit down, Dionysus shakes his coffee cup at me, never taking his eyes off his phone. I sigh and refill it for him, then I sit down and grab a *koulouraki* cookie from the tray, but my mother snatches it from my hand.

"You've eaten enough!" she says, and hands it to Dionysus. I lean back, half asleep. The Mets are in the sixth inning and losing, as per usual. Mama rubs Baba's aching feet with liniment that stinks. They look so old and frail. My brother is giggling to himself on his phone, swiping left.

"What is the prophecy about the sacred white bull?" I blurt out, startling them all.

"Why would you bring that up?" Mama asks.

"It's a stupid fairy tale, it doesn't exist!" my father cries.

Dionysus never looks up from his phone but then says: "The sacred white bull was the final prophecy from the Pythia at the temple of Apollo before she was murdered by the Christian marauders. The sacred white bull will be born in a strange land, and once it is slaughtered and we gods drink its blood, our power will return, and we will once again rule the Universe. Oooh!" he jumps up and says, "I have a meeting, going out!"

"An old wives' tale," my father says to no one, looking sadder than before.

I sigh again. "I'm going to bed," I say.

"Did you finish the laundry?" my mother barks.

"Yes, Mama," I say as I leave. She doesn't even say goodnight.

* * *

In my room I slather cold cream on my face. Why? I don't know. I am three thousand years old, and there isn't enough Oil of Olay on the planet to help me. I stare at myself in the mirror; there is no death for me, no end, just an eternity of slow disintegration. Orthopedic shoes, varicose veins, deep wrinkles, inflamed joints, thinning hair and swollen feet. What is left of who I once was? Do

I want to go back? I know I don't want to be here. I lie down, and stare at the ceiling. I shut my phone off.

Let him find his own bull.

* * *

That night I dream I am in the diner and the handsome man comes in, but instead of my regular beaten-down self, I become the sacred white bull, virile, strong, my horns sharp. I gore the man and spill his blood on the just-mopped floor. My mother screams as I run wild in the diner, destroying it, catching my brother by the pants with my horn and tossing him into the air. I jump on the old shitty grill, crushing it, and my father screams.

"I need an Adam and Eve on a raft, you motherfuckers!" I cry and bolt out into the street, flattening cars, crushing people. I am wild, primordial, electric sex that once caused the foams to rise in the Mediterranean and birth myself. Aphrodite. 'From the foam'. But then Hades snatches me, clips a ring in my nose, and I'm dragged to a temple. My throat is slit as I bellow and my blood gushes into a golden bowl. I collapse.

* * *

I awaken with a gasp. I check the time, and it is way past midnight. I get up and dress and quietly sneak down the hall. Dion is still out on one of his sexcapades. My parents are both snoring in their bed. Hephaestus is gurgling, his CPAP whirring. I head out down the stairs and to the bus stop.

I know what to do.

* * *

I arrive at the slaughterhouse. It's still dark and there is no one around. The doors are unlocked, and I enter. The animals are crowded in the paddocks, afraid, full of urine and shit. I search for him and there he is. The sacred white bull.

"You're late!" Hades cries, popping up out of nowhere, wheezing and coughing. His face is full of pustules and he's scratching at his arms. "Look at him," he says pointing to the bull. "Came from upstate, ready for slaughter, for burgers and meatballs at Citifield. Take him! Bring him to the park, we will be waiting there for you."

"We?" I ask, but he has disappeared again in a puff of sulfur and smoke. I wish he would stop doing that.

The white bull stares at me with his deep black liquid eyes from behind the stall. He is full of life and sex and juice and meat. He huffs from his nostrils, the steam clouds out around him. He has a halter with a line. I take it and quietly open the gate. He walks out slowly, subserviently, as if he knows it's his time.

I lead him out of the slaughterhouse and down through the park. The cars are just starting to pick up, as rush hour is beginning. I hurry down the path and make it to the open field.

Hades stands in the middle of the field with a group of strange beings in dark suits, with not one other Greek god to be found.

No Zeus or Dionysus or even Hera. Who did I think would be drinking the blood from the bull?

"Diti, you and I, together forever," he calls to me as his minions close in on me. "Hurry! It is time!!"

A gleaming dagger sits in a circle, surrounded by stones, and a tarp is laid down with a golden goblet at the center. The leaves in the trees rustle with the wind; lonely pink lights of the early dawn peek from above the horizon.

"Hurry up!" Hades hisses, scratching at himself, "I can't be out here too long! Slit his throat and we will drink and we will finally be back home!"

We.

I nod.

I pick up the dagger and just as I am to slit the majestic bull's throat, I pierce him on his haunch, enough to draw blood. I let go of the lead as the bull screams and kicks, and then rushes towards Hades and his minions, knocking them over like bowling pins.

Hades screams as the bull runs wild, then deep into the park away from us.

"Aphrodite will NOT take your order now!" I howl.

"What have you done, you stupid girl?!" Hades cries.

"Sending you back where you belong," I scream as the sun comes up. "You were never gonna get us home! You were gonna take all the power for yourself, and leave us behind, again!"

"I was going to take you, for me!" he screams and just as Hades and his gang turn to smoke:

"Enjoy the rest of eternity in this shit hole!" he howls, and they all disappear.

"Enjoy the pool you can't swim in, asshole," I say to the wind. The park is quiet, still. The bull is nowhere to be found. I head back to the bus stop.

On the ride back, I feel a strange yet familiar tingling. I upload Tinder on my phone and peruse the men.

* * *

When I arrive at the diner, it's bustling. The early morning breakfast crowd has filled the booths.

"Where were you?" my mother screeches, the furrow in her brow deeper than ever. The same handsome man with the *NY Post* enters and takes the last seat at the counter. He looks up at me with a gasp.

"Hey! You look different Afro-di-tee!" he says, staring at me bewitched. I ignore him. Something catches my eye on the TV mounted in the corner.

"Aphrodite will take your ord—" my mother starts, but I interrupt with a "Sssh!" holding my finger up.

I raise the volume. A news story reporting a rare wild white bull that escaped a slaughterhouse in Queens and ran amok in the park. He's already been caught and adopted by an animal rescue group; he will live the rest of his life eating, sleeping and banging cows.

"Good for you!" I say aloud. My phone pings. I look, and a handsome man stares back at me. I swipe left.

"Aphrodite! Get to work!" my mother howls. She glares at me. I brush past her, grab a donut from the counter, wave it in her face, take a violent bite and head to the door.

"Where are you going?" she screams. "Go downstairs and get the jar of pickles!"

"Dion can get it," I say, fluffing my hair. "I have a very important meeting to go to."

And I take another bite of my donut as I flounce out the diner, then head out down Steinway Street.

The Heart of a Warrior
Angelina Chamberlain

The staff cut through the morning air with practiced precision, each movement a memory preserved in muscle. Tasting the salty sea air, Aphrodite moved through her forms with fluid grace, her black Nike training shoes shifting silently on the cool Malibu sand.

Here, in these moments before sunrise, she found peace in movement over stillness, in strength beyond beauty. A peace needed after yesterday's frustrating training session with a new student – a newly made god who treated every lesson like summer camp rather than survival training.

She wore no elaborate styling or haute couture clothes, just Lululemon training wear and the weapon that had become an extension of herself. How different from the murals and statues depicting her lounging in splendor, eternally imposed as an object of desire. How different from the Instagram filters and internet trends that portrayed her, or the myth retellings that got *slightly* closer to the truth.

Aph adjusted her grip and began again, staff spinning in complex patterns as she moved through the techniques Hephaestus had taught her millennia ago. Memories of his patient instruction brought a small smile to her lips. Those early morning lessons in his forge had changed everything – had changed her.

Five centuries had passed since her last morning training with Heph, but she could still feel the ghost of his calloused hands adjusting her stance from their beginning lessons, hear his gentle encouragement, his breath brushing her cheek. The beach behind Poseidon's Malibu home wasn't his forge, but in these predawn hours, when the world was still quiet, she could almost pretend…

Her chest stuttered, and she shoved those thoughts away.

The heavy ancient training staff whistled as it cut downward in a strike that would have felled any mortal, immortal or monster she battled. In her mind's eye, she saw herself that first day, trembling and uncertain, clutching the practice weapon as though it might bite.

"Power isn't about force," Hephaestus said, his kind eyes, one brown one green, crinkling at the corners. "It's about knowing yourself, trusting yourself."

Behind her, a sleek glass and white stone mansion rose against the cliffs, its architecture somehow modern and timeless, imposing and invisible to mortal eyes.

Or at least, it was supposed to be.

A sound broke through her reverie – fabric scraping against stone, a stifled gasp. Aphrodite stilled; staff held loose but ready at her side. She'd have thought a stray animal breached the wards, but the gasp…no, that was entirely human.

No mortal should have been able to find this place, let alone breach magical wards hiding the few of them who remained. The fact that one had—

Her divine senses reached out, testing Poseidon's ancient protections. They felt thin, stretched, like fabric worn too long in the sun.

Troubling.

Another sound, this one distinctly human: the shaky intake of breath that follows tears.

Aph approached the rocks near the property's edge. There, wedged into a narrow space between two boulders, huddled a young woman, maybe nineteen, with tanned skin and dark hair. Her vibrant pink party dress, clearly new, was torn at the shoulder and hung awkwardly from her body. Her eyes, wide as dinner plates, watched Aph while she clutched her phone against her chest.

But Aphrodite saw herself in that moment – another lifetime ago, crouched beside a forge's hearth and desperate for sanctuary.

"You're safe here," Aph said softly, lowering her staff. "No one will harm you."

"I...I'm sorry," the girl stammered. "I didn't mean to trespass." She squinted, head tilting, disheveled curls falling to the side. "Are you glowing?"

Aph followed her gaze to her hands, to the divine light she sometimes forgot to suppress during intense training. She made a decision, but hesitated. As a goddess of love, she could sense and influence emotions – calm fears, soothe anxieties, even inspire trust. A power she rarely used on mortals; she believed mortals should have sovereignty over their own feelings. But the girl's terror was a living thing, wild and threatening to overwhelm her.

Enough to prevent panic, Aph thought, letting the slightest tendril of calming energy flow toward the girl. She didn't alter the girl's thoughts or force acceptance – merely dulled fear's sharp edge enough to allow rational thought. A betrayal of her principles, perhaps, but better than letting the poor thing suffer a breakdown.

"I've gone by many names over the years," she said, watching the girl's posture slowly relax, "but the most recognized today is Aphrodite."

The girl's fear gave way to skepticism, her brows knitting together, but there was less panic in her voice. "Right. Like the Greek goddess? Next you'll tell me this is Zeus's beach house."

"Poseidon's, actually." Aph strengthened her divine aura a fraction, her hair lifting in a non-existent breeze. The sea behind her responded, waves calming to mirror-stillness despite the predawn wind. "Though I understand your doubt. The world has changed much since mortals believed in us."

The girl squeaked, pressing herself further into the rocks, but Aph sensed her terror morphing – shock and disbelief, yes, but mixed with scholarly curiosity. The girl's eyes widened as realization dawned. "You're really her. *Aphrodite*. I've read so much about you in my Classics courses, but I never thought…" She paused, then laughed nervously. "My BookTok followers will never believe this."

Aphrodite raised an eyebrow. "BookTok?"

"It's a…never mind." The girl shook her head. "I just…I can't…this is impossible."

"No more impossible than finding your way onto a magically protected beach." Aph gestured at the mansion behind them, letting the mortal's sight fully penetrate the wards for the first time. The girl gasped as the house's true form revealed…a luxurious multi-story estate nestled into the Malibu hillside. The soft white walls gleamed against the backdrop of clear blue skies, and palm trees swayed in the ocean breeze, framing the building like nature's curtains. "Though you getting here is…concerning."

The girl's legs gave out, and she slid down to sit in the sand, dropping her phone. But her eyes carried a spark of academic excitement. "Oh my god. Oh, my gods? Which is it now? I mean…I can't believe I'm actually meeting you. You're actually real."

"Very real." Aphrodite unzipped her light training jacket and held it out. "You're safe here. Will you tell me what brings you to my beach at such an early hour?"

The girl's gray eyes darted between Aphrodite's face and the offered jacket, disbelief warring with desperate hope.

"You have nothing to fear," she whispered, keeping her distance. Seeing the trauma still tight around the girl like a shroud, Aph made another choice. *A touch more*, she thought, *enough to let her speak of it*. She subtly flicked her fingers, allowing a gentle stream of calming magic to flow into the frightened girl.

"I…there was a party next door" she began, voice hushed. "Everyone had been drinking and partying since sundown…"

Aphrodite nodded, understanding what remained unspoken. She draped the jacket over a nearby rock, close enough for the girl to reach. "What is your name?"

"Elena," the girl answered, slowly emerging enough to grab the jacket. Her shoulders relaxed as she wrapped it around herself. "And you're the Goddess of Love and Beauty. Everything I know about you comes from mythology and children's books. You're supposed to be…" She hesitated, her cheeks reddening.

"Lounging on clouds, causing trouble with love potions, starting wars over golden apples?" Aph's smile never wavered, but it held a trace of bitterness. She nodded toward the staff at her side. "They never mention this, do they?"

"No," Elena admitted, studying the staff, her phone forgotten beside her, pulling Aphrodite's borrowed jacket tighter around her shoulders. The goddess remained standing, her ancient wooden staff planted beside her, giving the girl space. The sun climbed higher, turning the Pacific into a canvas of rose gold.

"I was at this party," Elena finally began, her gazed downcast, one sandal lost somewhere in her escape. "One of those Malibu beach mansions, you know? At first, it was amazing. The music, the drinks, the view…" Her fingers worried at a tear in her cocktail dress. "Then I noticed how some guys were watching me. Tech bros. The way they looked at me…" She shuddered. "Like I wasn't even a person. Just something to be—"

"Possessed," Aphrodite finished quietly. "Consumed."

Elena looked up sharply, surprise flickering across her mascara-streaked face. "But you're a goddess. How could you possibly understand?"

A bitter laugh escaped Aphrodite's lips. "Even goddesses can be reduced to trophies in others' eyes." She sat on the sand, close enough to talk comfortably but maintaining distance. "The stories they tell about me – the ones carved in marble and painted on pottery, the ones in movies, on Instagram, even in books – they all share one thing in common. They reduce me to nothing but beauty and desire."

"I overheard them," Elena continued, her voice barely above a whisper. "Talking about spiked drinks, pills... I saw a girl stumbling, looking dazed. Three of them got handsy, too close, grabbing me..." She hugged her knees to her chest. "I panicked. I just ran. Somehow ended up here."

Aphrodite's expression hardened. "You did the right thing, Elena. No one has the right to take your choice away." She paused, centuries of pain and anger flashing behind her eyes. "Not mortal, not god, not anyone."

"How do you deal with it?" Elena asked. "Being seen that way all the time?"

Aphrodite smiled, running her hand along the smooth wood of her weapon. "Would you believe me if I told you that for centuries, I thought those stories were all I could be? That my entire existence was meant to be nothing more than a prize to be won, a trophy to be displayed?"

She rose in one fluid motion, taking up her staff again and moving through a simple defensive form. "Every movement has purpose. Each stance tells a story of its own." The staff spun in her hands, blocking imaginary strikes. "I learned this from someone who saw past the surface, who understood true beauty lies within."

Elena tilted her head, considering the goddess before her. "Let me guess, Ares taught you? God of war and your lover, right?"

Her veins burning with lava. Rough hands forcing her down. A hard slap stinging her cheek. Sweet ichor, salty tears and metal on her tongue as the same hand kept her quiet—

Aphrodite's grip on the staff tightened imperceptibly, her knuckles whitening for just a moment. The waves behind them grew choppy for a heartbeat before settling.

"No," Aphrodite said, her voice carefully controlled. "Ares did not teach me."

The goddess took a deep breath, remaining composed.

"It was Hephaestus," Aphrodite continued, her tone softening. "My husband. He saw beyond the surface, beyond what everyone else expected me to be."

"Hephaestus?" Elena echoed, surprised. "The god of fire and forges? I thought...well, the stories always made it seem like you two weren't—"

"The stories often miss the truth," Aphrodite said, a wistful smile playing at her lips. She extended her hand to Elena. "Come, let me show you what Hephaestus taught me about real strength and love."

Elena hesitated briefly before taking the goddess's hand. Aphrodite's watch chimed, reminding her she'd need to return to New Olympus soon.

"First lesson," the goddess said, taking a defensive stance. "True power isn't about force. It's about knowing and trusting yourself. It's about awareness, balance, and using an attacker's force against them."

The forge's heat pressed against her skin, beading sweat along her brow. Her hands shook as she gripped the wooden staff, its weight unfamiliar and intimidating.

"Before we begin," Hephaestus said, "we breathe." He laid a gentle hand on her shoulder. "Close your eyes, Aphrodite. Feel the air fill your lungs, your body, your very essence."

She did as instructed, surprised to find the trembling in her hands subsiding with each breath.

"That's it," he encouraged. "Power starts from within. Know yourself, trust yourself. The rest will follow."

"First, we breathe," Aphrodite echoed the memory, setting aside her staff. "Power starts from within." She demonstrated a deep breath, the kind that filled not just lungs but spirit. "That's what Hephaestus taught me my first day, when I could barely hold the staff without trembling."

She paused, pondering her next words as they breathed together. The sun had fully risen now, turning the sea to sparkling diamonds. In the distance, a gull wheeled and dove for its breakfast.

Her heart raced as she stumbled into Hephaestus's forge, the echo of grabbing hands and possessive words still fresh in her mind.

"Our story began with me running, much like you did tonight. I was fleeing from—" she took a breath, "from unwanted attention. I found myself at his forge, seeking sanctuary from another immortal who thought my beauty made me his claim."

A crackling hearth fire painted shadows on rough stone walls. Exhaustion seeped from every muscle, every bone, her silk peplos torn and stained with dirt and tears. The forge's warmth wrapped around her like a cocoon, lulling her into an uneasy sleep.

A shuffling step roused her slightly. Through half-lidded eyes, she saw Hephaestus approach, his strong silhouette backlit by the forge. Her heart raced, muscles tensing to flee once more.

But there was no hunger in his gaze, no reaching hands. He simply draped a woolen blanket over her trembling form, its weight unexpectedly comforting.

"I fell asleep by his hearth, exhausted from fear and flight. When Hephaestus found me there…" Aphrodite's eyes grew distant with the memory. "He didn't leer. Didn't try to charm or seduce. He simply covered me with a blanket and kept watch through the night."

Aphrodite demonstrated a stable stance without the staff, feet shoulder-width apart, Elena following as she spoke. "The next morning, seeing my trembling over returning to Olympus, he offered to teach me self-defense. Said 'beauty doesn't equate to helplessness'." Aph demonstrated a palm-heel strike so sharp Elena gasped. "Day after day, between crafting weapons for the other gods, he taught me. And day after day, I saw him differently."

"You fell in love?" Elena asked, her voice laced with romance.

Aphrodite lowered her arms, a genuine smile warming her features. "I fell in love with his heart first. His gentle wisdom. The way he saw me – truly saw me – when everyone else only looked. The love came slowly, built on trust and understanding, like tempering metal in his forge.

"The others…they never understood our bond. They saw his scars, his limp, his work-roughened hands, and thought him beneath me. Hera especially." Her jaw tightened. "She'd thrown him from Olympus as a baby, you see. Her own son, cast out for not being perfect."

"That's horrible," Elena whispered, following Aphrodite's movements as they began basic blocking positions and elbow strikes.

THE HEART OF A WARRIOR

"It was. But Hephaestus grew stronger for it, learning his craft on Lemnos. When he returned to Olympus, he was the finest craftsman in all the realms." A proud smile touched her lips. "And the kindest soul I'd ever known."

She adjusted Elena's elbow gently. "Like this – you want to protect your center. The same way I had to learn to protect my heart."

Aphrodite moved through her forms with the spear, each strike precise and powerful. "Ares has asked for my hand," *she said, her voice carefully neutral.*

Hephaestus's steady hammering faltered momentarily. "Oh," *he said, resuming his work.* "What did you say?"

Aphrodite's next strike came down harder than necessary. "He didn't ask me. Hera informed me she plans to bless the marriage. I'm just...what he desires."

The forge fell silent. Aphrodite felt Hephaestus's gaze on her, warm as his fires. "Is this what you desire?" *he asked softly.*

She turned to face him, the leather training armor he'd gifted her shifting with her movement. Their eyes met, and in that moment, all their unspoken feelings hung in the air between them.

"You know what I desire," *Aphrodite whispered.*

Hephaestus's face fell, his frown pulling at the scars across his face. "Aph—"

"Tell them!" *The words burst from her.* "Tell Zeus who you want."

"He will be King of Olympus one day—"

"That doesn't matter to me!"

"But it matters to my mother."

Tears pricked Aphrodite's eyes. She blinked them away, drawing a long breath. "I see," she said, her voice barely audible over the forge's crackle. "Then I suppose beauty truly is helpless after all."

With that, she fled, leaving Hephaestus alone in the forge's silence.

Her voice softened. "When Hera planned to force my marriage to Ares, Hephaestus crafted an enchanted throne that trapped her." Aphrodite showed a defensive sweep. "He refused to free her until I was given a choice in my own fate."

She watched Elena attempt the move. "Good. Keep your feet grounded, like tree roots. No one can move you unless you allow it."

They practiced in silence for a few minutes, the waves' rhythm keeping time. When Aphrodite spoke again, her voice carried a pained edge. "But even divine relationships face trials. During the Trojan war, while Heph was away..." She stopped, the old wound on her soul still stinging at the memory. "Let's just say I learned that all the training in the world can't protect you from every harm."

Elena stumbled in the next movement, catching herself. "What happened?"

"When Hephaestus returned and found me—" her voice caught. "He challenged Ares, wielding a weapon of terrible power. The price was his ability to walk without pain, but he never regretted it. Said my heart was worth any cost."

Elena watched as Aphrodite guided her through a complex series of movements, seeing beyond the training to the truth behind Aphrodite's words. Aph felt her warm understanding,

THE HEART OF A WARRIOR

her sharp sadness, but ignored it. "That's why I'm telling you this, teaching you these forms. Strength isn't just in the body. It's knowing your worth, in rising again after you fall, choosing who to trust with your heart."

Aphrodite exhibited another blocking stance, fighting back the familiar ache in her chest.

Metallic clashing, villagers' screams, Ares' cruel laughter... and Hephaestus, her beloved, falling – dying – threatened to overwhelm her.

For eight decades after that day, Aph lost herself. In wine, in the arms of countless lovers – men and women alike. Anything to numb the pain, to forget her failure.

Unbidden, the memory of a dream surfaced.

Hephaestus, whole and strong, his gentle eyes were crinkling as he smiled. "You're still the warrior you've always been, love." His calloused hand warmed her cheek. "Our village, me...that wasn't your failure. It was Hera's and Ares' cruelty."

"True strength," she told Elena, her voice thick with emotion, "comes from within. From surviving, from rising again after you fall." She tapped her heart, then her temple. "It's here, and here. No one can take that from you."

After executing a perfect block, Elena's face lit from within, a bright triumphant smile. "Is that why you're here training at dawn like a fantasy book heroine?"

Aph smiled, retrieving her staff. "Partly. I train to honor Hephaestus's gift to me. To remember I'm more than what others see. And sometimes, to help others discover the same truth about themselves."

She stepped back, displaying a simple strike. "Would you like to learn how to use it?"

Elena squared her shoulders, muttering something about always wanting to be a Valkyrie, the last traces of fear falling away. "Yes please."

As the morning wore on, Aphrodite guided her mortal student through basic spear forms, weaving in more of her story between instructions. She spoke of when the gods eventually left Olympus, spreading all over the world. Of her and Heph living peacefully, settling in a village in France where they were accepted, and of loss and love and finding strength in the darkest moments.

Aph noticed a change in Elena. Her movements became more assured, her focus sharpening. For a moment, it seemed the girl had forgotten about whatever had driven her to this secluded beach. In its place glimmered new-found strength.

"You're a natural, Elena," Aph proclaimed. "Perhaps there's more warrior in you than you realized."

The sun hung high over the water now, turning the morning mist into memory. Elena sat in the sand watching Aphrodite perform one final demonstration. The goddess moved like the water lapping along the shore, each motion flowing into the next, the staff an extension of her divine grace.

"The myths," she said as Elena rested, winded. "They paint me as faithless, flighty, focused only on passion. They were written by those who never understood that true love – the kind that transforms you, that makes you more than you believed possible – is the greatest strength of all."

Aphrodite and Elena completed their final forms. Elena's movements, while not yet perfect, carried a newfound confidence.

"Well done." Aphrodite planted her staff in the sand. "Let's rest."

They sat side by side, watching the waves. Elena pulled out her phone, then hesitated, seeing notifications piling up. "My sorority sisters are probably wondering where I am. And I should really post something..." She sighed. "Sometimes I wish I could just write and share my stories without worrying about likes or follows."

Aphrodite nodded in understanding. "Social media. A new arena where beauty is both celebrated and weaponized. The modern equivalent of temple paintings and marble statues," she mused. "Idealized life and beauty standards nearly unattainable." She gestured to their footprints in the sand. "But real beauty? Real strength? It leaves marks on the world. Changes things. Changes people."

Elena looked at her phone, then decisively powered it off. "I never realized someone like you would understand."

"Beauty and strength aren't opposites, Elena. They're two sides of the same coin." From a hidden pocket, Aphrodite withdrew something that caught the sunlight – a small bronze pendant on a leather cord. "Hephaestus made this for me long ago, when I first mastered the staff." She held it out to Elena. "Now I think it should be yours."

Elena gasped as she accepted the gift. A perfect miniature of a staff crossed with an olive branch, the pendant worked with such skill that it seemed almost alive. "I couldn't possibly..."

"You can, and you will." Aphrodite's voice was gentle but firm. "Wear it to remember what you learned today – not just the forms and stances, but the truth behind them. You are not merely something to be desired or possessed, online or off. You are a whole being, capable of both beauty and strength."

As Elena fastened the pendant around her neck, Aphrodite rose and retrieved her staff. "The morning's almost gone. Your friends will wonder where you've been."

Elena stood as well, squaring her shoulders in a way she hadn't when she first emerged from the rocks. "What do I tell them? About where I was, about...?" she touched the pendant.

A familiar look flickered in Elena's eyes, the spark of creativity, of stories waiting to be told. It reminded Aph of the bards and poets of old, always seeking to capture the essence of the gods in their works.

"Tell them whatever truth you choose. Or tell them nothing at all. Your story belongs to you now." Aphrodite's smile held centuries of hard-won wisdom. "But know this – should you ever need to find your strength, this beach will be here. And so will I."

As Elena prepared to leave, she stood taller, more confident. The party dress that had seemed so out of place before now looked like a warrior's garb. She turned to thank her divine teacher one last time, but Aphrodite spoke first.

"One more thing." She fixed Elena with an intense gaze. "The stories they tell about me and Hephaestus? About love and beauty and worth? Whether in ancient myths or modern posts?

THE HEART OF A WARRIOR

Challenge them. Question them. Write new ones, truer ones. That's how change begins."

Elena nodded, tears gathering in her eyes. "Thank you, Aphrodite. For everything."

They parted there, mortal and divine, each carrying a piece of the morning's truth with them. Aphrodite watched until Elena disappeared, then turned back to her private beach. The waves still crashed their eternal rhythm, the sun still sparkled on the water, but something had shifted – as it always did when truth replaced myth, when strength grew from vulnerability.

She took up her starting stance, staff held ready. There would be other mornings, other lessons, other souls in need of finding their own strength. For now, though, she simply moved through her forms, at peace with all her powers – those of love, of beauty and of the warrior's heart beating beneath it all.

Through the wards, she heard distant laughter – youthful voices carried on the morning breeze, probably from one of the nearby mortal beaches. Aphrodite smiled, wondering if any of those carefree souls could imagine their goddess of love and beauty was also a warrior goddess, here on this quiet beach, staff in hand, writing her own story with every strike and sweep and turn.

Some truths, after all, were too beautiful for filters to capture.

Best Served Cold
C.B. Channell

Aphrodite scowled at her husband. He glanced once at her, sniffed, and turned back to his work. Hephaestus's dedication to his craft was as solid as the ores he bludgeoned into form. Unfortunately for his wife, his temper was as hot as his roaring forge.

She turned, wanting to get away from the heat and smoke and the smell of slag. She wanted to be outside, growing her bright flowers and green grasses. She didn't even make it two steps.

"Where do you think you're going?" he demanded. He never lifted his attention from his project, but his god-sense was acute when it came to her. She sighed.

"Outside," she replied flatly, knowing full well what was coming next.

"I don't think so. Not without me, or an appropriate chaperone. After what you and Ares pulled? You belong to me! I earned you."

Her head snapped around. "You purchased me through trickery and by hurting your own mother! You earned nothing."

Hephaestus carefully set his tools in their places and dialed down his forge before turning his smoky-black visage toward his wife. He limped to her slowly, then leaned over into her face. She cringed from the sight and smell of him.

"Trickery? Hurting my mother? She cast me from Olympus! She only gave birth to me to punish your father, Zeus, for his adulteries. And you're just like him. They all come to worship you, don't they? The lechers and the prostitutes. You…you've never truly suffered a day in your existence. Everything comes easily for you. Everyone wants to praise your beauty! Well, you are the only prize I have ever had, and I have had to work for everything! I work myself to the bone and receive no respect. Even when I showed the rest of the gods your blatant adultery they laughed! Laughed at *me*! The victim! So yes, I have earned you. And you will learn to treat me with respect. *And* you will not go outside alone. Understood?"

She glowered at him, refusing to answer. She could see him redden beneath the blackened oxide. For a moment, she saw a tear sparkle in the corner of his eye, but then it was gone. Perhaps she imagined it.

She retreated to their bedchamber and sank onto the mattress with a heavy sigh. She ran her hand along the bedclothes, thinking of the times she'd spent there with Ares, meeting his violent and tender loving with her own. He should have been her husband. They could have raised a family that could challenge Zeus himself had they the freedom. But Zeus and Hephaestus were too clever. She never doubted that her misogynistic father had set Ares up to fail in his quest to win her legitimately. And now she was trapped in eternity with a broken, foul-smelling, angry man and his forge.

She didn't know how long she sat there. It could have been an hour or a year; what was time to an immortal, anyway? Hephaestus came in, saw her looking tenderly at the bed. His eyes narrowed in anger, recognizing who was filling her thoughts.

"I have to go," he said.

She looked up a little too quickly. He was cleaned up and wearing fresh clothes.

He smiled, the evil look that never touched his cold eyes. "Don't get any ideas, wife of mine." He held up his hand, and though she couldn't see them, she knew he was holding the invisible chains he'd used to trap her and her lover. She paled.

"I'm going to chain you here. You won't be able to reach out to him or leave, or even move. If he shows up, he'll believe you're gone or ignoring him. Either way, you two will never share each other's company again. It's time the love goddess learned what it is to be alone."

Her heart sank. She didn't even resist as he bound her to the headboard. She focused on keeping in her tears; she wouldn't show him her suffering for anything in the world. He leaned into her face to try and get a reaction but she only looked through him. Finally, disappointed, he pulled away.

As always, Ares appeared at the entrance as soon as Hephaestus was well gone. Their bond always told him when she was left alone. He pounded the door and she could hear all the eagerness in his rap. She opened her mouth to call out, but nothing came. The enchanted chains bound her in every way. The tears she'd held in while in the company of her husband rolled down her cheeks now, dripped onto her breasts, soaking her gown in salt water. A river poured from her eyes, carrying all her rage with it, filling the bedchamber, rising to a whitewater roar.

A figure rose in the midst of the little ocean and for a moment she thought her blurred vision deceived her. She blinked away the tears, ceased the waterfall, and gazed at her aunt, Amphitrite.

"Why have you summoned me, niece?" she asked. Her voice was kind.

She opened her mouth but nothing came out. Ares pounded again. Amphitrite, wife of Poseidon, looked over her shoulder toward the door, then at Aphrodite's arms, bound behind her, and understood. She, too, had been present at Hephaestus's ill-fated revelation.

"You wish me to defy my brother-in-law and your husband," she said.

Aphrodite dared not move. Though her aunt wasn't one of the children of the Titans she was wed to one. She knew the consequences of crossing the higher gods. Poseidon loved his wife and was fond of her, but that didn't mean he couldn't be dangerous.

"Aphrodite!" called Ares.

Amphitrite leaned over and gazed into her eyes. "If I do this for you, there is no turning back. The consequences will fall where they fall."

Aphrodite held Amphitrite's gaze. She didn't tremble or look away. The thought of never seeing Ares, of being trapped in this flaming hell with Hephaestus, cast off by the King of the Gods, was more than she could bear. What consequences could be worse? She nodded firmly. Amphitrite nodded back. Then with a gentle flick, she tipped her trident, hooked a link, and broke the chains.

"Oh, aunt! Thank you, thank you!" she cried as she ran to the door. She flung it open and threw herself into her lover's arms. Amphitrite swirled once, twice, then disappeared, taking her niece's salty tears with her, leaving only a dry bedchamber with broken chains.

"My love," said Ares between kisses hotter than even Hephaestus's forge, "we must away. I have something you must see."

"Anywhere," she replied and smiled. As her lips curved upward the shining love goddess emerged, emitting a golden light no mortal could gaze upon. Her hair, formerly filled with soot, now flowed down her back in stunning red-gold waves. Ares smiled and took her hands and they dissolved into the air, flying free across the sea.

They landed on a rocky outcrop overlooking the blue Mediterranean. Warm breezes blew around them as they materialized, he a dark sky behind her shining star.

"Why are we in the mortal world?" she asked, turning to take in the sprawling city below. "I thought we would find a place of our own, away from everything and everyone."

He kissed her fingers. "Do you trust me?" he asked. She nodded. "Then come." He led her down to the teeming crowds. They cast illusions over themselves to keep the mortals from going mad. The crowds opened around them, never quite touching, never quite seeing, not even realizing they were doing it. Aphrodite watched Ares' face while keeping pace with him, but his expression remained guarded. Finally she allowed herself to look around, absorb the ebb and flow of humanity.

She felt a twinge of recognition. She tried to remember if she'd ever visited this place before. It seemed like she had, but she had no memory of it. Still, the sensation niggled at the back of her mind.

At last Ares stopped. They stood before an ancient temple. The sensation in her mind grew stronger, more insistent. One word burst forth from her memory.

"Paphos," she said. Ares smiled and she felt as if the sun had risen just for her.

"Go inside," he said, and she did.

With each step, her memories began to emerge and stitch themselves together. Memories from before the time of Olympus, when she was the Lady of Cyprus, the passionate one, the goddess of love and battle. Memories which she now recognized that Zeus had stripped from her. Wonder slid into anger. Ares backed into the shadows, let her mind heal itself. She found the frieze representing her birth from Gaia's waters and Ouranus's blood. A fresh goddess standing on the bloody foam of the sea. Blood that was shed by her brother Kronos, Zeus's father. The breadth of Zeus's treachery made her blood flow hotter.

She let her senses open to the worshippers in the temple. She listened to their prayers: let my daughter find love in her marriage, save me from the husband who beats me, give me the power to vanquish my enemies. Feeling her powers rise once again she granted each petitioner their prayer. She again sought Ares and offered him a feral smile.

"That blasphemer Zeus was never my father. Therefore he had no right to give me to Hephaestus." She strode to her lover and grasped both of his hands and cast away their illusions. For the briefest moment the faithful saw the dark-and-light glory of the gods and then they were gone.

They flew to the sky and alit on a cloud, far above what she now knew to be her home. The anger within her only made her shine all the brighter.

"I will have my vengeance," she said.

"On Hephaestus?" he asked, a note of eagerness in his voice.

She snorted, a surprisingly sensuous sound. "No. Him I will ignore. To go after him would validate his existence, which is all he ever wanted. Leave him to rot in his forge, wallowing in self-pity. But Zeus…I want to upend his world."

"I'm glad to hear you say that."

She turned to him. His eyes were filled with the light of warfare and his smile predatory. "You and I will work together, my beautiful goddess of love and destruction. And you'll begin it with a visit to an arrogant young mortal."

The skies and the clouds flew past them and they shortly stood over another city, this one built high and surrounded by strong walls.

"Troy," she said. She spun herself into her most alluring vision. "Young Paris shall set Zeus's world on fire, and we shall stoke the flames!"

She pressed a passionate kiss upon Ares' lips, then descended to the city to pay a visit to Paris, prince of Troy.

A Mortal Breaks Aphrodite's Heart

Ev Datsyk

Aphrodite is heartbroken, and all anyone is talking about is her brand.

She is biting her nails into ragged, uneven moons, tasting blood while they make a fresh pot of coffee.

She is thinking about the pain of this – how it cannot be out-thought, out-ignored or even out-fucked. It is something gritty and perseverant, that laughs from its perch high in her chest when she says, *I am done with feeling you.*

Her PR team says this is no problem. They hand her collagen face masks and reapply her makeup and tattoo her eyebrows on – which is the rage, apparently. They erase her aching, her longing and her wishing with brushstrokes and careful wording. They want to confirm they have the mortal's NDA on file.

In the beginning, Aphrodite used to ask why. Couldn't she just have this day off? Doesn't she deserve to stuff her face with marshmallows and watch at least two seasons of *Gilmore Girls* back to back?

Pity shadowed her team lead's eyes, and Aphrodite thought, *Thank the Gods*, she was going to go home and order takeout and eat Chinese food with a fork and listen to Natalie Imbruglia on repeat.

But then he said, "Babe, if they," *they*, the team's catch-all for the entire mortal population, "find out you didn't want it to end, they're going to start wondering if love is even real." Then he handed her cucumber slices to reduce her under-eye swelling.

She overheard the team rolling their eyes in the lunchroom afterwards. "*We* don't take days off when *we* have a break-up. Work with your fucking broken heart like the rest of us."

"What a diva."

To this day, she finds this extremely embarrassing. These clips play in her mind often, reminding her it is better to be a doll in their hands, a plaything on which to apply copious rouge, than it is to be unlovable.

Now, she sits at the table, listening while they debate how to frame this breakup. Should they call it a fling? Should they suggest it was an affair of passion that burned bright before it sizzled? Either way, it is imperative people understand it was Aphrodite who pulled the trigger. She must be seen as beautiful, confident and laughing at a joke no one else has heard, looking nothing like the goddess who cried all weekend and wished for a mortal to take her back.

"And you should find someone new. Quick." This they all agree on, nodding vigorously around the table.

The ache inside of her amplifies. It almost throbs. It's so big her ribs rearrange in her chest to make room for the grief.

But she is not a diva. *Diva* is not conducive to the type of love she wishes to manifest in the world, so she says, "Of course."

"Who could it be...?" they muse amongst themselves. "Do you have a vision?"

Her head spins.

Her vision is that the mortal will appear at her door tonight, having run to her in the pouring rain to say, "I've made a terrible mistake. My love, forgive me." After, they'll lie in bed and eat chocolate-covered orange peels, whispering, "I missed you," giggling about the annoying infomercial jingle they both have stuck in their heads.

She closes her eyes. The blackness is so thick and far-reaching she could almost fall asleep.

"Maybe not another mortal," the table decides while she tries to unstick her tongue from the room of her mouth. They put their little bobbleheads together, and she tries to listen while they scheme, but there's a ringing in the ears that sounds like the earth, how it cried when it was young.

She loves dating mortals. She is no different from the other Olympians in this, but she feels very virtuous about it – falling in love with mutual respect. No deception, no lies. None of the things antithetical to love.

Once, stirring honey into her tea, Hera observed mildly, "It's still manipulative." Aphrodite was hot off the heels of an affair, trying to recover, but Hera's eyes gleamed; she has never found a knife she won't twist. "Your power dynamic is off. Mortals'll date you just because they're afraid you'll smite their bloodline."

Aphrodite retorted, "Well, *I've* never turned anyone into a cow to keep someone interested in me," because it was easier than admitting that Hera was right.

Even in this body, even on their earthly plane, she is a goddess.

If she set her sights on someone, she could easily become the object of their desire. She could slide her gender along a scale to match their sexuality. She could wear any mask: any person or creature or, gods forbid, inanimate object. But she does not.

She's chasing true love, which doesn't hold up under illusion.

She adores mortals earnestly. She's fascinated by them: their ever-evolving beauty, from smooth cheeks to laughter lines, from dark hair to wispy silver. She loves the weight they place on time, how they value their finite lives. She is curious, watching them live as if they might die tomorrow or might never die at all. They look behind them constantly or only ahead, with blinders on. They are so varied as they hunt for meaning in their lovely, precious purposelessness.

At the table, the unlovable mortals on her PR team turn to her. "What are your thoughts on Hephaestus?"

How can she explain it to them? She's had many lifetimes for dalliances with immortals, but they have grown stale in their sameness, their ageless wisdom. Mortality complicates everything, but to bite into it – it is the freshest fruit, the juiciest berry, the richest meat. Olympians taste to her like canned preserves, pickled things and dried apricots.

She has lost her taste for them.

But she nods and says, "He's fine."

Sitting across from him the following evening, she tears her cocktail napkin into fine shreds while he finishes an email on his phone.

"I'm really sorry," he keeps saying, but the email gets longer and longer and longer. She watches his thumbs for a while – like the rest of him, they're thick and square, decorated with coarse dark hair – but loses interest eventually. Her eyes glaze over on the window behind him, where rain smears a red light all across the street.

She met the mortal on an app. She felt it was her duty to ensure that love could be found there despite the cynicism and frustration she saw.

She found it in a pale, freckled woman with a high forehead and mouse-brown hair, whose first photo was of her in a plant nursery with a cart full of creepers. Her profile read:

Yet another day of buying twee things in flea markets, procrastinating on my PhD and lamenting the cost of grapes in this country. Looking for a relationship with someone curious, feminist and pro-plaid who won't mind getting texts from a night owl about the meaning of life...or ceramic cats.

Aphrodite honours love fully. She bought the mortal flowers every week, replacing the last bouquet just as its petals began to wilt. She texted her, *I'm thinking of you!* when she was – which was often: when she heard a song with a poignant lyric, when she saw two mourning doves picking apart a pretzel in a back alley, when she saw anything vaguely heart-shaped, when the air was light with the scent of fresh-baked bread, when the stars were bright and the moon was full, when a candle was burning low, when she was lonely or when she wasn't.

The mortal said, "You're so sweet, Dita, but I don't need all this," and she said it so softly that Aphrodite's heart melted. Still, she didn't know how to stop. She is moved when she is in love, and she speaks all love languages fluently. Equally. Loudly.

The next conversation was different. "Dita, this is *too much*."

But she still didn't know how to stop.

"I'm *so* sorry," Hephaestus says, and she realises he is done, finally.

She replies, "It's fine," though it's not. Only Olympians can spurn Olympians like this. A mortal would never dare, fearing that they might be transformed into a pigeon or a worm or something else easy to kill.

Still, Hephaestus is very sorry and says as much one more time before explaining in a wishy-washy way, "That volcano in Iceland, you know."

She shrugs noncommittally. She knows about the volcano in Iceland – she reads the news like everyone else – but she's afraid if she appears overconfident in his domain, he will hate her.

"The media keep calling, and it's so…" He takes a very long drink of the cocktail he's ordered. His nostrils flare as he does. His drink is pungent, cinnamonny. "Well."

"Mhm," she says. Aphrodite does not wish to relate, though she does to a degree. When she gets media calls, it's usually because there's been a widely publicized domestic violence incident and they would like her to explain how love could look like this. How could she make it so? "That must be difficult," she says diplomatically.

A part of her soul is already leaving her body. She feels it evaporating into the bar and out the window and into the rain, where it is cool and lovely and she is with the birds.

She misses evenings with the mortal. The mortal would take Aphrodite's hands in her own and kiss every dainty knuckle like a prayer before they ate. It was a form of worship she took for granted.

"Sorry," he says for the fourth time. "I don't want to bore you." His shoulders slump. "I was actually really happy when your office called."

His earnestness yanks her soul back from the fog. "Really?"

He nods, and his shaggy hair bounces on his strong brow. "You're always so quiet in meetings. I feel like I don't know anything about you."

He's wrong there. She hasn't *always* been quiet. At their round tables, she used to advocate for her people. She used to argue, what gets them out of bed in the morning? It's love. Love that rouses them. Love for a bright morning and the people they meet under the sun.

But then Achilles would say their health. And Hermes would say work.

And she would say, but what motivates them? What really motivates them? What force could be strong enough that it unfolds them from the safety of their nest and lures them into the wild world beyond? For what would they sacrifice their time and their comfort?

Then Plutus would say money. And Artemis would say wisdom. And all of Aphrodite's points would dissolve like the sea foam that made her.

"There's not a lot to know," she says. Time with the mortals has taught her humility. Sometimes, it's hard to remember her as she was once: a goddess rising from the sea, standing above the waves amidst circling warships, their sails cracking from the winds, their hulls snapping in the grip of a many-armed creature reaching from the depths. People forget she can be bloody, since no one wars in the ocean anymore. Though, with increasing regularity, she's getting calls about whales attacking yachts.

Hephaestus shakes his head. "Pardon my Latin, but there's no fucking way that's true."

Her cheeks burn. *Are you so lonely that you're falling prey to a man's flattery? A god's flattery? Surely you know better* – no, she's tickled. Her stomach flutters.

"I mean it. You have the best portfolio of all of us."

"Really?"

"Absolutely. You really get to know people as people."

Aphrodite flinches. The butterflies in her tummy dissolve into dust.

She's spent centuries reading between the lines of comments like this. He's making her work small. But she's more than love letters and chocolate. The mortal understood that.

Before she can stop herself, she's counting on her fingers. "I get media calls about domestic violence, incels, and kids dating AI." She ticks another finger. "The internet is blaming me for the gay agenda, as if we weren't all gay since before they were born." She lifts a third finger. "And, like, every week, my team lobbies to legalize sex work. Every. Week."

Hephaestus opens his mouth, then closes it again.

"*And*," now that she's riled up, she can't quite seem to stop herself, "while you all kill-fuck-marry whoever you want, I have to go on *fake dates*," she gestures viciously between them, "to make people think I'd rather have fun than a future."

Anything she had said to humble him is forgotten. "Fake dates?" Confusion creases his forehead and spreads to the corners of his mouth, flattening his lips into a guarded line.

Her anger stutters, "What did you think this was?"

"I didn't know…they just asked for a meeting."

"You think this is how I take a meeting?" She lifts her hand, gaudy with bubble-hearted acrylic nails, and indicates to herself: her skin-tight ruby-red velvet dress, her lipstick thick as blood.

"I…I guess?"

She stares at him. It has been many years since she threw a drink at someone. But she's tempted.

Finally, she sighs and gulps her cocktail. The cherry liquor makes her tastebuds pucker and her teeth hurt. She sets the glass down hard; a hairline fracture appears in the stem. "Unbelievable."

Even as she steams in her seat, part of her wants to apologize. *Sorry that this meeting is tabloid fodder, a meaningless headline designed to show the world my heart has never been anything but whole. Sorry for wasting your time, for assuming you knew what this was.*

Hephaestus has been staring at the table, looking down with a slightly horrified expression.

She almost dreads him ending his silence. She sits on a ledge, waiting, and he must be careful; the wrong words will unleash her, and she will soak something in poisoned blood for him to wear around his shoulders til it eats through his skin.

"I'm sorry," he says finally. "You're not what I thought you were."

She blinks. No one has ever apologized for that.

Her work is frivolous to the other gods and she knows it. They have temples and shrines, offerings of milk and honey, where entire villages kneel and pray for bountiful harvests and another year of peace. Meanwhile, Aphrodite has altars raised by teenage girls who proffer restaurant breath mints and beg to be noticed by a K-Pop star from their dreams.

She wishes this were not a point for comparison. Worship to most is a form of commerce. Payment for a duty done. But, over time, prostitution has been added to her portfolio, and surely she knows the difference between love and business.

She wishes love in all its forms on everyone – those who don't ask for it, just as much as those who do. It is not her right to profit from what humankind deserves unilaterally.

"You're right," she says, turning her nose up. "I'm not."

Sensing the fight has left her, Hephaestus's features relax. She's surprised he isn't leaving. "Why are we on a fake date?"

Aphrodite sags in her chair. "Because someone broke my heart." Her voice cracks with the effort of saying it plainly.

"Do you want to talk about it?"

"You want to hear about it?"

Their eyes meet over the table, both a little surprised.

"I do," he says. "Tell me about the real Aphrodite."

Pandemos – Skotia – Areia
Voss Foster

The smell of mud and copper filled the air, like the floor of a butcher in the heat of summer. Ikarios huffed, swiping sweat from his brow as he sprinkled fragrant resin over the coals in the brazier. It was never sufficient to keep the stench of war out of the tents, but it was better than nothing. Soldiers came to them for a reprieve. Small and insufficient it may have been, a breath of differently scented air, a cup of mead, and the touch of another were welcome luxuries amidst the terrors of war.

"We have celebrants gathering already."

Ikarios turned to see a large-bodied man, oiled so his skin shone in the dim light within the tent. His hair was shorn close to the scalp, though it did little to hide the threads of silver peering through the black.

"They can wait, Maro." Ikarios breathed deeply of the perfumed smoke, the mixture of acridity and bright pine notes familiar and welcome. So close to the brazier, he could *almost* close out the stink of combat from outside the tent. "The matrons have not yet allowed any celebrants entry, and neither shall we. If they are so impatient as to besmirch the good graces of the Whispering Mistress, then let them, and may she show them no mercy."

"Of course, Ikarios." Maro was older, but he had not been a courtesan anywhere near as long. Yet his age seemed to get the better of him, as even when he inclined his head to point his gaze to the floor, he continued to question. "I only brought it to your attention as there are *many* celebrants gathered. These are warriors, and I fear what they would do if kept waiting."

"This is the hallowed ground of our Whispering Mistress. Wherever we make our beds and halls open, that is a temple of Aphrodite, and only fools would dare anger her." Their tents were not omnipresent on battlefields, but they did their best to collect offerings and pay tribute to Aphrodite wherever they could. In silent agreement, none dared bring the war inside the walls of the tents, no matter which side of the conflict they represented.

A loud bell rang, vibrating through the air and shaking Ikarios's teeth. He walked to Maro and lifted the older gentleman's head, tilting it until he again stood straight and proud, displaying his physique. "You see? The matrons next door are well capable of handling the celebrants." Men and women worked in separate tents, as they catered to every taste in their worship. Any outside the strict duality were given their choice. And of course, all could move freely between the tents, so long as proper offerings were given to the Whispering Mistress. With enough sacrifice, one soldier could have every courtesan worshiping their body at the same time. Though no mere soldier had such riches.

"Go await a guest, Maro." He stroked a hand along the man's chin, then patted his cheek and sent him along. Ikarios glided through the fabric-walled walkways of the tent as other courtesans scurried to take their places. Most stood in the makeshift doorways to their bedchambers, posing their bodies seductively. Others stood by to serve wine and mead and honeyed bread, while others still kept oil warm over gentle coals to be used for massage.

Ikarios was the most experienced courtesan in this tent, so he stepped lightly outside and into the wretched miasma of a half-fought battle. In the distance, the sound of screams and grinding metal filtered in, but the fabric and canvas of the tent was thick enough to mute it.

Maro had been correct. Many celebrants had already gathered. Two dozen, perhaps, and though Ikarios had no line of sight to the matrons' tent, he could see the crowd of celebrants extending into his vision. That meant they all had a busy day ahead of them.

The celebrants in front of Ikarios began to jostle toward the front for position. Among them were handfuls of drachmas, jars of wine, cages carrying doves within, slabs of meat that only added to the stink outside.

Ikarios bowed to them. "We welcome you in the name of our Whispering Mistress. May she take of these bountiful offerings and be pleased, and may some measure of her grace be available to you before you return to the glory of combat." A tired speech, but that made it no less true. "May Aphrodite take what meager offerings we can arrange and lay her glory upon us all!"

The celebrants cheered as Ikarios stepped aside, allowing them to file into the tent. Two others, armed with spear and shield, kept the crowd from growing too rowdy. It was rare that the courtesans' guards had to step in, but it was well known that they *would*. Often, other soldiers would as well, to maintain the neutrality of their wandering temple.

Ikarios stayed long enough to gauge the emotions and gather impressions. It was important for him to keep himself apprised of all things, even when he would be seeing celebrants. If emotions seemed tense, he would have to postpone his own part in the worship to ensure the smooth management and function of their day's offerings.

By grace or luck, no one seemed agitated, merely eager to make their offerings and partake of what the temple could give in return. Doves were handed over, and silenced with the quick bite of a knife before they were thrown to the ritual fires. Meat was charred in the same flames. Drachmas collected and set aside to be spent in the glorifying of the Whispering Mistress. Wine was spilled into goblets and allowed to overflow onto the ground. They had their own wine for celebrants – this was for Aphrodite.

When he saw that all was well, Ikarios returned to his own chambers. He tried to, at least, but a hand landed on his shoulder, rough and gritty. He turned to see a young man with brassy hair lashed back by a strip of red-dyed wool. He was streaked with patches of dried dirt, and the outline of his breastplate was still visible, carved into his chest and shoulders by long hours of wear. Those shallow grooves were normal, and Ikarios could tell what side of the conflict they came from by the pattern. This one was from Athens. Or at least, he was fighting for Athens.

Ikarios took the man's hand and laced their fingers together. "You wish to worship with me?"

"If that's acceptable." He didn't make eye contact for longer than a moment or two before his gaze slid somewhere else, then darted back again. Not typical for the battle-hardened men and women who visited them here. Not unwelcome, but it made the man stand out a bit.

Ikarios turned and led the way, keeping his grip firm, but not painful. He had a skillful touch after so long, knew exactly how to guide celebrants through the tent. His own bedchambers amid the swaths of fabric were close to the entrance, but still far enough away to close out the bustle and noise from the front. Which was good. All praise to the Whispering Mistress, but the screeching of the doves, however rapidly cut off, did not lend itself well to their worshipful joining.

Once they were inside and Ikarios had untied and closed off the doorway to his chambers, he gestured to the pile of cushions and blankets on the ground. "Take this chance for comfort while it's available. Wine? Mead? Water?"

"Water. Please." The man didn't sit immediately, instead loosening his robes so they could fall around him. Ikarios kept the man in his peripheral vision as he filled a cup from the ewer. He had a lovely physique, and was well-blessed by the Whispering Mistress already.

Ikarios turned and offered the water. "You're free to sit."

The man drank down the entire cup, then repeated his routine from before, making fleeting eye contact, then darting away. "I was informed there was a chance to bathe? I wouldn't want to dirty the temple."

"I can bathe you." Ikarios ran his fingertips down the man's jaw, his neck, across his chest, and pulled away at his lower abdomen. "If that would be beneficial."

"If you…if you can." His voice had grown hoarse and quieted. A normal reaction. The power of the goddess could buckle the knees of even the most stalwart fighters.

Ikarios went back and grabbed the entire ewer. Then he removed the cloth from his waist, revealing himself fully, and laid it on the floor. "You can kneel here."

The man did so, eyes wide and hungry, and Ikarios took the cup from his hand. He dipped it into the water, then reached up with his other hand and undid the wool tie on the man's hair. It was just as dirty as the rest of his body, so Ikarios streamed the water through, combing and pulling the strands apart as gently as he could. Mud trickled out, leaving trails down the man's back as it dripped to the floor, and the fabric beneath him. It took three cups before the water ran clear over his scalp.

Ikarios shifted so he was fully behind the man, leaning around him and wetting his hands before rubbing across the man's chest. "Would you care to share a name?" It didn't have to be his, but it made things easier to call him *something*.

"Alexandros."

Ikarios rubbed his knuckles over the dried dirt, washing Alexandros's chest entirely by feel. He leaned close and whispered. "In the worship, you'll only sweat again." Finally, he let his fingers dip lower, beneath the man's navel, and relished the shudder that passed through him and into Ikarios's own body. "I'm happy to bathe you a second time, of course, but I would not want you to delay your prayer to the Whispering Mistress." He brushed his lips against Alexandros's ear. "Or we can stay in *this* ecstasy and celebrate her glory." His own body had begun to react to the closeness, and he shifted so Alexandros could *feel* that.

Alexandros leaned his head back and pressed his lips to Ikarios's. When they parted, he groaned out, "For the glory of Aphrodite."

"For her glory." Then Ikarios led the man to the cushions and blankets, knocking the ewer over into the dirt in the process, and they worshipped Aphrodite Pandemos – the goddess of the people, and of earthly love, and of carnal passions.

* * *

The fighting had slowed to nearly nothing. Ikarios never knew precisely what had started the conflict. He'd heard shifting rumors over the weeks since they'd opened their tents to the warriors. Some said it was over resources. Some said a jilted nobleman had launched an attack on his former lover. Others claimed it was part of some greater conflict that had spilled over from the east. Or the west, depending who delivered that rumor. And, as always, some attributed it simply to the whims of Ares or Nike or Athena or any of a dozen others.

None dared lay this bloodshed at the feet of the Whispering Mistress. Not in her own temple.

As the evening wound away and Ikarios gave a final kiss to his last celebrant, exhaustion tore at his muscles. The soldiers and other functionaries in the fight had paid many great offerings to

Aphrodite. He had encountered Alexandros three more times since his first visit. The ravages on the bodies of the courtesans was normal, but all in the glory of the Whispering Mistress.

She would not, however, begrudge any of them for complaining. What they did in her honor was difficult work, and acknowledging that was only further confirmation that they offered her value in their worship.

Ikarios took one final breath of the incense smoke, then doused the coals in the brazier with water. There had been terrible fires at temples in the past, and he would not be responsible for such an accident.

He had already established a plan for the evening. He had spoken with Maro, and would take advantage of the man's strength to work away what tension and knotting he could before retiring. He wrapped himself in a blanket against the encroaching cold as more and more of their braziers were put out. Only the sacrificial fire in the entrance was kept constantly alight, and as he walked through, he saw half a dozen courtesans already settling in to sleep around the warmth. As the wind bit against him, even through the blanket, Ikarios considered whether he should join them.

He let himself into Maro's chambers and saw the man still had his brazier glowing orange from the coals. They weren't gving out much heat, obviously, but enough. He looked Maro up and down, then swiped a thumb across the man's cheek with a frown, removing a dot of red. "Were you attacked?"

"The worship was intense." He pulled down his lower lip to show the inside broken and bruised. "I bit myself."

Ikarios's tension lessened. "Come. Mint should soothe you." The massage could wait. Ikarios was responsible for the other courtesans. "She doesn't require that we stay in pain." The fact the throes of his worship had injured him at all was enough of a sacrifice. He had spilled blood in the name of the Whispering Mistress.

They had a small selection of medicinal herbs at the entrance, to be used in the event celebrants needed some relief. The mint was still only half-dried, but he shredded the leaves into a splash of mead to rehydrate fully. Then he mixed them into a paste with a pestle. "The mint will soothe the pain, and the mead will address any tension still in your body." The next sentence pained him, but it was only right. "And sleep will do wonders." He took some of the paste onto his finger, already feeling the tingling cold, and gently applied it inside Maro's lower lip. "Take the remainder with you and rest."

"We had agreed—"

"I will recover." He took the small, partially used bottle of mead and tucked it under his arm. "I have my own ways to relax my muscles."

Maro hesitated, then took the paste and nodded. "Sleep well."

"Heal well."

Maro walked back towards his chambers and Ikarios heaved in a deep breath, ready to sigh.

Copper caught on his tongue, and while it shouldn't have alarmed him…why was it so strong? He looked around, then saw the red still swiped over his right thumb. He doused it with water—

Flames licked up the front of the tent, peeling away the fabric. Those clustered around the sacrificial altar shouted and scurried back, and Ikarios threw his mead at the entrance, knowing it would do nothing to quench the fire. "Out the back. Go!" He ushered them through, keeping his eyes fixed on the growing flames. Someone had left a brazier lit, knocked it over?

But no. That would have burned from the back. As he pushed the other courtesans along, he saw his first glint of metal, and the wash of copper filled the air. More than a single drop on his thumb could have possibly accomplished.

"Dogs and scum!" a man's voice roared out as the flaming entrance was hacked away by a xiphos. A xiphos streaked in brown mud and red…fluid. "They harbor the enemy!"

Ikarios's tense muscles disappeared as he ran for the spear near the door. He got a hand around it and ran backwards, keeping the point of the weapon forward and shouting as he moved through the tent. "Flee! Avoid the entrance! Go!" Almost everyone would have been able to get out from under the tent without leaving their chambers, if the panic would allow their minds to consider that option.

A dozen armored warriors marched in. The sacrificial altar was upended, spilling flames and cinders across the ground and catching everything else on fire.

Then Ikarios heard the first scream. The second. The third. As others ran past, their wind kicked up the flaps in front of the bedchambers and he saw the tent ripped open. Two more men, dressed in armor he did not recognize, had already plunged daggers into the chest of Gelon, one of the first courtesans to join after Ikarios. They carved apart his body like a trussed stag.

Ikarios was not certain how or when he escaped. He found an exit, already held open, and scurried out nude on his hands and knees. All he knew was the flames at his back and the agony in his knuckles from gripping his spear. He could not let it loose. He could not leave himself or any of the others unarmed, unprotected.

Eventually, the screams silenced, or they moved too far away to hear. A hand landed on Ikarios's shoulder and he whipped the butt of the spear around, but someone caught it. A young man who, finally, held eye contact. Ikarios wasn't certain his voice would work when he opened his mouth. "Alexandros."

"You're safe. All of you." He closed his hands over Ikarios's and pried his fingers up, releasing the spear and handing it to someone behind him. "You're under the protection of Athens for now."

You are under my protection.

The voice was so loud, Ikarios wrenched his hands away to cover his ears, but it did no good. As he kneeled down, he saw the other courtesans with him doing the same. Not nearly enough. Not nearly all of them. But everyone who had escaped did the same as Ikarios as the voice continued, like a chorus and a scream and a blazing fire all at once.

You have served me. You have honored me. You have given your bodies in my favor. On this night, know that I mourn for those who will never again worship me.

Ikarios barely perceived it through the agony pounding in his skull, but he saw the flames in the distance, their tents, their temple, snuff to nothing. The flaming torches around them followed suit. The stars themselves winked away, and the moon vanished from the sky. The killer of men. The gravedigger. The dark one. Aphrodite Skotia had made herself known, with the fury of a shattered heart.

The pressure finally eased as the voice quieted, and Ikarios stood. The Athenians had backed away, though none brandished their weapons. A few among their number had fallen to their knees, Alexandros among them. Not in pain, but in supplication.

A new light pierced through the black veil. At first, a simple sliver of gold, but it crawled from the earth, stretching toward the sky and branching. Within seconds, it revealed itself as a tree of pure gold, festooned with apples of brilliant, faceted garnet.

The voice, this time, was clear, but not painful.

I take no sides in these combats. But some have harbored my servants, while others have slain them. This night, you rest. Come morning, I demand you once again offer your bodies in my service.

The apples crashed to the ground, shattering apart. From within the heart of each grew a spear or a sword.

* * *

Phylas rubbed the sleep from his eyes. The battle was nearly won, and they'd made their displeasure known to the whores who comforted their opponents. By choosing no side, they had chosen Athens, and they had reaped their rewards in turn.

He left his tent to head for the latrine, and it took several steps for him to internalize the quiet. Yes, he had awoken before dawn, but he was never *alone* in such behavior. Yet the camp remained still.

Until it did not.

The golden light of dawn intensified, shifted, raced towards him until he realized…no. Not dawn. Not light. A spear of gleaming gold, borne by a man in no more cover than the wind itself. Blood spattered across his bare chest, glowing like a constellation of rubies set into his skin.

Phylas rolled aside. The man turned on his heel and gave chase, swiping with the oversized spearhead. An unwieldy weapon, but it whistled through the air, just above Phylas's head. He crawled into the nearest tent, shouting, "Attack! Ambush!" His throat, dry from slumber, gave out too quickly.

Then he noticed the smell of copper, and the slickness on his hands. Inside the tent, what should have been a dozen warriors were instead a dozen corpses. All of them slain, and all of them with golden sprouts growing from their wounds.

The tent was sliced open. The blood-splattered man marched for him, accompanied by an armored Athenian pig and a woman bearing two swords of the same glowing metal, and a similar pattern of blood sprayed across her naked body.

Phylas ran, tripped in the mud and blood, and pain bit into his shoulder. He looked up to see that the woman had stabbed him. With her other blade, she cut across the backs of his ankles and he found his voice anew, screaming to the heavens.

A foot caught him in his ribs, then gauntleted hands hauled him to his feet. The Athenian. "Unhand me!" He spat at the man's helmet.

"You will not suffer these *indignities* for long." The spear-bearer approached slowly. The gleam of his weapon increased and, as he came nearer, the sprouts in the wounds on his soldiers grew, as if reaching for the man. "You should not have trifled with the Whispering Mistress." The light – so bright, somehow growing brighter with each ragged breath – now emanated from his eyes, formed a halo around his head. "The goddess can buckle the knees of even the most stalwart fighters." He hauled his spear back and, try as he might, Phylas could not escape the grip of the Athenian.

The man's eyes were pure gold now. "You are cowardly swine, so she was not to be bothered. I will buckle your knees instead."

As the spearhead drove forward, the light took on visages, flashing a woman rising from the sea, a woman with her foot on the head of a giant, a woman holding a spear, mirroring this man.

She who postpones old age. The mistress. The armed one. Aphrodite Encheios – the spear-bearing.

No wound had ever burned like this before. Phylas shrieked as the spear carved through his gut. When it pulled out, he collapsed, his ankles no longer able to hold his weight. The man loomed above him. He allowed the blood to drip from his weapon onto his chest, where it glowed with all the others. "Ikarios offers this body for the glory of Aphrodite Areia."

Aphrodite the warlike. Phylas's vision blurred and blackened, but not before he saw a golden branch extrude from the wound in his stomach. And not before he felt the roots scratching into his flesh, curling through his intestines.

Hymn to the Pain
Luna C. Galindo

When I reached the sea, my knees were rattling. Their instability made my whole body quake, and I resented them for it. The morning mist cooled me to the bone, more so after walking across the night without a coat or a hat on. The chill had settled inside of me, gnawing at every inch of my body. My legs, shaky and tired, were struggling to support my weight. New injuries atop old ones ached and throbbed.

I breathed in the brine in the air like it was my only lifeline, like it would heal me when it reached my lungs. No matter how much air I breathed in, it wasn't enough, and I collapsed on the sand, gasping. My knees hit the ground, sending a jolt of pain coursing through my body.

The sun was tentative to arrive, still hidden by the retreating night. The lightening sky spread above me. On the horizon, I could see the star that was not a star, its bright light reflecting across the water. The star of sunrise. Of sundown. The brightest planet. I closed my eyes.

"I did it," I mumbled to it. I couldn't yell it out, but the need to hear it aloud pushed the words past my lips. A quiet plea, fleeing with the night.

I was wheezing, every breath a shard of glass running from my mouth to my lungs. My chest was being lashed with lightning, hot flashes of pain every time I inhaled.

Holding my silence, I pulled my prayer beads out of my pocket and pushed them against the sand, my hazy eyes fixed on the star. The pearls shone in the wet golden sand, the blood from my split knuckles staining them and the shore. The sun, tucked away like a secret, was by now a halo at the start of sunrise. But the pearls shone all the same, radiant in the light of the morning star.

When the salt white waves came, I smiled. As the sun rose, a nonsensical song filled my ears. Made of the breaking of the waves, the chirping of the birds and the ringing of wind chimes.

She came out of the water; more specifically, she became out of the water. She was a wave, then she was a woman. Then she was standing, bathed in sea foam and glistening with salt, dragging her long dress behind her like a fog blanket. Her bare feet left indents in the sand; the water did not wash them away. The pink and blue fabric of her tunic diaphanous, pinned in place by pearls.

She had never come to me in this way before, so corporeal, so real. I've never doubted her presence, yet I've never seen her. Her soft rose-kissed skin, decorated with gold paint; her long wavy hair, pinker than her skin, dissolving into the water. I never wavered in my devotion, I never wavered in my love, and my reward is this. She has come for me.

Below my astonishment, the heat of shame enveloped me. She was seeing me as I am now, cold and disheveled in the aftermath of what I've done, my own damnation painting my skin. I could not meet her eyes like this, wounded and aching and so full of hate.

"I am not worthy of you," I breathed out. I plastered my forehead to the sand, closed my eyes and extended my hands to her. That was all I could offer, a battered, battle-ridden body, mangled and scarred beyond repair. I was nothing, but I was all I had, and I'd give it up willingly to her.

And then she said: "I'll make you worthy."

And I rose, because I ought to.

Her hand pressed to my head, light as a feather. I felt the grains of sand clinging to my scalp as she combed her fingers through my short hair. Up close, she was so much bigger than me; I had to crane my neck up to see her face. She tilted her head, a beguiling smile on her lips. She was magnificent.

"How do I appear to you?" she asked, leveling her head to mine. "How do you see me, I wonder?"

"Beautiful," I breathed out, because what else could I say? And she smiled at me like it was a secret, just for the two of us to know.

"Describe me," she commanded. And I complied.

I told her about her eyes, blue like the ocean, dark and saturated, big and open. I told her about her skin, pink and unreal, soft as a petal. About her long hair melting into the wet sand like cotton candy would, leaving only a trail of pink. I told her about her cheeks, round and welcoming, framing her smile. The cruel tilt of her lips, and the kind pucker balancing it. The false dichotomy of the two, not opposing forces, but the same in different iterations. I told her about her dress, the layers of fabric, the strings of pearls on her shoulders, on her neck, over her head. She touched my cheek when I finished.

"How fun," she said, and it sounded like thank you. I was grateful as well, for her. I've never felt her so loving, so gentle and tender, as if her touch alone would make me float away like a soap bubble. Yet in her eyes I could see my own hate and pain reflected back at me. A mirror of understanding.

The torrential bout of feeling coursing through my body brought me to tears.

Love was her, I knew, and love was an emotion ever present. Just like anger required love. And sadness wouldn't come without it. It was the same for tenderness, bitterness and protection. All actions come first from a place of love, from a place of loving oneself or another. She thought me that, I could feel her reminding me in the way she cradled my head. Love seemed purer, knowing all this. Loving her seemed unavoidable, like breathing. I loved her in all of her forms. That is the reason I did what I did.

I've seen her rage-filled, righteous with madness, claiming death and destruction alike. I've seen her tumbled over the waves, rolling on her own sea of tears, quivering with earth-shattering grief. I've seen her extend a hand to tuck away her lovers and her friends behind her unwavering protection, her neck craned like a swan and her eyes bright with fury.

I've seen Aphrodite do all this without seeing her at all. I've known she'd done it. She'll do it for me if she felt I needed it. Like she feels I need the gentle caress of a mother now.

"You did it?" she asked, soft like a breeze. I nodded, now unable to speak it aloud. Her hands came to rest on top of mine, still holding onto the prayer beads, still bleeding from the knuckles.

"How was it?"

And I sobbed to her. Everything that I was barely containing spilled out at last. Because it was horrible. It had been a thunderous, bone-chilling thing, and it had felt so right I could not find remorse in any place of my body. I had brought death to men like I had offered love to her, in a radical attempt to protect myself and every woman from them. I had destroyed them so they could not destroy me anymore.

All I had lost in the process were not things I had to begin with. All they'd taken allowed me to take life from them. My new injuries, my next scars, meant something different from what the old ones did.

"I did it for you," I sobbed out. Because she must know, she must know. All I did was for her. To be worthy of moments like this. Of her soft hand caressing my scar, trailing its ragged edge from my forehead to my cheek, across the ridge of my broken nose. Of her other hand, clinging to mine and the prayer beads, smudged with blood and dipped in sand. I knew she understood me better than I did. She remembered all, like I did.

I was young when it happened. Guilty of the crime of being common and ugly, I was but a scrawny child. And I was punished for it. For being who I am, for not being with them, for being born with a crooked smile and a loud voice. They imparted their judgment and their wrath. With their hands they broke my ribs. With a rock they cracked my skull and my face. With a wooden stick they had their fun shattering my knees.

I was ugly then, alive but destroyed. And in that sorrow, I found her. When I was no more than blood and broken bone for months, I found her waiting for me. She had loved me into loving what I could do. She had protected me, taught me to demand protection. She had angered me and directed me to them. And, a few hours ago, in her name, I had broken their skulls, shattered their legs, and ended their lives. I had never felt so loving as when I did so.

Now, at the time of confession, I could only find one source of guilt.

"I am not worthy, still," I confessed to her. "I hate it, my face, my hands, my scars. I hate everything."

She shushed me and kissed my cheeks, her eyes thunderous blue, torrential rain, infintely kind. She looked back to the shoreline, where the salt waves crashed, white with foam and bubbles, and took me by the hand.

"What makes one worthy is not what they think of themselves," she said simply. "I make you worthy. My loving, my care, my anger. My feelings alone make you worthy of me," she sighed, dragging me along through the sand. "You can only make yourself worthy of you. Which is nothing now, and it will continue to be nothing, until you make it everything."

She walked me by the hand until my feet felt the wash of the waves, cool and soothing on my skin.

"Tell me, my dove," she said, sounding like another wave, crashing against the shore with fuzzy foam. "When you love me, you love my beauty and nothing more?"

And I told her no. When a mortal loves a goddess like I love her, the mortal must love everything there is. I told her I love her need for pain, her thoughts of blood baths and destruction. And

HYMN TO THE PAIN

I love her salt tears, white as clouds, bittersweet with pent-up emotion. And I love her scolding hand, the reprimands of love, vicious and vile. And I love her playful mischief, her joy when she sees pain, when she sees grief, her amusement over a broken heart. She is all of this at once, and I love it all so completely that I fear it might consume me sometimes. That I might as well become one of the pearls adorning her, only so I could love her and nothing more.

We walked together, tracing a path around rocks. The water reached my knees, lapping at my skin in warm undulations.

"When I love," she said to me, with the sternness of a mother imparting a lesson, "When I love, I love the uglier parts first." She breathed in the air and extended a hand out towards the horizon, where her star had been.

"When I love my husband, Hephaestus, I love his mended bones first, his grief and resentment; I love the pain I left within him; and the joy I bring, I love last. I love all this, with my company and my words." She let go of my hand and raised both hands to the sky. "When I love my lover, Ares, I kiss his deepest battle scars first, I savor his defeat and his bitterness and I fight him and for him. The gentle caresses, the soft sweet quietness of contentment, comes sweeter if given at the end." She paused once more, lowering her hands, but keeping her head high. "When I take a mortal, as a lover or as a friend, I find what he or she hates most in the world, what causes them most pain and most suffering of all; and I hold it tenderly, and I raise it to my lips. With all the disgust and shame they feel, I love this first. Then I love their pride, then I love their lust, then I love and I love and I love." She looked at me at last. "This is the nature of my love, and sometimes love looks like hate, and sometimes it's unfair and hurtful, but it is love, and it's what I have for you today."

I was breathless.

She dipped her hand into the water, dragging her palm along the surface before submerging it and bring it back up. Her hand, empty before, now held a red and yellow apple, glistening and wet. She smiled at it, brought it to her nose and sniffed it, inhaling the scent. The droplets of water slid against her skin, glimmering as if made from stars and not water.

She reached for me, using her free hand to touch my short hair, running her fingers in it. I felt it latching onto the back of my skull. Her eyes became tormented when she brought the apple to my lips, pushing my jaw open and letting me bite from her hand, letting me eat the sweet fruit from her own fingers. The salty water and the sweet apple dug a hole in me, a hole of want and pain. Tears prickled my eyes and slid down my cheeks as I chewed. As I ate, I felt the hole grow bigger and fill up at the same time. Before I had time to understand, there was no apple left. I had eaten all of it, even the hard core and its seeds.

"My dove," she called me, loving and sad; and I realized she was crying as well. Thick, glistening white tears, smooth and pearlescent, glided down her round cheeks, dropping from her chin. "You are worthy, as it is now."

When she plunged my head into the water, I was startled, but I didn't fight. I made myself limp and pliant. I let my body drop like a rock and turn soft like a plum in her hand.

The iron grip on my scalp, the water rushing into my nose, my ears, my mouth, invading my body and pouring into the hole the apple had left. Over the sound of the muffled waves, the echo of her weeping reached me and struck me like thunder. I fought then, to be let up and gasp for air. I felt my lungs giving up inside of me, battered and tired. They had not much left to give. I tried not to; I tried to stay put for her, to control my body and my need to breathe. And then I heard her voice, racketing against my skull.

"Fight, my dove, like you always have."

And I did. I thrashed and kicked. I reached out of the water to grasp at her dress, at her arms, finding only air and loose fabric. Nothing to grip, nothing to make a difference. The water surrounded me, painted with sand, floating up from the bottom in a reproach with each of my kicks.

When my body stopped the fight, I became angry with myself. I reprimanded myself for giving up for, my letting go. And she pushed me deeper, sent me down into the sand. I felt my cheek touch the bottom, my body heavy and unmoving.

The sand, opening below me, claimed my limbs and my head and my body. Swallowing it down like I had swallowed each bite of fruit.

When I emerged, I didn't gasp for air. I just came up.

The world unblurred to reveal the soft hues of the sunrise. I was no longer on a gloomy beach in the north, but in a warm pool of the bluest water, floating among water lilies and rose petals. A fountain rose up in the center, pouring out more blue water and sea foam.

Around me, crowding over the edge of the pool, were women and men in soft flowing gowns, wet and glimmering, their hands touching the water, their eyes joyful and their smiles sincere as they beckoned me over. The inviting song of the wind chimes and the birds resonating above me.

The sunrise, eternally warm, was leaking in between the columns, painting them and the stone floor with soft hues of orange and pink. The silks hung in between each column did nothing to hide the bare sky. I felt it seeping into my skin, calming my aches.

Eager to see more, I made my way to the edge of the pool. The people there pulled me out by my arms, gently, like plucking a flower off its stem. They tucked roses in my hair and rubbed oil over my arms and legs. My skin was no longer its usual tan color but, as it came out of the water, it was blue. Rich and unblemished in its new hue, reflecting the light, slick with holy water and oil. They pinned a tunic to me. They moved me and touched me on my shoulders, on my hands, on my head, as I passed along the path they made for me. In front of me stood marbled stairs, adorned in silky carpet and scattered with pillows all the way up to the high dais. My knees still rattled with each step, my lungs still throbbed from the lack of air, yet I'd never felt so healthy.

I climbed up with my head low. Unspilled tears pooled in my eyes as I reached the feet of the dais, where she lay reclined on cushions and ate pomegranates seed by seed. I dropped to my knees in front of her.

When she spoke, her sweet voice sounded different here. More thunderous, stronger.

HYMN TO THE PAIN

"This is my court," she said, "and this is you."

Aphrodite held out a circular mirror in front of me, her grip lax. In its reflection, my blue face looked back at me. My same hollow cheeks, with a scatter of dark blue freckles over each cheekbone. My same short dark hair, from which my ears peeked out, round and silly. My same droopy eyes with my short lashes, dark and unremarkable. My same thin lips, and the little mark I have there. And, across my forehead, over the ridge of my broken nose, tracing down to my cheek, my scar.

I smiled at my reflection, ecstatic to see it there, still worthy to be with me when I was perfect.

I might hate it all, but it didn't make me love it less.

I looked up at Aphrodite. And, with a jolt of boldness and joy, leaped into her arms. Her warm embrace enveloped me. Her fear and anger and resentment too. Her sadness and grief and amusement as well. Over all, her joy and sweetness and love.

And I loved her, like a pearl pinned to her tunic.

Feasts of the Fair and Fowl
Ali Habashi

She hatches, as all sirens do, on the foamy crest of a wave. As she matures, she pursues several flocks before finding acceptance in a group with only two others. Neither yet have their adult plumage, being young enough that downy fluff still layers their bodies like white algae over a rock.

Aphrodite (the name the others have bestowed upon her) still waits for the first of her feathers to protrude from her skin, and begins to grow self-conscious as they fail to appear, leaving her with a complexion as soft and bare as a human's.

This weakness, this wrongness, becomes very evident when they are forced to migrate from the ship graveyard that they have constructed about themselves in their earliest youth. The flock settles upon a small island with no soft sands to perch upon, and Aphrodite feels the scrape of the gray stone each time she dives into the water to thrust her sputtering prey beneath the waves.

The way that the sailors' limp bodies bob on the water is only a mild comfort.

"What will you do, Aphrodite," says Aglaophonos, "when our feathers grow as thick as the green weeds that wash ashore in great clumps? When our wings are strong and we alight like goddesses upon the air to snatch the sailors from their posts?

What will you do with your bare arms, smooth and pale as the inside of a shell?"

"The sailors play a game with the sirens who cannot fly," says Molpe. "The men stop their ears with wax so that they cannot be swayed by her voice, nor be driven mad by her song. They hunt and capture the flightless siren and cook her when they go ashore. The humans host a feast with music that rings out over the water while the meat blackens over the fire and they drink her blood watered down like wine."

"My feathers will grow," declares Aphrodite, but she is unsure. The feeling shrinks her.

The merchant ships are always her favorite to draw towards the rocks. When they run aground, they spill forth their goods into the water like an offering. She smashes open wooden shells to sample their treasure – salted meats and olives, sweet honey, white cheeses, and bitter wine that makes her head swim deliciously. Her sisters taunt her for her evolving tastes, but the teasing is worth it for the fine accompaniment these offerings make to her usual meal of man.

Blood rises in clouds around her as she chews her way through flesh and figs.

She much admires the weapons, the talons that the humans have crafted from metal that gleam like the sun upon the water. There is also pottery, which makes a pleasing sound when it too is shattered. Some of the pottery is adorned with painted stories, men dressed for war, monsters bent in supplication and gods that tower over all else.

It is a merchant ship that captures her.

Aglaophonos and Molpe have spent weeks now gliding languidly through the skies as easily as they did through the water, Aphrodite's unblinking stare upon them. Now that all of the infant fluff of their bodies has been replaced with sleek plumage the color of cloud and shadow, they have taken to calling her ugly, flexing their wingspans so that each perfect feather drips in a majestic cape from their arms.

Her sisters are outfitted in their new colors, from their breasts to their scaly feet. Aphrodite feels acutely each breeze that blows across her bare form, an unwanted touch, an admonishment.

Ugly.

It is her sisters that draw the attention of the merchant crew, their song ringing out in harmonious layers overhead. Aphrodite raises her voice as well, although she is sure she sounds far away to the ears of her companions and her victims.

Her sisters, at last, move towards her perch and she swells with anticipation, awaiting the ship's adjusted course. Instead, it slows to a stop, the great wooden hull stubbornly pointed away from their trap. Infuriatingly, the ship still seems captained by someone in their right mind, and carefully, the ship turns, its oars crawling many-legged towards her.

Aphrodite slips into the water and dives beneath the blue. This, at least, she can do. She moves with a swiftness strengthened by the promise of fresh meat. Soon, the sailors would splash, muffled, into the brine with her. Then she would wrap her fist in their hair and drag them so deep that only the bottom feeders would find what she left behind.

The surface is disturbed, and Aphrodite hurtles towards the ship to begin her work. This is much needed, after the days she's spent confined to land, head tipped back to glare at the open sky.

Her fingers, grasping, are abruptly ringed with line, and too late she finds herself entangled in a net. She thrashes, incensed, but has only a moment before everything tightens around her. There is little more jarring than being pulled from the water and into the air, and she gasps and thinks foolishly for a moment that she is flying.

The net scrapes and bumps against the side of the ship, where the oars have been drawn in on one side. Hands grasp at her, roughly handling her over the side and onto the deck.

Her sisters' song is silent, and she wonders at the quiet. This is the only reason she does not sing.

Instead, she stands, slowly, and the net falls from her easily enough.

A crew of men, watching her with trepidation, face her aboard the ship. Their eyes skip over her breasts, greedily skim over the expanse of her body.

"She is no siren," says one man, turning to the crew member next to him. Aphrodite sees, as he turns his head, that his ears are plugged with something like thick grease.

Wax, she thinks. *The song will not work.*

"A woman pulled from the sea in siren territory certainly seems a siren to me," responds another man.

Their eyes promise pain. There is an eager, unsympathetic gleam to their stares now, at once hungry and mindless. It seems an unfair scenario, that they should be clothed while she shouldn't. Once, after she had scraped her legs raw upon the rough rocks, she was pursued through the water by a shark that had tasted of her blood. The vulnerability of being pursued had felt, in a way, exhilarating. Natural.

This is different.

There is a danger distinct to humans, one that is manipulative and clever and vicious. A danger that drives them to craft their own talons from metal, and then justify their use against entire populations.

Aphrodite knows this; she has seen the pottery.

Fear twists at her gut as she pictures the game her sisters had described. The hunt. Aglaophonos and Molpe are no longer overhead, and even if they were, rescue would be unlikely. For all of their posturing, her sisters much prefer to snatch their prey from the sea, waterlogged and flailing.

"Are you a siren?" asks one of the men.

Aphrodite shakes her head, no. She feels that her rocky perch is shrinking behind them as they sail onwards, and she is careful not to look back.

"A woman?"

Their eyes are still on her body, ravenous, waiting.

No, instinct demands she tell them. She knows from the painted pottery that there is only one being that towers over all else.

"Neither beast nor woman? Then what?"

"Unstop your ears. If she tries to sing, then we will kill her."

"I think that attempt is best left to you, my friend."

One man, brazen in youth, steps forth and digs the wax from his ears.

"Who are you?" he asks, voice breaking over his words.

She can feel the fear of discovery rush hot and cold over her skin, pound at her chest, crawl up her throat. Everything in her screams at her to sing, to drive these men, or at least this one man, overboard with the last of her breath. She opens her mouth.

"I am the goddess Aphrodite," she says. "And I have saved you from the sirens."

It takes surprisingly little to lie to these men. She is fascinated to discover that her voice holds sway even with no melody to accompany it. Evidently, she has a gift for storytelling.

Aphrodite tells the men that she has risen from the waves to help them on their journey and keep them safe from sirens, who will snatch men from the deck of their ships only to drop them like shellfish upon the rocks. She tells them that no siren would dare attack a ship with her favor.

They ask many questions, and she answers them in ways that she suspects will please them.

What is she goddess of?

Pleasure and procreation.

Will she bless them with lovers upon their return to shore?

Of course, for she is also the goddess of love.

Had she the favor of any other gods?

Yes, for when she first strode fully formed from the sea foam, many gods were charmed by her visage and wished to make her their lover.

The crew's expressions have changed with each unfounded declaration, until their predators' stares are gentled with curiosity and wonder.

"Surely, you are the most beautiful among the goddesses?" asks the young man that first exposed himself to her voice. His eyes flick nervously between her face and her body, attempting and failing to show respect.

Aphrodite, who has never been called beautiful before, finds herself pleased by the title. She smiles in the way that her sisters do when they are preening under her jealous gaze. The boy's embarrassed stare drops to his feet under the warmth of it.

"There is no radiance that can match sweet Aphrodite's," another man agrees. She bestows her smile upon him as well.

"What offering do you prefer, Aphrodite, goddess of beauty?"

She thinks greedily of everything she has tasted, of what may be stored on this very merchant ship. She imagines singing the men overboard, now that their ears are open to her.

"When your voyage is over," she declares, "we will celebrate your safe return with a feast, and music that carries over the waves. This way we may taunt the sirens, our most hated enemies. Until then, I will require a covering, to keep my modesty and virtue among you, my brave sailors."

She only wants a small taste, she thinks, of what humanity has to offer her. Then she will return to the sea and her sisters. Her rocky outcrop that scrapes holes into ships and into her knees.

Upon dry land, no one asks her to prove her godhood. Weaving stories, she finds, is enough. There are endless humans, desperate to follow the direction of another. And so she leads them.

Feasts beget offerings beget sacrifices.

Men are happy to praise her beauty, benevolence, and grace. She sees in their faces what they do not say. Lust oozes from their pores in her presence. It wafts from them.

The word beautiful still pleases her, despite the stink of it.

Artists clamber to chip her likeness into stone, usually depicting her in some state of undress. Temples are erected in her name, many in port cities, and she herself resides in one with a bath at the center. She has her attendants pour ocean water into it, and she rests in her slice of sea as worshipers flood through her doors. She wears a chiton now that clings to her wetly and rests lightly in ripples around her. It is immodest to a degree, but it also denies the men the nakedness they have come to expect of her.

Men and women alike bring her armfuls of roses and myrtle, and she tears the petals from their stems and scatters them in her waters. She does the same with the pearls that are bestowed upon her, so that the smooth rounds of their bodies wink temptingly from the bottom of her bath. There are several species of birds that are gifted to her in cages. These she frees.

The humans, blessedly, also bring food, gifts that she had once stolen like an animal, to consume damp and salty.

She plucks at pomegranates, admires as their jeweled seeds burst and bleed down her wrist. Sailors bring her every meat that she misses – plates laden with oysters and cockles, carved swordfish, savory tuna and eel. One man makes a habit of bringing her fresh apples, skinned and candied with golden honey.

Aphrodite endears this man to one of her lovelier worshippers – one Helen of Troy.

Women often take her advice on love and on childbirth. Love is easy enough to lie about, she finds. The humans prioritize passion over peace, so even the most wretched of her suggested affairs do not condemn her as a fraud. In fact, these failed or violent relations only further serve her purpose, as the humans insist that these are merely punishments for any woman who believes herself more beautiful than Aphrodite.

On the matter of human procreation, she is less well versed, and nearly gives herself away with her earliest advice on the safest place to lay one's eggs before their hatching. It is of no consequence. Her mistakes are explained away by her worshippers, ignored or forgotten by her attendants. Contradictions, hypocrisy and logic are nothing in the face of human faith.

There is only one offering she must still take for herself.

Sparingly at first, then more frequently, she calls upon men to visit her in the late evening, when the worshippers have cleared away and her attendants are at rest. Aphrodite is selective, choosing only the most smugly confident. She reads the superiority in their smirks, sees that they expect her to be impressed by them, no matter how insignificant their feats, or how dull their lives.

She, a goddess.

They steal into her temple and she beckons them into her bath. They shed their himations, their chitons, their tunics, and slide into the water naked and eager. Aphrodite glides to meet them, chiton flowing around her, and weaves her fingers in their hair.

Then she presses them down, thrashing, into her nest of pearls.

Rumors abound about the men that are seen for the last time vanishing into her temple.

They are Aphrodite's lovers, of course, say the humans. Perhaps they are even the gods that so admire her. Nerites. Dionysos. Poseidon. Ares. Hephaestos. There are even a few mortal men who bed her, they say.

A divine punishment, that last one.

The humans cast her in whichever role suits them best: sensuous lover, reluctant wife, promiscuous adulterer, adoring mother. There is always a level of condemnation to each title, Aphrodite notices. Gods do not seem to receive the same level of judgment.

But then again, there are no gods. Only her, and her endless appetite.

Ever since her first feast ashore, she has insisted upon them as often as is appropriate. It has been an age since she last sang, and she so enjoys the hymns that swell at her presence, the tables laden with food that stretch before her.

She drapes herself in the rarest of colors, the finest of materials, the most ostentatious of her jewelry. She picks the blood from beneath her nails and between her teeth, and she beams beatifically at her worshippers, their voices merry and harmonious.

It is on a particularly hot day that this feast is held. Aphrodite longs for her salt sea bath, swirling cool around her. Her skin is dry with the want.

She is sat upon a marble ceremonial chair, and absently she brushes her fingers down the carved pattern of the arm rests. Her attention is arrested with the arrival of the men in armor.

Aphrodite enjoys men in armor. They sink remarkably fast. Their offerings, too, are good, although the smell of blood sometimes still lingers around them.

This day, their gift is shrouded in cloth.

"Beautiful Aphrodite," one says. "Goddess of love, of pleasure, and exalted protector of sailors. Please accept our gift to you. Your most hated enemies, captured and silenced."

They draw back the curtain to reveal a set of cages beneath, larger than any she has yet seen. And within, their wings clipped and mangled, their mouths sewn shut, are Aglaophonos and Molpe.

Her sisters.

Aphrodite has not felt this way since she first rose from the net to stand naked before the merchant crew. Aglaophonos whimpers as her gaze falls upon her. In Molpe's eyes, she notices, there is a dull sheen that is near lifeless in its apathy.

She has never seen her sisters so…

Ugly.

It enrages her. It pleases her. It scares her.

Her gaze lifts to the humans, their eager faces, and to the ocean beyond. Aphrodite has always known that she would return one day to the sea, no matter how reluctant she was to do so. Sirens, too, grow old.

And a goddess of beauty must not grow old.

Aglaophonos and Molpe, despite their teasing, were her flock. Her family. No matter the years that passed, they would still be so once she returned. But an old, flightless siren would find no love, even cruel love, with a new flock.

And what of these humans? If they ever discover her secret, her lies, was this to be her punishment? Caged and voiceless?

No, she knows. *It will be worse.*

Aphrodite is not so naive now. Humans delight in their punishments, and their powerplay. The rumors that flow around her in a never-ending tide are all tinged with critical condemnation. She is locked in the body of a woman, and made vulnerable by it, even in godhood.

It has been ages since she last sang.

I can do it now, she thinks. *Sing them all straight into the sea.*

Then they three can return, flightless, to the water together.

She gazes longingly at the table laden with food, at the humans that cluster around it, shiny worship on their faces. The ones that call her beautiful. The ones that bring her every treasure they can spare. The ones that listen to her stories and forgive her missteps with barely a blink.

The ones that steal into her pool without even a song to guide them.

Aglaophonos and Molpe, she thinks, never loved her half as much as these humans do. Will never love her so, even if she sacrifices every pleasure for them. Even if she drowns the world, wrenches open their cage bars, and tears open their mouths to free their voices.

Would they worship her too, for their rescue? Or would they simply sneer, and declare that she was just as hideous as the day that she vanished?

Surely a goddess deserves more than that.

"Does this please you?" asks the man that has captured her sisters.

Aphrodite lifts her face to address the crowd, and opens her mouth.

All's Fair

Xoe Juliani

There is a saying, among the mortals, that love is cruel. It is not. Love is a force, like any other, and it cannot be kind or cruel, it can simply *be*.

Aphrodite is not kind. She knows that. She does her best not to be cruel.

It is cruel, perhaps, what she is doing to the girl. The mortals whisper that it is, that Aphrodite has targeted her because of her beauty. *"She has offended the goddess,"* they whisper, *"and the goddess will take her revenge."* Aphrodite lets them whisper, and she does not argue. The truth of it does not matter, not to them.

The truth of it is that Aphrodite's cruelty is only to prevent something far worse.

There is a prophecy about the girl, about who she will marry. More specifically, about *what* she will marry. The Fates have said that her husband will be a cruel, evil creature that even Zeus would fear. Zeus dismissed it as folly, but Aphrodite knew who the girl's husband would be the moment she heard the words.

There is little that can be done to stop the Fates once they have spoken. She will still do whatever she can to protect this girl from her son.

The girl is brave, at least. Aphrodite watches as she stands on the rocky crag, her head held high. Her outfit is a wedding dress and a funeral dress all in one, but she wears it with pride. Aphrodite has always respected pride.

The girl's hands tremble slightly, the only break in her facade.

When her wedding procession is entirely gone, Aphrodite flicks her fingers. Beside her, Zephyr moves obediently, curling the girl up in his grasp. Aphrodite lets him take her, not daring to follow them to the grove. The girl is only safe if no one knows where she is, and Aphrodite is expecting a visitor.

"Mother."

Aphrodite turns. "Eros."

"Where is she?"

Aphrodite had sent Eros out to find a monster for the girl to fall in love with, something horrible enough to fulfill the prophecy. She'd expected him to be gone longer, but she dared not plan for it.

"I sent her away, to wait. Have you found something sufficiently horrible for her to love?"

Eros's eyes narrow, and Aphrodite realizes with a sinking horror that the mania in them is worse than normal. He is the child of Love and War, his sanity never stood a chance, but this is something more. She looks down at his hands, and she sees golden blood trickling from his finger. She knows what arrowhead made that wound.

This is what happens, she thinks with regret, when anyone, even a god, tries to deny Fate.

"She will love me," Eros says.

Aphrodite is a goddess. She has lied to Zeus himself, right to his face. She does not let Eros see how her heart plummets. All of her plans are crashing to the ground around her, but she is far from helpless.

She is a goddess. She will make a new plan.

"She must not know who you are."

Eros tips his head to the side in confusion, and for a moment, all Aphrodite can see is the little boy he once was, back when the madness was just an occasional glimmer in his eye. She reaches out an unthinking hand to cup his cheek, but he scowls and bats it away before she can touch him.

"Why not?"

"You know what happens when mortals look upon the splendor of gods," Aphrodite says. "If she looks upon you in your full glory, she will burn."

It is a gamble, to think Eros would care. He can be even more bloodthirsty than his father, and the life of one mortal means little to him. But if he has trapped himself in his own power, then perhaps his sense of possession over the girl will be strong enough that he will want to keep her safe, and he has never been good at hiding himself from mortals.

"Then I will hide from her," Eros decides, and Aphrodite does not let even a glimpse of her relief show on her face. "But she will be mine. Where is she?"

There is no more point in hiding her. "Zephyr brought the girl to a grove, where a great house awaits her. She will be safe there. But you must not go to her until after nightfall."

"I will not," Eros promises. Aphrodite hopes he's lucid enough to mean it. "Will you go to her, Mother? Will you make sure she is comfortable?"

Too often, Aphrodite has to refuse her son, for his own sake or for the sake of others. Now, she can do what he asks, and she does not have to regret it.

"I will. She will want for nothing."

Eros nods. Aphrodite is about to leave when he moves forward. "Wait."

"Yes, my son?" Aphrodite asks, looking at him with eyes that reveal none of her fear. She is close, so close. But she knows well that Eros is unpredictable, and if he has changed his mind, there is little she can do to change it back.

But it seems he has not, because all he asks is, "The girl. What is her name?"

Aphrodite lets out a slow breath. "Psyche. Her name is Psyche."

* * *

Psyche, when Aphrodite reaches her, has found the house. Her eyes are wide as she examines it, but there is something guarded in them, even while she is alone. She must be wondering who her new husband is. She must be wondering what sort of monster could provide something like this.

Psyche is the daughter of a king. She has lived her whole life in splendor. None of this will be new to her, but if she is smart – and Aphrodite cannot help but think that she is – she will know that it is not easy to obtain. She will wonder how her new husband has obtained it.

Perhaps, if she is daring enough – and Aphrodite has a suspicion that she is indeed – she will wonder whether or not her new husband is mortal.

If Aphrodite shows herself to the girl, she will have to disguise herself as a human. She did not lie when she warned Eros; if Psyche sees any god in their true form, it will destroy her. But Aphrodite knows well that mortals often see through the guises of the gods, even if they pretend not to. If Psyche sees Aphrodite, she may suspect.

It is not so dangerous if she suspects her husband is a god, but it is best if she does not realize which one he is. Aphrodite will watch over her, but Psyche will not see her.

It takes little effort for a goddess to make herself unseen; Aphrodite is invisible as she steps up to Psyche. A goddess is also soundless, unless she wishes otherwise, and Aphrodite's footsteps are silent. She would have Psyche hear her words, though, and she says, "You may make yourself comfortable."

Psyche startles, whirling around. There is panic in her eyes, but she does not lose herself entirely. Aphrodite is glad to see it. She will need every advantage if she is to survive Eros.

"Who's there?"

Aphrodite ignores the question and opens the doors to the house with a wave of her hand. Psyche peers inside cautiously, but she does not step forward through the doors.

"You may enter," Aphrodite tells her. "The house is yours now. You may do as you wish. A feast will be ready for you when you are ready to eat. Your husband will visit you tonight."

"And who is my husband?" Psyche asks.

Aphrodite does not let her grief tinge her voice. "You know the words of the oracle, child."

Psyche closes her eyes, and for a moment, she looks nearly as old as Aphrodite feels. Resignation follows closely, and when she opens her eyes again, her youthful beauty has returned.

"Your husband will visit you tonight," Aphrodite repeats. "You must not look upon him."

Psyche is clever, and Aphrodite hopes she will not be taken in solely by beauty. But Eros is love itself, and if she sees him, her fear may lessen. Her only hope is if Eros's obsession remains one-sided and fades. His obsessions never last long. With time, he will move onto something else, and with luck, that will leave Psyche free.

"I cannot look upon my own husband?" Psyche repeats. Even to a goddess, her tone is unreadable.

"You cannot," Aphrodite confirms. "I am sorry."

The apology is for more than Psyche can ever know.

* * *

Sometimes, Aphrodite wonders if Zeus was more far-seeing than he seemed when he gave her in marriage to Hephaestus. Not because he thought she would love him, but because of what their child would be. Or, perhaps, what their child would *not* be. Hephaestus is the god of metalworking, of blacksmiths, of craftsmen. A child of Love and Crafting would be passionate, but not dangerous.

But Aphrodite is not one to be bound to only one man, and she was not nearly far-seeing enough when she lay with Ares. She had thought it to be an entertaining dalliance, one pleasant enough to repeat when the urge struck her. She had not thought about their child. She had not thought about what they would be. Even when her womb had quickened, she had not thought about what she would bring into the world.

She loved Eros, when she bore him and swaddled him and held him to her breast. She loves him still, even now. If she could reverse time, if she could warn her past self, she does not think she would, not if it meant the loss of her child.

But that does not make him any less of a danger to everything around him.

Aphrodite is his mother. All she can do is take responsibility for her son and hope that someday, she will be strong enough to stop him.

* * *

Aphrodite played little part in Zeus's vengeance with Pandora. She made the woman beautiful, as requested, but it was Zeus's vengeance, not hers; she cared little for it. She did wonder, though, how something so simple as curiosity could cause the doom of all humanity.

Now, as her plan teeters on the brink of ruin, she understands the danger that curiosity can bring.

Psyche's sisters set the events in motion, but it is Aphrodite's own fault for not anticipating it. Psyche had wanted so desperately to see her family again, and Aphrodite, more fool her, had not seen the harm in it. She had urged Eros gently, in the roundabout way that Eros could sometimes be urged, and he had agreed. Zephyr had been sent out for Psyche's sisters, and he had brought them to the grove, where they had dined with Psyche in her grand home and looked at the splendor of her grand life and burned with curiosity as to the identity of her grand husband. Psyche had been curious too, but she had been restrained. She had been cautious, wary. She had remembered Aphrodite's warning, Aphrodite thought, and she would heed it.

But her sisters had urged her otherwise. Aphrodite can only blame herself for not seeing it coming. Of course her sisters would wish to know the truth. Whether out of familial concern for their younger sister or out of envy at her decadent life, they would surely want to know who their sister had married, and Psyche could only hold out against her curiosity for so long. If she were pushed…

And so she had not listened. And so she had looked. And so she had discovered, at long last, the truth.

It would not have been so dangerous, except that Psyche wounded herself on one of Eros's arrows in her shock, and now she is searching for her husband.

The only saving grace is that Eros fled when the hot oil spilled on him instead of attacking. Aphrodite had found him and corralled him, and she has been able to keep him contained since, but she knows she will not be able to forever. But if she can keep him at bay for long enough, then she hopes the effects of the arrows will wear off, and ideally, neither Eros nor Psyche will retain any love for the other. If she can simply wait until Eros becomes disinterested, until his wild mind latches onto something new, perhaps Psyche can still be saved.

The arrow has not worn off yet, at least not for Eros. "Leave the girl," Aphrodite tries to urge him as she tends to his wounds. "She is not worth the trouble."

"She is mine," Eros replies coldly. "I will have her, Mother."

He is steadfast. Aphrodite will have to wait.

Psyche cannot be allowed to reach Eros, of course, but Aphrodite cannot be obvious in her machinations. As subtly as she can, she guides the girl to temples of her fellow goddesses, ones she hopes will take pity on her. Psyche prays in the temples of Demeter and Hera, and both give her what favor they can. But they cannot take a stand against another god, they will not risk war on Olympus, and even if it is with regret, they still send Psyche on her way.

It is dangerous for Aphrodite to step in herself. It could easily go wrong. Eros still languishes with her, and Aphrodite fears to let him and Psyche get too close. Even she does not always understand the power of Eros's arrows, and she knows their proximity will bring risk.

But she is the only one who can help Psyche, and she will do everything that she can.

She delays Psyche as long as she can, and then finally, she lets her arrive. The girl is worn and desperate, a far cry from the beauty in the grove. Her beauty remains, but her mania has sharpened it. It reminds Aphrodite of Eros, and she hides a shudder at the thought.

"I know my husband is Eros," Psyche says. "Your son. I know he is here."

"You should find yourself a new husband," Aphrodite tells her. "Go now. You are beautiful enough to manage it with ease."

Psyche shakes her head. "I cannot." Eros's mania glints in her eyes. She will not listen to reason until it wears off.

Aphrodite will simply have to delay her until it does.

"Then you must prove yourself worthy of him," she says. "You will serve me."

Psyche only hesitates an instant before she drops her to knees. "Yes, my lady. What would you have me do?"

Aphrodite brings her to a barn full of mixed grains. "You must separate them all by type. Each must have its own pile."

Psyche looks around the barn in despair. "It will take an eternity."

"You may leave instead," Aphrodite offers. "Find a new husband. Forget the old one."

Psyche steels herself, her back straightening. She still does have the confidence and strength that she did before, only bent in a more dangerous direction.

"I will do it for my husband."

"Very well."

The task is nigh on endless. Aphrodite designed it that way. If Psyche can be delayed with the mindless task, her feelings toward Eros will wear away.

Only some small creature decides to help Psyche, thinking itself to take pity on her, and the task is completed in a single night. Psyche stands before the piles of grains, her head held high.

"May I visit Eros?"

Aphrodite shakes her head. "Your tasks are not yet done."

* * *

Aphrodite cannot blame the world and its creatures for taking pity on Psyche. She is pitiable, and anyone who did not know the reasons behind Aphrodite's tasks for her would think them torture. No one can know that they are to save her.

But because no one knows, Psyche is repeatedly helped, and that means she has been able to fulfill Aphrodite's tasks far more quickly than expected. She has gathered golden wool and black water, and the effects of the arrow have shown no signs of wearing off. Aphrodite is a goddess, she does not feel desperation, but even she must admit that she is growing close.

What she needs is to buy more time. Her plans to do that have failed so far, but there is one further option, one she has thus far not needed to resort to. Now she has no other choice, so she calls Psyche before her, and she sends her to the Underworld.

It is a risk. Most mortals cannot go to the Underworld and return. But Psyche has the blessing and support of goddesses and nature spirits alike, and Aphrodite cannot help but think at least one of them will help her. And the season is right for the Underworld to have its queen, and Persephone, Aphrodite knows, will help. Persephone, who has struggled for so long to bear a child of Life and Death, is one of the few that Aphrodite has dared speak to of the depths of Eros's madness, and Aphrodite is confident that she will understand the truth behind her actions. Persephone will help.

Aphrodite sends Psyche to the Underworld with the command that she return with a box of beauty, and she trusts Persephone will remember their old joke and know what it means.

And Persephone does, for when Psyche opens the box – as of course she does, with her mortal curiosity; Aphrodite knows it well enough to plan for it now – she finds it is filled with sleep, enough to send her into an immediate and deep slumber. She falls, and Aphrodite prepares to go and collect her.

She forgets, in her haste, that Eros is mostly healed. She forgets that the effects of the arrow on him have not faded, or they have woven themselves into his normal mania. She forgets that he will do whatever he thinks is necessary to find his wife.

Aphrodite finds Psyche, but Eros finds her first.

* * *

Long ago, Hephaestus caught Aphrodite and Ares in one of their trysts and captured them in a net strong enough to hold even the gods. It was the end of their ill-fated marriage, but to the surprise of both, they grew fonder of each other as friends than they ever were as spouses. Eventually, Aphrodite dared to approach Hephaestus and tell him of Eros's madness, of her fears of what he might do, and ask that Hephaestus make something that might trap him, as he had once trapped his parents. Hephaestus told Aphrodite he would do his best, and a few days later, he gave her a delicate golden chain he claimed was unbreakable. It was beautiful enough that Aphrodite could drape it over herself as jewelry, and so she did, wearing it always. Sometimes, she almost wished she could pretend the chains *were* just jewelry, but she knew better. She knew that one day, she would have to use them.

As she faces Eros, Psyche asleep between them, she fears the day has come.

"She is my wife," Eros tells Aphrodite. "She is *mine*."

"She is a mortal," Aphrodite counters. "Do you not wish for a goddess?"

"I will make her one. I will feed her ambrosia, and she will live beside me always."

If Aphrodite could believe that Eros would be true, that he would love Psyche and care for her, she would gladly allow it. But she cannot trust it. She knows her son too well. She knows his capriciousness, knows his possessiveness, and she knows that he would stifle any wife he could find. Psyche is strong, but even she could not survive that.

Psyche is strong, and she may have another option.

"Wake her, then," Aphrodite urges Eros. The effects of the arrow have not worn off for him, but she fears they never will. For Psyche, however, Aphrodite is almost certain they must have.

She was afraid of her husband, before she knew who he was. She knew the prophecy. If her mind is clear once more, Aphrodite can only hope that her fears remain.

Eros leans down and draws the sleep from Psyche, replacing it in the box. It takes a long, breathless moment, but Psyche's eyes flutter open, and they meet Eros'.

"Oh!"

Aphrodite feels a wash of relief. That was not the sound of a woman seeing the man she loves, but the sound of a startled woman seeing a man she fears. They still have a chance.

"My love," Eros whispers, drawing Psyche into his too-tight grip. Aphrodite can see the panic in her eyes.

"Eros," she urges gently, "you are hurting her. You are holding her too tightly."

She knows, even as she speaks the words, that Eros will not care. His is the type of love that would rather break something than let anyone else have it. Sure enough, his grip only tightens.

"She is mine."

"You are hurting her. Leave her be."

"She is *mine*."

Psyche's eyes meet Aphrodite's over Eros's shoulder. Aphrodite has taken too many gambles already, but she takes another anyway, letting her jewelry slither into her hand as a chain. She angles it slightly so Psyche can see it, and she hopes the girl will understand.

She does. "Kiss me, husband," Psyche tells Eros. "If you love me, close your eyes and kiss me."

And Eros, Fates be thanked, does. His eyes fall shut as Psyche presses her lips to his, and his grip loosens just enough. Aphrodite spares a single instant to hope she can someday be forgiven for what she is about to do, and then she flicks her wrist, and the chain curls around Eros.

Hephaestus is well-known for the quality of his work. The reputation is more than fair. It only takes an instant for Eros to be bound.

"Mother?" he asks, looking at Aphrodite, and he sounds so much like a child again that her heart shatters in her chest. She wishes she could free him. She wishes she could close her eyes. She can do neither.

"I'm so sorry, my son."

Psyche takes a step back as the chains settle into place around Eros. She looks at Aphrodite with wide eyes.

"Were you trying to protect me, all along?"

"I did what I could."

"Thank you." She looks down at Eros, still bound between them. "What will become of him?"

Aphrodite dares to look down at her son. He has hardly fought the chains at all since they wrapped around him, and she cannot help but wonder why. She cannot help but hope that some part of him recognizes that he had to be stopped.

"He cannot be freed," Aphrodite says. "At least not now."

"What will the world do without him?"

"The world needs love," Aphrodite says. "I will do what I can."

Psyche looks down at Eros for a long moment, then she looks up at Aphrodite. "Can I help?"

"Do you offer this truly?"

"I do."

Aphrodite feels a small smile spread across her face, and she takes Psyche's hand.

Venus Descending
Vanessa Ziff Lasdon

The cliffs of Akrotiri are a solitary throne. The wind's cold fingers tangle my hair and salt air kisses my skin as I stand beneath the heavens. Above, Helios drapes gold and crimson across the sky. Below, the sea roars and seethes with waves of phosphorescent fire as if Poseidon himself rages against my silence.

With good reason.

Love has gone quiet in the world, and the silence is unbearable. I see the mortals' dead eyes. They forfeit embraces and hurl careless words. Once, I could hear the music of every heart, pulsing in a symphony that crested and bowed before me, constant as a lover's breath. Now, even gods grow weary of passion, our glorious entanglements poisoned by scorn.

My flame – once a boundless force that blazed within – now dims and sputters, fragile as a dying ember. I can hardly remember the last time a love story inspired me. Is this how it begins, the slow diminishing of power? Will even I – Aphrodite, goddess of love – flare out as a forgotten relic tossed into oblivion?

Tonight, the sea churns like my restless soul. Endlessly, it comes and goes, insistent and indifferent as time itself. I tighten my grip on the myrtle branch in hand; delicate buds tremble.

This is not a storm. It's a summons.

A shadow flickers in the corner of my vision, and I turn to see Hermes in his winged sandals, blocking out the rising moon. He's all light and motion, but his face carries an unfamiliar hue. Hesitation? It doesn't suit him.

"'Lo, Aphrodite." He bows.

"'Lo, Hermes."

"The Quintessence, dear heart." The mirth in his playful smirk fails to reach those golden eyes.

"You're early, Harbinger." I mock his tidings to mask my fear, but the tone is sharper than intended. He was my lover once, and we share Hermaphrodite after all.

Still, Hermes brings my reckoning front of mind. This day has pressed closer with each passing century. Every god and goddess faces the Underworld's gauntlet, but a Quintessence is the treacherous crucible that coincides with Hades' 5,000-year celestial alignment; it is meant to test the very essence of my power and my merit to possess it.

"If I refuse?" I turn away in dread, focus instead on a jeweled horizon fading into twilight.

"Without your flame, the seasons falter. Without renewal, all balance breaks."

"Indeed!" I laugh. "Is that all?"

"And Hades comes for you."

These are slashing truths; I parry with disdain. "Ho, Death himself!"

It's then the myrtle bursts into flame, crumbling to embers in my hand. I tuck them into my cloak pocket and curse my petulance. Hades, of course. He's listening, growing angry.

"Aphrodite..." Hermes' hands rest on my shoulders. "The Quintessence will show your truest self, for better or worse. So choose to reclaim what you've lost. Succeed, and soar."

"Or fail, and fade." His nearness is a balm, but my fear has become a wicked thing: a nightmare with teeth that gnash our words in wrath.

Helpless before my fate, I refuse to meet Hermes' eyes. The heavens expand into infinite gray. Every lover I've graced, every brokenhearted soul left in my wake – they wait for me below. Demanding retribution. Threatening to undo me.

"Desire, despair, jealousy, resentment, regret. Are they worth the wrenching pain, for love?"

Hermes doesn't reply. My own yearning sparks though, soul-deep and resolute. A torch in the dark. I turn at last to clasp Hermes' outstretched hand. He squeezes tight.

Ready or not, let the Quintessence begin.

* * *

My island falls away in a rush of wind and shadow. Hades hastens our arrival through a cold, heaving, stygian dark that swallows light, sound and breath alike, leaving only the memory of an echo in my mind. The chill here wants not flesh but spirit.

Dead silence. Underworldly. Hades reminds me what I have forgotten.

Only Hermes' golden sandals cut faint arcs through the gloom. He kisses my hand then releases me, his warm glow receding far behind. I don't turn to watch. My feet are planted on ancient, barren soil that seems determined to root me into place.

Eyes adjusting to the dark, I lock onto a trail of dancing lights and don't let go. They bend around some unfathomable space, and it's here that I find him: the carver.

He stands in a room of polished stone, back to me, chiseling maniacally upon grotesquely shaped marble. The metal on stone is a glorious spike of sound in the suffocating quiet.

"Pygmalion," I whisper.

He's driven by an obsession that twists mind and hands alike. Yet at his name, he freezes: knuckles white from the death grip on his chisel, handsome face contorted with anguish.

"Aphrodite," Pygmalion laughs. Brittle shards of sound ping off stone walls. His fevered eyes rake over me, but the heat in his gaze is not adoration; it's accusation. "You've ruined me!"

"I delivered you," I correct. "You asked for beauty. I gave you perfection."

"It's never enough! Look at her." The carver spits on his marble ruin. "My immaculate idol!"

I want to seethe with righteous indignation. Blame his misery on selfish mortal desires. But I hear the despair in his jeers and watch him pace like a caged animal.

"Night and day I see her, crave her, chase her; the curve of her lips, the lines of her neck. I slave for a masterpiece that masters me, for all beauty pales in your cruel brilliance! You've cursed me, Aphrodite."

I'm the muse who blessed Pygmalion's hands, the goddess who fills his dreams. But he's right. Perfection is a cursed myth. And I showed him all-consuming beauty without parallel.

"Do you know what that does to a man?" he continues. "To love the unattainable? To see the world as dull and lifeless compared to the visage... *of you?*"

I yearn to make amends. To give Pygmalion peace. "What do you want?"

"Take back your gift," he pleads. "These eyes are blind. They're not my own. Let me see the world as it is, not through this unbearable lens."

The Underworld exacts a terrible price for truth. I must surrender my beauty to heal what is broken in Pygmalion. He is an artist of exquisite talent. I will help him remember and lighten both our hearts. With excruciating intent, I let my skin dull and my hair lose its luster, let this precious immortal veneer peel away like old paint.

When I open my tired eyes, Pygmalion's own are bright with tears. "Thank you," he whispers, freeing a shudder from his chest. I am old, but he is new.

The contours soften on his marble carving; her asymmetrical lines captivate the eye. Pygmalion slides a tender finger down her cheek, marveling at the imperfections that make her unmistakably human and real. "She looks at me now," he says softly. "Not past, nor through."

He too is remade. "Regrets?" he asks.

I catch my reflection, taking stock of loss and gain. "Not yet." *But a shade of doubt.*

Pygmalion studies my unfamiliar ordinariness with an appreciative eye. His hands on the stone move with a new purpose. I leave him to his work.

"Aphrodite?" he calls. I pause. "Even unadorned, you are still, well... *undeniable.*"

I grin before stepping back into darkness. "Stick to sculpture, Pygmalion. That's *your* poetry."

* * *

How long have I traveled? An hour? A year? Time warps here, minutes stretching into eternities, centuries collapsing into heartbeats.

My beauty ebbs and still I surge forward in Hades' black tide. The shadows press close. They cloak my wounds and keep me whole. They whisper of another soul waiting.

The air is first to shift, a sharp wind that smells of sea brine. The waves and gulls come next, crashing and squawking from a cavern bathed in pearl, watery light. Far inside, I find a strange, stormy expanse trapped within the walls like a miniature in a bottle. A ship rocks in the tumult, its sails tattered, its hull listing precariously with every ocean swell.

On the deck stands a man. He is tall and broad-shouldered, face weathered by salt and sun. His hands grip the wheel with a desperation that speaks of years spent fighting an unwinnable war. Even from a distance, I can see his stubborn-set jaw and pride etched into every line of his face.

"Captain!" I call, my voice cutting through the chaos.

His head snaps up, eyes narrowing in recognition. For an instant, the ship steadies and the gales subside as if they too await his response.

"You," he growls. "You dare return."

Water foams around my feet. "I go where I am needed." The shoreline is curiously detached from storm and ship.

"Needed?" he scoffs, and the wind snaps. "Was it *need* that drove you to me all those years ago? Or *amusement*?"

The man is a prickly sort. "Be careful, Captain." My voice is seashell-soft but edged. "You would not speak so boldly if you truly understood what it is to amuse a god."

He juts his jaw and scowls. "Tell me, Aphrodite. What do you call it when a goddess gives a man the sea and then watches it swallow his world?"

"A shitstorm, Captain. One of your own making." I let that one sink in. "You came to me, begging for my favor, for the strength to command the seas. Do not cast blame if the cost was dearer than you bargained for."

"The cost!" he rages, suddenly by my side. "Family, duty, honor! I was peerless in them all! No wave could sink me, no storm break me."

No gold or glory slake you.

"But you lied, Aphrodite. When the sea rose against me, when my ship floundered and my family fled or drowned, you were nowhere to be found."

Fool. So arrogant is his pride that he's forgotten what it means to be mortal. Yes, yes, I lured him to this downfall – hook, line, and sinker. He deserved the old bait-and-switch!

"Commanding the high seas is one thing, Captain. A noble pursuit. But no man grasps a god's power to bend waves to his will and survives. I'm sorry for those you lost."

He surprises me with a nod. "I bear the scars and sorrows of all my failures." He gestures to the ship. "And now I am stranded without loved ones to help weather this storm."

This is not a great man, but he is decent at heart. And alone. I dread the bill that comes. "Name your price, Captain. If it's mine to give to ease your storm-tossed heart, you will have it, I promise."

The man's eyes widen in surprise and he drops to his knees. "Goddess, have mercy," he pleads. "Strip me of this vainglory pride that binds my fate to the sea. Shelter me from the storm and grant peace within my heart. Let me go."

Pride is my fortress too; its unshakable walls surround my certainty that I am more than the sum of my gifts. I loathe to surrender such powerful defenses for the sake of one mere mortal. Who is he to strip me, Aphrodite, of precious armor so painstakingly crafted to my soul? And what pitiful thing lies underneath, naked and exposed?

With heavy reluctance and not a little wrath, I tear at the part of me he begs me to destroy. When it clings like a barnacle, I yank with all my might to crush its imminent uprising. The glow of my essence flickers as it rips away with the remnants of my resentment.

The change is immediate. The storm subsides, the captain's stance softens, and I...I feel a lightness, strange and ancient, wrap its essence around me – what is left of me.

Without words, he and I find ourselves sitting in the sand, watching the sunrise in wonder.

My pride is gone, and with it, the goddess that's always been. Two mighty pieces Hades has claimed. I bow my head in supplication to the goddess I remain.

* * *

Down I twist and tumble, in-out-into pools of ink.

The air is laced with something electric that raises fine hairs on my neck and arms. It smells of charred cedar and copper, sharp and metallic – a warning, or perhaps an invitation.

I feel his force before I notice him, and my whole body craves his touch. Stripped of beauty and pride though, I keep my head down and watch.

He emerges from the darkness limned in gold. Familiar heat rolls off in waves, prickling my flesh and stirring the embers of my fading flame. His armor is scorched, the breastplate sooted. The burns only strengthen his firepower. "Aphrodite?"

"Ares." His name is a warm whisper on my lips.

The god of war tilts my chin up to examine what I've become. "Look at you, Aphrodite. What's happened to you?" He drinks me in with molten eyes, and I can't decide whether to shrink away or melt toward him.

"Ares..." But where I'd normally declare *I love you, I need you, I miss you, my beloved*, now the words lodge in my throat and fill me with hot tears.

All my immortal life, I have come to Ares an equal, with a beauty and pride to match his own. We seek and spurn each other with insatiable lust and reckless abandon, we gods of love and war. But it's been an age since he and I were one; now for the first time in my existence, I want to crawl back into the shell from whence I came, feeling ugly, pitiful, and wholly inadequate in Ares' presence.

"I've lost much of my fire in the Quintessence," I manage, clutching my frayed cloak like a wilting wallflower. "Surely you do not mean to punish me further."

Ares smirks and leans in, a charismatic lion flirting with its prey. "Oh, but I do, my heart. Unless we can help each other? You burn in me, Aphrodite; the burning never stops. You feed me flames and leave me smoldering in ashes. Let us go on petting and punishing, shall we?"

His words kindle my defiance. "Do you menace Phobos like this when he needs his father? You mistake passion for ruin, Ares. Is it my fault you wield it like a bloody indiscriminate blade?"

"As if I have a choice!" he rages. "You filled with fire long ago, Aphrodite, knowing I'd grow to worship the heat. It's because of you that I crave destruction equal to victory! And when the flames of jealousy and wrath consume me, you just disappear."

His accusations rip through me, their edges sharpened by the truth in Ares I have too long refused to acknowledge.

"I disappear," I counter, matching his glare, not his pitch, "when passion blinds you to boiling point. My flame was never meant to sustain you, Ares. The gods know, I now have little enough left even for myself. This passion was meant to...to...*inspire* you." The last part I barely speak aloud, hardly daring to believe the notion.

Ares doesn't catch on, so intense are the feelings he seeks to contain. He rattles his fists like the damn war god he is. "What choice do I have? With this conflagration wild in my veins? Shall I burn and plunder for all time, caught in a maelstrom of fury and regret?"

Passion is a dangerous force in a warrior's heart; it's a raw, chaotic energy that builds as much as it destroys, and Ares' unavoidable nature has turned our eternal fire into a curse. One from which only I can free him.

"No, Ares, love." *My life. My heart. My soul. My body.* "You've suffered enough. I will take it away and release you." *Possess you no longer. Though how I will miss you.*

With a quivering breath, I summon the spark that drives lovers to madness and gods to ruin. Hesitantly, I reach for it, the glow of my essence flickering as I grip the ember that remains. It resists, clinging like two lovers in one last desperate embrace. I close my eyes and steel myself against the terrible ache. My passion has always been a gift; now it demands sacrifice. To deliver Ares from suffering and offer him peace at last is worth the torment of losing him.

I let it go, reduced to faint smoke, cold and subdued, curling at the edges of my fading self, and watch his beautiful, proud face shudder into stillness, like ripples on a pond.

"Oh, goddess," he whispers, dropping to his knees with a sob. "Bless you, Aphrodite."

Ares will always love the burn, but his scars no longer need be made by love's fiery tongue.

And I...I return to the shadow path alone, empty of everything.

* * *

The darkness this far down smells of parchment and damp earth. I find myself wandering heavy-footed amongst a grove of ancient trees whose gnarled branches claw at the canopy as their roots slither across the uneven forest floor.

My steps slow from an unbidden heaviness that settles over me until I simply cannot go on and I slump against the nearest tree. The trunks all around are carved with lines of text, words etched deep into the bark. Peering closer, the markings grow clear – snatches of poetry, fragments of prayers.

There, at the base of a large oak across from me, sits the poet who died young, consumed by a longing that haunts me still.

His shoulders are hunched, his head bowed; dark hair falls in loose waves around a face that was handsome once. In his hands, he cradles a thin sheaf of papers, their edges tattered, the ink smudged. His fingers tremble as they trace words, trying to hold onto what's already slipped away.

"Orpheus."

He glances up and blinks on seeing an old friend. "You've changed." His eyes don't miss much.

I laugh, a willowy sound. "You haven't."

He flashes a fleeting smile. "That's the trouble, isn't it? Nothing here ever changes. Not the trees, not the air. Not her." His voice cracks on the last word while his gaze shifts inexorably toward a shape just visible through the murk.

Beautiful Eurydice stands at the edge of the grove, her form pale and indistinct, as though made of mist. She doesn't stir, but her head tilts slightly, listening for something beyond the silence.

"She doesn't know me anymore," Orpheus whispers. "I've called to her, sung to her, written for her. But the words...they fade." He looks down at the papers in his lap and his hands tighten on the edges. "I can't hold them. The memories. The songs. They slip away, and she slips with them."

I move closer, kneeling before him. "Orpheus," I say gently, "why have you brought me here?" I feel suddenly very tired.

"Because you are memory, goddess. You are the keeper of love's first touch, its last whisper. And you have the power to give her back to me."

I shake my head, the ache in his voice carving its way into my chest. "I promise, I have no power left to offer. Besides, I cannot give what was never mine to keep. You chose to look back, Orpheus. You chose to lose her."

"Then let me lose myself," he says, his voice rising with desperation. "Take my memory, Aphrodite. Take the words, the songs. Take everything that ties me to her and let me forget."

The pull of the Underworld surges again, cold and unrelenting like Orpheus's pain.

I've spent lifetimes collecting the memories of love's beginnings – stolen moments of joy and fleeting sparks that burned bright and brief – those are sweetest of all. To surrender even a fragment of that cherished immortal vault is unthinkable. And yet, what have memories done for me? What good is holding onto that which has already faded?

I reach out to grace Orpheus's trembling hands. Songs, poems, and professions of love dissolve beneath my touch, their ink bleeding onto my fingers before fading into nothing. The pull sweeps through me, drawing out pieces of myself that I've never dared release.

The words are first to go, followed by faces and voices. The echoes of a thousand stolen moments fade into silence, leaving only the ache of their absence.

Orpheus looks up, eyes wide with wonder. "She's gone," he whispers. "Truly gone."

"She always was," I say, for both of us.

He stands, deliberate and tall, perhaps for the first time in a hundred years. "Thank you, Aphrodite, for letting me go." Eurydice's form is now indistinguishable from the mist. Orpheus doesn't look back.

"I will miss you, dear friend." Yet even as I say this, the memory of him flees, and all vestiges of the boy in the wood vanish from thought as the fog gathers in my mind.

* * *

I'm sliding down a frost-slickened corridor of jagged black stone. Hades pulls out all the stops down here. It's not enough that I'm stripped bare – beauty vanquished, pride relinquished, passion extinguished – now even memory surrenders to the void.

I do not remember why I've come, only that I have no choice but to keep sliding, treacherously – until I tumble into a clearing – to spot at its center a vast, still pool. A mirror. And at its edge, Persephone, her queenly figure carved in sharp relief against the ashen sky.

She turns as I approach, sable hair glinting in dusky light. Gods, she is beautiful! Her gown of autumn colors – amber, emerald, wine – clings to her form before blurring into the shadows. Her violet eyes harbor secret worlds.

"You don't remember, do you?" she asks.

I stop a few paces away, unsure whether to kneel or run. "Remember what?" I ask. My voice is strange to my ears.

Her full lips curve into a mocking smile that's not unkind. "No, of course not. You've cast away the pieces of yourself that would tell you." She gestures to the pool where her reflection ripples. "But I remember everything, Aphrodite."

The name resonates with a mighty hum somewhere deep and unreachable. "Who are you to me?"

She laughs, then shrugs. "You have forgotten." Then her gaze snaps back to mine, composure cracked. "You forgot how I loved you. How I waited for you. How I gave you my joy and watched you squander it for fleeting pleasures. You forgot how you abandoned me."

In vain, I search through the empty vault of my mind; to my horror, I can find no betrayal. But I *feel* it. Feel her heartbreak frosting over my heart – slick, jagged, deadly. It fills the empty spaces in the hearth fires where my divine gifts once bloomed with life.

What can I do? I drop to my knees. "Your sorrow, Persephone, it is mine now too. Ours to share. And I'm so very sorry. Truly. Please forgive me."

Her expression softens, though her eyes stay guarded. "Look." She gestures again toward the pool. "Look into the Mirror of Souls and see what you have hidden from yourself."

I hesitate, hunched. Cold air bites at my bare and broken skin. "What will I see?"

She steps closer, her gaze piercing. "The truth."

At the mirror's edge, I fix my eyes on a shifting reflection. At first, I see only myself – pale, hollow, utterly unadorned. Then the image fractures, splitting into countless versions of me.

In the mirror, I am Inanna, bold and fierce, descending into the Underworld to claim my power. I am Ishtar, weeping as love turns to vengeance. I am Astarte, forgotten yet enduring, my name whispered in foreign tongues. The goddess of love wears many faces, but each carries the same bitterness, same yearning, same fears – of being unlovable, hidden beneath centuries of vanity and pride; and I see the transience of physical beauty, the fleeting adoration it inspires.

Then I see the garden.

It's overgrown and wild, the flowers strangled by thorns, their petals faded to gray. Love has withered here, forgotten and abandoned. And I see myself in its center, clutching the last ember of light, unwilling to release it.

I would double up in agony were I not already crumpled on the ground.

"Do you see now?" Persephone asks. "Love is not perfection. It is not possession. It is sacrifice, vulnerability, faith."

Faith. Faith is not holding on; it's letting go.

The pull of the Underworld surges again. It will swallow me this time, I am sure. I am too weak to go on or give more. I face Persephone, desperate and disconsolate. "What must I do?"

"The joy here is gone, Aphrodite. Taken by time, by loss, by the weight of the Underworld itself. But you remember it, don't you? The joy you once carried, the spark that could ignite a thousand hearts?"

She sits beside me, her hand resting on mine. "This Garden of Joy will bloom again, but it requires the Quintessence – the purest part of yourself. Such is our First Law Under the Heavens: that Change is the only constant."

The words pierce through the fog of my mind. I am Aphrodite. Inanna. Ishtar and Astarte. My love is strength and sacrifice, faith and joy. I reach for the last thread of light that binds me to the heavens and release it into the Mirror of Souls.

The garden stirs to rise from its silent grave. The trees shiver, the fountain froths, and wind sings through tall grass and bent posies alike.

Persephone rises, her silhouette lit by a golden light that comes from nowhere and everywhere at once. "Aphrodite, you've come far. You have done what no goddess before you could," she says. "You have restored the faith and joy of love itself."

I nod, rather numb, though the ache in me is a sweet pain. My Quintessence is gone, yet I feel no loss – only change.

Persephone extends her hand and her radiant smile. "Come. Let us speak with Hades. Spring awaits!"

* * *

Diminished though I am, my heart gladdens with Persephone's hand in mine.

As our fingers brush walls and bid shadows farewell, the Underworld shifts and releases its merciless hold. Our silence is a prayer while I grapple with a disquieting truth: it is not the Underworld so changed, but I.

Hades waits at the gates.

The God of Death is ever-imposing as he fixes his eye darkly upon me. I meet his cold glare with quiet defiance and feel a warm hand squeeze tight. Then Persephone's fingers slip from my grasp to embrace Hades as Springtime Incarnate.

"She has given enough, beloved." Persephone's tender touch softens Hades' wintry countenance and my wizened own. "You are brave, Aphrodite," she says with eyes of gold. "Brave and beguiling and divine."

I blush. In her words, my empty chambers ignite anew. I hope she will visit me soon.

Hades' gaze relaxes to betray a glint of respect. "Go then. Ascend, Aphrodite," he declares. "You have earned your spring." With a wave of his hand, the gates groan open to spill light on the hidden path ahead. Already I am awash in its glow.

"And take heart, Fair Goddess of Love!" His voice echoes in the shadows behind. "Thy eternal flame shall never be yours alone to bear."

* * *

I stand again at the world's edge, windswept by swelling salt waves.

The mirror of the sea no longer reflects a goddess fickle or fleeting, unravaged by time, unyielding in power. Her face is mine, yes, and hardly a stranger's. Crone, mother, maiden. I embrace all of my everlasting self – this wild hair and weathered skin, these keen eyes that see to the heart – like a lost love found.

I know well that love is enduring. It changes. It grows.

Spring takes root in the myrtle ash and seed I now press to the earth. Tiny buds rise along delicate stems, unfurling into sprays of white blossoms on evergreen boughs.

From this young shade, I step full into the sun. Dawn bathes the cliffs of Akrotiri in her steady glow, and I reach, boundless and reborn, to catch her kiss on my cheek.

The Constraints of Love
Russell Hugh McConnell

At first, I think she must be a trick of the light, an effect of the late afternoon sun that glitters on the surface of the wine-dark Aegean, dotted with German patrol boats. Whatever the cause, I cannot quite tell where she comes from, cannot tell where the sea foam ends and her white dress begins as she walks up the beach past the deep treads left by the Panzer III tank that is now parked beside the Ariti Hotel, where the Nazi officers are about to have their meeting. And somehow, against all reason, I am not concerned about her safety, even though we are under Axis occupation, and no one is safe anymore. Unlike the rest of us, she somehow seems to be in no danger at all. And when she walks right past Major Schäfer and he does not so much as glance in her direction, the impossibility of the whole scene is only confirmed.

It would be extreme arrogance – hubris even – to suppose that this golden-haired goddess would want to speak to me. But naturally I can suppose nothing else, and with the inevitability of a dream she walks right up to me. I am a tall man, but I have to tilt my head upwards to meet her gaze, and meeting that gaze takes all my strength.

"Nikos," she says, "you have loved."

"I have," I reply, although I cannot now remember whom I ever loved, nor when, nor why. Her face and body fill all my thoughts, press their contours into my most intimate memories, so when I try to cast my mind back to my past loves, I see and feel nothing but her.

"When you loved, I was there," she says in a voice that murmurs like the soft Aegean waves. "I was within you, and thus came to know you. I know you now. And you know me."

"Aphrodite," I say, and she does not even deign to nod her confirmation. "Are you, uh, are you—" I struggle to speak under the gentle yet overwhelming pressure of her gaze. But she does not interrupt and eventually I manage to get the words out. "Are you here to help us win? To stop the Nazis? To prevent the armies of evil from stomping their jackboots though our antique land, and over the face of all the earth? Have the Olympians come back to turn the tides of this war?"

She regards me with eyes as bright as the sky and as deep as the sea. "Of course not," she says winsomely. "I am here for a man."

"A man?" I gasp, my disappointment drowning in hope. Her face exceeds all loveliness and every curve of her body whispers sensuous promises. Even though I know I am the greatest fool in the world, I cannot help but fantasize that she man she seeks might be me.

"Will you help me?" she asks.

I cannot refuse. No man on earth could, and perhaps no woman either. Gorgias was right about the *erôtos anangkais*, the constraints of love: love is irresistible, and those who obey her are blameless.

"What do you need me to do?" I ask helplessly.

She raises her hands up near my face, and between them I think I catch a glimpse of the faintest golden shimmer in the air. "This took me so long to recover," she says. "I did not know what had happened to it." She sees my puzzled squint and smiles a little more widely, holding out her hands even closer. The scent of roses fills my nostrils. "Look, but do not touch," she says. The shimmer in the air is tantalizing, as if something is hovering just this side of invisibility.

"You can see why it was difficult to find," she says. "There was a time when I hated it so much that I wished never to see it again. For centuries I gave no thought to where it might have ended up. But then I realized that it was the very thing I needed, and by then it could have been anywhere. And therefore I searched – over the sacred mountains, and under the troubled seas, and through the undergrowth of ancient forests, and up and down the bustling streets of the cities of men. For over a thousand years I sought it, the strongest and subtlest thing in the world. Fine enough to be invisible, yet strong enough to bind a god."

"The golden net!" I exclaim, remembering the story. The stories say that Aphrodite was married to Hephaestus, god of smiths. When he suspected her of infidelity, he used all his art to create a net of gold, a work of divine craftsmanship. Its threads were so fine that they could not be seen, and yet so strong that even a god could not break them. He set a trap, using the net to capture Aphrodite in bed with her lover Ares; then he dragged them before the other Olympians, to expose their wrongdoing. It had not occurred to me until now, but the stories say nothing at all about what happened to the net afterwards.

"This is what trapped me, and bound me to my former lover," says Aphrodite. The way she says "lover" makes the word sound both infinitely alluring and totally without shame. "And now, I shall lay a trap of my own."

She makes a movement with her hands that I cannot comprehend. It seems at once utterly simple, a mere upward thrust of her palms as if she were tossing the net into the air, yet at the same time her fingers seem to be performing manipulations of unimaginable complexity. I blink, and the golden shimmer is now nowhere to be seen.

"What is my role in this trap?" I ask.

She does not quite look pitying. She is too grand for that, too distant. But she comes close. "You are a mortal, Nikos, and therefore a pawn. Today you are the bait to my trap. And you shall enjoy no reward. Love offers no rewards. Love offers nothing at all. Love only demands, and it will keep demanding until you have nothing left to give." Her gaze travels up and down my body in a manner that sets me tingling. "You have a pistol," she says.

"Y-yes," I say. "I was planning..." Under her cool gaze my words wither and die. My plans and goals are not relevant here. Her mere presence sweeps them aside like autumn leaves.

It is true that I have a pistol secreted under my shirt, wedged uncomfortably in the small of my back. Before the goddess walked out of the sea, I had been just about to use it to shoot Major Schäfer. It was not a considered plan, but rather the wild impulse of a desperate man. Only this morning, I overheard a young lieutenant remarking to a friend that he wanted to ask Major Schäfer something about fuel shipments at the meeting at the Ariti Hotel that afternoon, and the idea had sprung fully formed from my mind, like Athena from the brain of Zeus. I realized that I now knew exactly where Major Schäfer was going to be, and when. And I had a gun: my father's old Ruby M1914 pistol, buried deep in the tatty linen in the trunk beneath my bed.

I knew I could get close enough. The Major slightly knows me, believes that I am compliant. I have had some limited freedom of movement ever since they determined that I had no Jews working for me at the print shop.

Killing Major Schäfer would not win the war. It would not drive the evil from my native land. It would undoubtedly get me killed. But it would be *something*. It would be a way to feel that I was still a man, a way to tell these invaders that Hellas did not belong to them, that their inhumanity and wickedness could not triumph forever on these ancient and noble shores. When the idea came to me to kill the Major, I actually felt happy for the first time since the Germans had arrived. It was a harsh, ferocious happiness, welling up from the conviction that I could *do* something, that I could resist.

But Aphrodite extends her hand. "Give it to me," she says.

Unhesitatingly I dig the pistol out from under my shirt with a trembling hand. It feels incredibly heavy, and so greasy with sweat that I am ashamed to hand it to her, but I do. It looks so incongruous in her delicate fingers.

"Know that I am not sorry," she says. Then the goddess of love shoots me in the stomach.

I feel no pain. I just hear the sharp crack and then feel an icy numbness seize my abdomen. Slowly, I look down to see the blood blossoming on the front of my white shirt. The dreamlike feeling has returned, the same sense of unreality that I felt when I first saw her walking up the beach.

"I am not insensible to the cruelty of this action," she says delicately. "But I do not apologize. You agreed to help me, and this is necessary."

I try to form the word "why" but my mouth contorts grotesquely, refusing to obey my will. Nevertheless, she seems to understand.

"You have been slain by a goddess," she says. "This fact entails special procedures."

A cold wind hits me, colder than any springtime wind should ever be, colder even than my insides. The sky seems to darken. I see the newcomer arrive, but I cannot tell where he has arrived from. It is as if he has just stepped through a doorway that isn't there. He is an old man, gaunt and white-bearded, wrapped in a dark grey cloak. On his back are great feathery wings, the color of charcoal. His eyes are twin black marbles.

He bows to me with the dignified patience of ritual. "My name is Thanatos," he says in a voice like freezing rain, "and I have come for you."

He steps forward and extends his right hand, and I can feel the world dimming as my soul is drawn towards him. Before this moment I never knew I had a soul, but now that I feel it, I wonder how I ever could have missed it. It is so palpable, so undeniable, so much realer than my frail body ever felt.

But then my eye catches the faintest of shimmers in the air above Thanatos's head, and the golden net drops down on top of him. He gasps and falls to his hands and knees, immobile. The goddess of love laughs triumphantly, and the sound of her laugh drives away the cold and dark, making the sky bright and blue once more. She places one perfect bare foot proudly upon her captive's back in a pose of triumph.

I realize that my wound has stopped bleeding. I look down and the great scarlet patch is still on the front of my sweaty shirt, but it no longer feels cold. It feels like nothing at all.

Then I hear something, although I also do not hear it, because it is not really a sound. But whatever it is, it is overwhelming. It seems to fill the air around me and shake the earth beneath me, and I feel as though my bones are vibrating with it. Words cannot describe it, but it is as if the whole cosmos is emitting a great, terrible groan.

"He is here," Aphrodite breathes. "It did not take him long." And then a nightmare surges up out of the earth. It has a face, but its form is shockingly inhuman: it resembles nothing so much as a black mountain crowned with black flame, seeming to fill the whole landscape at once. Then the vast form wavers, like a distant view on a hot day, and it shrinks down, the craggy features morphing into something that could almost be mistaken for those of a human being, but that are still as unreal in their fierce ugliness as Aphrodite is unreal in her sensuous beauty. He appears now as a large, dark-haired man in a black linen suit, but even if I had not seen his true form a moment earlier, I could no more have mistaken him for a mortal man than I could have mistaken her for a mortal woman.

"Aphrodite," he rumbles dangerously, "what madness is this?"

"I want him back, Hades," she says. "Return him to me."

"The road to my realm goes only in one direction," he says. "Those who enter may never leave. Thus it has always been, and thus—"

"Persephone," says the goddess. "Theseus."

He glowers, "You must understand—"

"Herakles. Alcestis. Orpheus."

"That's not—"

"Odysseus. Aeneas."

"Enough! You cannot—"

"Psyche. Hippolytus. Sisyphus."

"*FINE!*" roars Hades and his voice booms and cracks like a violent storm. The earth lurches beneath us. Yet immediately after this outburst, Hades looks suddenly cowed. His eyes flick upwards towards the sky, just for a moment.

"No thunder," chides the goddess, waggling one long, elegant finger. "Thunder is still his, remember? Now give my Adonis back to me, and I will free Thanatos. If you refuse, I will keep him imprisoned, and Death shall be undone forevermore."

"You are mad," says Hades.

"How many men and women have died since the dawn of humanity?" the goddess asks. "Perhaps a hundred billion? No doubt you keep records of such things. Imagine a hundred billion people pounding their fists on coffin lids, rattling the doors of their crypts, sprouting up from old battlefields like the warriors of Cadmus. Imagine them cracking open sarcophagi and marching up out of the sea. Imagine your realm disgorging *all* its prisoners to overwhelm the mortal world."

"It cannot be!" cries Hades.

"It is happening already," she replies. "Listen!"

And once again I hear but do not hear that terrible, calamitous groan – the wail of the cosmos itself as it strains against the unimaginable weight of the dead. I imagine for a moment that I can hear that terrible pounding of bony fists, that I can see millions of dead men staggering out of the Aegean in their rotten sailors' rags. I imagine that the mass grave that the Germans dug just west of town is now a seething mound of living bodies, clawing their way back up out of the dark earth.

"You will undo everything!" cries Hades, and now I hear real fear in his voice, the kind of fear that should be unimaginable to a god. The fear of finality, of unmaking. The same fear that he and Thanatos present to mortals like me.

"Bring me Adonis," says Aphrodite, a tower of beauty and strength. "And all will be as it was."

There is no puff of smoke, no clap of thunder. Hades does not so much as speak or wave his hand. All he does is vanish, and in the place where he stood there is now a nude young man of impossible beauty. Aphrodite embraces him with a cry of delight and the two of them cling to one another blissfully.

"My Lady," pleads Thanatos, still on his knees.

Aphrodite casts him a glance that would be scornful if it were not so indifferent. She flicks her wrist, and the faint golden shimmer appears in her hand. Although nothing else changes perceptibly, it feels as though the whole world breathes a sigh of relief. In my mind's eye, the bony fists cease their pounding, the mass grave stops seething. "You are free," she says to Thanatos. "Do as you must." And hand in hand Aphrodite and Adonis stride away down to the shore without so much as a backward glance, and walk together out onto the surface of the glittering sea. And although I cannot see for sure, it looks to me as though she carelessly tosses the golden net into the waves.

My vision blurs and my breathing falters. As I slump down on the hillside next to Thanatos, I notice that my wound has started bleeding again.

"Why me?" I ask him. "Why not Major Schäfer? Or the lieutenant? Or that Nazi sympathizer Dmitrios? Or anyone else? Why did I have to be the one to die?"

"Many are chosen by love," says Thanatos. "Rarely do any of us know why. She comes and goes according to her own mysterious will, and it is by that will that she chooses. She never justifies herself."

"She used me," I grunt. "She used me and then threw me away as if I were nothing."

"We have both of us been used," he agrees.

"She is a goddess," I say. My voice is so quiet now, just a hoarse whisper. My blood feels boiling hot where it has spilled over my icy cold hands. "With her power, she could have helped us. She could have turned the tides of this war, swept the Germans from our coasts."

"That is not her way," says Thanatos, "that is not the way of love. Aphrodite neither makes wars, nor ends them. Wars are not her purview. She cares for neither war nor peace, good nor evil, justice nor injustice. She cares only for the love that she herself embodies – the love that rolls within and among all of us, mortal and immortal alike, as blind and ruthless as the sea, as full of life and death."

He turns to face me. "I still have a job to do," he adds sadly, and extends his hand for a second time.

As the sun sets and the light fades, my last vision is of the white sea foam, cast upon the sand by the ceaseless waves of the wine-dark Aegean. These waves roll on forever, out of the deep Homeric past, and forward into a nameless future.

Aphrodite's Promise
Melody E. McIntyre

Helen leaned out of the palace window to get a better view of the chaos below. Spears hurtled through the air to sink into flesh or ricochet off shields. Short swords found purchase in their enemies sides. Cries of anguish and bloody triumph filled the air. The armies were so close now. She feared it would not be long before they reached the palace interior. Helen retreated into the bedroom where she and the other women hid. She cast her eyes toward her sister, Clytemnestra, who was usually so brave and calm. Instead, Clytemnestra was drinking undiluted wine and eyeing the sword Agamemnon had left her.

Little hands tugged at Helen's robes, and she bent to scoop up her daughter, Hermione. A red, splotchy face covered in tears and snot looked up at her. Cleaning her daughter's face gave Helen something productive to do. Ever since they fled Sparta and holed up in Mycenae, Helen felt useless. Grateful for the sanctuary of her sister's home, but unable to contribute.

"There, dear one." Helen smiled the most radiant smile she could manage and kissed Hermione's forehead. "Now go play with the others." Helen watched the children play and tried not to worry about their fate.

Bony fingers dug into Helen's arm, and she winced at the pinpricks of untrimmed nails biting into her pale flesh.

"That smile may have fooled the little ones, but I can see the panic in your eyes," Clytemnestra hissed in Helen's ear and pulled her to the corner farthest from the others. "Did you see anything out the window? Was it Agamemnon? Is he all right?"

Helen removed her arm from her sister's stony grip and checked it for marks. Clear, not even a red smudge. As Aphrodite's favorite, Helen never suffered the indignity of wounds or blemishes. She sent a thank you to Aphrodite in her mind and reached into the folds of her robe to caress the seashell token the goddess had given her.

"I did not see him," Helen said. "From here, the men blur together, and I cannot recognize their faces."

"Ugh, we should have gone to Ithaca." Clytemnestra started biting at one of her nails. Helen lifted a hand to bat her sister's hand away from her mouth, but then decided that it didn't matter anymore. She hadn't lied to her sister. Dust covered the battlefield, and all the men wore similar armor. Helen hadn't mentioned that even from her poor vantage point, she could tell they were losing.

"You think we'd be safe in Ithaca? I've heard the Trojans have conquered everything."

"Not safe *in* Ithaca. It's a tiny, pathetic island. The Trojans would have overrun it no problem. No, I meant we'd have been better off running to our cousin Penelope. She and Odysseus are the smartest people we know. Surely they would have a clever plan for escape."

"You know Agamemnon would never have run away with us," Helen said. *Neither would Menelaus.*

A loud crash interrupted them. Hermione wrapped herself around Helen's leg as a second crash landed and shouting filled the palace.

APHRODITE'S PROMISE

"What on earth?" Clytemnestra pushed her way through her own children to the window.

The door to their room burst open.

Slaves poured in and began barricading the door with what furniture they could. Helen cringed, remembering when slaves had burst into their palace in Sparta. Except, instead of barricading doors, they'd brought Menelaus on a stretcher, gored by a spear. Infection soon took him and the only treatment she could offer him was a concoction made from poppy seeds for the pain.

"Mommy, what's going on?" Hermione asked. Helen stroked her daughter's hair, unsure how to answer.

"He's coming," said Clytemnestra.

Helen's heart sank into her stomach, and her whole body shook. She pushed Hermione away and ran to the small shrine to the gods. Clutching at the seashell token she wore around her neck, Helen begged Aphrodite to protect them. Through the din of battle and the clatter of the barricade, Helen heard her sister muttering her own prayers as she knelt next to her. With her free hand, Helen grabbed Clytemnestra's and squeezed.

"I'm not sure how much help Aphrodite will be for us, but she's always favored you," Clytemnestra said when their prayers were finished. She touched the hand Helen had wrapped around the token. "Ever since she gave you this, you've been blessed with beauty and love."

"Until I lost it all in Sparta." Helen stood up and resisted the urge to smash the small shrine. "Love and beauty are great in peacetime, but they're useless against the onslaught of the Trojan army." Tears stabbed at her eyes, but she refused to let them fall. "What good is a goddess's favor if it cannot keep your husband alive?"

CRASH!

Something smashed against the door, rattling the furniture barricade. Clytemnestra sprang into action. She ordered the slaves to pile more furniture and to press their bodies against it. She marched over to her sword and snatched it up. Her son, Orestes, stood at her side, holding a dagger.

CRASH!

Soldiers shouted through the door, promising mercy if they surrendered peacefully. Clytemnestra growled in reply. Helen wanted to scream, but the sound lodged in her throat. *Not again, not again,* her mind repeated. Memories of her brothers fighting off Trojans as she snuck herself and Hermione out of Sparta. She'd watched her brothers die protecting her and now she would be forced to watch her sister and nephew die, too. Her stomach clenched, and she ran back to the window to vomit. Cursing her cowardice, she clung to the edge of the sill as she retched.

CRASH! CRASH! CRASH!

Soldiers broke through the door and climbed inside. They slaughtered the male slaves. Helen grabbed Hermione and Clytemnestra's daughters. She shoved them behind her and grabbed a discarded knife. She had no fighting skills, but she would try to protect them.

Clytemnestra screamed and charged at one of the soldiers, but instead of goring her, the man disarmed her with the ease of a seasoned veteran. Orestes charged forward to protect his mother. The man slashed his blade once and Orestes fell, blood pouring from his neck. Clytemnestra howled with agony and hatred burned through her eyes at the man as he bound and gagged her.

He came for Helen next. She brandished her weapon, but he cast her a dubious look. Helen let the knife fall. The soldier held her as the other men chased the young girls over to join the other women. Helen met the man's eyes, and he gasped. A red flush filled his tanned cheeks and his eyes grew wide. The power of the goddess took him and his hand trembled. Helen braced herself and wished for her veil, but instead of tearing off her clothes, he simply walked her over to join the other women.

"Women of Mycenae, your city, and your men have fallen to Troy," the man said. "I am Deiphobus, Prince of Troy. You will all clean and dress yourselves for inspection. I promise you no harm will come to you if you cooperate."

"Inspection? What does that mean?" one of the other noble women asked Helen.

"It's Paris. It's the way of his army. Have you not heard the stories?" Helen realized she was the only one here who'd faced the Trojans before. "It's why they fight this war. Paris is scouring the world for the bride he was promised. No one touches the women until Paris inspects them."

"Who is he looking for?" the woman asked.

"I don't know."

But I do know.

He's looking for me.

* * *

As a child, Helen's favorite game was hide and seek. She was the smallest of her siblings and knew all the best places to hide. One day, she wandered far from the others and wedged her tiny body into a cluster of bushes. As she waited to be found, Helios drove his chariot across the sky, and Helen dozed. A gentle kiss on her forehead woke her. Helen opened her eyes, expecting to see her mother's smiling face, but instead, a golden light obscured her vision. When it faded, Helen saw she was no longer in the bushes, but on a silver cloud floating in the sky. White birds with wings tipped in gold swirled around her. Helen laughed with delight.

Would you like to be the most beautiful girl in the world?

The mysterious voice thrummed with power. Helen's body hummed along with it.

"I want to be beautiful," she said.

Give me your heart and I will fill your life with love and beauty.

Helen nodded, and a fire blossomed in her chest. She cried out, but the voice whispered soothing words. Soon the fire settled into a pleasant warmth. The golden light solidified into the form of a beautiful woman. Helen drank her in like a sun-starved flower before falling back to sleep. When she woke in the bushes to a sky filled with diamonds, Helen was sure it was a dream. Yet, in her hand was a small, pink seashell. Helen slipped it into a secret fold in her robe and ran home.

* * *

Years later, the goddess came again.

I gave you the beauty you desired and now I have come to collect the heart you promised. I have need of it.

Helen trembled as the goddess pressed a burning hand to her chest. In her mind's eye, she saw a tall, dark-eyed man. Handsome and alluring, but there was a hunger in his eyes that made Helen nervous. Aphrodite presented Helen to him. He studied her body and Helen wished she had on more than just her nightclothes. Agonizing moments passed and Helen could feel the heat from his penetrating gaze. The goddess snapped her fingers, and he was gone.

"Who was that?" Helen asked, clutching a blanket to cover her body.

His name is Paris and you will belong to him.

Six months later, the war began.

* * *

Paris stood before the gates of Mycenae with Agamemnon's blood dripping from his armor. *Finally*, he thought, *she must be here. There is nowhere left to look.* He pressed his foot down on Agamemnon's body and pulled his spear free. The body lurched up against his foot and Paris winced at the squelching sound his spear made when it released.

"He fought well," said Hector as he came up beside Paris. "We should let them collect the corpse."

"He's our enemy," Paris said and gestured for a slave to come and wipe some of the blood off his armor.

"He deserves our respect, nonetheless."

"Hector, I grow weary of your soft heart. But, I suppose it does not matter. They can have him after I find her. She's here. I know she is."

"And if she's not?"

Paris glared at him. If anyone else asked that question, he'd have them killed, but Hector was his brother and even with the goddess's blessing, he needed Hector to keep the Trojans loyal.

"She is here. The goddess promised me."

"You said the same thing in Sparta," Hector said and started for the palace.

"I will not stop until I have her."

* * *

Years ago, Paris had fallen asleep under a tree after a rough day. He'd judged the local cattle show and even though he knew he made the right choice, not everyone agreed with his decision.

Another contest for you, sweet Paris.

He started awake to find three goddesses standing before him. Floating in the air in front of him was a golden apple. The task was simple, award the apple to the fairest one. He hesitated, thinking of the angry villagers, and wondering what the spurned goddesses would do to him. But their beauty dazzled him, and he accepted the task with pride. To buy more time to gaze upon each of them, he asked them to come alone and present their case.

First white-armed Hera came and dropped her robe. Paris's mouth went dry at the sight of her. His legs melted, and he fell at her feet.

Choose me and you'll have sovereignty over the nations of the world.

Cast out by his family, the King and Queen of Troy, because they feared a dark prophecy, Paris hungered for the wealth and power he was denied. His adoptive parents had done their best, and he was grateful for their love, but he wanted more than the life of a shepherd.

A stack of crowns for your head. The first one will be Trojan.

APHRODITE'S PROMISE

Next came the glorious War Goddess, Athena, shining in her armor. Her wise, grey eyes pierced Paris's soul, and she presented him with another tempting offer. With her by his side, he would amass the fiercest army. His prowess in battle would be unmatched.

Not even Hector, Breaker of Horses, Crown Prince of Troy, will be able to defeat you.

Aphrodite came last. Her offer was simple and pulled at the deepest part of him. She spoke not a word, but only raised her hand and showed him a vision of a beautiful woman. Lovelier than a sunset. Aphrodite in human form. Paris spent that night caught in fever dreams of her body in his bed.

When he woke, his decision was made.

* * *

Helen listened to the women in front of her muttering and fretting over which hero they would be given to. Paris always picked first, but rumour was he never took any for himself. People speculated he wasn't actually interested in women, but Helen knew better.

And now there were only a few women between her and him. Dread coursed through her veins. He'd almost had her in Sparta, but she'd fled with her sister while her brothers died protecting them. Helen had stolen a glance backward in time to see Paris sink his spear into her brother's side.

And now he was threatening her sister.

"Lift your veil," Paris demanded. Then he said to one of the soldiers, "Why are so many of these women veiled?"

"It is the way of Mycenae," the soldier said.

It wasn't normally, but Clytemnestra had ordered all the women to cover their faces after their baths. She knew about her sister's vision and wished to buy what time they could.

"I said remove your veil, woman," Paris said, but Clytemnestra stood firm and tall. He gestured and a Trojan soldier came forward and ripped off Clytemnestra's veil. Helen's heart swelled with pride as her sister did not flinch and instead fixed Paris with a withering stare.

"Not her, but a beauty, nonetheless. Who are you?"

"She is Agamemnon's wife," said the soldier who'd taken her veil when Clytemnestra refused to answer.

"The queen? Who would like to mount Agamemnon's wife?"

The men jeered, and Clytemnestra's hand disappeared inside her robes. Helen wondered if her sister had somehow smuggled in a knife.

"Paris, you killed Agamemnon, she is yours," said Hector.

Paris rose and walked forward. He studied Clytemnestra's face, and she held his gaze. "You do look a little like her." His eyes closed, and he tilted his head as though he were listening to someone no one else could see. With a nod, he opened his eyes and thrust out his hand to grab Clytemnestra's wrist. In one swift movement, he twisted her body around in front of him and the knife clattered to the floor. "You'll need a firm hand. Deiphobus, you can have this one. I heard you took care of her once already." Paris shoved her towards the large, hulking man from earlier. Helen caught the look on her sister's face and wondered how long her sister would wait before she avenged her son.

"Only one woman left, Paris," Hector said.

No! Helen's mind cried, and she clutched her seashell token tight. *Goddess, please.*

The moment froze, and gold light obliterated the world. Helen was back on the cloud with her goddess.

"Aphrodite, please, if you have ever loved me at all, do not give me to the man who killed my love, my brothers and my father."

You are what he seeks. Having you will end this war.

Helen thought about Menelaus, delirious with pain as infection took him. Paris covered in her brother's blood. Hatred scorched her heart, but how many more had to die for her? A thousand ships launched from Troy to hunt her down, and in their wake, the world had burned.

"Send me back," Helen said. "I'm ready."

* * *

Soldiers seized Helen's arms and thrust her at Paris's feet. Her knees collided with the floor, and she cried out in pain.

"Who is this?" Paris asked.

"I am Helen of Sparta, Menelaus's wife," she spoke in a loud, clear voice.

Paris seized her veil and tore it from her face.

"It's you," Paris said. A smile touched his lips and he trembled.

If it will stop these awful wars, Goddess, I will not resist him. I will even try to love him.

Helen felt a fresh wave of strength and beauty surge through her and the goddess's kiss on her brow.

Your heart is as kind as you are beautiful, my child. Forgiving and sweet. Yet I am a goddess.

And we do not forgive.

Time froze as the goddess sent her one last vision.

* * *

A younger, less battle-weary Paris lounged under a tree and twirled a golden apple in his hands. A tall, fierce goddess in shining armor approached him.

"My apologies, War Goddess, but I will announce my decision at dawn when the others arrive."

I know that Hera offered you sovereignty over the known world, but it is to Aphrodite that you will give the apple. Her prize is irresistible.

"Then why have you come?"

With my army, there is nothing you can't have. No crown you cannot wear, nor woman you cannot have. You can have everything you desire.

Paris placed the apple in Athena's hand.

* * *

Paris winced as his eyes went dark and swam out of focus. He rubbed at them with his hands and when his vision finally cleared, he looked again at the woman before him. A moment ago, he swore it was finally her, but something wasn't right. She was beautiful, but her eyes were blue instead of green and her hair was a mousey brown, not sun-spun gold.

"No, you are not the one. I thought for a moment, maybe."

He remembered the apple gleaming as he placed it in Athena's hand. The shrieks of the spurned goddesses still stung his ears.

Every crown but Troy's.

Every woman but her.

"Hector, you take this one. Now, bring me a map. We must plan our next assault. I hear Penelope, the Queen of Ithaca, is quite beautiful."

Someone will remember us
Fiona Mossman

Aphrodite was reclining in the gardens of Olympus when the news came of Sappho's death. Around her the great discordant family of gods ate and drank and paid no attention to the little sparrow that fluttered towards her, perching on her shoulder, its talons airy nothingnesses against her robe and its beak cool against her ear. Aphrodite heard the message and propelled herself from her seat in an instant, her cup of ambrosia clattering to the ground.

"Leaving the party so soon?" called Zeus. She glanced at him, the loud, loutish god, legs akimbo on a silken couch and nymphs scattered like cushions beside him.

"What is it to you if I am?" she replied. Any mortal would fall upon their knees hearing their goddess's melodious voice so arch, so full of disdain. Zeus merely laughed and waved his hand in dismissal. Aphrodite stalked away.

Fuming at his disrespect kept her distracted as she walked without a destination nearly halfway around the expansive gardens. Eventually she came upon the bower. Ah yes, of course; this was where she had been heading. Bowers had always been sanctuaries for Aphrodite, and the one on Olympus was no different. The delicately draped plants, the soft sound of water running by, the generous curves of the path as it led deeper and deeper, and the privacy: that was what she needed.

Roses and hyacinths climbed the archways that she passed under and the heady scent of iris and myrtle filled the air as she brushed past their flowers, setting their heads nodding.

"Aphrodite?"

Her eyes threw daggers over her shoulder at the intruder. A thin, pale face framed by black hair emerged from the shade of the roses. Hades.

Of all her immortal relatives, she had never quite been able to pin this one down. His domain was death. He was funereal, grim, a keeper of the rules. She had never liked rules; and it was where life bloomed most fiercely that she always gravitated towards, people risking their hearts, their minds, their souls for a chance at feeling alive. But despite their differences there was something fascinating about him – something that bound their two domains together. She was the flame that consumed and moved on. Hades was whatever happened when the flames went out. She usually kept her distance, despite that whole Persephone business that had somewhat put him in her debt. And now, with news of Sappho's death – and presumably her journey to the underworld, where Hades ruled – he was the last person she wanted to see.

"You seemed upset at the feast. Tell me, gentle goddess, what's wrong?" he asked. He sounded genuinely concerned, but then again, he probably just had a good bedside manner. Aphrodite couldn't say the same, despite the many beds she frequented. Sickbeds and deathbeds she stayed away from.

"Oh, as if *you* don't know."

Hades' brow furrowed, giving him more than a passing resemblance to Zeus. Aphrodite shook her head.

"Don't tell me you don't know, oh *god* of the *dead*." The words were spat like pomegranate seeds from her lips.

The furrowed brow disappeared and in its place was understanding. Aphrodite had to look away, staring instead at the intertwined roses than climbed the sides of the bower.

"Who was it?" he asked softly.

It was her turn to frown, hard, still not looking at him. One arm rose up to meet the other and she crossed them protectively in front of herself. "Sappho," she said, and stopped.

She found herself listening for his response. He moved slightly, one foot to the other, she thought. "Who was that again?" he mused. "Ah – your priestess on Lesbos. Was that her?"

"You tell me, king of the underworld."

"Hmm. There was one such – yes."

Aphrodite turned then, peering into the black pools of his eyes. "You have her? She's crossed the River Styx?"

"She has," he confirmed.

His calm, deep voice did nothing to steady her. She took a breath, inhaling iris and rose, myrtle and hyacinth.

"Aphrodite," he rumbled, taking a step towards her. "Are you quite well?"

Aphrodite closed her eyes. Death was a travesty. Bad enough that mortals grew old and feeble, only living in their memories of past beauty; that they should die too was simply unconscionable.

"Don't tell me you cared for this one?" Hades said, placing one long-fingered hand on her waist. Aphrodite did not lean in. Her skin grew icy where his fingers lay. "You've lost lovers before. You know that you can visit them throughout time. Why are you so consumed?"

"You do not understand, do not pretend that you do," she spat, loosening some of that anger at last. "This is your fault. Things should not *end*—"

Hades withdrew his hand with a sharp intake of breath. "Honoured Aphrodite. You must be crazed with grief. I thought I heard you say that things should not end?"

She glared. "You heard me. Desire is ever-renewing, it brings us towards the future, lets us mould the future to our will. Love has no limits. Pleasure is endless. Why should anyone die? Why should any of it end?"

Hades tilted his head, not backing off an inch despite the fury that burned around Aphrodite, enough to turn the air around them to a heated shimmer. He seemed, if anything, calmer than before. Aphrodite nearly growled at the sight of his self-satisfied smile.

"How far have you gone into the future?" he asked. The Olympians, being gods and the murderers of time, had a looser relationship with linear chronology than humans did. Forwards, backwards, sideways – it was all much of a muchness.

"Far enough," she said. She didn't know where he was going with this evasion, but she forced herself to make the words light, to tamper her flames down a notch. It would not do to burn the bower down around their feet.

"Have you been to the end?"

"The end?"

"The end of humanity. As far as we can go."

She frowned. "Not the end of the world?"

His smile deepened. "Oh, the world carries on after the humans are gone. But they come to an end; as do we. We are human gods, after all."

Aphrodite lifted her chin and sniffed disdainfully. Did Hades think to impress her with apocalyptic talk? He wouldn't be the first or the last to try that move. "What of it? It's far, and I have what I want right here."

"Yes…" Hades put a finger on his chin and tapped. "Desire, love, pleasure, beauty… You do have those things. But I think you should come with me. Let's go to the end. If desire always leads towards the future, I say you should see it through. Will you accompany me?"

There was no reason to go. She had not asked for interference, not from the god who denied all pleasure, who dwelt beneath the earth and smelled like a sepulchre. But the feeling that she had been born with, the feeling of lack, of something missing, the feeling that drove her burning night after night into the arms of mortals and gods alike – that feeling was there. And there was no reason not to go.

"Very well," she said. "Lead the way."

* * *

She never knew, in the days that followed of grief and rage and powerlessness, whether that choice – following the god who fascinated and repulsed her in equal measure to a place where nothing mattered, where people were dying and could not or would not help each other, where the very sky and ground and oceans waged war – was a mistake or not. She walked forwards and backwards across time, bounded on the one side by the death of Kronos and on the other by the failure of humanity; she wept, she cursed and she watched. She visited her favourite lovers, Adonis, Don Juan, the sheer thoughtless fucking of Ares. And finally, she paid a visit to Hades and Persephone in their underground home. She needed to talk.

"Honoured Aphrodite," Persephone greeted her with respect, holding out a tray of refreshments with her eyes lowered so that all Aphrodite could see was the girl's lustrous hair, which seemed to glow even in this lightless place. She took a goblet of ambrosia with slight distaste: who wanted skulls on their drinking vessels? Honestly, these two really leant in a bit too hard on their whole death-focused deal.

"Greetings," Hades called, hurrying over from where he had been conferring with an underling. Here in his own domain, he appeared larger, more confident. What read as unusual or sombre in the world above seemed only fitting down here.

"Hades. Persephone. Thank you for letting me visit your realm."

"It's not often we have visitors, but you are always welcome," said Hades. "Come, let us sit somewhere comfortable." Persephone's mouth curved up into a private smile as she raised her head and gestured politely for Aphrodite to follow her husband.

Hades led them through several corridors of the palace that he and Persephone shared, the black velvet fittings failing to dampen the hollow echoing sound of their steps, shades shimmering at the edges of the rooms like the memories of candles. Aphrodite searched those indistinguishable faces as they passed, but if Sappho was there, she could not see her.

She summoned herself a thicker garment as they turned another corner and Hades finally gestured for her to enter a slightly brighter, slightly more hospitable room. There were couches for reclining on, a small water feature, and a few vases of flowers as yet undecayed. This room seemed more of the springtime goddess than the grave god.

They sat on the couches, Hades and Persephone on one and Aphrodite with her legs up on another. One of the servants had carried Persephone's tray of refreshments through, furnishing each immortal with food and drinks before retreating to a shadowed corner. A musician took up his station and began to play. Of course, it was a lament.

Aphrodite felt on the edge of control, ready to fracture, though why or into what she did not know. "Can you not play something cheerier?" she snapped at the musician, who hesitated a moment with a neutral expression and then bent over the lyre again, changing the melody but hardly the mood. Aphrodite sighed.

"Listen, king of shades," she said to Hades, more roughly than she intended. "Ever since we went so far into the future, I have been...troubled."

Hades took a long draught of ambrosia. "I know."

Aphrodite sighed again. "I cannot believe that it will end that way."

Hades and Persephone exchanged a glance that riled Aphrodite even more.

"It is wrong!" she burst out. "It was so...*ugly*."

Persephone spoke up then, her voice quiet but sure. "Do you not believe in the ugliness of humans? You, who know of their desires and their greed?"

Aphrodite glared at the younger goddess. "I know better than you of their desires."

Persephone was unruffled. "Then you know that they are capable of acts of great cruelty, as well as love. Sometimes both together." She paused. "They will bring it upon themselves, you know, and take other creatures down with them."

Aphrodite shook her head. "I don't care! It's *wrong*."

"I'm sorry that it was hard for you to see," Hades said. "Everything ends, though. Even Zeus's time is limited, though he, like you, refuses to hear of it."

"Do not compare me to him. I am nothing like Zeus," Aphrodite retorted, tight-lipped.

"My apologies," Hades said mildly.

Aphrodite felt the rage rising further, saw the flames flickering at the edges of her vision. In this gloomy place they cast new shadows. "That is not how it goes! There are other ways. There are other worlds."

Hades set down his goblet. "How do you know?"

"Because I desire it so."

"Desire is not destiny."

"But I am the goddess of desire, which looks only towards the future. There is no fulfilment. There is no stillness save the stillness of constant motion. Desire creates desire, and in creating, continues. I create the future. I am Aphrodite."

"Do you not think I know what it is to love life? My wife, whom *you* helped me win—"

Aphrodite rolled her eyes but Hades leaned forward, raising his voice.

"She is life to me. She is my life, which I both possess and can never possess—"

"Don't lecture me about my own domain—"

"If I'm not to tell you of desire then you must not talk to me of death. Everything ends, Aphrodite. There is no gainsaying it. Everything ceases, one day. You can burn up all the hearts and bodies you like on your way, and never look back at the ashes, but that does not change the fact that you will lose all there is to lose, because we all do."

There was silence in the room then as Aphrodite glared at Hades and he stared straight back. Persephone laid a gentle hand upon Hades' arm. "I think it's time we let our honoured guest retire," she said.

"I was leaving anyway," Aphrodite bit back. As she swept from the room in her fullest, most regal manner, she brushed against one of the vases of flowers and did not look back as it toppled and shattered.

* * *

The sickroom smelled of earth and rot, a curiously sweet smell, overlaid with the heady scent of the flowers that were piled up on every available surface, riots of purple and green that overspilled onto the marble floor. Aphrodite bent to pick a fallen violet as she entered.

There was a gasp from the bed. "My goddess!"

The woman in the bed made to struggle upright and Aphrodite closed the distance between them with swift steps. "No, lie back down," she said, pressing the flower into Sappho's fingers. They were wrinkled, gnarled like old olive bark. Sappho lay back down abruptly, breathing hard. She lifted the violet towards her face, far more lined than last Aphrodite had seen it. But those eyes were the same. They fixed first upon the violet, which trembled a little in her grasp, then they moved towards Aphrodite's face. Those eyes were bright with unshed tears.

Neither of them spoke for a long while. The silence was broken by a girl rushing into the room, exclaiming, "Are you well, my lady—" and breaking off with a strangled sound. Aphrodite shielded the maiden's eyes from her own beauty; it would not do to send the girl mad.

"You may go," she said, sketching a blessing in the air between them. The girl, eyes fixed on the floor, backed away until she reached the doorway and then turned and fled.

Sappho and Aphrodite found themselves sharing a grin. "I try to find good girls, but they are hard to come by these days," Sappho commented. Her voice was dry but those eyes were dancing with mischief again.

"What, even on Lesbos? I had thought this isle was flooded with them, with all the petitions and hymns you sent to me, this girl, that girl."

Sappho laughed. "And who says that those girls were good?"

The laugh turned to a cough and Sappho hacked into a square of silk, each sound tearing the air. Aphrodite half-raised a hand, but there was nothing she could do. When it was over there was silence again between them.

Sappho broke it this time. Her fingers closing around the bloodied silk, she carefully avoided Aphrodite's gaze as she said, "I did not think you would come to me, now."

Aphrodite looked down at the mortal woman on her deathbed. This poet, this singer, this human who had pursued beauty nearly as fervently as Aphrodite herself did – this priestess who had lain with so many women, who had taught them the ways of the goddess and of worship – this human who was maybe, strangely, the one who knew her best: she lay withered and pale, breathless. Dying.

"I saw the end. I went to the end of humankind." The words were wrung slowly from her almost without intent.

Sappho looked up. "And what did you see?"

"I saw the fires, I saw the floods. I saw suffering. Things I cannot even describe. And I also saw…" Aphrodite looked at Sappho, her wizened hand resting on the bedspread. "I saw violets. They still grew."

"Ah." Sappho sighed and the sound was like the wind upon the burned-up riverbed.

Aphrodite frowned. "It pains me to see you so reduced."

Sappho's mouth formed into a smile that did not reach her eyes. "I am honoured that you should grieve for me, my goddess."

Aphrodite was in no mood for platitudes. She began to pace, her robes sweeping the marble every time she turned about in the confinement of Sappho's bedchamber. "And you? Do you grieve for yourself?" she demanded.

Sappho did not reply at once. "I do, indeed," she said slowly. "But…I have lived a good, full life. I have many memories."

"Memories!" Aphrodite shook her head, still pacing. "What use is memory? A pale shade of what really matters…desire, the *now*, the possibilities…"

Sappho smiled again, a real one this time. "Ah, but my memories are sweet," she said. "So sweet I might die of them at times. You should know, Kytherea, my goddess. All those times you answered my pleas, came to me on your sparrow-drawn chariot, brought me each garlanded girl I longed for. And the time we first met, in my bower, when we…"

Aphrodite paused, but Sappho did not finish the sentence. Eventually she resumed her pacing.

"You know, you remind me of that time, now. I recognise this mood of yours. Aflame, and sweet, but sad all the same."

"Do you remember it, then?" Aphrodite asked. "How it felt to burn with desire—"

"Yes."

"Longing—"

"Yes."

"Ardour—"

"Yes."

"Worship—"

Sappho's eyes flicked upwards to meet the goddess's. "Yes."

They fell silent. The air between them was warm and elsewhere on Lesbos people were risking it all for a chance at feeling alive, or simply going about the everyday miraculous mundanity of living.

"'Someone will remember us, I say'," Aphrodite murmured, quoting Sappho's own lyrics. "'Even in another time.'"

Sappho nearly laughed. "Every time I sang, I thought of you," she said. "Sometimes I wonder how long I really will be remembered. Those days are behind me, my sweet Aphrodite. I have burned. Now I fade."

Aphrodite looked down at her dying priestess, whose words would be destroyed, mistranslated, clung to and misunderstood, casting shadows down the long centuries. Sappho was still smiling, and her eyes were shining. There was the trace of a tear track down her cheek.

Aphrodite leaned down and kissed the salt of that absent tear. "Goodbye, beautiful Sappho," she whispered.

Then she turned and walked out of the chamber and into another time, an older time. The island of Lesbos opened up around her, the air full of cassia and myrrh, the sun warming the skin of mortals and immortals alike. She made her way around the isle to a place she knew. The delicately draped plants, the soft sound of water running by, the generous curves of the path as it led deeper and deeper, and of course the privacy. But in this violet-strewn bower, at this time, she knew, there was someone waiting for her.

"There are other ways," she whispered to herself as she prepared to draw aside the flowers. "There are other worlds."

Then she smiled, and went in to meet Sappho again.

Sorry, But We Really Don't Need a Love Goddess Right Now

Noah Ross

"Oh, almighty gods of Olympus. I humbly ask for your help in this, our moment of greatest need."

The young shrine maiden knelt in the temple of the gods. Her eyes closed as she prayed for all she was worth. Outside the temple's marble walls, the blue night sky was lit up ominously by fires in the distance, as sinister shapes moved in the shadows.

Pyrrha had entered a meditative-like state that she thought was bringing her closer to the gods. If she just tried a little more, then maybe they would answer.

"Have they heard you yet?"

Pyrrha sighed as her concentration was abruptly broken. "No, Tantalus, not yet."

Tantalus, the greasy-haired, lanky head of the temple, stamped his foot in frustration. "Then you must not be doing it right," he said.

"There is no right and wrong way to pray. If the gods are listening, they'll hear me," Pyrrha said.

The door to the temple's innermost chamber opened, and an old man with a white beard walked through. "We've finished evacuating the villagers and are hiding everybody in the temple's basement," he said.

"Good job, Aristophanes. At least you're doing more than complaining," Pyrrha said, shooting a glance at Tantalus.

"Well, of course I'm complaining," Tantalus said, his expensive gold-trim robes looking more ruffled than usual. "When that army of monsters is done burning down the village, they'll come here and kill us all."

"Not if the gods send us help," Pyrrha said, turning back to the altar. She wiped down her white robe and began to pray again, small statues of the gods staring down at her.

"Oh, what's the point? The Olympians don't care about our small village," Tantalus moaned. "Maybe we should hedge our bets and start praying to those animal-headed gods from the desert."

"Could you please stop whining for two seconds?" Aristophanes said.

"It's all right for you, old man. You've already lived your life. Dying doesn't mean anything to you. But I've still got so much life ahead of me! Except now I'm going to get killed by monsters because Pyrrha sucks at praying, and the gods aren't coming."

Pyrrha did her best to block out his words. "Oh, gods of Olympus. Please hear my plea and send us aid, and maybe that will shut him up." As soon as she said that she regretted it because surely the gods weren't going to answer a prayer like that.

Just as she was about to beg the gods for forgiveness, a brilliant light shone down through the temple window from the heavens.

Pyrrha, Tantalus and Aristophanes stared up in amazement, their mouths hanging open as what appeared to be a giant clam descended in the radiant light. Heavenly harp music sounded through the temple, seemingly coming from nowhere.

The giant clam grew still, and then slowly the two halves started to separate, light pouring out from inside. Like a shining pearl, a woman was revealed. Her radiant blonde hair flowed down her back like a majestic waterfall. She wore a gorgeous pink dress that complemented her hourglass figure, and when she smiled, it was like a thousand rainbows shone into existence at once.

"I am Aphrodite, goddess of love," she said. "And I'm here to help."

The three mortals stared at her for a long moment.

"Oh no," Pyrrha said.

"How unfortunate," Aristophanes mumbled.

"Oh, come on, seriously?" Tantalus complained.

Aphrodite's warm smile faded from her face as she looked at the despairing mortals. "Oh, what's wrong? I thought you were praying for some divine intervention. Did I get that wrong?"

"No, my lady, we were," Pyrrha said. "But, sorry, we don't really need a love goddess right now."

"Yeah, we need one of the other gods or goddesses," Tantalus said. "We need someone who can kill those monsters invading our village."

"Oh, I'm sorry, but the others are busy at the moment," Aphrodite said sheepishly. "The whole of Greece is under attack by an army of monsters led by Typhon, and everybody else is busy defending the biggest cities. I was supposed to stay on Olympus, but when I heard Pyrrha praying, I knew I had to come and help, so here I am."

"Well, thank you for coming, my lady," Pyrrha said.

"So how can I help?" Aphrodite asked eagerly.

"Could you destroy the monsters attacking our village?" Aristophanes asked.

"Mmmm." Aphrodite thought for a moment. "I'm not very good at destroying things, unless it's someone's love life, and only if they really deserve it."

"So that's a no, then?"

"I told you, she is useless. We are all doomed." Tantalus threw up his hands, tugging at his greasy hair in frustration. "Any of the other goddesses would be better than her. Athena or Artemis would save us in an instant, but *nooooo*, of course, we get stuck with the one who is really good at ruining dates."

"I am sorry," Aphrodite mumbled, looking down at the marbled floor.

"Tantalus, be nice. I'm sure there is a way she can help us. She is a goddess, after all," Pyrrha said. "My lady, surely you have some godly abilities that could help us."

"Oh, yes," Aphrodite said, perking up. "I can do this." She thrust her palm out and a spray of bubbly foam sprang forth. A soapy smell filled the air as the bubbles coated the floor of the temple.

"Foam? Well, I guess that's something," Aristophanes said. "You can make foam because of your origin, right? According to the legend, you were born from the sea foam when Uranus…"

"No, stop," Aphrodite said quickly. "I really don't like thinking about that."

"Sorry, my lady," Aristophanes said.

"Oh, good, foamy bubbles. That should mildly inconvenience the monsters before they chop our heads off," Tantalus said.

"It's also really good for your skin," Aphrodite added cheerfully. "Just add some water and soak for an hour and you'll come out with skin silky smooth."

"That's great. We can all look our best as the monsters are slaughtering us," Tantalus shouted. "I told you, she is completely useless. We're all going to die, and it's her fault."

"She is trying her best," Pyrrha said.

"Well, if this is the best she can do, then she shouldn't have bothered coming at all. I'd rather get no help at all than help from a useless, big-chested bimbo."

"You can't talk to her like that. She is a goddess," Pyrrha said.

"Hey, that's rude." Aphrodite pouted.

"Well, it's true. She's nothing but a ditzy blonde who is utterly useless," Tantalus continued to rave.

"No, I'm not," Aphrodite insisted. "I'll prove I can be useful. Watch this." She made a love heart symbol with her thumb and index fingers and pointed it at Tantalus.

Before anyone could do anything, a bright pink love heart shot out from Aphrodite's hands and struck him in the chest.

Tantalus slumped over, his mouth hanging open, staring sightlessly forward. "You are now in love with," Aphrodite scanned the temple for a moment, "that bowl of fruit," she said, pointing.

Tantalus's head immediately snapped towards the bowl, and his eyes widened. He ran his hand through his greasy hair and fixed his clothes before strutting over. "Hey there," he said in a smooth voice.

The fruit did not reply.

"I couldn't help but notice how ripe you look today," he said.

"Tehehehe," Aphrodite giggled. "That never gets old." She turned back to Pyrrha and Aristophanes who were staring at her. "What?"

"That was amazing, Aphrodite," Pyrrha said.

"Oh, hehe, thank you," the goddess said sheepishly, playing with her gorgeous blonde hair.

"Yes, this is great. You can make the monsters fall in love with rocks or something, and we can make our escape," Aristophanes said. "You truly have saved us."

"Yay!" Aphrodite said excitedly, and then she frowned. "Oh, no, wait, I can only make mortals fall in love with things. It doesn't work on monsters. Something about them not having any concept of love."

"Ah well, back to square one then," Aristophanes said. His wrinkled face sagged in disappointment.

"And may I say, you have a very nice pair of pears," Tantalus said, still trying to chat up the fruit bowl.

"Oh, I know," Aphrodite said. "I can ask my boyfriend for advice."

"Boyfriend?" Pyrrha asked, but Aphrodite didn't answer. She reached into her hair and rooted around before bringing out a beautiful blue shell.

She brought the shell up to her ear and waited for a moment, with Pyrrha and Aristophanes looking at her in puzzlement.

Suddenly, sounds of screaming blasted out from the shell, accompanied by the sound of metal on metal and the stamping of feet.

"Hi, honey, are you there?" Aphrodite said into the shell.

"Oh, hi babe," a gruff male voice came from the shell.

"We've got a little problem here and I was wondering if you could give me some advice," Aphrodite said cheerfully.

The sound of something sharp being swung at high speed came through before the voice said, "Yeah, sure, anything for you, darling."

"Well, you see, I'm in a small village under attack by monsters, and I was wondering how I should go about defending the lovely mortals here," Aphrodite said, but her words were drowned out by a guttural scream coming from the other side of the shell.

"Sorry, could you repeat that?" the shell asked.

Aphrodite held the shell to her mouth. "I said, how do I beat up monsters?"

"Oh, I was thinking about this the other day, battle strategies that are perfect for you, utilising your special skills to destroy the monsters. All you need to do is…" The sound of an explosion and several people screaming in agony, then a monster's roar, blasted out of the shell.

"Ah drat. It grew back all of its heads. I should probably go kill that before it eats all those mortals," the voice said. "Sorry, my pretty Pegasus. I've got to go. Talk to you soon. Love you lots."

"Oh, okay. Love you too, stay safe," Aphrodite said.

"You too. AAAAAAAAAAGGGGG! Die, you monsters!" the shell shouted one last time before growing silent.

"Was that the god of war?" Aristophanes whispered to Pyrrha.

"Can't believe he called her his pretty Pegasus," she giggled.

Aphrodite put the shell back into her hair and smiled. "See, I knew asking him would help. Now I just need to remember what the battle strategies were…" Her face fell. "Oh, he didn't actually say it, did he?"

Pyrrha shook her head.

"Ah, phooey," Aphrodite said. "I guess we'll just have to come up with something else."

"Is that a banana in your bowl? Or are you just happy to see me?" Tantalus said, still trying to chat up the fruit bowl.

"Well, we'd better come up with something quick, because I think the monsters have finished ransacking the village and are on their way here," Aristophanes said, peering out the temple's window.

"Oh no," Aphrodite said in a slight panic. "Maybe I can distract them by giving them dating advice whilst you guys escape; I'm pretty good at that. People always come to me for advice on Olympus. I can't count the number of times Zeus asked me how to woo a certain woman. I had to stop when Hera found out, but now he—"

"My lady, Aphrodite, calm down your rambling," Pyrrha said.

"I know, I'm just panicking," Aphrodite said, flustered.

"Don't worry, I'm sure we can find a solution," Pyrrha said. "What if we tried—"

The wall of the temple exploded. Everybody yelled as they were pelted by rubble. A giant figure loomed in the newly created hole in the wall.

The monsters had arrived.

A giant hoof slammed down onto the temple's marble floor as a humongous creature entered. A muscular man's body was topped with a bull's head. Wicked horns shot up from his temples. The Minotaur held a sharp, black obsidian axe in one huge fist. The handle was shaped like a screaming face. He snorted like a bull as he saw the terrified humans staring back at him.

Other monsters lurked outside the temple, but their general got first dibs on the humans inside.

"So, this is where you've been hiding. Which one of you mortals should I dispose of first?" The minotaur scanned the room. "Maybe that young maiden or the old geezer, or that lanky guy hiding in the corner who really likes fruit." Then his monstrous eyes finally rested on Aphrodite.

"Holy cow, you're a goddess!" he said, stumbling backwards in surprise.

"Huh? I mean, yes, I am," Aphrodite said. She stood up on her tiptoes to make herself taller and puffed out her chest. "I am a goddess of Olympus, and I demand you leave these people alone."

"What is an Olympian doing in a backwater town like this? I thought they were all defending the big cities," the Minotaur said, continuing to back up quickly. His huge body suddenly looked more awkward than intimidating.

Aphrodite strode forward, making a shooing motion with her hand. "Yes, begone monster or I'll be forced to smite you."

"Yes, of course, I'll leave right away," the Minotaur said, one hoof already out of the hole in the wall. "Just don't hurt me Athena, or are you Artemus? Or…" The Minotaur paused and stared at her.

Aphrodite blushed, but still tried to look as imposing as she possibly could.

"No, you're not Athena or Artemus," the Minotaur said slowly. "You're not even Hera or Hestia."

"I am too, Athena," Aphrodite lied.

"Oh yeah?" the Minotaur stepped away from the hole and walked up to her. "Then say something wise," he challenged, looming over her.

"Mmmmmh," Aphrodite thought. "An apple a day keeps the doctor away?" she mumbled.

The Minotaur snorted air from his nostrils, blowing her hair. "That doesn't sound very wise."

"Mmmmmh," Aphrodite mumbled, starting to sweat.

In that moment Aristophanes faked a coughing fit, which distracted the Minotaur long enough for Pyrrha to slip a piece of paper into Aphrodite's hand.

The goddess unwrapped the paper and read. "The only true wisdom is in knowing you know nothing – Socrates."

"Knowing nothing? That's not wisdom. I knew it. You're not wise," the Minotaur accused, pointing one giant finger at her. "You're not Athena, with that hair, and that figure and your clothes. You're just Aphrodite." The Minotaur wiped some sweat from his brow. "Phew, that's a relief. I thought I was in real trouble for a minute, but you're just some useless love goddess."

"I am not useless," Aphrodite insisted indignantly, stamping her high-heeled foot.

"Yeah, yeah, whatever you say," the Minotaur continued, then with one massive hand, pushed her aside. Aphrodite squealed as she stumbled. "Now, let's get back to the mortal killing."

"No, don't worry, my love. I'll protect you," Tantalus said, clutching his beloved fruit bowl close.

The Minotaur eyed him. "Okay, maybe I'll let one of the other monsters kill that weirdo." Then he turned to Pyrrha and Aristophanes. "All right, who wants to get up close and personal with my axe first?"

"Strike me down, you monster," Aristophanes said, stepping in front of Pyrrha. "You make a run for it whilst he is killing me."

"No," Pyrrha said, dashing in front of him. "Kill me first."

"No, Pyrrha, I'm an old man whilst you have your entire life ahead of you," Aristophanes said stepping in front of her again.

"But you're the wisest person I know. You need to pass your wisdom down to the younger generation. I can't offer them anything," Pyrrha said, elbowing him aside.

"You're a smart young girl, in time you will become wise," Aristophanes said pushing her out of the way. "But only if you don't die here."

"Stubborn old man."

"Foolish girl."

Pyrrha pulled on his beard whilst Aristophanes mashed his palm into her face.

"Oh my gods, shut up!" the Minotaur shouted. "I'll kill you both at the same time if that will make you stop arguing."

Pyrrha and Aristophanes stopped pushing each other and stared in terror as the Minotaur raised his giant axe.

"Now hold still," he said.

"No, stop!"

"Grrrr, what now?" the Minotaur growled, lowering his axe.

Aphrodite walked forward, a determined look on her face. "I have a deal for you, monster," she said. "I, Aphrodite, the goddess of love and one of the twelve Olympians, shall become your prisoner."

"What?" the Minotaur and the two humans said at the same time.

"I promise I will not try to escape," Aphrodite continued, "and you can use me as leverage against the other gods. But only if you promise to leave all these mortals alone."

"Aphrodite, no!" Pyrrha shouted.

The Minotaur rested his axe over his shoulder and stared down at the goddess. "You'll become my prisoner if I don't kill these mortals?"

"And any other mortals too," Aphrodite quickly amended. "And that goes for any other monsters under your command as well."

The Minotaur thought for a moment, scratching his chin. "Mmmmh, I do enjoy killing mortals, but delivering one of the Olympians to Typhon would definitely get me a promotion. Okay, you have yourself a deal, little miss love goddess."

"Good," Aphrodite said in relief.

The Minotaur bent down and lifted her up, throwing the love goddess over his shoulder. "Well, looks like you get to live another day, humans," the Minotaur said before walking out with his prize.

"You can't do this, Aphrodite," Pyrrha shouted.

"I'm sorry, Pyrrha," Aphrodite said, as she hung over the monster's shoulder.

"Nooooo," Pyrrha said. "We have to do something. We can't just let her sacrifice herself for us."

"But what can we do?" Aristophanes said.

"We have to fight back."

Before Aristophanes could stop her, Pyrrha grabbed the first thing she could find, which happened to be the fruit bowl that Tantalus was clutching. He let out a horrified cry, but Pyrrha ignored this and hurled the contents of the bowl at the retreating Minotaur. The fruit splattered against the monster's back, and he paused.

"Pyrrha, nooo," Aphrodite said as the Minotaur turned around.

"So, you want me to kill you, little human?" he asked.

"I can't let you just take Aphrodite like that," Pyrrha said, refusing to be intimidated by the huge monster standing in front of her. "She may be useless at fighting monsters, but she still came to help when no one else would. She has a kind heart and that's worth a thousand slain monsters."

"Aw," Aphrodite said.

The Minotaur placed the goddess down on the ground and approached Pyrrha, raising his axe again.

"No, you can't kill her. We made a deal," Aphrodite shouted.

"I'm not gonna kill her. I'll just break all her bones, but she'll still be alive," the Minotaur said.

Pyrrha pushed down her fear and stared up at him, refusing to back down. Just as the Minotaur got into swinging distance, he stumbled, almost tripping face-first into the shrine.

"Hey, watch it."

It was Tantalus crawling on the floor. He was crying his eyes out and picking up the remains of the smashed fruit Pyrrha had thrown. "No, this can't be, my beloved," he said through messy tears.

The sight of this man crying over a pile of smashed fruit was so bizarre, it stopped the Minotaur in his tracks. "What in Tartarus is up with him?"

"My love, noooooo!" Tantalus cried.

"He's really upset about the fruit," Pyrrha said, her brain running a million miles an hour. "Because it's special. Isn't that right, Aphrodite?"

"Oh, mmmh yes, very special," Aphrodite said, nodding her head rigorously. "It can turn mortals into gods."

The Minotaur's eyes widened. "What?" *That sounded too good to be true, but if it was a lie, then why was this mortal crying like his heart had been broken?*

"Yes, that's why I came to this temple actually," Aphrodite explained hurriedly. "I was delivering these special fruits to these mortals so they could become gods and help us fight off all the monsters, but now you've discovered our plans. Silly me. Whoops-a-daisy," she said, doing her best impression of an airhead.

"Hahaha, foolish love goddess," the Minotaur laughed. He batted Tantalus away with one hand and picked up the remains of the fruit. "Now I can become a god. God of the monsters. I won't have to take orders from Typhon anymore." He then proceeded to devour the smashed fruit in a rather disgusting display, licking his hands clean while pungent slobber dripped from his mouth.

Everybody stared as he finished off the smashed fruit. "Am I immortal yet? I don't feel any different," the Minotaur said.

"It can take a couple of seconds to kick in sometimes," Aphrodite said.

"Still don't feel any different," the Minotaur said. Then he sniffed. "Wait a minute, I smell something. It smells flowery, like soap."

"Yes, that's it," Pyrrha said, subtly stepping in front of the foam on the floor. "I've heard when you become an immortal you suddenly smell soap."

"Yes, that's all your mortal impurities being washed away, so it smells like soapy foam," Aphrodite said.

"YES! I am immortal. I am a god," the Minotaur bellowed. "Now Zeus himself shall fear me," he laughed. "I'm going straight to Olympus to take my rightful place on the throne."

He swung his axe back over his shoulder and went to leave, pausing as he walked past Aphrodite. "Thank you, love goddess. I guess you're not useless after all, as you doomed your fellow gods." Then still laughing, he exited through the hole in the wall.

"I AM NOW A GOD!" he proclaimed to the monsters waiting outside. "Now we march to Olympus."

The humans watched in disbelief as the triumphant Minotaur led his army of monsters away.

"Wow, I can't believe that actually worked," Aristophanes said.

"Tehehe. He didn't expect a ditzy love goddess to be able to trick him," Aphrodite giggled. "He shouldn't underestimate me just because of my looks."

"Now we need to run before he realises what has happened," Pyrrha said.

"I don't think that will be necessary," Aphrodite said. "When Zeus sees an army of monsters approaching Olympus, he will hurl a thunderbolt at them, and if the Minotaur thinks he's immortal, then he won't attempt to dodge."

"Haha, I wish I could see that," Pyrrha said.

"Me too."

Pyrrha clasped Aphrodite's hands in her own. "Thank you, Aphrodite. You saved us."

Aphrodite giggled and blushed. "No, Pyrrha, I only helped you save yourself."

"We all worked together," Aristophanes said, nodding.

"Did you really mean what you said before?" Aphrodite asked.

"Of course," Pyrrha said. "I think it's obvious that the goddess of love would have the biggest heart."

Aphrodite couldn't help herself as she pulled Pyrrha into a hug. "Thank you so, so much."

"Don't let anybody call you a useless love goddess again."

Their tender moment was ruined somewhat by Tantalus moaning from his prone position on the floor, his hands smeared with what used to be fruit. "My beloved is gone, devoured by that monster. Now I am all alone."

"Oh, I should probably lift the spell on him now," Aphrodite said.

"No, wait, just a little longer," Pyrrha said. "This is hilarious."

The Love Goddess's War
Zach Shephard

The other prisoners in the yard were split into their cliques, or gangs, or whatever you want to call clusters of women in too-tight orange jumpsuits and mandatory makeup. I'd only been there an hour, so I didn't have a group of my own – and I wouldn't be around long enough to join one. I was just there to get some answers and be on my way. I'd probably keep the orange jumpsuit, though. I looked cute in it.

Lots of heads turned as I crossed the yard. Not just the guards, but the women, too. Guess they'd never seen a millennia-old love goddess before. I nonchalantly drew a lock of black hair behind my ear, letting my finger drag down the golden tan of my neck. People eat that stuff up.

Nina al-Dulaimi leaned against the chain-link fence, arms crossed. She was a few inches shorter than me, with a band of freckles bridging her cheeks across her nose. Punkish purple hair rose from her head like snapping flames. She definitely looked like someone with enough "fuck it" to try and blow up a robotics factory. My job was to find out who her co-conspirators were, and where they were hiding.

I couldn't care less about those questions. I had my own agenda.

Nina and her two pals saw me coming. I stepped into their circle, squinting against the sun beyond the fence.

"Let me guess," she said, looking me up and down. "The incels in D.C. made a law banning 'unconscionable temptation.'"

I laughed politely. "Close. I removed my ankle tracker without my boyfriend's permission."

"Welcome to the club, sister. Half the women here are in for that."

"But not you. Rumor has it you're here for something a little more explosive."

"Correction: something *almost* explosive. Those VulCorp guard-bots were a lot smarter than I'd hoped. Faster, too."

"Sounds like a fun story. Maybe you can tell me the full thing after we talk about the Cult of Inanna."

She looked me in the eye like she was deciding whether or not to chat about that particular subject, but I knew where she'd end up. People don't say no to me.

Nina dismissed her pals with a gesture of her head. They left to join a basketball game.

"All right," she said. "What do you want to know?"

"You formed a cult. Why?"

Nina snorted, her freckle-band scrunching. "Sister, look around you. We get arrested for not wearing our ankle trackers; for leaving the house without permission. For having the *audacity* to exercise free speech. And then we stand trial in a court run by a man, with a jury that's down to only six people because half the population is no longer allowed to serve on one. We can't vote, can't work, can't live a life without the permission of our husband or father or *government-assigned handler*. So why did we form a resistance? Because in the dystopian shitstorm that is 2047, someone *had* to."

"But why a cult? And why Inanna?"

"Because this movement needed a symbol. Someone to worship. Inanna was the Sumerian Queen of Heaven; the goddess of love and war. The women of this world tried love for a long while, and it got us nowhere. So now it's time for war."

Worship. It had been *centuries* since I was last worshiped. Sure, I could turn heads in a prison yard, but that wasn't the same. All the cults of Aphrodite had died out a long time ago. Were things really changing back? I needed to know more.

My next question got cut short by screams from the basketball court. Personally, I'd have been willing to ignore the distraction, but – Nina? Not so much. She sprinted past me toward the action.

The guards were throwing around some of the women. Nina scooped up a rolling basketball mid-charge and hucked it into the fray. It bounced off a guard's head. He turned his sights on her and came forward, baton held low.

Nina raised her fists like she was ready to box the guy. Gotta give her credit for bravery, but I wasn't about to let her get walloped before she told me more about the cult.

"Hey," I said. The guard looked my way just as he and Nina were squaring up. I moseyed in between them. "It was an accident. You can let her go."

He gave me the same look Nina had earlier, considering his options. He sneered.

"Back away, lady."

Oh, no. No-no-no. That wouldn't do at all.

I'd made kings melt at my feet with a smile. I'd been the start and end of wars. I'd seduced the goddamned gods themselves. I wouldn't be refused by a dickless goblin with a stick.

I repeated my hair-behind-the-ear trick from earlier, adding a coy smile to the performance. As my finger came down my neck, the guard grabbed my wrist and yanked me to the ground.

No one had raised a hand against me in three thousand years – not since the siege of Troy. I didn't know how to react. I froze.

The rest of it was a blur. I saw a streak of purple hair flash overhead as Nina dove in to help. I saw a swarm of gray-uniformed guards swallowing us up. I saw nothing else after that, because all I could do was cover my head against the fists and feet.

* * *

Every cell in the prison had a mirror so inmates could do their makeup. I was using mine to check my bruises. Flashbacks of Troy shot through my mind like Diomedes' spear had shot through my hand, all those centuries ago. It felt like the wound was opening all over again. My heart raced at the thought, and not in the way I normally like.

I still couldn't make sense of what had happened in the yard. It'd been years since I'd needed to put serious effort into my charm, but it should have been like riding a bike. I'd never had it fail before. What was going on?

The door opened behind me. "Meal time."

I turned. The guard looked me over. A slimy smile crawled up one side of his face, like a slug migrating north.

"I'm not supposed to be here," I said.

"Sure, cutie. Just like everyone else."

"No – listen to me. I'm not a real prisoner. I'm just here to do a job for my husband. Ask the warden."

He came into the room. He stood too close. His breath smelled like greasy onion rings.

"Well I don't see your husband here. Maybe you could do a job for *me* instead." He grinned, letting out more onion fumes.

I gave him a look. *The* look. The one that makes men throw themselves onto puddles so my shoes won't get dirty. The one that turns CEOs into my personal footstools. Onion-breath didn't even react to it. He just kept grinning, like he was deciding which part of me to sample first.

"After dinner," I said, and brushed his hand with a finger as I walked past. I didn't stop. Didn't look back. I just got out of there as fast as I could without looking rushed.

What in the *hell* was happening? I was Aphrodite – goddess of love and lust, charmer of anything-she-damned-well-pleases. And now I couldn't even convince a half-brained swamp-troll to let me out of a cage? Something was wrong. Something was really, really wrong.

I got to the meal hall, with its plain white walls and rows of tables. Someone scooped three ladlefuls of three different slops onto my tray. I took it over to the table where a beacon of fiery purple hair sat. Nina, bruised like I was, nodded at me mid-chew. She gestured with her fork at the bench across from her. I sat.

"Nice try with the guard outside," she said. "You're probably used to that sort of stuff working, huh?"

"Yeah. I must be off my game."

She smiled around a mouthful of food. "Straight-up siren. Just like I figured."

"Huh?"

"Siren. It's what the rest of us call women like you. Someone so irresistible she doesn't have to live like a twelfth-class citizen. Don't worry – I'm not mad about it. Jealous? Sure. But not mad. I'm glad anytime a woman gets ahead in this world. I just wish it weren't limited to the supermodels among us."

"For what it's worth, this siren's lost her song. The guards aren't having it."

Nina nodded, stirring her slop. "That's the growing trend these days. Men barely even see us as human beings anymore. No wonder you can't wrap anyone around your finger – it's hard to call the shots when you're just an object."

I browsed the meal hall. The women all looked dejected and downtrodden. The guards leered at them, occasionally approaching to do whatever they thought passed as flirting. The women just had to sit there and take it.

Look, I'll admit: I never really paid attention to how other people lived. I always had it easy, hooking up with whatever king or warlord or rock star could give me the cushiest life. The only time I noticed other women was when they had the gall to challenge my beauty. But finally seeing the world from their point of view was a serious eye-opener.

"I'm Nina, by the way. Short for Ninshubur."

I wasn't able to hide my surprised look, but Nina couldn't have known what I was thinking.

"Not my real name," she said. "But everyone in the Cult of Inanna picks something like that. I chose Ninshubur because she was Inanna's handmaiden – totally loyal to the goddess we worship." She swirled her fork at me. "What can I call you?"

What the hell. When in Rome . . .

"How about Aphrodite?"

Nina smiled. "Sure thing, 'Phro. Although we're at war these days – we could use more Athenas than Aphrodites."

Sure, if you wanted a bunch of butt-ugly gutter-hags to join your resistance. I decided to let the comment slide; old grudges weren't important just then.

"Why were you so curious about the cult, anyway?" Nina asked.

She wouldn't believe the real reason, so instead: "I wanted to know what kind of group would attack the VulCorp factory."

"The kind that doesn't want to be hunted down by an army of misogyny-enforcing robots. If Henry Festus has his way, women everywhere will be living in a police state. More than we already are."

"And you think blowing up VulCorp would have made things better?"

"'Would have'? I think it *will*."

"I don't know if you've noticed, but we're sort of in prison. Probably not much demolition you can do from here."

She smiled. "Inanna's got a lot of worshipers on the outside, 'Phro. And they're ready to change the world." She looked at the clock on the wall. "Duck."

"Huh?"

"Duck!" She dove under the table, just as the entire prison shook.

The booming sound sent everyone for cover. Alarms blared. Guards ran off, yelling into their radios over the chaos. Another boom hit, raining debris from the ceiling.

Nina and I scrunched together under the table. She grinned at me. "Goddess of war, baby. You ready to get out of this hellhole, Aphrodite?"

After the incident in the prison yard had dredged up some trauma from Troy, I wasn't eager to join any fights. But I also wasn't keen on sticking around in a place where my usual weapons weren't working.

I gestured at the world beyond our cover. "Lead the way, Ninshubur."

We escaped through the panic and falling rubble, into one of two waiting transport helicopters. Nina's cultists provided suppressing fire against the prison guards as inmates piled in around us. With everyone on board, the white vehicles carried us away, soaring through the sunset like swans over water.

* * *

We sat strapped into the helicopter's seats, along the walls. The woman across from Nina wore urban camo and matching face paint. The fingers of her right hand were tattooed with a letter apiece, spelling out "FEAR" for anyone on the wrong end of her fist.

"Thanks for the save, Pheebs," Nina said.

A bone-white grin split the black-and-gray camouflage. "Don't look at me – it was your plan."

"And I was hoping we wouldn't have to use it. We really screwed up at VulCorp. How're things looking?"

The grin faded. "Not great. Security at the factory increased after your attack. It'll only get worse once Festus hears you've been sprung."

Nina leaned forward, elbows on knees, index fingers tapping together. I'd seen looks like that before – in generals, warmongers, revolutionaries. She wasn't just thinking; she was witnessing the next battle in her mind.

"What's the call?" Pheebs asked.

"I need a minute. This is Aphrodite. I've got a good feeling about her, but she's the supreme queen of mega-sirens, and is just now figuring out how bad things are. Fill her in while I think."

And so Pheebs did.

She told me all about Henry Festus, the CEO of VulCorp Robotics. He wasn't technically a politician, but he was rich enough to buy his way into a presidential advisory role, so he wielded power like one. Most people credited him with masterminding the "War on Women" that had led to – well, to the state of affairs that allowed average-Joe prison guards to resist a love goddess.

A lot of the misogynist laws on the books were Henry's doing. His latest masterpiece would strip women of their few remaining rights, and his robots were slated to enforce it. The attack on his factory, Pheebs said, had been meant to show legislators women wouldn't go down without a fight. It hadn't convinced them.

Nina looked up at the helicopter's ceiling. Hanging there was a small bundle of reeds, swaying like an ornament as we cut through the sky. She smiled.

"I've got it." She elbow-nudged me and pointed at the reeds. "Symbol of Inanna. When in doubt, ask what a war goddess would do."

"And what's that?"

"Stop thinking so much, and go to war." She yelled to the pilot: "Change course to Henry Festus's estate. We're kicking down the front door."

Everyone cheered. They chanted Inanna's name, pumping their fists at the hanging reed-bundle. I could feel their energy churning like the waters about Cyprus. They really did worship her.

No one had worshiped Aphrodite in years. And I finally understood why.

There was a time when I'd been a more active deity. So much so that I burned out. I couldn't take the responsibility any longer. So I headed west. I found Greece. The gods of Olympus invited me to be their love goddess, saying they wanted nothing else out of me. It sounded like the change I needed.

Still, it took me a while to break old habits. I occasionally tried doing more than my assigned duties. It never worked out: weaving on Athena's loom got me yelled at; descending to the battlefield of Troy got me injured by a mortal's spear. Going outside my lane wasn't working, so I did what the gods had asked, and stuck to love.

Over the next few millennia I ignored the world's problems, literally fucking my way through existence. The Aphrodite cults died off. And who could blame them? I hadn't given anyone reason to worship me.

The women in that helicopter worshiped Inanna. It was a beautiful thing to see. It made me want to return to that life before Olympus, when I was a true queen.

Nina offered me an automatic rifle. "What do you say, 'Phro? Wanna change the world?"

I accepted the gun. I turned it in my hands, taking in its lines, its violence. In my mind's eye, I saw battle again.

The spear of Diomedes flashed through my vision. I dropped the gun like it had bitten me.

"She might want to sit this one out," Pheebs said.

Nina picked up the gun, put her other hand on my shoulder. "It's okay. War takes getting used to. Maybe next time."

Everyone else was arming themselves: these mortal women in orange jumpsuits, only minutes out of prison, ready to fight under the banner of Inanna. Meanwhile I, an *actual* goddess, sat frozen in fear. It wasn't right.

"I want to help," I said.

"I know you do, sister. But Pheebs is right – she's seen what fear can do to a soldier in battle."

"So we don't battle. We walk in the front door."

The crowd laughed, shaking their heads.

"Sorry, 'Phro," Nina said, "but we're way past that point. You've seen how useful the siren approach is these days."

"It might not work on some random guard, sure. But I bet I could pull it off with Henry Festus."

"Why's that?"

"Because," I said, "he's my husband."

* * *

The reaction was about what I'd expected. Lots of angry shouting, a few pointed guns. Some of the women wanted to throw me out of the helicopter. But I'd had faith that Ninshubur, known for her loyalty to a goddess, would at least hear me out. And she did.

I told everyone the truth: that I had no love for Henry Festus, and that I hadn't even realized just how much damage he'd done to women until today. I was, after all, a "siren." Reality didn't much apply to me. I was with Henry because his wealth gave me an easy life. Same reason I'd seduced any number of kings throughout the centuries – although I didn't mention that part to my present audience.

"We can't trust her," Pheebs said.

"Hold on," Nina said. "Let me think."

"The story doesn't even make sense! If she's married to Festus, how'd she get arrested?"

"I didn't," I said. "Not really. Nina wouldn't talk to investigators after she hit the VulCorp factory, but I told Henry I could probably charm some info out of her. So he arranged to have me fitted for a jumpsuit. But that was just my excuse to get in. The real reason I was there was because I'd heard about the Cult of Inanna, and wanted to learn more."

The truth wasn't doing me any favors. Everyone only focused on the part where I'd been sent in as a spy for Mr. Misogyny himself. Lots of arguing followed. Nina's shout was the only thing that restored order.

"Hey! How many of you actually said a word to Aphrodite in prison? That's what I thought. She and I talked, and she *never* dug for information about the attack. It's like she said: she was only curious about Inanna. Yeah, she's married to an asshole. But she only did it to get ahead in a world where people like us don't have a hell of a lot of opportunities. And it's not like she's supported Henry Festus's War on Women." She looked over, held my gaze for a long moment. "I believe her. And if she's got a way to get us close to Festus, we're not wasting it."

And that's how a head-on suicide charge into Henry's mansion got turned into a small-scale infiltration mission. I'd get Nina in, she'd pull the trigger. Everyone else would wait a safe distance away in case things went south. We had it all worked out.

Things, unfortunately, would not work out.

* * *

Getting past the gate was easy enough. The guard-bot's facial scan identified me, despite the bruises. It waved me up the drive. Once we were clear, Nina folded down the car's back seats and crawled out of the trunk. She sat beside me.

"Jesus," she said, taking in the property. "Talk about living the high life."

Even at night, the place was a wonder. Floodlights shone from the trimmed lawn, illuminating lavender leaves on artfully spaced wisterias; each tree looked like its own museum display. Everything on the property was well-manicured: every blade of grass, every perfect bloom. It was nice having a fleet of robots designed solely for landscaping.

"Sounded like things went smoothly at the gate," Nina said.

"Maybe. The bot didn't recognize this car; it spent a little too long looking." I glanced at the change of clothes the cult had outfitted us with. "Pretty sure it realized this isn't my usual style, too."

"Think we'll have any problems getting in the front door?"

"I'm thinking we should skip it altogether. There'll just be another bot waiting for us. Better to try a window."

Nina checked the chamber on her handgun, let the slide click back into place. "You're the expert here."

I stopped the car well before reaching the mansion. Nina and I got out and maneuvered between the floodlights, sticking to the patches of darkness the exterior designer had left to boost contrast. At one point we had to dodge a squad of landscaping bots patrolling for imperfections; I thought we were toast when one of them turned its headlamps our way, but Nina yanked me behind a bush. It looked away and the group continued on.

Sprinting the final distance to the house's side, we flattened ourselves against the darkened wall. Nina gave me a look. Under the starlight, I saw a flash of her smile.

"I can hear your heartbeat from here, 'Phro. Exhilarating, isn't it?"

Exhilarating? Scary? Who's to say. Regardless, I couldn't remember the last time I'd felt so alive. It made me wonder if going to Greece had been a mistake all those years ago. Had I wasted the past few millennia being a do-nothing love goddess?

A bright light flashed on in the air overhead, shining down on us like Helios at midday. I raised my hand against it, squinting. Nina aimed her gun, but it was too late: the hovering security drone launched a silver net that enveloped us both and cinched up automatically. We dropped to the ground as a unit, my head bouncing off the house's faucet along the way. A trickle of blood ran down my temple. The net tightened further.

Great. *This* again.

* * *

I heard his mechanical footsteps before he came into view. Henry had lost his legs in a car wreck years before I'd even met him, and replaced them with prosthetics of his own design. It was part of the reason I'd married him – I knew I'd never need to do any of the physical stuff.

He stood before us, hands on his metal hips. Under the drone's bright spotlight, I saw just how ugly Henry was; his curly red hair seemed dirtier, his face craggier. Every flaw was exaggerated now that I'd seen the impact he'd had on the world.

Three bronze security bots stood with Henry, their lenses staring like we were being publicly shamed. The man himself shook his head in exaggerated disappointment.

"I was loath to believe it," he said. "When they informed me you'd fled with the other degenerates, I'd thought them mistaken. Surely the wife of Henry Festus was smarter than that. Surely she knew she'd be freed through official channels soon enough. But, alas. Here we are. You come to my home bringing your rabble and ill intentions. I'd hoped for better."

I felt Nina struggling to move her arm and aim the gun, but the net was too tight.

"Henry," I said, "you know I love you. I'd never—"

"Stop. I'll save you the effort by informing you we've located your reinforcements – the ones you believe to be so cleverly hidden in the hills. A squadron of my latest creations is on their way to apprehend them now." He smiled wickedly, the drone's light drawing knife-sharp shadows down his face. "I trust they'll resist."

Nina thrashed, spitting profanity. Meanwhile, I reached out with my mind. I called on the powers of the sea: the foam encircling Cyprus, that had washed away my old life and carried me into Greece. I asked for its help.

Henry knelt next to us, stroked my hair through the net. "I've never met a woman so beautiful as you, darling. You certainly are one of a kind. But as much as I'd like to overlook your disobedience, this is one betrayal we can't simply wash away."

"Don't be so sure," I said, and released the fury of the flood.

The faucet I'd hit my head on blasted out from the wall, propelled by a Poseidon-strength spray of foamy water. It cracked Henry's jaw and knocked him back. Before he could recover I summoned a strength I hadn't employed since my time before Greece. I spread my arms wide, ripping the wire net apart.

The bots rushed forward to rescue Henry. Two of them dragged him away. The third raised a wrist-mounted barrel to us.

Nina filled its metal torso with her entire clip before it could fire. The machine fell back, body spitting sparks.

I scrambled through the still-spraying water, ripped a leg from the fallen bot's body, and charged the others. The makeshift weapon was nothing like the ancient swords and spears I was used to, but times change. I was far too late in changing with them.

I swung the leg hard into the first bot, shattering both my weapon and its head. I dropped the leftover junk and grabbed the machine-man before he could tip over. He served as my shield against the gunfire of the third.

Hiding there behind my metal barrier, listening to bullets clang into the thing, I didn't think back to Troy. I didn't think back to the spear of Diomedes, piercing my flesh and retiring me from combat for the next three thousand years. No. Instead, I thought about the time before Greece. The time when I could terrify any man or woman on the battlefield, just as easily as I could seduce them.

Nina may have worshiped Inanna, but there was one thing she didn't seem to know about the goddess: when the Queen of Heaven tired of her responsibilities, she left the lands of Sumer and Babylonia, looking for something simpler. She found Greece. She met the gods of Olympus. And alongside them, she became Aphrodite.

Now, thousands of years later, Aphrodite was finally ready to reprise her original role. In a big fucking way.

I threw the mangled bot into its still-firing brother, knocking them both over. Like an angry lion I pounced on the final attacker. I controlled its wrist-barrel with one hand, while my other grabbed for the throat. Maybe not an especially vulnerable target on a robot, but old habits die hard.

I ripped a handful of metal and wires away. The machine shuddered. I slammed my fist through its bronze skull, planting its processor about four inches into the ground.

I stood and turned to Henry. A compartment on his outer thigh opened up, offering a handgun – a laser prototype he'd been working on. I stepped over and stomped his wrist before he could grab it. Bones crunched beneath my heel. I hadn't heard that sound in far too long.

Henry moaned in pain. I picked up the gun.

"This is something I should have done years ago," I said. "Like, three thousand of them." I leveled the gun at Henry's head. Before he could beg for mercy, I pulled the trigger. In the middle of his pale white forehead, a red rose bloomed.

My husband fell back, lifeless. Nina came to my side. Above the freckle-band, her eyes stood wide.

"Okay," she said. "I'm gonna need an explanation for what the hell I just witnessed."

In the distant night, gunfire rang.

"Later," I said. "For now, I've got some old rust to shake off."

We ran toward the sounds of battle, guns held ready. Somewhere in the hills, my cult awaited.

Froth

Lauren Talveryn

I've never understood the appeal of a bath. I don't love heat or bubbles or strong scents. I loathe the feeling of wet paper so much that I won't risk bringing a book with me. And I hate being naked. There's really not one aspect I can totally get behind.

But now I stand in my bathroom, feeling the cold tiles beneath my feet. Candlelight dances in the glimmering porcelain. I collected every candle I could find around my house. I only found five. That wouldn't be nearly enough. I had to make a special trip to the store. Thankfully, they had some on clearance.

Tiny glass jars rest on every surface: the sink, the back of the toilet, the shelves. I cleared off the lowest shelf of my linen cabinet to make more space. A potent medley of scents wafts to my nose: vanilla, rose, pumpkin, clean laundry, sea breeze.

The two tallest candles sit on my vanity. White tapers stand sentinel on golden candlesticks, slowly burning away. A burgundy, leatherbound book rests between them, opened to the center. Cursive etched in ink scrawls across the yellowing pages. The bottom of the page is nearly brown after decades, maybe centuries, of fingers turning it. The woman at the bookstore looked so ancient she might have been the author. But they did take Apple Pay, funnily enough.

My fingers wrap around the stem of the wine glass on the table. Thick, amber liquid sloshes against the sides. There is so much honey in the white wine it's become viscous. The book gave explicit instructions: the juice of a golden apple, oil of the narcissus flower, three fingers of honey, and an imperial pint of dry white wine. If I don't call it a potion, it doesn't feel quite so ridiculous.

I can't put it off much longer. My purple silk robe falls to the tiles, leaving me bare. Even alone and behind a locked door, my shoulders hunch to hide myself. My arms shift towards my chest and pelvis like a shield. I reach for the wine glass and step towards the tub.

I've lived in this apartment for three years, and I've never used the bathtub. I had to scrub it clean last night before using it. Pearly bubbles froth along the edges. The book said the water needed to be hot. Steam rises from the water's surface.

I hiss as I step in. It nearly singes my skin. I stand for a moment, waiting for my body to adjust. Slowly, I descend and displace the water. It rises up along the smooth white sides of the tub. The floral scent of the oils overpowers me. Essence of myrtle activates in the warmth. I relax in spite of myself.

I inhale through my nose and exhale through my mouth. The wine glass presses against my open lips. I swallow deeply. The golden nectar disappears down my throat. After half of it is gone, the sweetness burns almost as much as the water's heat. I force it all down.

My mind swims through the haze. I feel the wine coursing through my blood. My tongue feels leaden. I say the words before they vanish into the ether.

"I call upon you, Aphrodite. Goddess of love. Queen of beauty. Lady of desire. I beseech your favor. I honor you. Please grant me your divine gift."

The dripping faucet breaks the silence.

"I call upon you, Aphrodite. Goddess of love. Queen of beauty. Lady of desire. I beseech your favor. I honor you. Please grant me your divine gift."

I feel my heartbeat in my ears, but I hear no voice.

"I call upon you, Aphrodite. Goddess of love. Queen of beauty. Lady of desire. I beseech your favor. I honor you. Please grant me your divine gift."

My eyelids grow heavy. I crane my head back, resting it against the porcelain edge. This was madness. I never truly expected it to work.

I sit still, but water splashes across the floor. I hear it drip down across the tiles.

My eyes open. But the woman in front of me belongs in dreams. Golden waves fall from her shoulders and disappear beneath the water. Amber eyes stare back at me from behind sharp cheekbones. Every feature could be carved of marble. She could be a sculpture. But her full chest rises and falls with each breath.

Her voice is satin. "I have heard your call, my child. Now that I look upon you, I see you do not lack for beauty."

Blood flushes across my cheeks. It's not from the heat. Her smile stokes the flames. I mutter, "Thank you."

She leans in toward me. I force myself to meet her eyes, to avoid the bare curves lurking beneath the water. A bright white foam gathers around her. It glimmers as if it's made of a thousand tiny moonstones.

Her golden irises glow in the low candlelight. She proclaims, "I have clearly graced you with my first gift at birth. So you must want for my second? Love."

Words evaporate on my tongue. Wine courses through my veins. But the water laps against her chest. Glimmering bubbles cling to her perfect skin. Puddles form on the floor where she displaced the water. She is truly here. I'm in the presence of a goddess.

I answer, "Yes."

She fills the silence. "You have grown tired of solitude. You yearn for devotion. You are prepared to make the exchange."

"The exchange?"

Her gaze drifts across the dimly lit room. She gestures to the open book. Wax falls from the candles onto the thin pages.

"Surely those pages tell of what you must do. If you require one of my gifts, you must sacrifice the other. I fear I only hold dominion over two: love and beauty. Unlike some of my fellow goddesses. They have so many bounties I'm certain not even they could name them all. For centuries, I was extravagant. I bestowed them in equal measure. I squandered my blessings on ingrates too vain and too enamored to honor me. Now if I grant one, I must collect the other."

I've heard that I am pretty all my life from family, friends, and strangers. They don't mention my mind, my humor, or my heart. They praise my blue eyes, my bright smile, my thin waist, my flat stomach, and my long legs. So do my dates. It's always the first word they say. But it never captures them for long. They stay dates or friends or friends with benefits. Or they vanish. They never become boyfriends.

Beauty has yet to bring me love. But tonight it could.

I ask, "How will it happen?"

"It will not happen all at once. I am not cruel like so many of my fellow Olympians. I am no true daughter of Zeus, reveling in destruction. And the old powers are not as strong as they once were. It will fade gradually, as it does for most. For you, it will be faster. Each year you will lose more splendor. But as it wanes, your love will wax. Many loves burn strong but grow weak and frigid with time. I offer you a love that fortifies with each passing season. After long, it will become unbreakable."

The promise of infallible love led me to podcasts on folk magic, to the Classics section of the library, to the coven-owned bookstore, then into this bathtub. I've been chasing it for decades but have never caught it. I've never had a real boyfriend, never brought someone home to meet my family, never lived with a man. I know what I want, even if there is a price to be paid.

"That's what I want. I'll make the sacrifice."

Her smile grows even wider, somehow more alluring. The foam surrounding her gleams brilliantly. She's even more beautiful when she's revered.

Water drips from her flawless skin as she lifts her right arm. Impossibly long, thin fingers reach across and wrap around my shoulder. Warmth radiates through my veins at her touch. "Each turn of the sun, or each year as you mortals now say, you will perform this same ritual. You will reaffirm your vow to me. And I will reward you in kind. I will grant you a love without end."

Heat flows across every inch of my skin. It's as if fire surrounds me instead of water. My blood feels thick. My eyes fall shut. The backs of my eyelids morph into molten gold.

* * *

I performed the ritual faithfully for three turns of the sun. Aphrodite delivered on her end of the bargain. Cyrus approached me at my favorite bar two weeks later. When was the last time someone actually asked me out on a date in public? That was divine intervention, indeed.

We glided to each new milestone with ease: from first date, to talking, to dating, to exclusive, to boyfriend and girlfriend. There was no strife, no self-sabotage, no bullshit. We fell in love. My friends, my immediate family, and my extended family were as enchanted as me. They can't believe I got so lucky. He moved in. We got a dog.

I didn't believe Cyrus was truly human until I met his mom. She pulled out the photo albums and glowed with maternal love. I saw him as an infant, a toddler, a kid, a preteen and a teenager. Only then was I sure that Aphrodite didn't form him from dust and sea foam especially for me.

He laughs with you not at you. He remembers the little things. He whispers an inside joke to you when you really need a laugh. He drives with one hand on the wheel and one hand on my knee on long road trips. He runs his fingers through my hair when I fall asleep on the couch with my head in his lap. He says I love you before he hangs up the phone.

One of his best traits is that he cannot lie. He is honest. I don't have to sift through every sentence and message to find the subtext. His love is from the heart, and it's his only truth.

That means I saw the proposal coming a mile away. He suddenly had to go to the dentist once a week in the jewelry district. He left browser windows open on his phone and laptop searching for rings. He couldn't meet my eyes when he suggested I get my nails done as a treat last week. His voice wavered when he said we should dress up for our picnic on the beach.

My fingers grip the sink's edge. I glance down at my left ring finger. I envision the glimmering diamond that will rest on it in a few hours. Warmth spreads across my chest. It dissipates as soon as my eyes shift to the mirror.

Aphrodite gives just as she takes away. There's only so much manufactured beauty money can buy. Hair extensions only add so much volume. My white scalp peeks through my thin brown locks tauntingly. Shallow wrinkles etch into dull skin. Foundation fills them in. My cheeks and lips look gaunter each day. Fillers are too expensive to keep up with. But there's nothing you can buy to replace the light in your eyes. And I haven't even moved away from my face. I can hardly look in the full-length mirror anymore. I barely recognize myself.

Everyone else pretends not to notice. At first, they asked if I was tired. Was I getting enough sleep? Did I need to start taking vitamins? When was the last time I had bloodwork done? They're too kind, too loving to say what their eyes show. Everyone except Cyrus.

He tells me I'm beautiful every day. He means it. He doesn't see a wasting, waning woman. He sees the love of his life. I wish that was enough for me.

Disgust clouds my vision every time I look in the mirror. I avoid taking pictures. I stare at the ones we do take, cursing every flaw. I scroll back to old photos and feel nostalgic for the girl I see. She was lonely. She cried far too often. She yearned for the love I now have. But she was beautiful.

I know Cyrus hired a photographer for the proposal. He accidentally made the deposit on our shared card and made up some story about a birthday present for his mom. I don't want to hate these pictures. I want to feel beautiful and loved all at once. I don't think that's too much to ask.

The bathtub sits empty behind me, unused since last year. I should have performed the ritual last week. But I couldn't bring myself to do it. I just need to get through today. Then she can have another pound of my flesh.

Cyrus leans into the doorway. "Ready, babe? You look amazing. Car's packed, just come down when you're ready."

Nervous energy thrums in the air around him. He hasn't sat still all morning. His fingers drift to the pocket inside his blazer in spite of himself. A real smile spreads across my lips when I look at him. I grab my purse. "I'm ready. Let's go."

As I step towards the door, the faucet in the bathtub turns on. Water gushes into the porcelain for a few seconds. Then it shuts off. My blood runs cold.

"That thing's been acting up all week. I'll put in a maintenance request later, let's hit it." Cyrus rushes me out the door.

He chatters the entire drive to the coast. When he's nervous, he talks a mile a minute. I go silent. I force my mind to dwell on the nerves about the engagement, to my heart hammering against my chest. This is everything I wanted, what I sacrificed for.

But I can't ignore the pit in my stomach. It's been opening up more each day that I've skipped the ritual. Each time the faucet turns on of its own volition, it tears further. It's a warning. I just need to get through today with what little beauty I have left.

We pull into a parking spot. The lot beside the beach is nearly full as sunset approaches. People shuffle towards the sand in flip flops. Waves crash against the sand. Cyrus is out of the car as soon as he turns off the engine.

As he walks towards the trunk, a dove lands on the side mirror. Up close, I can see the shades of blue and green on the tips of its gray feathers. A black band circles its thin neck. It stares back at me with amber eyes. I sit frozen.

It looks at me for a minute. As it takes flight, I see a flash of gold in the mirror. It's there for an instant. Then it's gone.

Cyrus opens my door. The picnic basket rests on his left arm. He reaches for my hand with his right. "You coming? It looks like it'll be a great sunset."

Salt hangs in the air. Tall reeds and blades of sea grass dance in the wind. My dress billows with each gust. Sand drifts across the wooden boardwalk like the waves in front of us. I feel the grains against the soles of my feet. I focus on the feel of Cyrus's hand in mine, the breeze on my skin, and the briny taste on my lips.

Seabirds glide in the air above us. Swimmers disappear beneath the water. Kids run back and forth between their families on the shore and the ocean. Sandcastles along the water's edge withstand breaking waves.

As we get closer to the water, the sand becomes more compacted. Footprints pressed in the grains mark our path. Each step is less effort than the last. Sharp pain explodes across my heel.

"Shit!"

I look down at the sand. Blood seeps from a fresh cut. The crimson oozes, filling in the shallow imprints of my toes and arch. Granules cling to the wound's edges.

Panic consumes Cyrus' face. This isn't part of his plan. He rushes over, leaving the blanket and basket behind. He asks, "What happened? Are you okay? You got cut? Someone must have broken glass or something. No one gives a shit about the environment, I swear."

It wasn't glass. I spot the broken seashell beside my foot. Blood coats the edge, confirming it's the culprit. The pastel pink and white betrays its danger. It's as sharp as any blade.

I jump on one foot, trying to keep my cut out of the sand, and fall onto the blanket. I hiss as I gingerly touch the wound. "I think it was a shell. It's okay. It's not that deep, I'll be fine."

He shuffles over to the basket. His hand disappears inside, searching for something to help. He pulls out napkins and passes them to me. Red seeps through the white instantly. He smiles. "Good thing we came for a picnic. I'm prepared. Do you want me to grab the first aid kit from the car?"

That was his idea, too. He was a Boy Scout. Before him, I didn't do a lot that would cause the need for a first aid kit. I didn't spend much time outside. I assure him, "No, I'm fine. I'm fine. Let's just eat. Thanks for doing all of this."

His usual smile returns to his face, replacing the fear in an instant. The right side of his grin is slightly higher than the left. His jawline is strong but not sharp. It's a perfect smile. It's the first thing that made me fall for him. It brings me back to the moment. He's going to ask me to marry him. It's finally happening.

His eyes drift to the horizon, trying to time the sunset perfectly. He pulls plastic containers from the basket. I spy pomegranate seeds, chocolate-covered espresso beans, pretzels and apple slices through the clear plastic. He brought all of my favorite snacks, the ones I would pick out for myself at the grocery store. After three years, he still makes me swoon. I wrap my arms around my legs and rest my head between my knees. I watch him and forget the rest of the world for a moment.

He replies, "We haven't had a picnic for so long. We used to do this a lot at the beginning, remember?"

I pry the lid off a container. The apple crunches as I bite into it. I laugh. "I do. You always used the same line. 'I got us a reservation at this new spot.'"

He chuckles and finishes the line in his signature, goofy tone, "It's got a great view of the park. Amazed I got another date with that one."

I pretend I don't see the cork of a champagne bottle sticking out of the open basket. "My mom always said finding someone who makes you laugh is the most important thing. Everything else changes. But you always need to laugh."

"My mom said something like that, too. Once you find someone you think is both beautiful and funny, the game's over. And I started my last match a while ago."

It's happening. He shifts from sitting to kneeling. I feel light-headed. I see a woman walk down the shoreline toward us. I spot a large camera lens under her long cardigan. My heart races.

He continues, "I'm sorry, you know words aren't really my thing. I'm more of a doer. And you make me feel like I can do anything. I love everything we've done together so far, but I'm ready to do so much more. I want to get married. I want to buy a house. I want to have kids. I want to see the world. I want to sit in a rocker on our front porch and watch our grandkids. I love you. I want to be with you forever. Will you marry me?"

The world glows. The sun shines. The diamond reflects the orange of the setting sunlight. As his hand trembles, the prism refracts every color of the rainbow. It glimmers. The camera flashes. The world is light.

But all I see is a new patch of white on the ocean. The foam spouts from the water. It rises from the depths. It clings to the surface. It grows and expands, pure white against the dark blue waves. In the dim light of the bathroom, it looks opalescent. But outside, it is bright and blinding.

Then she appears.

Golden waves emerge from the blue. Ivory skin inches out of the water. Every curve is bared and brilliant. Long legs and arms unfold as she rises to her full height. Her thin, lithe neck holds her head, as perfect as a bust, high. Molten gold eyes bore into me.

"Did the text not forewarn what it means to anger a goddess? Of the vengeance I will seek when a gift is taken but a sacrifice is not returned?"

The sea foam draws closer. It does not rise and fall with the waves. It moves in a straight line, determined and true. She uses it to propel herself to the shoreline.

"I am born of the sea. You come to my realm. You flaunt the love I bestowed upon you. You revel in the bliss I have granted you. Yet where is my offering?"

Cyrus and the photographer stare at me expectantly. Do they not see her before them? Do they not hear the rage-filled melody of her voice? Do they see that she is as beautiful as she is terrifying?

"I forewarned you. You were born with beauty's touch but not love's. I proffered an exchange."

Cyrus still kneels in front of me, watching me. But his eyes are different. They don't meet mine. They don't know me. His brown irises are my home. Now they stare through me.

"Yet you dare to drink from both cups. You drink of my nectar. You eat of my ambrosia."

The skin on my face grows taut. An unseen force pulls at the edges. With much more pressure, it will tear. My hair loosens. I feel it fall onto the blanket beneath me. The brown locks rest against the blue fabric. My fingers fly to my scalp. The feeling of bare skin turns my stomach.

"You have learned of a goddess's grace. Now you will know of her wrath."

Biographies

Anja Ulbrich
Foreword
Anja Ulbrich has been the A.G. Leventis curator of Cypriot Antiquities at the Ashmolean since 2009. She studied Classical Archaeology, Ancient History and History of European Art at Heidelberg University, Germany, and completed an MPhil in Classics (Greek archaeology) from the University of Cambridge where she encountered and became fascinated with Cypriot archaeology. Back in Heidelberg she holds a PhD with a thesis on sanctuaries of female deities in Cyprus during the Archaic and Classical periods.

Benjamin Cyril Arthur
Those That Hunger for Warmth
(First Publication)
Benjamin Cyril Arthur is a graduate from the University of Cape Coast. He is a participant of the Canex Creative Writing Workshop 2024 and a winner of the 2020 Samira Bawumia literary prize competition. He has been published by *Brittle Paper*, Flame Tree, Tampered Press, *Lunaris Review*, *Ghana Pride* anthology, *L únl ún* and the Ama Ata Aidoo Centre for creative writing. When he is not writing, he spends most of his time behind his camera.

Bernice Arthur
Obaasima Aphrodite
(First Publication)
Bernice Arthur is a student at Ashesi University with a deep passion for Africa. As an emerging writer, she is dedicated to exploring and rewriting the African narrative in better ways that reflect the true African identity while celebrating African culture and its people. Influenced by the late Ama Ata Aidoo and Efua Sutherland, Bernice is committed to telling authentic

stories that capture the essence of the African experience. Through her writing, she seeks to honor her heritage and contribute meaningfully to the growing body of African literature.

Andrea Modenos Ash
Aphrodite Will Take Your Order
(First Publication)
Andrea Modenos Ash is a native New Yorker who graduated magna cum laude from Hunter College with a dual degree in Classical and Women's Studies. Her love of everything Ancient Greek filtered through a feminist lens has shaped her writing. She lives in Long Island with her husband, daughter and a menagerie of pets. Her debut novel, *Coven of Ashes*, will be released in the fall of 2025 by Van Velzer Publishing. For updates and new projects, visit her at andreamodenosash.com.

Angelina Chamberlain
The Heart of a Warrior
(First Publication)
Angelina Chamberlain writes from her home in NorCal's Sierra Nevada foothills, where she lives with her husband, three kids, and an ever-entertaining circus of pets. Her voracious reading habits – spanning encyclopedias, comics, and classics – naturally evolved into storytelling, with inspiration drawn from poetry, mythology, history and speculative fiction. She weaves romantic elements into all her stories, and she's currently querying a contemporary Greek story featuring Aphrodite and working on a standalone project.

C.B. Channell
Best Served Cold
(First Publication)
C.B. Channell is a Chicago-based author who spends part of each year in Los Angeles. She has a B.A. in Anthropology and has always had a passion for mythology. She has published alternative Greek mythology stories, including 'Persephone's Children' in *The Magazine of Fantasy and Science Fiction*, 'A Mother's Blessing' in the *Circe* anthology from Flame Tree Publishing, among other genre shorts. This is her third appearance with Flame Tree Publishing.

BIOGRAPHIES

Ev Datsyk
A Mortal Breaks Aphrodite's Heart
(First Publication)
Ev Datsyk is a queer, second-generation settler living on the land known today as Canada. She primarily writes short stories and is passionate about the Oxford comma and questionable puns. Her work can be found in Haunted Words Press and Divinations Magazine, with a full publishing history accessible on her social media. You can find her at @evdatsyk on most platforms.

Voss Foster
Pandemos – Skotia – Areia
(First Publication)
Voss Foster lives in the middle of the Eastern Washington desert, where he writes science fiction and fantasy from inside a single wide trailer. He is the author of the *Office of Preternatural Affairs* series, as well as *Evenstad Media Presents,* and has had work featured alongside historic classics in the *Heroic Fantasy* series, as well as by Vox Media. When not writing, he can be found admiring his ever-growing collection of carnival glass.

Luna C. Galindo
Hymn to the Pain
(First Publication)
Luna C. is a 25-year-old psychology student and avid Aphrodite devotee from Valencia, Venezuela. Her life has been influenced not only by the world around her as a young woman in Latin America, but by the worlds she has created and inhabited in daydream; art and writing becoming outlets for everything she has felt and lived. As a way to connect with others, stories became her whole life.

Ali Habashi
Feasts of the Fair and Fowl
(First Publication)
Ali Habashi lives in a city once condemned for its inescapably dark past, and now known for its fantastic Halloween parties. Her short horror stories have been featured on several podcasts and in even more anthologies, and she came in first in the Creature Feature category for *The Asterisk*

Anthology Vol II. Find her fiction on The Other Stories podcast, on The NoSleep Podcast, and in the Flame Tree anthology *Footsteps in the Dark*.

Xoe Juliani
All's Fair
(First Publication)
Xoe Juliani is an American writer living in the Netherlands. She started writing as a teenager and never really stopped. At any given moment, you're likely to find her either reading or writing – and if she's not, she's probably wishing she were. She has a degree in Literature and Creative Writing from Antioch University and has previously had short stories published in the Harmony Ink *Harmonious Hearts 2016* anthology and in *Sci-Fi Romance Quarterly*.

Vanessa Ziff Lasdon
Venus Descending
(First Publication)
Stories are spells, and Vanessa Ziff Lasdon weaves them with myth, history and heart. A Los Angeles-based author, editor, educator and founder of W.O.R.D. Ink Agency, Vanessa holds an MFA in Writing for Children and Young Adults and helps emergent writers discover their unique voice. When Vanessa's not writing, she's bingeing epic fantasy, dystopian sci-fi, gothic thrillers, crime dramas and sweeping romance alongside seven fur babies and a very understanding husband. In her latest work, Aphrodite's tale of sacrifice and self-discovery reveals the transformational power of love. Visit her Instagram page: @wordinkagency

Russell Hugh McConnell
The Constraints of Love
(First Publication)
Russell Hugh McConnell was born in Toronto, Canada, but has spent his adult life in Odyssean peregrinations through realms of gold (and, occasionally, realms of bronze, nickel and tin). Currently, he keeps his still hearth among the barren crags of North Texas, but as the veering winds shift, he could set sail at any time. He has published stories in *Dragonesque*, *Familiars*, *Last-Ditch*, and *Achilles*, and has work forthcoming in *Pulp Literature* and *Shadows and Signals*.

Melody E. McIntyre
Aphrodite's Promise
(First Publication)
Melody lives in Ontario, Canada and writes speculative fiction. She is also an avid reviewer who writes reviews and articles for *The Horror Tree, Ginger Nuts of Horror,* and on her blog. Melody is a member of Sisters in Crime and is the secretary for the Ontario chapter of the Horror Writers Association. She earned her Master of Arts studying Ancient Greek and Roman Studies and often infuses her work with elements of Greek mythology.

Fiona Mossman
Someone will remember us
(First Publication)
Fiona Mossman is a librarian and writer from the Scottish Highlands, now based near Edinburgh. She adores short stories and her writing is often inspired by myths and folktales. Some of her stories can be found in *Crow & Cross Keys*, the anthology *We Are All Thieves of Somebody's Future* from Air & Nothingness Press, *The Utopia of Us* from Luna Press and her first poetry publication is in *Door Is A Jar Literary Magazine.*

Noah Ross
Sorry, But We Really Don't Need a Love Goddess Right Now
(First Publication)
Noah Ross is 27 years old and lives in the UK. He runs a popular YouTube channel with over a million subscribers, creating animations. He also works as a Drama Assistant at a local after-school acting club. He has severe dyslexia, which makes reading and especially writing hard. He has used voice recognition software to write this story, because he believes the inability to spell shouldn't get in the way of writing.

Zach Shephard
The Love Goddess's War
(First Publication)
Zach Shephard lives in Enumclaw, Washington, where he dreams up fantasy, science fiction and horror stories. He frequently uses mythology in his writing, because it's a lot easier to explain bizarre plot choices

when capricious deities are at work. His fiction has appeared in *Fantasy & Science Fiction*, the *Unidentified Funny Objects* anthology series and several of Flame Tree Publishing's books – including the *Medusa* and *Circe* installments of the *Myths, Gods & Immortals* series. For more of Zach's work, check out zachshephard.com.

Lauren Talveryn
Froth
(First Publication)
Lauren Talveryn is an author rediscovering her love of writing. When she was young, she filled countless notebooks with tales of animal friendship and superhuman abilities. As an adult, she loves to craft fantasy and horror stories. She relishes in world building and creating a space for readers fragmented from reality. Her work has been featured in the anthologies *Children of the Dead: Lost Lullabies* and *Flash of the Dead: Halloween '24* from Wicked Shadow Press.

Myths, Gods & Immortals

Discover the mythology of humankind through its heroes, characters, gods and immortal figures. **Myths, Gods and Immortals** brings together the new and the ancient, familiar stories with a fresh and imaginative twist. Each book brings back to life a legendary, mythological or folkloric figure, with completely new stories alongside the original tales and a comprehensive introduction which emphasizes ancient and modern connections, tracing history and stories across continents, cultures and peoples.

Flame Tree Fiction

A wide range of new and classic fiction, from myth to modern stories, with tales from the distant past to the far future, including short story anthologies, **Beyond & Within**, **Collector's Editions**, **Collectable Classics**, **Gothic Fantasy collections** and **Epic Tales** of mythology and folklore.

Available at all good bookstores, and online at flametreepublishing.com